1

The Tales of Valhanor
The Mask of Melanthius

S. A. Richardson©2017

Other titles in the series

The Chalice of Knowledge

The Laurel of Victory

The Mask of Melanthius

Short stories by same author

The Tall Elf

Copyright

ISBN-13: 978-1548214319

ISBN-10: 1548214310

About the Author

S. A. Richardson lives in the historic town of Tutbury in the U.K. with his wife and two children. He graduated from school in 2002 and took a fulltime job at one of the largest poultry suppliers in Britain, where he worked until 2010 when a minor medical problem with his spine forced him to give up the job. Failing to find another job, he took up writing as a pastime and has continued it ever since.

Follow Author S. A. Richardson on:

Twitter @valhanor

Or

Facebook @s.a.richardsonauthor

The Mask of Melanthius

Is for my wife, Joanne, with love

Contents

Map of Market Barton

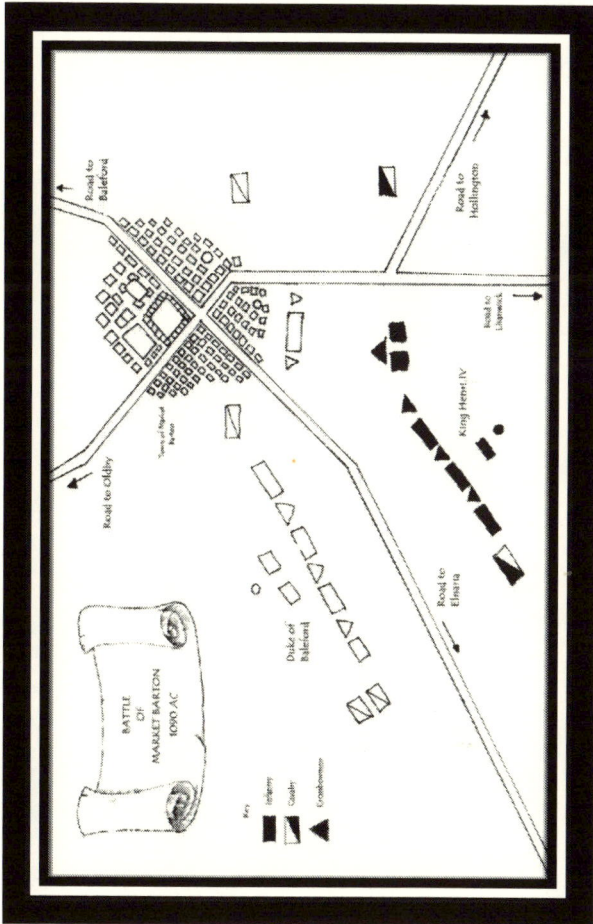

10

Prologue

Mahault's arms and legs burned from the effort of climbing the mountain. For the past three days he and Elmar had been searching for an entrance to an ancient tomb, a tomb many didn't believe existed. But for all their efforts, nothing had they found. Their hands were cut and blistered, their boots scuffed and split from the sharp, wet rocks. But still they climbed, desperate to prove that Mahault was right, and not the myth believing fool that many had called him.

"We should go back!" Elmar called up to Mahault. Elmar was cold, despite the thick woollen clothing he was wearing, tired and had given up hope of ever finding the tomb.

"No!" Mahault called back down to him. "We have to go on!" Mahault was a stubborn man driven by the need to leave a legacy for his children back home. Many in Arnon had warned him not to undertake such a foolish errand, but Mahault was an explorer, an explorer that had too often returned home having failed his quest. But not this time, he told himself. "We go on!" He called down to Elmar.

"I haven't the strength to hold on much longer!" Elmar shouted back. "I need to rest!"

Mahault glanced up and saw a flat ledge that looked large enough for them to rest on. "Follow me!" He climbed up on the ledge and held down his hand to help Elmar up. Both slumped down, breathing heavily.

Elmar took off his pack and pulled out his water-skin, draining the last of his water. He was a small man with wide shoulders, hazel eyes and short, dark hair. "Our quest is lost." He said tossing his empty water skin over the ledge. "The Satrap and his council were right. We should have stayed at Arnon."

Mahault, ignoring Elmar's doubts, pulled out an old parchment from a pocket on his tunic and examined it. The parchment was an old map of the mountains that showed the location to the tomb he was looking for. Around the edges were instructions, written in the eastern script, on how to find the entrance. "It must be near." He said folding the map back up and stuffing it back in his pocket. "It must be near." He repeated as he gazed up at the mountainside in hope of seeing some clue to the whereabouts of the tomb. There was a thin mist that clung to the mountain that made it difficult to see too far ahead. He stepped close to the ledge's edge and looked back down at the mountain disappearing into the mist below, thinking.

Months ago, he had left the eastern city of Arnon with a fellowship of ten men that had all sworn an oath to stay true to their quest until the bitter end. But the expedition had met with much danger. Twice bandits had attacked the fellowship, killing six. The remaining four made for the eastern sea where they purchased two small boats to crossover to what they called the Island of Ash and Fire. Three days into the crossing, black clouds rumbled overhead. High winds tore the boats sails and heavy rain lashed down on the remaining fellowship as they desperately tried to row against the high waves that slapped over the sides of their small boats.

"The great sea serpent swims!" Elmar had shouted. It was then that a wave turned over the other boat and both Elmar and Mahault had watched helplessly as their companions were swept away by the rough sea. Now there was only the two of them, and the greatest of dangers was yet to come.

"Do you have any water?" Elmar exhaustedly asked. "The mountain is cold and wet, yet the air is so dry."

Mahault went and knelt down beside his pack and pulled out a water-skin. "Only a little." He said passing Elmar the skin. He looked much similar to Elmar in stature, but had a weatherworn face that told that he was well travelled.

"We should go home." Elmar said as he took a small swing from the water-skin. "We have come further then many believed we would." He passed the water-skin back to Mahault and shook his head. "Maybe it was just a story."

"No!" Mahault replied sharply. "There is truth in the story, why else would the ancient scribe feel the need to record the tomb's whereabouts?" He added, angrily corking the water-skin.

"Yes, but that scribe lived hundreds of years later than the events he recorded." Elmar said as he stood and gazed up at the mountain. "I fear that we shall meet our ends on this foolish errand." He kicked a small rock in frustration, sending it over the edge and crashing down into the mist below. Covered over by the rock was a carving of an archer, arrow notched and pointing higher up into the mountain. "Mahault, come take a look at this."

Mahault walked over to Elmar and looked down at what he was pointing at. "The archer!" He quickly fished out the map from his pocket and unfolded it. "Trust the flight in thy arrow, and to the foot of the tomb shall you come." Mahault knelt down and brushed away the grit that blanketed the ledge with his hands. "Look another arrow!"

"Then let us put an end to this expedition." Elmar said as he shouldered his pack. "I am cold, wet and in need of my warm fire and bed back home."

Mahault folded the map and stuffed it into his pocket before he snatched up his pack and led Elmar ever higher into the mountain. For hours more did they climb, getting ever higher until a cold wind cleared the mist and brought snowflakes that dusted the top of the mountain. Twice they lost the arrows that were carved into the mountainside and were forced back upon themselves to find the right route. As the faded sun was swallowed by the mountains, they came upon another ledge where there was a doorway carved into the mountain. The doorway was framed by three large stones that were inscribed with words that Mahault didn't understand.

"How are we going to get in?" Elmar asked. As he spoke he saw a flash of yellow eyes looking down upon them. "What was that!?"

"What?" Mahault asked as he took off his pack and placed it by his feet.

"Eyes…. I saw a pair of yellow eyes looking down at us." Elmar stood rigidly, pointing up at the mountain.

Mahault looked up but saw nothing. "The air is light here, it causes hallucinations." He then looked out across the lava plains far below, knowing that somewhere down there was the Minoton, creatures said to guard the tomb.

"I know what I saw!" Elmar said, his anger building. "I am no fool!"

Mahault looked back at Elmar and saw that he was frightened by what he saw. "Then we must hurry, before our presence in discovered." He knelt down and opened his pack, pulling out a lantern that he lit from his tinderbox.

"How are we to get in?" Elmar asked again, slowly taking his eyes from where he had saw the yellow eyes.

"With this." Mahault said pulling out a small glass phial from his pack. He stood up and tossed it at the doorway.

The phial was filled with an explosive potion that had been mixed at the alchemist school in Arnon. It hit the stone and shattered, exploding in a sudden blast of fury that knocked Mahault and Elmar off their feet. Smoke and dust lingered in the air and it took a few minutes for the breeze to clear it. The rocks that were blocking the entrance were now gone.

"Elmar!" Mahault called as he painfully got to his feet. "Are you alright!?"

Elmar rose from ground, covered in dust and coughing from the smoke. "I'm alright." He said as he dusted himself down. "You have carried that all the way from Arnon?" Elmar said, surprised that it had not exploded in his pack, especially after all that they had been through.

Mahault shrugged at Elmar. "One of many risks I was willing to take on this quest." He picked up the lantern and

15

cautiously walked up to the entrance, peering into the gloom. There was a set of red painted stone stairs that led down into the darkness of the mountain. "Come Elmar." Mahault held his lantern out in front of him and began to climb down the stairs.

It seemed like hours had passed before they wearily came to the bottom. They found themselves in a long corridor lined with white marble columns inscribed in the same language that was written around the entrance. In-between the columns were carvings of trees and animals that dwelt in forests, a mighty elk splaying his elegant antlers, boars rummaging through the undergrowth, rabbits and many birds.

"A work of wonder." Elmar said as he gazed at the lifelike carvings. "A pity it should remain hidden in the mountain's darkness where none shall see it."

"A pity indeed." Mahault agreed. "But for good reason." He reminded Elmar.

They continued along the corridor until they came to an entrance of a chamber. The doorway was closed by a single block of stone and flanked by two statues of Minoton, horned beasts with the head and legs of a bull and the body of a man.

"Do you still disbelieve Elmar?" Mahault said as he raised his lantern to get a better look of the statues. They looked lifelike, as though they would spring to life at any moment and seize them.

"Disbelief has given way to fear." Elmar's voice sounded shaky. "And I fear that if we do not go now, then we shall perish here."

"We have not come this far too simply just turn back now." Mahault said turning back to look at Elmar's ashen face.

"We cannot move that." Elmar said pointing at the huge stone that blocked the entrance to the chamber.

"Hold this." Mahault passed the lantern to Elmar and pulled out the map from his pocket, examining it. "The furthest eye to the left, then the furthest eye to the right." He repeated the words from his map. He stuffed the map back into his pocket and climbed on the statue on his left, going to press the eye nearest to the wall.

"Wait!" Elmar called. "The furthest left eye."

Mahault stopped before he pressed the eye and jumped down. "Of course, left as from their stance." He climbed up the statue to his right and pressed in the left eye. Then quickly climbed back on the statue on his left and pushed in the right eye. There was a sudden sound of unseen cogs and chains scraping and pulling as the huge stone blocking the entrance slowly slid open.

"We're in." Mahault said taking back the lantern.

The doorway led into an ancient burial chamber, the chamber that Mahault had longed to see. It was circular with glow stones imbedded into the smooth walls that dimly lit the tomb. In the centre was a stone sarcophagus with a life-like effigy of a tall elf, holding his hands upon his chest pointing up as if he was in prayer.

"Melanthius." As Mahault whispered the name the light from the glow stones flickered and a soft sigh came blowing down the corridor.

17

"It's real!" Elmar said as he rushed over to the sarcophagus and ran his hands over the masked face of the effigy. "Help me remove this lid." He pushed the lid with all the strength he could muster and it creaked open a little, seeping out a black smoke.

"No Elmar wait!" Mahault shouted. But it was too late. As the lid slid open there was a sudden flash followed by a blast. Mahault quickly turned away to shield himself from the blast and fell to his knees.

Elmar screamed as his flesh burned, blistered and fell from his bones. Then fell face down, silent forever more.

Mahault rushed over to what remained of Elmar and turned him over. He was no longer recognisable and his face resembled more of a burnt ham than a person. "Forgive me Elmar, I shall remember you always." Tears fell from his eyes as he placed Elmar's hands over his chest. Mahault stood and walked around the sarcophagus, looking down at the bones that had lay undisturbed for thousands of years. Over the skull was a black mask with a gigantic rune for the letter M on its forehead, a mask Mahault had read much about and had longed to gain. He placed his lantern on the floor and picked out the mask, turning it over in his hands. "Such a simple thing," he said aloud to himself, "a thing of such power."

Sudden sounds of heavy hooves on stone came flooding down the corridor and Mahault quickly ducked down behind the sarcophagus, hiding. Through the door came three of the Minoton, carrying huge axes ready to slaughter those who dared to disturb the tomb. They were tall with black bull-like skin and sharp pointed horns on the side of their heads, glaring around the chamber with their frightening yellow eyes that would terrify the bravest of warriors.

"Who dares to disturb the bones of Melanthius?!" The voice was fierce and full of malice. "Know that death has come for those that enter this tomb!"

From behind the sarcophagus Mahault rose, but he was no longer himself, but in the form of Melanthius. He now wore a crimson robe with a hood pulled over his head. The black mask covered his face and in his right hand he held a staff with a blue gemstone fitted onto the end. "Kneel and rejoice, for your master has returned." Melanthius said, his voice muffled by the mask.

The Minoton, seeing the return of their master, knelt down and lowered their heads and said, *He who possesses the mask, possesses the power.*

Chapter 1

The two armies had stood facing each other, ready for battle, all morning in the blazing sunshine. They shouted insults to and fro as they sweated and awaited for the order to charge. The king's army had formed up from east to west on the hilltop known as Baden Hill. His position was strong as the hill overlooked the road to Langton Castle and gave command over the lower ground to the south. There on the yellow buttercup fields below was the Lord of Langton's smaller army, banners bright and snatching with the warm breeze. It had become a stalemate as the king was not willing to give-up the advantage of the hill and Lord Langton was not willing to fight his way up it. As the sun reached its height, the king's men began to sit down and take off armour thinking that there would be no battle that day. Yet the older men who had seen battle before stood ready, knowing that the order to advance could come at any moment.

Lord Langton rode his pure-white horse along his front line, a hand on his hip and his head held high as though he had already won the battle. His hair was long and blond, his face thin and youthful. Over his slim frame he wore expensive plate armour covered over with a tight fitting pure-white jupon with a red rose on his chest. Next to him rode his closest advisor, an older man with a stern face and a pursed mouth.

"Telescope." Lord Langton said as he reined his horse to a stop.

The old advisor reined in beside his lord and handed him his elegant brass telescope. "We should hold our ground." He said, knowing that his lord was eager for battle.

Lord Langton ignored his advisor's comment and snapped open the telescope, scanning over the king's army. "No discipline!" He said, surprised by what he saw. "They're sitting down!" He scanned back over the king's frontline and added, "Some are even cooking a meal! Just look at them! If they were my men, then they would feel the lash!"

"It is the heat my lord." The advisor answered. "It can sicken men and rob them of their strength. We should allow your men to rest my lord."

"We shall attack now." Lord Langton said, snapping shut his telescope and handing it back to his advisor. "While they are resting."

"Forgive me my lord, but our men are tired from standing too long in the sun. Their advance will be slow and by the time they had reached halfway up that hill, the king's forces would be ready for us."

"So what are you advising?" Lord Langton replied mockingly. "To cower from battle and glory?"

"My lord." The advisor spoke as though he was talking to a child. "Sometimes there is more to be gained by not fighting."

Lord Langton rolled his eyes and shook his head. "You are far too cautious old man. First you advise me to waste my gold on hiring that no-good Robert Hawkwood to delay the king at Lhanwick, but that failed to gain me more than a couple of days. Then you advise me to stay behind my walls and let the king attack me where I was trapped. And now that I am upon my field of victory, you would advise me to do nothing?"

The old advisor thought his lord young and foolish, a spoiled brat that had grown accustomed to getting his own way. His father had been different, considered a wise man by his council, a man that had a great understanding of many things and was wise enough to take counsel from his advisors when needed. "My lord the only battle we need to win is that of time. The king needs to defeat us quickly as the Duke of Baleford is moving against his back."

"So you would advise your lord to do nothing while others steal my glory?!" Lord Langton said, looking disapprovingly at his advisor. "How the bards would mock me." He added.

"The bards will sing only of victory, and those that won it." The advisor said, shifting in his saddle to get more comfortable. "Let them sing of how the tyrannical king longed for the blood of his own people and eagerly swooped down from that hill like a wave of death, only to be stopped by you, a man blessed by the Star Gods to save the kingdom."

With his ego stroked by the advisor's words, the lord smiled and nodded his head. "Very well, I shall bow to you counsel and wait for the king to attack me. Then we shall defeat him and march north to join Baleford's forces."

"It would be better if we were to retreat back to the safety of our castle's walls, and let the king tire himself out by attacking our walls." The advisor said, trying one last time to convince his lord not to risk his army in open battle.

"You risk losing too many men in an open battle, especially when the king's forces outnumber us." Many times he had counselled his lord to remain behind his castle walls, explaining that they could hold off the king until the Duke of Baleford's forces came south, trapping the king. But the lord was eager for battle and had foolishly refused to take the counsel given.

"I will not retreat in the face of my enemy. I will stand and repel the wave of a tyrant." Lord Langton said with a smug face that showed he was oblivious to the dangers of open battle.

"My lord," the old advisor tried once more to make his lord see sense, "the king has more men and the high ground."

Lord Langton shot him a look that said the matter was closed. He then nudged his horse and rode back along the line, with the old advisor reluctantly at his side, shouting words of encouragement to his men. "Today we shall end the rule of a tyrant!" They half-heartedly cheered, wanting nothing more than to turn back and go home.

The waiting went on as both sides seemed destined to watch each other and do nothing more than shout insults, insults that were not often heard because of the distance between the two armies.

Henri could hear the noise coming from the king's army along the hilltop. He was now a squire to a well-known knight called Sir Gregory Fitzwalter, a knight that disliked Henri and made things difficult for him. Sir Gregory had taken all of his other squires to battle, but had ordered Henri to stay behind and safeguard his pavilion from any man that cowered back from the fighting to plunder unguarded pavilions. Henri sat beside the entrance of Sir Gregory's pavilion, knees up and scratching the image of a knight on horseback into the ground between his feet with a stick. He thought that being a squire would be different, that he would be respected because of his rank. But instead he found that he was not wanted anywhere; the lower ranks saw him as a squire and was no longer considered a peasant like them, and the other squires and knights said that he was not a true blooded squire, so he was not one of them either. So Henri felt like one of those monsters that rose up out of their graves, not alive but not dead either and stuck in limbo where nobody wanted him.

"So Sir Gregory has left you behind." A young voice said to Henri.

Henri looked up and saw a young boy with a mop of straw coloured hair, wearing a brown tunic with a white lion rearing up on its back legs. "Hello Rylan." Henri said sulkily.

Rylan was a page in Sir Gregory's retinue. He was only ten years old and already considered to be a knight in the making. His family were wealthy and were well-respected as they could trace their ancestry back hundreds of years through a long line of knights that had loyally served the king. But Rylan was gentle in nature, preferring to tend to the horses and read books rather than honing his limited skill with a sword. "Why haven't you gone with the other squires?" He innocently asked.

Henri snapped the stick he had been using and tossed it onto the ground. "I have been ordered to guard the pavilion." He said standing and brushing off the dirt on his trousers with his hands. When he had been made a squire, he had been given a new pair of tall boots, black trousers and a red tunic with a yellow lion standing on its back legs embroidered on it. Often the Master-At-Arms would reprove him for looking dirty like a peasant, and instruct him to clean his livery. Even his hair had been cut short in an effort to make him look less peasant like. "I should be at the battle earning my spurs." He said looking down at the image of a knight he had scratched in the soil.

"Sir Gregory wants you kept safe." Rylan said, running his fingers through his mop of sweaty hair. "After all you are the saviour of the temple."

"Saviour of the temple." Henri repeated the words mockingly. It felt so long ago that he had led the Star Oracle out of the secret passageway. Then he had been hailed and awarded with the laurel of victory, but now it had seemed to be forgotten. "He wants me kept out the bloody way!" He added angrily. "It doesn't look good having a jumped up peasant in his retinue."

"You should feel lucky," Rylan said, "not many peasants have achieved the rank you have."

Henri knew this to be true. He had known of no other that had done what he had, but it seemed to matter little to Sir Gregory and the other squires. "Shouldn't you be with the horses?" Henri asked to take the conversation away from him.

"Sir Gregory has taken them all." Rylan replied. "There's nothing to do until he returns."

Sudden rhythmic beats of drums followed by cheers sounded from the hilltop and Henri angrily scuffed out the image of a knight with his foot. "I'm going to take a look at what's happening."

"No, Henri!" Rylan pleaded. "You mustn't disobey your orders!"

Henri shrugged. "He won't know unless you tell him."

Rylan reddened in the face. "But a knight should speak only truth."

"Yes, but we're not knights." Henri pointed out. "Nor am I ever likely to be." He bent down and picked up his short sword that was leaning against a wooden box outside of the pavilion. "Well are you coming?" He asked as he strapped the belt his sword was tied to around his waist and walked off towards the hill.

Rylan was still unsure, but as he watched Henri walk away he had a sudden fear of being left alone. "Wait for me!" He called to Henri as he ran to catch up with him. "We'll get in trouble if we're caught." Rylan warned as he caught up with Henri.

"We won't get caught." Henri reassured Rylan. "Sir Gregory will be with the other knights on one of the flanks. We'll take a look by that tree." Henri pointed out a solitary tree upon the highest point of the hill that he thought would be the centre of the king's line. As they climbed over the brow they saw the king's army formed up in its battles about a quarter of the way down from the ridge. Most were sitting and trying to shade themselves as best they could from the unrelenting sun that made things hazy when looking from a distance. Sweat trickled down Henri's spine and forehead, stinging his eyes as he stared down at the two armies.

"There's so many." Rylan said, looking at Langton's army on the lower ground to the south.

Henri wiped his forehead with the sleeve of his tunic and shook his head. "We have more."

"Why are they waiting?" Rylan asked. "Why don't they just attack?"

Henri just shrugged. "I wouldn't want to fight my way up this hill. Especially in this heat."

"Then why don't we go down and attack them?" Rylan said brushing his damp hair out of his eyes. "It would be better to get off this hill. It is a bad place to be."

Henri looked at Rylan, puzzled. "What do you mean?"

"Have you never heard of Baden Hill?" Rylan said, sounding shocked.

"Not until we got here." Henri admitted.

"Haunted." Rylan said in a hushed tone as though his words would rouse the spirits under the hill. "Haunted by the outlaw William Baden himself."

"William Baden," Henri said, "never heard of him."

"He was an outlaw that lived hundreds of years ago." Rylan said, pleased at the chance to show off his knowledge. "He made this hill his base and raided the nearby villages and plundered carriages traveling on the road."

"So what happened to him?" Henri asked, intrigued by the tale.

"Well, the then lord of Langton sent men, and they killed all of William Baden's followers, he was then captured and was taken to Langton Castle to stand trial. For his many crimes they brought him back here and hung him from this very tree, as an example to all others. Once dead, they cut off his head and stuck it on a spike on top of the hill." Rylan shuddered and looked around as though he were being watched. "They say that the headless ghost still wanders this hill, ever searching for its head." He added.

"So that is why it is called Baden Hill." Henri looked back down the hill and understood why the hill had been used by William Baden. The hill gave commanding views over the road and any rich carriage would be seen well in advance, giving him plenty of time to prepare an attack.

"Look." Rylan said pointing up into the tree. "You can still see the rope marks."

Before Henri could say anything, a group of horsemen trotted over the brow and reined in by the tree. "Henri?" A man dressed in a grubby white padded tunic with a black boar on his chest said. "What are you doing here?"

"Hollington!" Henri said surprised by the sudden appearance of the Duke of Hollington. "Sorry, I mean your grace." He quickly added as he remembered who he was talking to, and bowed.

The Duke of Hollington ignored Henri's clumsy bow and impolite tone as he dismounted and handed his reins to an aide. "Sir Gregory is on the left flank, why are you here?" He asked, looking at Henri with suspicious eyes.

"I got lost looking for him." Henri lied, knowing how stupid it sounded.

Hollington looked at Rylan. "Are you lost as well?"

Rylan reddened and looked down at his feet, unable to answer and not wanting to lie to the Duke.

"Lost indeed." Hollington said with a smile, fully aware that Henri was lying. "Well since you are here I might as well make use of you." He pulled out his telescope that was tucked into his belt and handed it to Henri. "Your eyes are young, tell me; do those fellows down there look like they will attack any time soon?"

Henri stretched open the telescope and scanned over Langton's army. "They look ready for a fight." He answered. It was a small telescope, yet powerful, and he was sure that he could have counted the number of rust spots on their armour, even at this distance.

"But do you think they will attack us?" Hollington asked, wanting an answer.

"No." Henri said after a moments pause. "I don't think they will attack." He then trained the glass on a swallow that had flown down onto a log that was between the two armies, pecking for insets. It was odd he thought, of how calm the day seemed to be; men laydown and joked, the sun shone brightly and birds sang and flew back and forth like normal. Yet at any moment it could all erupt and men would scream and die, the land below would become littered with blooded bodies and broken weapons. Such peace and beauty to be destroyed by men's' folly. "I wouldn't attack uphill, not in this heat." Henri said as he snapped shut the telescope and handed it back.

"My thoughts exactly." Hollington said stroking his bushy beard. He looked more weary and scruffier then he did normally. "It looks as though we will have to take the fight to them."

Henri stared down the hill at the king's forces that were now being ordered to their feet by their captains. "Permission to join the other squires." Henri asked, hoping that Hollington would grant his request.

Hollington shook his head. "The king has ordered that you are kept safe, and away from any fighting."

"But why?" Henri moaned. "All the other squires have gone, so why not me? I'm a better swordsman than any of them."

Hollington knew why, but never said. The Star Oracle had foretold that the *one* would rise from the dirt, and that the light of the stars would be with him. Henri had rescued the oracle and the temple maids during the final stages of the siege of Lhanwick, rising up through mud that concealed a secret passage into the temple. The king now believed that Henri was the one that the oracle spoke of, and wanted him kept safe. Though that was not the whole truth. Rumours had spread amongst the lower ranks that Henri was chosen by the gods, and the old tale of the one that would return the kingdom to light and free them from the chains of serfdom began to be spoken of once again. The king thought this a threat to his rule and wanted Henri kept out of the way until he was forgotten about by the lower ranks.

"Because the king has commanded it." Hollington answered Henri, unwilling to tell him the truth.

Before Henri could say anything else the king and his entourage cantered along the crest of the hill towards the tree. He reined in by Hollington and said, "It appears as though we will have to make the first move."

"My king." Hollington bowed. "It would seem that Lord of Langton is not as foolish as we had hoped."

"Foolish enough to have left his castle." The king said looking at Henri with distrustful eyes. "And I intend on punishing him for it."

"We should attack now." Hollington suggested. "Before he finds some sense and retreats back to Langton."

The king held out his hand and an aide leaned over in his saddle and instantly passed him his telescope. He unsnapped it and scanned over the battlefield. He had placed his men a quarter of the way down the slope with his centre battle positioned over the road that led to Langton Castle. In total he had three battles, each made up of Men-At-Arms and spear militia, formed up in a line from east to west. Between the battles and on the flanks were crossbowmen formed up in wedges, ready to release their deadly volleys. Guarding the east and west flanks were the knights and mounted squires, eagerly waiting for the order to charge and win glory.

"Have the crossbowmen advance within rage of their line." The king said taking his eye from the eyepiece. "It is time to take the fight to them."

Hollington mounted his horse and looked sternly down at Henri. "Go back to the camp."

Henri saw that the king was looking at him, though he never spoke a word to him. He and Rylan simply bowed to the king and walked back down towards the camp.

*   *   *

The people of Heath Hollow lined the streets to welcome the Duke of Baleford's army. His army had arrived the previous day and had made camp to the north of the town, the people feeling both excited and frightened by the sight of thousands of armed men on their doorstep. They had been awoken by the town crier ringing his bell and shouting that the rightful king would enter their town that morning, and that all were required to line the streets and rejoice at his coming. So fearful of what might happen to them if they disobeyed, they reluctantly took to the streets.

The Duke of Baleford led a procession of knights, all wearing expensive plate armour that shone brightly in the midmorning sunlight. Each carried a bright banner of purple silk with a golden head of a stag in the centre, and had long purple feathers on top of their helms that flurried with the gentle breeze. Their horses were equally as impressive as their riders, plated in armour and decorated in purple feathers on their heads. The people cheered and waved their hankies as they passed, some shouting, "Long live the true king!" But the Duke of Baleford was not one for getting ahead of himself, and refused that any of his men call him king until he had been crowned. He sat in his saddle looking rigidly ahead towards the castle upon the hill. Heath Hollow was a castle that he needed. It guarded the road north to Baleford and would offer his retreating army time to regroup if things should go wrong. He'd had to offer a high price in order to gain the allegiance of the Lord of Heath Hollow, the hand of his daughter to John Kinge so that he could call himself a prince, a price that he was never comfortable making.

Baleford thought the town shabby, and it smelt worse than pigsty. The city of Baleford had once been like this, he thought, but he had built sewers and punished anybody who emptied their chamber pots onto the streets. His city was now clean and his people spoke highly of him for it. Baleford himself was a short stocky man with greying hair and beard that he kept short. His left eye was blind, pure white and scarred from a hunting accident when he was younger. He was a straightforward man who had little time for fools, an efficient man that left nothing to chance which gave him a high confidence that all around him took comfort in.

The precession rode up to the castle gates that were opened up by soldiers that now displayed both the badges of the Kinge's and Baleford's on their tunics. They rode into the centre of the courtyard where they waited to be met by the Lord Aide of the town. But he was nowhere to be seen.

"We welcome you to Heath Hollow your grace." A captain said as he knelt before the Duke.

"Save the pleasantries Captain," Baleford said, looking down at the captain from his tall horse, "and go and fetch your Lord Aide."

"Forgive me your grace," the captain said as he stood, "but I was ordered to welcome you and escort you into the lord's audience chamber."

"Was you indeed?" Baleford said with a raised eyebrow. He dismounted and winked up at the captain, who was far taller than himself. "Better to be greeted by a real man, and not some pompous fool." He said, patting the captain on his shoulder.

The captain smiled but said nothing as he didn't want to risk his master finding out that he thought him a pompous fool.

Two of Baleford's knights dismounted and stood behind their Duke, hands on their hilts and ready for any sudden attack, but Baleford waved them off. "The good captain here will see that no harm shall come to me." He said walking towards the entrance to the keep.

The captain hurried along and escorted the Duke into the audience chamber where all the men of worth had gathered to swear their fealty to the Duke. At the far end, on a raised wooden floor, stood the Lord of Heath Hollow with his son, the Lord Aide at his side.

"I bid thee welcome to my town." The lord said, stretching out his arms in a symbol of friendship. He wore his usual attire, a long black robe that pointed up at the shoulders and a tricorn hat with a long red feather sticking out of the back. His face was ashen and betrayed nothing of what his thoughts were, his beady hawk-like eyes watched the duke, weighing him up.

The Duke of Baleford walked up towards the empty throne-like chair that was placed behind where the lord and his aide were stood, his heavy boots thudding loudly on the wooden floor. He unbuckled his sword belt and tossed it at John, who only just caught it. "Do you not know that it is customary for the Lord Aide to welcome nobles to their town?" He said, giving John a look that showed his annoyance.

"I thought the duty to be beneath a future prince." John said smugly as he handed the Duke's sword to one of the officials standing at the foot of the raised floor.

"You are not yet a prince!" Baleford snapped. "And what use is a prince that knows not his duty!" He looked away from John and at his father, the Lord of Heath Hollow. "I had heard that your son was a fool, but I expected better from you."

"My son sometimes forgets himself." The Lord of Heath Hollow said, stepping forward and grimacing with the sudden sharp pain in his stomach. "But he will learn." He added trying to hide the pain from his voice.

"Learn," Baleford scoffed at the word, "he has much to learn if he is to marry my daughter and call himself prince."

The lord saw that his son was getting angry with Baleford and quickly drew his attention away from him. "The king has marched south on Langton Castle." The lord said stepping forward. "This is no time to argue amongst ourselves."

Baleford looked at the lord and could see that he was in pain. "It is no argument," he said leaning forward in his chair, "your son is a fool and has much to learn." When he had made the deal for John to marry his daughter he had sent men to inquire about John, and what they had reported back, he disliked. They said that he was smug and sly, a man that rode on other people's success as a ship rides upon the sea's waves. He often neglected his duties and blamed others for his failures, yet reaped all the acclaim for himself when things went right. Above all he was distrustful, a man that would consort to unimaginable evil to aggrandise himself.

"Maybe." The lord conceded. "But he has his uses."

"And we need not remind you of your need of our alliance." John added with a sly smile. It gave John great satisfaction knowing that the Duke of Baleford had little choice, not if he wanted their alliance.

Baleford wanted nothing more than to break the alliance and smash his fist into john's smug face. But there was a war to be won, and he needed the castle of Heath Hollow as a safety net should things go wrong. "Then let us get on with this formality." He said, gesturing for the waiting crowd to come fourth and swear their loyalty to him.

One by one the rich men that owned property in the town stepped up before the Duke of Baleford and knelt down, swearing their allegiance and acknowledging him as rightful king. It went on for hours and Baleford began to tire of the constant stream of men that would have sworn their loyalty to a goat if it meant that they were left in peace. He knew it was all a show, a play that the lord had conducted to show the unity of his town. Once all were done, the Duke of Baleford stood and said to the lord, "Let us retire and talk more privately."

The lord, followed by his son, led the Duke through a doorway to their right and into a chamber with a large table in the centre. A large map of the kingdom was spread over the table with wooden pieces showing the position of the armies. "The king has reclaimed the temple at Lhanwick quicker than we hoped." The lord said as he leaned over the map and tapped on Lhanwick. "So we must move quickly."

Baleford noted that he used the word, we, and it irritated him. "The king has one army only, an army that has taken heavy losses at Lhanwick." He said as he walked around the table and moving the small wooden block south. "My spies report that the king has now marched south to face Langton's forces."

"Then we must hurry and attack him in his rear." John said as though he was well experienced in war.

"Fool." Baleford said as he looked at John. "It may sound a good idea, but we know nothing of what Langton might do."

"Does it matter?" John said looking down at the map. "We should just march on the king's rear quickly and put an end to his reign."

"If the Lord of Langton listens to his advisors and remains behind his castle walls, then I would happily march on the king and trap him between the castle walls and my army. But the last reports I had suggest that he is eager for battle and is readying to march north to face the king in open battle."

"I have heard the same." The Lord of Heath Hollow said, holding a hand to the pain in his stomach. "So what do you plan to do?"

"If the reports are right and Langton is foolish enough to engage the king's force in open battle, then we must leave him to his fate." Baleford said.

"You mean that we will do nothing." John said with scorn. "We won't win the war by doing nothing."

"I mean," Baleford answered, growing angry with John's lack of understanding, "I mean that it could go two ways." He pushed the small block that represented Langton's forces up to meet with the kings. "If Langton moves on the king and defeats him in battle, then the king will have to retreat back toward Market Barton and we will finish off what remains of his forces."

"But what if the Lord of Langton gains a total victory and captures the king?" John said as though it would somehow be a bad thing.

"Then the war would be over and I will be king." Baleford replied mockingly as though a child could have guessed that outcome.

"But what if Langton is defeated?" The Lord of Heath Hollow asked. "To my understanding he has a smaller army and would surely lose if he met with the king in open battle."

"If Langton loses, he would be forced back to his castle." Baleford tapped the castle marked out on the map. "But the king will have heard reports of my movements and will want to march north to defeat me."

"So we march south and defeat him." John said as though it would be that easy.

"My army is big," Baleford said, "and the march would be tough, tiring my men and battering their moral."

"So we let the king tire his already tired forces." The lord said, understanding the situation.

Baleford nodded and picked up the piece that represented his army. "I need not rush, after all I need only to crush the king's army once to win this war." He then placed the piece on the crossroads at Market Barton. "I will wait here until I have received further reports from my spies, once we know whether Langton is the fool that I expect him to be or not, then I will act accordingly."

The Lord of Heath Hollow cast his beady hawk-like eyes over the map. It made sense to him to wait for further reports. If Baleford was to rush south as his son suggested, then he risked misjudging the timing and the king could find a strong position in which to defend from. No, he thought, better to let the king wear out his men and be forced to fight on a field not of his choosing. "Very good your grace." The lord said, taking his eyes off the map. "But what of our other arrangements?"

Baleford glanced at John, then to the lord. "It will be as we agreed, but it is my understanding that your son is still married."

"For now." John said as though he could rid himself of Elizabeth at any time.

"And it is my understanding that she is now under the protection of the Duke of Hollington, along with your friend Henri Richards, who was awarded with the laurel of victory and made a squire." Baleford said with a note of admiration for Henri in his voice.

"He is peasant scum!" John angrily snapped. "And shall hang for his crimes!"

Baleford smiled at John and said, "That peasant scum is said to have survived the terrors of Dimon Dor and saved the star oracle and her temple maids. Which is more than you can say."

John was surprised by how much Baleford knew and it unsettled him. "I am the Lord Aide of this town and its future lord." He said proudly. "Far more significant than a jumped up peasant."

"Bah." Baleford waved a dismissive hand at John. "Handed to you on a silver platter by your father. You have done nothing for yourself."

John had wanted to lash out in anger, but he saw the hard look his father gave him from across the table and knew better. "I will take my leave." He grudgingly bowed to the Duke and stormed out of the chamber, feeling bitter.

"If we are to be allies," the lord said in a calm manner, "then we should help one another." The pain in his stomach suddenly flared up and he was forced to sit on a chair placed up against the wall. "Can you not have one of your spies kill my son's wife?" He asked, getting straight to the point.

Baleford shook his head. "I will not have a woman killed for that fool. No, he should be rid of her one way or another, but I will not help in the matter." The truth was that he hoped John would never be free from his marriage to Elizabeth, but somehow maintain the uneasy alliance with them without the need for his daughter to marry John. The best outcome was that the silly bugger got himself killed he thought.

"The agreement was that my son was to marry your daughter in return for my support." The lord said giving the Duke a threatening look. "If you do not honour your side of the agreement, then I shall not honour mine."

"What and change back onto the king's side?" The Duke said sneeringly. He thought about it for a moment and knew that he could not risk losing the lord's support. "I cannot have a hand in the murder of his wife directly, but I shall assist him in any way that I can."

"And my son is to be given a position of command?" The lord asked with a raised eyebrow. "It would show your trust in him and show that our two houses are united."

Baleford sighed, knowing John was a fool he didn't trust. But he had little choice. "Yes, but I will place a man I trust to act as his advisor."

"Very well." The lord said standing. "Let us go and feast and drink to our alliance."

Both left the chamber feeling uneasy that their alliance would hold, but it would have to if Baleford was to seize the throne and John to become a prince. For the pieces of war were moving and there was a war to be won or lost.

Chapter 2

"Henri," Rylan pleaded, "we should go back to camp like the Duke told us to."

"You can go back if you want." Henri replied. "But if I can't fight in the battle, I might as well watch it." He walked towards the western flank where he climbed back up the hill and laydown just below the brow.

"We're going to get in trouble." Rylan warned as he lay stomach down next to Henri.

Henri ignored Rylan's concerns and poked his head over the top of the hill. The king's crossbow men had advanced further down the hill where they were within range of Langton's frontline. They sent constant volleys down onto the tight formations below, and Henri watched as men fell to the ground as they were caught by crossbow bolts.

"What's happening?" Rylan asked, not daring to look over the brow.

Henri looked back down at Rylan. "Come take a look."

Rylan shook his head. "I don't know, I don't want to get killed."

"You're quite safe here." Henri said gesturing for him to come and have a look.

Curiosity got the better of Rylan and he crawled up next to Henri, poking his head over the brow. He watched, mesmerised by how efficiently the crossbowmen reloaded and loosed their deadly bolts. "Who is that?" Rylan asked pointing down at a man riding behind Langton's battle line. The man was mounted on a pure-white horse and shouting instructions. He must be a captain Rylan thought.

Henri looked and shook his head. "I don't know, but he looks impressive." The man stood out in his white jupon with a red rose on his chest, and Henri thought it stupid to wear such bright clothing and be so close to the crossbowmen that would surely aim for him. "An impressive fool." He added.

Langton's crossbowmen loosed a volley of their own, but their bolts fell well short of their target. Henri and Rylan watched as the mounted man in the white jupon shouted and pointed up the hill. There was a sudden horn blast and the two wedged shaped battles began to advance, keeping their tight formation. At first they walked and were an easy target for the constant peppering of bolts that rained down upon them. "Close up!" The captains shouted. "Close up!" They cursed the stupidity of advancing in a tight wedge and wanted nothing more than to give the order to form a loose skirmish line that would help protect them from the barrage of bolts that sent men crashing to the ground, screaming. Men stumbled and fell as the advancing wedges began to lose their cohesion as men began to run uphill to get within rage quicker. Behind the two battles was a trail of dead and wounded men that traced back to their original position. After taking much punishment, the captains gave the order to form a skirmish line, shouting as they pushed men into place, ordering them to shoot back. It took a few minutes, deadly minutes in which they were constantly barraged by the king's crossbow men, before they were in place and began to shoot back.

"There're fighting back!" Rylan said, sounding both excited and scared.

Henri traced a volley from Langton's men with his eyes and noticed that a few bolts were still falling short or flying harmlessly over the heads of the king's men. "We'll have the better of them." He said confidently. "It's easier shooting down than up."

A handful of the king's men were snatched back by bolts, but it was nothing compared to the casualties that Langton's men were taking. More than half of the king's force was made up of crossbowmen, men that had been formed up into four wedges that had quickly advanced into a skirmish line halfway down the hill.

"Keep shooting!" A captain of Langton's men yelled as his men began to waver and edge back. "Hold your ground and shoot back!" A bolt buried its self into his neck and he fell to the ground, rolling and gargling his last breath.

A trumpet sounded from behind the king's battle line, and advancing from the flanks were the knights and mounted squires. The Lord of Langton saw the threat to his crossbowmen and ordered his knights to engage with the king's. It was a sight that the bards sang of, the poets wrote of, and young boys dreamt of, a sight that many thought glorious and noble. The king's knights trotted forward, keeping their tight formation, but they rode not for the crossbowmen who were now retreating, but straight towards Langton's knights who foolishly charged uphill to meet them.

The Lord of Langton had fallen into the king's trap.

Behind the knights on the king's western flank was a small battle of Men-At-Arms armed with long, crude billhooks. They remained hidden behind the knights, keeping pace, until their time to attack came. The steepness of the hill checked Langton's charge and slowed them until they had almost stopped. The king's knights seized their chance and charged. It was like a hammer hitting an anvil as the two formations of knights clashed. Steal clashed on steal as they fought desperately from their saddles. The small battle of Men-At-Arms charged in on Langton's knights and noblemen clad in expensive armour were pulled down off their horses and killed by poor men armed with a crude weapon. On the eastern flank Langton's knight had fared no better. They were outnumbered and were quickly defeated by the sheer weight of numbers. Along the hilltop, the king's three battles of infantry advanced. His crossbowmen formed back up into wedges and re-joined with the advancing line.

"This battle is over." Henri said as he watched Langton's knights being killed as they tried to retreat. He glanced over to the west flank, where the king's knights were pursuing what remained of Langton's knights, and thought that he should have been there, charging forward and winning glory. "Do you think that Sir Gregory will come back?" Henri said, in hope that he might not.

Rylan looked at Henri as though he had just committed a crime. "Of cause he will, Sir Gregory is a fine swordsman."

"I've never seen him." Henri replied. "I'm not allowed to train like the other squires." He added with scorn.

"He's won seven tournaments." Rylan said, choosing to ignore Henri's scorn. "So I've heard anyway."

A sudden eruption of shouting sounded as the king's battles crashed into Langton's line and the killing began. To Henri and Rylan it look a chaotic mess, a mass of men screaming and stabbing at each other in a blind fury.

"How do they know who is on whose side?" Rylan asked staring at the slaughter below.

Henri just shrugged and said, "I'd kill anyone trying to kill me."

They watched in silence as the knights and mounted squires on the flanks regrouped and charged to attack the rear of Langton's line, routing his army.

"Come on." Henri said standing. "Let's go back."

The walk back towards the camp was grim. Wounded men limped and staggered from away from the fighting, leaving bloody trails behind them. The sound of battle and the moans of the wounded hung heavy in the air as the king's constables rode amongst the wounded, arresting any with no wounds. It was an easy excuse to help a wounded man to the infirmary and get away from the fighting, but it was an age-old trick that the king had forbidden. Any man caught would have their names taken and flogged; if caught a second time, then they would be hung for cowardice.

A wounded man with a crossbow bolt through his left thigh saw Henri and Rylan and called out to them. "Help me!" He shouted, waving a bloody hand. "Please help me!"

Henri went over to the wounded man and helped him up. "How did you manage to get this far?" He asked, knowing that with a wound that bad, nobody could have walked back from the fighting alone.

The wounded man whelped as a flash of pain shuddered up from the wound. "I had help." He said though gritted teeth. "But those swine arrested the man who was helping me." He was wearing a steal cap, a leather jerkin and had a short sword scabbarded at his waist.

"You're a crossbow man." Rylan said as he took an arm, trying to help.

The wounded man nodded. "I was in the thick of it when a stray bolt found its way through to my leg." He whelped as another stab of pain shot up from his wound. "I would have been trampled to death had not my friend helped me."

"The same friend that brought you here?" Rylan asked.

"I lad, but the bloody swine took him and left me here to bleed to bloody death!"

Henri knew what he meant by swine, he meant the constables. The constables were made up of wealthy men that had purchased their rank. They were hated by the lower classes because of their wealth and power over them, and that they were never involved in any of the fighting. The king's enforcers of rules, rules that kept the lower classes in their place. A mounted constable that was nearby saw them and suspiciously rode over.

"Bloody hell!" Henri swore as the constable reined in close to them.

"Are you injured?" The constable said looking for any signs of wounds on them. He wore the navy-blue tunic with white trousers and tall, well-polished riding boots. At his waist hung an elegant sword that had never clashed with another blade nor tarnished by blood.

"This man is badly injured and needs help to the infirmary." Henri answered with a note of dislike in his voice. With Rylan's help, he placed the wounded man back on the ground, expecting trouble.

The constable looked at Henri's red tunic and recognised the yellow lion standing on its back legs on his chest. "You're a squire to Sir Gregory." He said with a raised eyebrow. "What is a squire and a page doing helping wounded men?"

"Part of the code of chivalry is to help the weak." Henri answered evasively.

The constable was an older man, wise enough to know when someone was hiding the truth from him. "I think that you are cowering from the battle." He said as he dismounted. "In fact, I don't think that you're a real squire."

"You can think what you like!" Henri snapped back at the constable. "Now get out of my bloody way!"

"How dare you speak to one of the king's constables like that, do you know who I am?" The constable said as though his words were enough to frighten Henri into subjection.

Henri just laughed. "I know what you are. A pompous prat that has paid to avoid getting near to any of the fighting." He laughed again. "If you were poor they would call that cowardice, but because you have money they call in honourable."

"Insolence!" The constable yelled as he drew his sword. "You're under arrest!"

Henri, as quick as a flash of lightning, drew his own sword. And in a swift movement that the constable didn't expect, disarmed him and knocked him onto the ground.

"Henri stop!" Rylan yelled, fearing that he would kill the constable.

Henri stood over the constable, the point of his sword held in front of the constable's face. He was full of anger, frustrated by being held back by Sir Gregory and for not being considered to be a true squire. "Bugger off." Henri said removing his sword from the constable's face.

The constable got up and picked up his sword. "I've heard of you." He said, ramming his sword in its scabbard. "You're the peasant the king made a squire." He mounted his horse and looked hard at Henri. "I shall see you stripped of your title and hung for the cowardly peasant that you are."

Henri, still angry, turned and slapped the constable's horse on the rump with the flat of his sword, sending it speeding off.

"You should not have done that." Rylan said, shocked by what he had seen. "Sir Gregory will surely take away your title of squire now."

Henri just grunted and rammed his sword back in its scabbard. "Was I really a squire anyway?" He put the wounded man's arm around his shoulder and helped him back onto his feet. "Let's get you to the infirmary." He knew there would be trouble for his actions. A squire was supposed to uphold a noble manner that reflected upon the knight that he served. But Henri, who had not come from a privileged family, often found himself in trouble with Sir Gregory for his lack of decorum. Once he found out that Henri had drew his sword on one of the king's constables, he would come down hard on him, like a hammer striking a nail.

The wounded man grunted in pain as he took a couple of steps and said, "Thank you."

They slowly made their way back towards the camp, but they were not alone. Many other wounded men staggered back from the battle, some had bad wounds and had managed to crawl away from the fighting, only to bleed to death on the slopes of the hill. The king's constables rode up and down the slope, arresting any they found with no wounds and taking them in chains to a makeshift dungeon close to the middle of the camp. The infirmary was on the outskirts of the camp, and it was already overflowing with the wounded. Outside of the entrance were wounded men lying on the ground. As they passed a pole that had been painted with red and white stripes that was the sign that the pavilion was the infirmary, two physician's apprentices carried out a bloodied body from the entrance.

"We have a wounded man!" Henri called to them.

The two apprentices placed down the body they were carrying and glanced over towards Henri. "Take him inside." One of them said, jerking his head at the entrance. They were young, a similar age to Henri, and wore brown leather aprons that were wet with blood. Without saying another word they walked back through the entrance.

Henri helped the wounded man inside and as he stepped through the entrance, the smell of blood and slaughter hit him. Wounded men lay wherever there was room, bleeding and dying. Men moaned and death hung heavy in the stifling air. There was a small space beside a man with a deep cut from a sword on his left shoulder and they placed the wounded man down and glanced around the pavilion, looking for a physician. At the far end there was a physician holding a bloody pair of tongs that he used to pull-out a crossbow bolt embedded in a patient's forearm. Henri watched as the two apprentices he'd saw outside held the patient down as the physician pulled the bolt out. The patient grunted and bit down hard on the piece of wood that had been placed into his mouth as the physician slowly wriggled the bolt out.

"It hurts just watching it." Rylan said, looking suddenly very pale.

Henri then noticed a woman giving the wounded men water from a pail that she carried. Her back was to him so he walked over to gain her attention. "I have a wounded man in need of help." He said placing a hand on the back of her shoulder.

"They are many wounded in need of help." She said as she turned to face Henri.

Henri instantly recognised Elizabeth. After the siege of Lhanwick she too had been taken under the protection of the Duke of Hollington. At first she had acted as a cupbearer for the duke; but vile rumours soon spread that the duke had took her as a mistress, and so he assigned her to help the physicians to put an end to the rumours and avoid any scandal. She was dressed in a simple white dress that looked grubby, and a brown leather apron that was spotted with blood. Her hair was tied back with a strip of leather and Henri thought that she looked tired, older. She seemed different, tougher, much changed from the woman he knew working her father's stall at Heath Hollow. But thinking back on all she had been through, Henri couldn't blame her; after all he was no longer the same boy that had stolen a bag of gold from the lord of Heath Hollow.

"Henri!" Elizabeth said, surprised by his sudden appearance. Since he had rescued her from Dick at the end of the siege of Lhanwick, she had seen him little. "Are you alright?" She awkwardly asked, her cheeks reddening.

Henri nodded his head. "Yes I'm fine. But I have a wounded man in need of help."

"They are many men in need of help." Elizabeth tiredly answered. "He will have to wait his turn like everybody else."

"But he'll bleed to death by the time a physician tended to him." Henri didn't know if that would be true, or why he even cared. But the thought of a man dying because of being made to wait, angered him.

Elizabeth exhaled deeply and said, "Ok I'll take a look, but he will still have to wait for a physician."

Henri led Elizabeth over to the wounded man he and Rylan had carried in. She knelt down to inspect the crossbow bolt that was deeply embedded in his left thigh. Blood trickled out of the wound as Elizabeth took out a small pocketknife out of the pocket on her apron and cut open the wounded man's trousers. She could see that the crossbow bolt had gone in at an angle and had broken the bone.

"Can you pull it out?" Henri asked.

Rylan, who was stood behind the wounded man, was getting nervous. They had spent too long away from their duties and he feared that they would get into trouble, even more trouble than they were already in. "Henri we had better go." He said in hope of a quick exit. In truth it was not just the thought of the Master-at-Arms punishing them that troubled him, it was the sight in the infirmary. He kept on looking over to the large table at the far end of the pavilion. Beside it was a pile of limbs, sawn off and dumped as though the physician was a butcher carving up joints of meat for the market. The thought of the physician slicing through flesh and muscle, then taking a saw and sawing through bone made Rylan feel queasy. "Henri we had better go." He said again, his face once more turning pale.

"Well," Henri said to Elizabeth, "can you pull it out?"

Elizabeth examined the wound closer. "No, that is not my job." She said as she stood. "The best I can do is bandage it up and make him comfortable." She then took Henri's arm and led him out of earshot of the wounded man. "I fear your friend will die." She said bluntly.

Henri looked over at the wounded man. He had gone pale and quiet, and barely moved. "He only needs it pulling out." He said with a hint of anger.

Elizabeth shook her head. "The bolt has broken the bone. If a physician pulls the bolt out and any bits of bone, fever will soon set in and most likely kill him." Elizabeth lowered her head as if she was ashamed. "I doubt any of the physicians will even treat him."

"Surely he deserves a chance." Henri said looking at Elizabeth.

Elizabeth looked up and met his eyes. "I'm sorry, but I can do nothing more than make him comfortable."

Henri reluctantly nodded and wondered if the wounded man had a family back wherever it was he'd come from. Then he thought back to the temple of Dimon Dor. The spirit that dwelt there had told him, *"If thee doth not flee the path thou has set upon, then thou heart shall know pain."* And since he had drank from the Chalice of Knowledge, he'd known nothing but pain. His best, and only friend had been killed, his mother had died whilst he was imprisoned, then he had been secretly rescued by the king's Arcani, only to be sent on a dangerous mission. After succeeding in that mission, he had been rewarded with the Laurel of Victory and made a squire, but even that had turned sour. Now he had tried to help a wounded man, only to be told that he would most likely die. Would everything good he did turn bad?

"Elizabeth!" The physician called over from the table. "Come and hold this man's hand!" Two of his aides had pinned a wounded man down on the table, but he fought and thrashed about to save himself from the physician's knife, crying and calling for his mother.

"I had better go." Elizabeth said. "They find that my presence soothes men as the physician hacks away."

"Elizabeth!" The physician called again as his aides struggled with the wounded man.

Henri watched as Elizabeth rushed off without saying another word. He had loved that woman once, and a part of him still did. But much had changed since that night of summer's end when he was going to ask her hand in marriage. He was no longer a foolish peasant, but a squire, a disliked squire, but a squire all the same. And she was still married to John Kinge, a man he considered his enemy.

"We had better go." Rylan said as he came and stood beside Henri.

Henri looked away from Elizabeth and back at the wounded man, feeling saddened. "Let's go."

They walked out of the pavilion and both were glad of the fresh air. Henri looked back towards the hilltop and saw men sitting and lying, exhausted from battle. Men's moans carried with the warm breeze and the sound of battle had eased. "It must be over." Henri said, walking back towards Sir Gregory's pavilion.

"We'd better hurry." Rylan said. "Before we get into more trouble."

"Henri!" A voice shouted over the moans of the wounded.

Henri turned and saw the Master-at-Arms angrily striding over towards him.

"Where the bloody hell have you two been!" The Master-at-Arms shouted at them. He was a stern looking man, short and stocky with a bold head and a broad, flat nose. His tunic was blue with a yellow lion standing on its back legs embroidered on it, and he had a deep scar on his left cheek that made him look as if he were half smiling. "Well, what have you to say for yourselves?!"

Henri, who stood taller than the Master-at-Arms, looked down at him and said nothing, staring at the deep scar on his cheek.

"You were ordered to guard Sir Gregory's pavilion!" The Master-at-Arms then shot an angered look at Rylan. "And you I expected better from!"

"Rylan only left his post to fetch me back." Henri said, trying to take all the blame.

The Master-at-Arms grunted and said, "You have neglected your duties and Sir Gregory will deal with you."

"I am a squire!" Henri angrily replied. "It is not my duty to guard a pavilion!"

"Your duty!" The Master-at-Arms snapped back, grabbing a fistful of Henri's tunic. "Your duty is to do as commanded!"

Henri instinctively smacked the Master-at-Arms fist off his tunic and shoved him back. He never meant to do it, but his anger for the man had slowly built up over time. Too often he had found himself in trouble with the Master-at-Arms for things that the other squires did, yet where they had gotten away with it, he'd found himself being punished, all because of his low birth.

The Master-at-Arms saw the anger in Henri's eyes and kept his distance. "Your actions are not worthy of a squire!" He gripped the handle of his sword and said, "You both are to follow me!"

Henri momentarily thought of drawing his sword and ramming it in the Master-at-Arms face. But he managed to control himself. They followed the Master-at-Arms back to Sir Gregory's pavilion where they were made to wait outside. The pavilion was a burgundy colour with two blue and white banners standing either side of the entrance.

"Do you think we'll get off with just a good telling off?" Rylan nervously asked, pacing a few steps forwards and then back.

"You will." Henri said, still angry. "But they'll not be so forgiving towards me."

The Master-at-Arms poked his head out of the flaps of the entrance and told them to enter. Inside was hot and stuffy, and Henri could feel the tension hanging heavy in the air.

Sir Gregory was stood with his arms stretched out at his side as two squires unstrapped his armour. He was short, stocky with a full head of blond curly hair and had a youthful face, despite him being in his early forties. His family boasted that they could trace their lineage back to the founding of the kingdom, tracing it all the way back through a long line of knights that had loyally served the king. As he saw Henri enter, he shot him a look of utter disgust. "You have disobeyed my orders!" He snapped in his privileged voice. "Both of you!"

"Rylan came to fetch me back." Henri said to defend Rylan, who just stood beside him looking sheepishly down at the ground.

"Is this true?!" Sir Gregory asked angrily swiping at a fly that flew close to his face, irritating him further.

"Yes Sir Gregory." Rylan answered. He had wanted to tell the truth, that he willingly went with Henri. But if Sir Gregory found out Henri was lying, then he would only get him into more trouble. And so he lied. "I told him to come back, but he wouldn't listen."

"Rylan, you are from an upstanding family of high merit, do not let that name be tarnished because of this peasant." Sir Gregory said looking at Henri with utter disgust.

"I'm no longer a peasant." Henri said. "I'm a squire."

There was an awkward silence as the two squires unbuckled the last of Sir Gregory's armour and dutifully left the pavilion to clean it. Sir Gregory walked over to the table he used to write his orders and sat on the chair beside it. "You are a squire in title only!" He said as he picked up a goblet filled with a sweetened red wine. "It is quite clear that you are not worthy of such lofty privileges." He paused to take a swig of his wine. "I will speak with the king to have your title removed, until then you will take up duties with the pages. You will clean the horses and their equipment, and serve on the other squires." Sir Gregory drained the remainder of his goblet and angrily added, "You will never become a knight!"

"It is not proper for a squire to be doing the duty of a page!" Henri angrily replied.

"And it is not proper for a peasant to be a squire!" Sir Gregory roared, standing from his chair. "This is not a matter to debate, now go clean my horse!"

The Master-at-Arms grabbed Henri by his scruff and pulled him out of the pavilion. He was taken to a large canopy where the horses were kept and told to start cleaning.

"Damn them all." Henri muttered to himself as he picked up a brush. "Damn the king and all the kingdom."

*   *   *

The king sat on his great warhorse, watching as knights rode up before him with captured banners. They ceremonially tossed them down at his feet and said, "Victory for you my king." before inclining their head and riding aside to allow the next knight to present his captured banner. Gathered behind the knights were the Men-at-Arms and spear militia, looking on and grumbling. And they had good reason too. As Langton's army was surrounded, it had tried to flee. They dropped shields and weapons in a blind panic, holding up their hands and shouting for mercy. But little did they find. Many were killed and their pockets searched for anything of value, the banner-men suffering the worst. Their banners were ripped their out of their grasp as they were brutally cut down and mutilated. They waved the banners high in the air and shouted victory, but the knights, wanting glory for themselves, took the banners off them, sometimes having to use violence. Now the knights reaped the rewards and boasted amongst themselves of how they had captured them.

The Duke of Hollington reined in beside the king as the last of the banners was placed at his feet. "My king." He greeted, inclining his head to show respect. "Langton's forces have been totally routed…"

"Yes I known that!" The king snapped. "But what of the Lord Langton, has he been captured?"

Hollington turned in his saddle and waved at two of the king's constables, who were behind him, and they came forward holding an old man, blooded and defeated. "This is the aide to Lord Langton." Hollington said, gesturing at the old man.

"My king, mercy, I ask for mercy." The old man shakily said as the constables forced him onto his knees.

The king nudged his horse forward, trampling over the captured banners. "Where is your lord?" He asked in a tone that showed he was in no mood for the usual pleasantries expected when a man of rank surrendered.

"Dead my king."

"Dead?" The king said looking to Hollington for an answer, the tone of his voice seemingly lighter.

"It is true," Hollington confirmed, "I have seen the body."

"He died fighting my king, and deserves a proper burial as befitting his rank." The old aide said, trying to gain some dignity in this defeat. He had been with Lord Langton as his small battle of bodyguards had been surrounded. Many times had he pleaded with his lord to escape the killing, but he had refused. Instead of running for his life, which he said was cowardly, he desperately fought on, foolishly still claiming that he could gain a victory. In the end it had been a crossbow bolt that had pierced his heart that brought him down. With their lord dead the remainder of the bodyguards had lay down their weapons and surrendered.

"He was a traitor!" The king roared at the old aide. "And you will treated as such!" He waved for the constables to take him away and turned to Hollington. "Come, let us take a tour this field of victory."

Hollington nodded and followed the king. The on-looking soldiers cheered the king and his victory as he rode through them. But Hollington knew that it was not over yet. Though the king had won his victory, a small number of Langton's men had managed to flee and Langton Castle still needed to be taken. And besides all that, there was the Duke of Baleford's army to defeat.

"What are our losses?" The king asked, reining in beside a cluster of blooded bodies.

"Hollington shook his head. "The final count has not yet been made, but I don't expect them to be too heavy."

"Have the captains call the rounds." The king said as he took his eyes off the dead bodies. "I want to march on Langton Castle before nightfall."

"You should allow the men some rest, they are overtired from the heat and battle." Hollington understood that they needed to quickly capture Langton Castle, but attacking a castle with tired men would be reckless. "Give them this night and march at first light." He added, seeing that the king was eager to get his army marching.

The king glanced around the battlefield, tiredly thinking. He still needed speed. Though Langton and his army were defeated, Baleford was not. Reports of his army marching south had reached his ear and the last thing he wanted was to be trapped between the castle walls at Langton and Baleford's army. Speed would decide the future of his reign. "No we must march to take Langton." He said closing his eyes to relieve the dull ache behind his eyes.

"My king, what of our dead and wounded?" Hollington said, wiping his sweaty forehead with the sleeve of his grubby tunic. "And they are the prisoners to consider."

The Marshal of the constables rode up towards the king, weaving around the dead bodies. He wore an elegant navy-blue tunic with a silver brooch of shackles pinned to his chest and white trousers with tall, well-polished, riding boots. "My king." He said as he reined to a stop in front of the king. He was a middle-aged man, short and flabby from his easy lifestyle. His straw coloured, curly hair was greying and his face was red and sweaty from the heat.

"Marshal." The king tiredly greeted. "What ill news do you bring me?"

The Marshal opened a saddlebag and fished out a folded parchment. "A list of cowards that fled the fighting." He said passing it to the king.

The king unfolded the parchment and scanned over the names. "How many?" He asked, looking up from the parchment.

"One hundred and forty-seven." The Marshal replied as he uncorked his water canteen and drank deeply.

"One hundred and forty-seven." The king angrily repeated as he passed the list on to Hollington. "Have them all flogged, no hung as an example."

"My king, would that be wise?" Hollington said nudging his horse closer to the king. "We need all the men we can muster for the coming battles."

"And what of discipline?!" The Marshal interjected as he tied his canteen back on his saddle. "My king if you were

63

to show leniency in this matter, then your entire army would flee at the sight of the next battle."

"After the losses at Lhanwick and now here, you will need the men." Hollington said. "Our numbers are a little over half of what we set out with."

"There'll only be more losses if you don't punish the cowards." The Marshal warned. "They'll start to desert in the night."

"Enough!" The king tiredly snapped. He thought both were right, he did need as many men as he could muster. But on the other hand he needed his men to fear him more than the enemy, or else they would just simply run. "Have every fifth man on that list flogged and shamed, and make sure that they are all in the frontline for the next battle." And he knew there would be more battles to come. Since the campaign had begun he had won two victories, one at Lhanwick and one here at Baden Hill, but the rebellion was not yet crushed. Yet one decisive victory for Baleford would see his reign end. "See to the floggings." He dismissively ordered the Marshal. "And make sure all the cowards watch it."

"My king there is another couple of matters that require your attention." The Marshal said pulling a cotton handkerchief out of his sleeve and wiping his sweaty forehead.

The king tiredly sighed. "What now?"

"A number of Langton's soldiers have been captured and are being closely guarded by my men. But we have nowhere to put them." The Marshal said, stuffing the damp handkerchief back up his sleeve.

"Hang them all and be done with it." The king coldly replied.

"It will take days to build the scaffolding." The Marshal warned, feeling sweat trickle down his back.

"Days!" The king snapped. "We leave at nightfall so you have hours only."

"Forgive me my king, but it cannot be done."

"Then what is to be done?!" The king said, angrily slapping his thigh.

"You could grant them a pardon." Hollington said, an idea forming in his head.

"You would petition the king to pardon treason?!" The marshal both sounded and looked disgusted. "It would be bad for discipline."

"Have them fight for you." Hollington said, looking at the king in hope that he would listen. "Offer them a full pardon if they swear loyalty to you and fight bravely."

The king tiredly rubbed his face, thinking.

"My king, it would not be wise to pardon high treason." The Marshal said, seeing that the king was considering it. "It would make other lords declare against you."

The king took a moment to think about it. He didn't want to pardon those that had betrayed him, but there was little choice. The Duke of Baleford had a much larger army that was fresh, where his army had been diminished by battle and was dog-tired. He needed the men. Besides that, once word reached Baleford's army of how merciful the king had been, then his men would be more willing to surrender. "Very well." He replied to Hollington. "But have any that refuse my pardon executed."

The Marshal shook his head in disbelief.

"And the final matter?" The king asked. The pain behind his eyes was growing worse and all he wanted to do is return to his pavilion and sleep.

"One of my constables was assaulted by that peasant you made a squire!" The Marshal sounded angry. "I ask your permission to arrest him and make him stand trial for his crime."

The king thought back on what the Star Oracle had told him, the *one* must be kept safe as his destiny was linked with his own. He had only made Henri a squire in order to give him some protection, but now he feared that it had been a mistake. All he had heard was of how Henri was failing, and that none accepted him as a true squire. The common men had liked that one of them had won glory, but the nobles had disliked it and had branded him foolish for doing such a thing. "The *one*." The king said softly to himself. This *one* needed to prove himself he thought. "I will deal with it." He said, waving his hand to dismiss the Marshal.

"As you wish my king." The Marshal was not happy with the king's decision and reluctantly turned his horse and rode off, feeling as though the king cared little for justice.

"It was a mistake making Henri a squire." The king said watching the Marshal ride off.

"You remember what the oracle said?" Hollington said. "He needed to be protected as his destiny is linked with yours."

"But what if she was wrong?" The king asked raising his eyebrows.

Hollington shrugged. "She was right about how you would identify him."

The king thought back to when he had visited the temple in the winter and could hear the star oracle's words. *From the dirt he shall rise, and the light of the stars shall be with him.* And that prophecy had come true. At the end of the siege of Lhanwick, Henri had risen up through mud that had concealed a secret passageway, along with the star oracle and the temple maids. After, the oracle had confirmed to him that Henri was somehow chosen; but chosen for what he didn't yet know. "Come," he said turning his horse, "we need to make further plans."

The king and Hollington rode back to the camp where men tiredly lay around small fires with pots of runny porridge hanging above them. They lowered their eyes and fell silent as the king passed them by. In the centre of the camp was the king's pavilion, a huge purple and yellow striped structure filled with all the comforts of a palace. Servants rushed forward and took the reins of the king's and Hollington's horses as they dismounted. Inside was hot and humid. A large table used for council was in the centre, and sitting at the table was a man wearing a dark-green tunic and trousers, and a steel cavalry mask that concealed his face.

"My king." The man said standing and bowing, his voice muffled. As he stood upright, he removed his mask.

"Commander Symond." The king greeted. "What news do you bring me?" He asked as he took his seat at the head of the table.

After the siege of Lhanwick, Symond had been promoted to commander and was in charge of a small force of Arcani that shadowed the king's army.

"I bring you news of Baleford." Symond opened a pouch on his belt and pulled out a report. "My informer has reported that Baleford's forces are at Heath Hollow."

"So he plans on marching south and striking my rear?" The king asked, taking the report and glancing over the words.

"He will march as far as Market Barton and decide on a course of action there." Symond said, sweat trickling from his brow.

"My king," Hollington said, "We should use this time to quickly finish off Langton's resistance."

"We should turn and face Baleford immediately." The king stood from his throne-like chair and walked over to a small table at the side and poured himself a goblet of wine. "Before he convinces more lords to join his cause."

"If we don't take control of Langton Castle, they will only appoint a new lord and regather their strength." Hollington warned. "Better to deal with them now before they regain their strength."

"His grace is right my king." Symond interjected. "It would be better to capture the castle and appoint a lord who is loyal to you."

The king took a mouthful of his wine and sat back at the table. "But sieges are time consuming and costly in men." He banged down his goblet on the table. "And Baleford would surely attack my rear."

"News will soon reach him of your victory here," Hollington said, "and of the death of Lord Langton. He will know that the castle will not hold out for long. With their lord dead and his army beaten they will have little choice but to surrender to your mercy."

The king picked up his goblet and thought about it. "Very well, have the army ready to march at first light." He drained the remainder of his wine and stood and leaned on the table with his hands. "Inform the commanders."

"Yes my king." Hollington bowed. "I will see to the orders now." He left the pavilion, leaving the king and Symond alone.

"My king." Symond bowed and went to leave.

"Wait a moment." The king said holding up his hand. "I want you to speak with Henri and tell him to stop his foolishness."

Symond had not seen Henri since after the siege of Lhanwick. After Henri had been rewarded with the Laurel of Victory, they had stood on the wall that overlooked the burnt remains of the village where they had talked. He had congratulated Henri and said his goodbye, saying that he had been ordered back to the Arcani. "What is it he has done?" Symond asked.

"He has assaulted one of my constables." The king replied, anger building in his voice. "Tell him that if he persists in acting like a peasant, then I shall make him one once more and make him accountable for his actions."

Symond bowed. "I shall return to my company and bring them near to Langton, I will speak with him once your army arrives."

The king nodded his agreement. "Good, and make sure that he understands. One more transgression against my law and I will string him up!"

And the king meant it.

Chapter 3

Not a year ago, Catharine had all she could have ever wanted. She had lived in a large house filled with servants to tend on her every needs, the most fashionable dresses and jewellery, and work on her father's stall. She had often complained about being made to work on the stall, saying that it was beneath her and more suited to the servants. Yet now she missed the noise, the hustle and bustle as people bartered for the lowest price. But those days had now passed. Since Elizabeth had married John, and her father had been murdered, things had gone downhill fast. Like a pebble sinking to the bottom of a lake. Now their family home and stall was gone, sold off so that John could fill his own coffers. The money that her father had promised them in his will had never come and Catharine and her mother were now left with nothing.

When John had returned home, deserting the king's army at Lhanwick, he had sent armed men to drag them both out of their home. Catharine's mother had protested and desperately tried to grip onto one of her bedposts. But the armed men had forced open her grip and dragged her out onto the streets. John had been there, sitting on the pure-white horse that had been a wedding gift from Catharine's father, smugly smiling as Catharine and her mother were thrown into the dirt. A few of the town's folk had gathered around to watch the commotion, silent and shocked they watched as Catharine and her mother were led off in chains.

At first they were placed in a damp, dirty cell and were guarded day and night by guards that continually mocked their downfall. But after spending what seemed to be a lifetime in that cramped cell, they were summoned before the lord. The guards escorted them to the lord's office where he sat behind his desk, scratching at a parchment with his quill. He had been dressed in his usual grim attire and still wore his tricorne hat with a long red feather sticking out of the back, even though it was warm. He never took his eyes off the parchment as Catharine and her mother were shoved before him and continued writing. There they waited, silent and uncertain of what might happen to them.

"I have decided to show you mercy." The lord had said as he dipped the tip of his quill in the inkpot and signed the document he'd written.

"Mercy?" Catharine's mother had said with a hint of anger in her voice. "Mercy from what crime?"

The lord placed down his quill and sat back in his chair, resting his hands on his stomach. "You are the family of a traitor." His beady hawk-like eyes looked hard at Catharine's mother. "Your daughter Elizabeth has abandoned her lawful husband and has took refuge with that tyrant we call king."

"If we are traitors, then so are you!" Catharine had angrily snapped back at the lord. "After all we're all family now!"

The lord took his hands from his stomach and placed them in front of him on his desk, leaning menacingly forward and giving Catharine a sinister look that showed his annoyance with that matter. "Not for much longer."

"You cannot do anything without Elizabeth." Catharine's mother had said, knowing that Elizabeth would have to agree to a divorce.

The lord had waved a dismissive hand and replied, "A mere formality that can be overcome. But it is you two that I must deal with first."

"So have us executed; take our lives like you have taken everything else away from us!" Catharine's mother had said, defiantly holding back her tears.

The lord sat back in his chair and shook his head. "You have a debt to me, a debt that must be paid."

"What debt?!" Catharine's mother had said with disbelief. "We owe you nothing!"

"Your debt is for your imprisonment and my protection." The lord had taken another blank parchment from a pile on his desk and took up his quill. "A substantial sum that you both will work off." He dipped the nib of his quill in his inkpot and began writing on the parchment. "Find them a room in the servants' quarters." He ordered the guards, not taking his eyes off the parchment.

So it was that Catharine and her mother were forced to mop floors, wash dirty linen and tend to whatever the lord commanded. Their room in the servants' quarter was small and dull with no window to let in any light or fresh air. The walls and floor were bare stone and cold, their small beds were pushed up against the walls, and a small table with a single candle was placed between the beds. It was little better than the cell Catharine decided, but it would be something she would have to get accustom to as there was no chance of ever paying off their debt.

The lord had trapped them. He had kept them in the cell long enough for them to accumulate a large debt, then had shown mercy and offered them a chance to work it off. Only now they were charged for their food and lodgings with the servants, so their debt would never be paid. It had all been a political move. The lord's spies had reported that there had been unrest amongst the men of rank in the town caused by the mistreatment of Catharine and her mother. So the lord had the ringleaders of the unrest secretly murdered and had shown mercy to Catharine and her mother while keeping them as prisoners in all but name. But why the lord needed them kept as prisoners they didn't yet know. After all they had no wealth nor power to give him concern, so why not just get rid of them?

Catharine was now standing at the edge of the castle courtyard, hanging rugs over a wooden frame and beating off the dust with a wooden pole. She had once prided herself on dressing as a lady of status, wearing expensive dresses and silk ribbons that decorated her hair in the latest fashion. But now she was dressed in a simple brown woollen dress and a white grubby apron tied around her thin waist. Her hair was simply pulled back and tied into a ponytail at the back of her head with a strip of brown cloth. She took down the rug she had been beating and folded it up, placing it in a wicker basket. The day was hot and sunny and she found the work hard, so she paused for a moment and looked around the courtyard.

A crowd had gathered in the courtyard and there was a hive of activity as stable boys rushed to ready horses and servants loaded up carts with all the comforts that John wanted on campaign. Stewards barked out orders and constantly shouted at the servants carrying boxes of wine to be careful. But worst of all was the dust that had settled over the cobblestones. Later, Catharine knew that she would be made to sweep it clear.

A trumpet blast sounded and all in the courtyard turned towards the keep. Catharine watched as John came out of the doorway. He was dressed in expensive plate armour that caught the sun as he moved and a tight fitting jupon made of blue silk with a red feather on his chest. He walked with the confidence of a conquering hero, proudly strutting as a peacock. Walking a pace behind him was a knight clad in equally expensive armour as John. He was a slender man with thin lips and high cheekbones. Under his arm he carried an elegant helm, decorated with well-polished brass that shone like gold and a plume of scarlet and white feathers. The wealthiest people of the town had gathered in the courtyard to watch the Lord Aide and his knights ride to war. They applauded as he mounted his heavily armoured warhorse and the women whispered of their admiration for the Lord Aide.

Catharine stared at John and thought that he looked smug, thoroughly enjoying the attention he was getting. She watched as he smiled and accepted tokens, a silk bit of cloth scented with perfume, from foolish young ladies who thought that they could gain the affections of the Lord Aide by such mere trinkets. But not so long ago Catharine herself would have been among their number, hopelessly believing that a piece of silk could win the affections of someone high ranking. There was another trumpet blast that drew her attention back to the doorway, and out came the lord. He was leaning heavily on a walking stick and seemed to be in pain with every step he took. Catharine thought that he looked deathly pale, tired, stressed and frail, and yet still his presence dominated all around him. He slowly walked over to John, holding a hand to the pain in his stomach, and spoke a few words that Catharine couldn't hear. Fed up with the sight, she turned away and hung another rug over the wooden frame and began beating off the dust with the pole. She beat the rug as though all of her frustrations were weaved into it, and bashing it would somehow free her. "Fickle." She said to herself. "They're all fickle." She repeated, bashing the rug as hard as she could.

The crowed once more applauded as John and his company of knights rode out of the gates. The lord watched them leave, his ashen face betraying nothing of what he might be thinking, before turning and painfully walking back inside the keep.

"Clear the courtyard!" A captain of the guards shouted as the last of the wagons rumbled out of the gate. "Come on!" He shouted, waving his hands to hurry the crowd on.

Catharine folded the rug and angrily tossed it down into the basket as she watched the captain usher out the remainder of the crowd. She saw a young boy run out of the doorway to the keep and straight across the courtyard towards her. "What do you want?" Catharine said sharply as the boy came to a stop in front of her.

"His lordship requires that you bring him some honey-water." The young boy said, panting to catch his breath. The boy was a groom to the lord and was dressed in a tailored black tunic made of velvet. He was only seven and was the son of a wealthy merchant that had paid a hefty price to have his son serve on the lord.

Catharine picked up her basket and gave the boy a disgruntled look as she passed him. She hated having to take orders from him, a child that knew very little of the ways of the world. But there was little other choice.

"Hey!" The young boy called out to Catharine.

Catharine turned around to see the young boy sticking his tongue out at her. And so in childlike manner, she stuck her tongue out in retaliation and did as she was ordered. She went and fetched a jug of honey-water from the kitchens and took it to the lord's office, only to find that he was not there. An aide who was sat at the lord's desk told her to take it to his bedchamber and Catharine carefully carried the jug up the many stairs to the lord's bedchamber. The door was closed and Catharine could hear muffled voices inside. She tried to make out what the voices were saying, but they were speaking too quietly to understand; and so she knocked on the metal studded door.

The door was pulled open by a tall, thin man with a long crooked nose tipped with small, round spectacles. He wore a scarlet tunic with a white feather on his chest and white trousers that were stained by ink where he had wiped his quill. "Well!" He snapped at Catharine. "Don't just stand there!" He opened the door wide and waved Catharine in.

Catharine hurried in and felt the stir of air as the door was quickly closed behind her. The chamber was lit by many candles as thick, heavy curtains had been pulled over the windows. It was warm with the smell of incense hanging heavy in the air and packed with many of the lord's officials that stood around his bed holding parchments for the lord to sign. The lord himself was sat upright in bed, signing parchments that his officials handed to him one by one.

"Place it over there." The lord's steward said, pointing to a small table in the far corner of the room. "And pour out a goblet." He pulled out a handkerchief from up his sleeve and wiped his bold patch on top of his head. "Well get on with it!" He snapped at Catharine, who seemed hesitant to move.

Catharine reluctantly did as she was told and took the jug over to the table where she carefully poured a goblet of the honey-water. She listened to one of the officials complaining to the lord that the cost of arming men had doubled as armourers could not produce arms quick enough, and that more money than originally planned would be needed. Catharine turned around to leave the chamber and noticed that the lord was looking at her from his bed.

"Clear the chamber." The lord ordered, his voice sounding weakened. "Catharine come closer."

Catharine could feel his gaze, his beady hawk-like eyes menacingly watching her every step as she walked over to his bedside. "My lord." She said as she curtsied.

The lord waited until all of his officials had cleared the room before he spoke. "What do you think of my son, John?" He asked, his voice suddenly sounding full of strength. He was still dressed in his long black robe and tricorn hat, refusing to change into his nightgown, saying that it would weaken his presence.

"What?" Catharine replied, surprised by the question.

"What do you think of my son?" The lord repeated, his eyes narrowing as though Catharine had somehow annoyed him.

"He is both handsome and strong." Catharine answered tactfully. "A credit to your lordship."

"Bah!" The lord spat waving a liver spotted hand at her. "Don't tell me what you think I want to hear. But the truth, you will not be punished for it."

Catharine was unsure if she should tell the truth. Did the lord really want to hear what she thought of John, or was this some sort of trap? Unsure, she remained silent, fearing that she would only bring more trouble for herself and her mother.

"Well!" The lord snapped. "Tell me!"

But Catharine remained silent and looked down at the floor.

"Pass me my goblet." The lord ordered, realising that he would not get an answer from her. In truth he didn't need one as he knew what his son was like, a drunk womaniser that cared little for his duties. His son was not the man he had wanted him to be. He had wanted his son to be more like himself, efficient in his duties, calculated, and above all, feared. But many thought his son a joke, a court jester dressed in silk that commanded little respect. And a man that was not respected by his enemies, was not a man to be feared. And one could not rule without fear.

Catharine passed the filled goblet to the lord and watched as he drank deeply. "Would that be all my lord?" She asked, wanting to return to the servants' quarters.

"No." The lord replied, passing the goblet back to Catharine and giving her a suspicious look. "Have you heard from your sister?"

Catharine shook her head. "No my lord."

The lord remained silent and stared at Catharine as if he was weighing her words for truth.

"Though if your lordship in his mercy would soothe my concerns with any news of my sister." Catharine said in hope that the lord had received news that Elizabeth was coming home.

"Elizabeth is under the protection of the Duke of Hollington." The lord said, a trickle of sweat running out from under his hat. "She will most likely remain with the king's army until the war is over." A sinister grin spread across his wrinkled face and he added, "If she is not killed before that." As he spoke a stab of pain in his stomach made him flinch and cry out.

Catharine stood, surprised by the lord showing his pain. Normally he kept a strict discipline over showing any emotion; and never in all of her years had Catharine seen him like this. "My lord are you unwell." She asked, feeling suddenly sorry for the pain he was in.

The pain eased and the lord looked at Catharine, his beady eyes angered and full of rage. "Speak to no one of this!" He snapped at her. "Or I will have your tongue removed!"

Catharine never doubted the threat and sullenly nodded her head. "I won't tell anybody." She said softly.

The lord wriggled his body to make himself more comfortable. "The physicians have advised me to rest in bed for a few days." He said, still angrily staring at Catharine. "You will act as my chamber servant."

Catharine was shocked to be given the position of chamber servant. Normally that would be reserved to a high-ranking official's son, not a woman that was not so long ago called a traitor and locked up in the dungeon. "Thank you my lord."

"It is not out of kindness that I offer this!" The lord said sharply. "But out of need."

"Need?" Catharine repeated, wondering why the lord would need her.

"I have many servants," the lord explained, "but none I trust not to talk of my illness. You I don't trust either, but know that I can easily have killed should you speak." The lord's words were full of evil intent and his hard eyes filled with utter hatred for Catharine.

"I won't say anything." Catharine said again as tears welled in the corner of her eyes. "I promise."

The lord looked at Catharine as though he disbelieved her. "Many have said as much, but I have learned that it is better to keep your enemy close."

Tears rolled down Catharine's cheeks. "I have done nothing to offend you my lord." She sobbed.

"It matters not, now go." The lord ordered after a moment's silence. "Bring me some bread and another pillow." It gave the lord great satisfaction knowing that Catharine had once come from a wealthy family, and that now she would empty his chamber pot. Though it was not just the satisfaction of her family's fall; but it showed the other merchants that they were not beyond his reach and a similar fate awaited them if they displeased him.

Catharine turned and left the chamber, felling trapped and alone with no hope of ever regaining the former life she once had.

* * *

Oldby was an ancient fishing village that could trace its origins back to before the founding of the kingdom of Elnaria. During the mass migration of men in the Dark Age, men had a camped on the eastern coast for a brief time while they fished to replenish their depleted stores. They found that the sea was rich with exotic fish and a few decided to remain when the migration moved on. There they built a wooden village and the men became expert fishermen and renowned for their seamanship. Over time they built up trade with nearby settlements where they sold a portion of the fish they caught from boxes filled with herbs and salt. The other settlements nearby thought the villagers of Oldby to be superstitious and gossipy, especially the women. While their men were out at sea, they would gather on the shoreline each morning and whale as they tossed sand over their heads until the sun was at its height. Then they would begin making a broth out of fish guts, which they fed to the children, believing that it would ward off any disease. Upon the return of the men, they would divide their catch amongst all so that none would starve. But the greatest portion they left on the shoreline for the tide to sweep back into the sea as an offering to the great sea serpent, Strabo. Ever shall the village be safe, so long as Strabo protected them.

But now many believed that Strabo had abandoned them. Days ago the sea had turned calm and quiet, turning as still as the water in the village well. A thick fog had slowly swept across the sea, forcing the boats to remain ashore until it had passed. There was barely a ripple as the tide had seemed to have stopped, and many believed that Strabo had vanished from the waters. Now, as the days passed and the fog only thickened, the villagers gathered in the hall to voice their concerns to their Mayor.

The hall was a large rectangular shape built from stone with a thatched roof. Inside the walls were plastered white with paintings of exotic fish, and in the centre was a stone fire-pit that gave heat and light to the hall. The mayor sat at his chair in front of the large fire that crackled and spat its embers up towards the roof, listening to the many tales of ill omen that the villagers told. He was old with long white hair and beard, and dressed in a long grey robe with a chain of office shaped like fish around his shoulders.

"I tells ya." A fisherman said stepping forward from the crowd. "I sees it last night." The fisherman was thin with long, dark hair and missing his two front teeth. "I was out smoking my pipe when I decided to take my nightly stroll as I usually does. The fog was thick and the night dark; I could barely see the tip of me nose and I walked plum dumb into someone. I offered my sorry to the man, but nothing did he says. So I bid him a goodnight and Strabo's blessings as is proper and began to walk away, feeling somewhat annoyed by not being bid a goodnight and Strabo's blessings myself. Then it called to me, asking for a match to light its pipe. I being of good heart took out a match from my tinderbox and lit it, holding it out so that it could light its pipe. As it got close I noticed that it was wearing a dark cloak with the hood pulled over its head so that I could not sees its face." The fisherman fell silent, unsure if he should go on.

"What did you see?" The mayor asked, wanting the fisherman to go on.

The fisherman shifted from foot to foot. "Something evils." He said shaking his head as if he disbelieved what he had seen. "When it grabbed the match the first I noticed was its hands; scaly like a lizards with long, sharp claws. Its cloak then fell open and instead if have legs like you or I, it had bent legs like a cow, but scaly like its hands. Then it held the match up to its face." He paused a moment before continuing. "It had large sinister eyes as yellow as the summer sun, a broad flat nose and two sharp tusks on its lower jaw. It smiled at me, and in horror I turned and fled."

The mayor stroked his beard and leaned forward in his chair. "Had you been drinking?" He asked in hope of finding an easy explanation to the tale.

"No, I swears to the great Strabo I had not touched a drop." The fisherman replied. "I knows what I saw, a demon."

"He speaks the truth." Another man said stepping forward. "I saw it also. Late in the evening, two days ago, I heard the sound of hooves outside of my home. I went out to take a look and saw hoof prints in the mud nearby. I turned back towards my house and noticed a short hooded figure, its sinister yellow eyes staring at me. A demon!" He said holding up a figure. "I took a step back in terror, then noticed a fishing spear leaning up against my smoking shed. Finding my courage I snatched up the spear and ran at the demon. But it too ran, fast, as if unnatural powers drove its legs on. I gave chase as fast as I could, but it leapt clean over houses to evade me."

The crowd began to mutter as others said that they too had seen such things. The mayor had received many reports, all telling of a yellow eyed demon stalking their village. "We must learn what this creature is." The mayor said, holding up a hand to quiet the crowd.

"We know what it is." An old, blind woman said. Her daughter took her arm and led her before the mayor. "The great sea serpent, Strabo, is angered that its offerings have ceased."

A few in the crowd muttered their agreement and the mayor once more held up a hand to silence them. "I have already considered this." He said as the crowd fell silent. "The best and bravest of our fishermen have gone to sea and once they return, we shall make our offerings."

"They were sent days ago." The blind woman said, her voice old and croaky. "And should have returned by now."

The mayor knew this to be true and himself feared that they were lost. "They are most likely delayed because of the fog, but the beacon shall guide them home." He said in hope. When the fog had first swept across the sea, the mayor had ordered a huge fire lit on the beach to serve as a beacon to guide their boats home. But as the fog grew worse, men feared the water and the boats stayed ashore.

"The great Strabo knows our plight and is testing our belief in him." The blind woman held up both of her hands as she spoke. "This fog is nothing more than the great serpent's breath, and to show our devotion we must gather our remaining stores and send them out onto the sea. Only then will the great Strabo vanquish this fog, and the demon that terrorises us."

The crowd began to argue amongst themselves as they were split on what should be done. "If we send out the remainder of our stores, we shall starve!" A man with a mop of red hair angrily shouted above the noise.

"It is because of that lack of faith, is why the great Strabo sees fit to test us." The blind woman calmly replied. "There was a time when we would fill a boat with our finest fish, along with offerings of gold and silver." The crowd had fallen silent, giving way to the sound of the crackling fire. "It was not just Fish and gold, but the most beautiful virgin in our village."

"Surely you cannot be suggesting that we sacrifice one of our daughters?" The mayor said, his face full of horror and ashen. "We have not done such a thing in hundreds of years."

"And our faith has wavered and faded in that time." The blind woman's voice strengthened, "And now the great Strabo wills it."

"She's right!" A woman from the crowd shouted. "We must show or faith."

The crowd once more burst into argument and the mayor shouted and pleaded for calm, but they would not listen. Then the doors to the hall burst open and a woman with bright red curly hair staggered in, whaling and holding at scratches on her blooded face.

"Demon!" The woman cried. "The demon!" Blood oozed out of her wounds and dripped onto the stone floor. She fell to her knees before the mayor, sobbing. "The demon!"

"Tell us what you saw." The mayor said as two women came forward to tend her wounds.

The woman shook with fear and her trembling hands could barely grip the goblet of water she was given. "I....I saw it." She managed to say before sipping at the water.

"What happened?" The mayor asked, his voice full of fear.

The woman took another sip as the blood was wiped off of her forehead. "I was walking here when I heard footsteps coming from down an alleyway. I went to look, but because of the fog I could see nothing." She paused to take another sip. "I foolishly walked down the alleyway, believing that it was a child playing tricks on me. I picked up a stick that was lying on the ground and hit the wall, calling for whoever was there to come out." She shuddered at the memory. "Yellow eyes pierced though the fog at me. The demon leapt at me flapping its claw-like hands at me and scratching my face."

"Where did it go?!" The mayor asked, standing from his chair.

The woman shook her head. "It leapt clean over the house and disappeared into the fog."

"Arm yourselves!" The mayor roared at the crowd. "Let us find this demon and send it back to the underworld!"

The men, angered by the attack, lit torches and grabbed anything they could use as a weapon before taking to the fog concealed streets. For hours did they search but find nothing. Gangs of men continually stalked through streets, poking their fishing spears into rubbish heaps in hope of flushing out the demon. From the beach a young boy watched the flickering torches weave in and out of the fog.

To him it looked like orange and yellow orbs dancing through the mist as though some silent music were playing. He could see nothing of the gangs of men that carried those torches, but he could hear their shouts and banging's as they searched for the demon.

The boy's father had instructed him to keep the beacon burning and to remain there until he had returned. He eagerly agreed, not wanting to come face-to-face with a demon. As the night went on, he added fuel to the fire from a pile of wood that he and his father had stacked earlier. But something in the night unsettled him. Regularly he would stop what he was doing and look out across the sea, into the fog as if something was watching him. Yet he could see nothing, but felt sure he was being watched by an unseen pair of eyes.

Hours later his father returned with a jug of warm ale and a loaf of bread. "Here you go lad, get this down ya." He was a small, broad man with a weathered face and a flat nose.

The boy greedily bit into his bread, his young eyes still staring out into the fog covered sea. "Did you find the demon?" He asked, willing himself to tear his gaze away from across the sea.

The boy's father placed down the jug of ale into the sand and shook his head. "No lad, but it is only a matter of time."

"Is it truly a demon father?" The boy asked, focusing in on a spot in the fog where he thought he saw movement, a brief shadow sweeping through the fog.

"There is something evil stirring this fog lad." The boy's father said picking up the jug and taking a swig. "And demons are never far from us."

The boy had grown up hearing such tales, but had never once saw one, nor known of anyone seeing one until a few days ago. He picked up a pebble from the sand and tossed it out into the fog, feeling sure that it would stick in the fog as it was that thick. But seconds later he heard it *plop* into the sea.

"What are you looking at lad?" The boy's father said as he stood and walked beside him.

The boy shook his head. "Nothing, I can't see anything other than this fog."

The boy's father stared out in the direction his son was looking. "What do you see?"

"I thought I saw movement." The boy answered, pointing out into sea, his hand disappearing into the fog.

"It must be the breeze trying to clear the fog." The boy's father replied. "Is there something else?" He then asked, seeing the concerned look on his son's face.

"I feel as though I'm being watched, as if someone is peering at me through the fog at me." The boy stared at the spot where he felt the eyes. "I feel it now."

His father ruffled his hair and said, "Nobody can see far in this." He went and sat back beside the fire and took another swig of ale. "It's your imagination."

The boy wanted to believe that's all it was. But something deep-down within himself told of terror and impending doom. He picked up another pebble and tossed out into the sea. *Plop*. There was a sudden creaking sound as if the wooden planks of a boat was moaning against the strain of the water. "Father come listen!"

The boy's father rushed over to his son side and listened. "The creaking of a boat!" He said excitedly. "The others have returned!" There was a sudden surge of water that lapped around their ankles. "Wait." He said as his son rushed off to make the announcement. "Something isn't right."

"What is it father?" The boy asked, coming to a stop. But before any answer was given, something shot out of the fog and struck his father in his chest. He rushed back to his father's side, who was now lying on his side, his blood spilling out into the sea. "Father." The boy said falling to his knees beside the body of his father. "Father." He wept.

Out of the mist came a longship, its wooden beams black and its sail blood red. Its bow ran aground on the sand and horned demons jumped over the side. They were tall and heavily muscled with the body of a human and the head and legs of a bull. Their skin was thick, black and as tough as leather, their eyes a sinister yellow and full of malice. In their hands they carried huge axes and swords as big as two men.

The boy tried to scramble away, but was pulled up off his hands and knees by one of the demons. "Let me go!" He screamed as he thrashed about in an attempt to free himself. The demon turned him, and the boy fell still with fear as he gazed into the face of a Minoton.

"Give up whelp." The Minoton said, its voice deep and full of evil. It tossed the boy back down onto the sand and pulled out the throwing axe that was stuck in the boy's father's chest. "Your fate is doom."

The young boy's hands and legs were bound with a thick rope that had been enchanted never to come loose. He listened as women screamed and men died, children cried for their mothers as they were rounded up and placed next to him on the beach. The women suffered the same fate as the children, only they were kept in a separate group away from the children. But no man was spared from death. The buildings were set alight and plundered for any wealth, which they piled up before the prow of their longship.

It was then that the young boy noticed a figurehead of a bull carved into the bow of the ship. Its eyes were yellow glow-stones and its horns steel. The boy thought that it looked frightening and realised that it was those eyes that were staring across the sea at him. He tore his gaze away from the figurehead and watched as a gangplank was lowered over the side. Down the gangplank walked a tall, masked man. He wore a long crimson robe and carried a staff with a blue gemstone fixed onto the top. His mask was black with a white gigantic rune for the letter M on its forehead.

"Has the village fallen?" The masked man asked a Minoton that knelt down before him in subjection.

"Yes my master." The Minoton answered. "We have stripped it of wealth and captured its women and children." The Minoton was slightly bigger than the others and wore a gold torque around its thick neck. "The men folk we killed."

The tall, masked man glanced over at the group of captured children, frightening them with his sinister presence. He walked over and pointed to the young boy. "Bring him to me." He ordered. The Minoton obediently plucked out the young boy and tossed him down at the feet of the masked man. "Do you know who I am?" He asked, his voice muffled by the mask.

The young boy looked up at the mask and noticed that they were no eyes behind the mask's eyeholes. "No." The boy said, frightened.

The masked man knelt down and looked straight into the boy's eyes. "I am Melanthius." A shudder of fear swept through the villagers and a few of the older women sobbed on hearing the name. "And I am in need of your service." He placed a hand on the boy's head and the ropes that bound his arms and legs fell off. From his robe he pulled out scroll that he handed to the boy. "Take this to your king. Tell him what has happened here and that other towns and villages will share your fate if he does not agree to my terms."

The young boy looked down at the scroll in his hand and noticed that it was dimly glowing red. "I don't know the way." He said sombrely.

"It matters not." Melanthius said standing. "You shall find him."

The Minoton grabbed the boy by his dark-green tunic and pulled him onto his feet. "Go." He furiously said.

The boy wept as he reluctantly walked away from the village. He walked up a nearby hill and looked back down at the burning village. It had been the only home he had ever known, and now it was nothing more than an inferno of doom and dread. The fog had almost lifted and the way forward seemed suddenly very clear to him. Find the king, he told himself, the king would avenge his father and the village. Before he turned to leave, he saw a figure leap over a burning building and off into the fields below. "The demon." He said aloud to himself.

Chapter 4

Langton Castle had been held by the Langton family since
its founding in 458 Ac. King William II had granted a
knight called Alard Langton land that guarded the pass
through the mountains of Azaroth for his victory in the
king's tournament. The tournament had attracted the
greatest of knights from all over the kingdom, all of whom
wanted the winner's purse of a lordship. The tournament
had gone on for days with jousts, swordsmanship and
archery competitions taking place. But the event everyone
wanted to see had been the thirty man battle of champions,
where you were eliminated if you were knocked down.
The thirty men had fought all afternoon, the crowd
cheering and waving small flags of their favourite knight,
until only Alard remained standing. The king had crowned
him with a laurel of red roses and handed him a scroll that
gave him the title, Lord Langton.

At first the castle had been built from wood, a simply
motte-and-bailey stronghold where Lord Langton had
consolidated his power. The early years of his lordship had
been difficult as the ground was hard and stony and the
farmers were unable to grow much. But once the lord
ordered the mountains to be mined, his fortunes changed.
From the belly of the mountains came precious gemstones
that were sold in the market to jewellers, and the lord
became rich. The wooden walls and keep gave way to
thick stone and merchants and men flocked to the rose
banner of Lord Langton, offering him their allegiance. The
castle became a seat of wealth and power, and the lords

that followed Alard became one of the most powerful lords in all the realm.

The huge stone keep was now protected by a thick inner curtainwall that ran from the western mountain, along the brow of the old motte and back into the mountain. There were five huge round-towers along the wall and a fortified gate on the east wall that guarded entrance into the old motte. On the lower ground below stood two more walls, one to the north, and one to the south. Both ran from the mountains in the west to the mountains in the east, following the brow of the old bailey. Each wall had six round-towers and a fortified gate that barred the road south to the town of Elwood, so that any wishing to travel south would have to pass through the town.

The king's army was now spread out on the plains before the northern wall. At midday the king's outriders had been spotted and the town's bell had been rung in warning. Many gathered along the wall to see the arrival of the king's army, and nervously watched as his men made camp.

"I hope that we need not lay siege." The king said staring at the high walls though his telescope. "I doubt that we have ladders long enough."

The Duke of Hollington was stood beside the king, staring up at the walls. "Their army is defeated and their lord dead. I doubt that they have the stomach for a fight."

"The walls look strong." The king said, taking his eye away from the eyepiece. "If they make a fight of it, it will cost me dearly in men." He snapped shut his telescope and handed it to an aide who was dutifully stood a few paces behind him and added, "And time."

"We should have the men stand ready for an assault on the walls." Hollington suggested. "The more we frighten them the better."

The king nodded his head in agreement. "Send fourth the herald, give them one hour to surrender."

"Yes my king." Hollington said, bowing and walking off to carry out the king's orders.

The king's army positioned itself for the attack as the herald rode up before the walls. He carried a white banner that told the men on the wall that he wished to parley, and they obligingly shouted to hear his terms.

"What have you to say?!" A captain on the wall called down to the herald.

"Your lord has fallen and his army defeated at Baden Hill!" The herald called back up to the captain. "The king wills that you yield the key to the castle, and in his mercy you will all be speared!" He was clad in shining plate armour which was covered over with a quartered yellow and purple jupon, and rode a grey warhorse that was as equally impressive as its rider.

"And what if we don't!?" The captain shouted, already knowing the answer.

"Then the king shall attack and spare no one!" The herald pulled out a scroll from his saddlebag and held it up. "These are the king's terms to which you have an hour to agree." He tossed them down at the foot of the gate and rode back towards the camp.

The captain watched the herald ride off before he called down to a solider stationed at the gate to collect the scroll.

It was then taken to the Lord Aide who had gathered his officials in the lord's audience chamber.

The king's terms were short and simple. The castle was to surrender and its men of rank were to swear their loyalty to the king, and all would be shown mercy for their treason. If not, then the king promised to take the castle by force and kill all who have defied him. To the Lord Aide there was nothing to debate. News of Lord Langton's defeat had reached them a day before the king's army had arrived by a man that had survived the battle. Their numbers were too few to defend the walls and their moral was depleted after hearing that their lord had been slain. And so the Lord Aide told his council that they would surrender to the king, and pray to the gods above that he stays true with his offer of mercy.

The king was sat on his throne-like chair under a purple canopy being held up by four brass poles that shone like gold in the sunlight. He wore full plate armour covered over with a silk, purple jupon that had silver stars stitched into it, and above his brow a white crown of stars. His face was calm, calculated as if he expected nothing other than the castle's complete surrender. As he watched the castle's Lord Aide and his entourage approach him, he felt disappointed that there would be no siege, believing that it would be better to show his might and destroy the castle for its treason. "Perhaps I should send in men now, while their gate is open." The king said aloud.

"No man would follow a king who did not keep his word." Duke of Hollington replied. He was stood beside the king and dressed in his usual grubby gambeson with a black boar on his chest. "Our enemies would only use it to persuade other lords to join their rebellion."

"I jest my good Duke." The king said in high spirits. "A simple jest."

"Very good my king." Hollington replied with a courteous smile.

As the Lord Aide and his entourage came before the canopy, they fell to their knees. "O' merciful king forgive us for we are but humble servants that foolishly followed Lord Langton's orders." The Lord Aide pleaded. He was an odd-looking man with a flabby body and round bulging eyes. The red tunic he wore was fading and looked more pink, and the chain of office he wore was tarnished and in need of a polish.

"You are treasonous dogs that have rebelled against your rightful king!" The king said in a serious tone, his earlier good mood seemingly vanquished.

"No my king, it was not us." The Lord Aide's hands shook with fear. "I and my council tried to tell Lord Langton not to take up the rebellion against you. But he would not heed our counsel."

"Do you take your king for a fool?!" The king roared and stood from his throne-like chair. "I wonder if you would have said as much if your lord were the victor at Baden Hill?!" He strode up to the Lord Aide and placed his armoured foot out in front of him.

The Lord Aide lowered his head and kissed the king's foot. "Mercy my king, mercy!" He pleaded.

The king snatched his foot away and went and sat back on his throne-like chair. "You have read the terms?" He asked, his eyes showing his anger at the Lord Aide.

"Yes my king." The Lord Aide shakily answered. "Me and my council have read your most gracious terms and summit ourselves to your mercy." He turned to an aide kneeling behind him and took the small wooden chest he was holding. "I, the Lord Aide of Langton Castle, surrender the castle and its holdings to you, King Henri IV, the rightful king of Elnaria." He said holding out the chest.

Hollington stepped forward and took the chest off the Lord Aide. "The key to the castle." He said opening the lid and presenting it to the king.

The king leaned forward in his chair and looked down at the key. It was not a useable key where one could open a door with it, but symbolic. When a man became a lord, he was presented with the key to a castle and a scroll that confirmed his lordship. The key had become a symbol of sovereignty over the castle, and it had become traditional for it to be presented to a victorious besieger in times of war. Now the king owned the castle and all its holdings.

"We surrender to your mercy my king." The Lord Aide said as he lowered his head in subjection.

The king took the silver key from the chest and cut off the white and red ribbon tied onto the head with a dagger scabbarded at his waist. "Do you renounce the rebellion and the traitor Lord Langton?"

"Yes sire, with all that is righteous." The Lord Aide replied, keeping his eyes low.

The king dropped the ribbon onto the ground and placed the key back into the chest. "You and your council are hereby stripped of your office." He said waving a hand for

Hollington to take away the key. "You shall return to the castle and make the announcement of your surrender and instruct all men of rank to gather in the lord's audience chamber where they shall swear their fealty to me." The king once more stood from his chair. "Any that fail to do so shall be executed for treason as the law permits, is that understood?"

"Yes sire." The Lord Aide shakily answered. "I shall gather them at once."

The king waved a dismissive hand at the Lord Aide and watched as he took three steps backwards, bowed, turned and walked back towards the castle. "Is my entourage ready?" He asked the Duke of Hollington.

"You may enter the castle as you wish." Hollington replied, indicating that the king's entourage was ready and waiting for him.

"Good, then let us get this over with." The King stood from his throne-like chair and mounted his horse that was brought over to him by a groom. He led a procession of knights and officials through the gate into the castle, only to find the streets were almost empty. The sight of only a handful of people, who silently watched as he passed them by, angered him. He had expected the populous of the castle to be thankful of his mercy. To be applauding him and throwing flowers onto the cobbled street before his horse. But instead, the people chose to hide inside their houses in case the king went back on his word. "Damn them!" The king snapped. "Are they not grateful for my mercy!?"

"They are afraid my king." Hollington replied. "But they shall soon return to their normal ways."

101

The king and his procession followed the main road up towards the inner gate that led up to the old motte. There, in the castle's courtyard, the king and his procession dismounted and entered into the keep. At the entrance was a short, thin man with a mop of curly hair waiting for them. He bowed to the king and led him into the audience chamber where the men of rank had hastily gathered. As the king entered, the chamber fell deathly silent and his heavy footsteps echoed off the stone floor as he walked to the lord's seat at the far end.

It was a dull, rectangular room with faded tapestries hanging on the walls. The chamber was built in the centre of the keep, so there was no windows to let in any light, and was lit by hundreds of candles that clouded the room with the smell of molten wax.

The king sat on the lord's high-backed chair and beckoned for the first man to come forward and swear his loyalty. One by one, the men of rank knelt before the king and swore their fealty to him and denounced the rebellion and the traitor, the Duke of Baleford. It went on for hours as the king accepted their loyalty and promised each man a pardon for their treason. Once the last man had sworn his loyalty, the king rose from his chair and tiredly asked for his chamber. He was led up to the highest room in the keep, where a bedchamber had been hastily prepared for him. He lay down on the four-poster bed and closed his eyes to relieve the dull ache behind his eyes. But minutes later he was disturbed by a loud knock on the door.

"Sorry to have disturbed you my king." Hollington said as he walked through the door. "But plans need to be made."

The king sat up and tiredly rubbed his face. "Can it not wait?" He asked.

"Tomorrows orders." Hollington waved in a servant carrying an inkpot and quill. "You need to sign them." He plucked out a folded piece of parchment that was tucked into his belt and placed it on the table where the servant had placed the ink and quill.

The king went over to the table and signed his name at the bottom of the parchment. "Is that all?" He asked, hoping that he could lay back on the bed and sleep.

Hollington took the parchment and handed it to the servant. "Have this copied and given out to the captains." He ordered.

"What else would you have from your king?" The king asked, seeing that there was yet more Hollington wanted.

"Sir Gregory Fitzwalter asks for an audience with you."

"Well he can wait!" The king angrily snapped. He knew what Sir Gregory wanted; he wanted to release Henri from his retinue as it had damaged his reputation amongst the other knights. But it was a problem the king cared little for.

"You keep on denying him an audience." Hollington spoke as though he was speaking to a frightened horse, so not to anger the king further. "I fear this matter will only grow worse if left without your judgement."

The king deeply sighed and shook his head. "Show him in."

Hollington bowed and went out of the bedchamber only to return moments later with Sir Gregory.

"My king." Sir Gregory bowed. "I thank you for granting me this audience." He was dressed in a crimson tunic that was pulled in at his waist by a blue belt that was studded with brass lions standing on their back legs.

"It is getting late." The king said as though he was irritated with Sir Gregory. "Spare me the pleasantries and get to your issue."

"I wish for Henri to be removed from my retinue forthwith." Sir Gregory said, pushing a lock of curly hair out of his eyes. "I can no longer tolerate one so lowly born in my retinue."

"Is it not a blessing to have one so blessed by the star oracle in your company?" The king asked raising an eyebrow at Sir Gregory. The truth was that he knew having a lowborn in your retinue was seen as a scandal. That the other knightly classes would mock and whisper of dishonour at the king's folly for rising one so low into the rank of a squire. But the oracle at Lhanwick had told him to keep Henri safe, that their paths were intertwined. So he did as the oracle had bid, not that he truly believed in the oracle's words.

"My king," Sir Gregory went on, "His very presence in my retinue is an insult to my good family name. And his conduct has only tarnished it further." He took a step closer to the king and held out his hands as if pleading his case. "As you will be aware my king, his resent actions of assaulting one of your constables has caused me great trouble."

The king held up a hand to stop Sir Gregory. "I have already dealt with this." He said in a tone that showed he was irritated with the matter being brought to him again. It was a problem that had been plaguing him for the past week. He had ordered Symond to speak with Henri, to put him in his place. But Symond was with a company of Arcani a few miles away from his army and was unable to speak with Henri until he arrived a Langton.

"Forgive me my king, but he cannot be allowed to transgress in such a manner and still remain a squire. It reflects badly upon me and my family name." Sir Gregory said, his anger beginning to rise. "If he is not removed, then it can only be seen as a great insult to me!" He added sharply.

"So what is it you want?!" The king said abruptly. "To have him hung!? To banish him from the kingdom!? No, he shall remain in your retinue!"

There was a moments silence as both considered their next move. "Very well my king." Sir Gregory conceded. "But if he is to remain in my retinue, I demand a reward that compensates the damage to my family name."

The king looked long and hard at Sir Gregory with suspicious eyes. "What have you in mind?"

In the last couple of days Sir Gregory had thought about it, planned this moment he would ask the king. "I wish to become the new lord of Langton." He said in a self-righteous manner.

"That is a lot to ask of a king!" The king said with disbelief. "You are only a knight and cannot jump straight to the rank of a lord!"

"No more so then a lowborn peasant jumping to the rank of a squire!" Sir Gregory argued. "It would be a fitting reward for the trouble he has caused me."

The king shook his head. "I need time to think on this matter."

"Go now." Hollington said to Sir Gregory. "The king shall summon you when a decision has been made."

Sir Gregory bowed to the king and left the chamber feeling as though the lordship was already his, that the king had little other choice if Henri was to remain a squire in his retinue.

*   *   *

"The horse can feel your anger." Rylan warned Henri as the horse they were cleaning stamped its front legs. "You need to be soft and yet firm at the same time."

Henri bent down and dunked his brush in a bucket of water and shook off the dirt. "I shouldn't be doing this!" He said standing back up and wiping sweat off his forehead with the sleeve of his tunic. "The king himself crowned me with the laurel of victory!" Henri angrily tossed the brush into the bucket of water and walked out from under the canopy where Sir Gregory's horses were stabled. It was a sunny day with a clear blue sky with little breeze to cool it. Birds sang and frolicked in the perfect sky above as the king's army made use of the time by resting and repairing weapons. He looked over towards a group of squires stood at the edge of a clearing between two pavilions belonging to knights. They were cheering and shouting encouragements to the two squires thrusting and swinging at each other with blunt swords.

"It's not that bad." Rylan said as he came and stood next to Henri. "You just need to get used to it."

"They're having a tourney!" Henri said with spite, ignoring Rylan.

Rylan looked over to where Henri was staring and watched as a squire with dark, shoulder length hair parried a blow and countered with a clumsy swing of his own. "It's too hot of a day to be fighting with swords."

"I should be there!" Henri shook his head in anger. "I could beat any one of them."

"Your time will come." Rylan said seeing the anger in Henri's eyes. "You just need to grateful in your duties. Then Sir Gregory will soon place you back with the squires."

Henri looked at Rylan with disbelief. "You think that I should be grateful for mucking out his horses!?"

"You was born a peasant Henri." Rylan said as though Henri was missing his point. "And now you're a squire. Not many can speak of such achievements."

"No Rylan." Henri replied, looking back over towards the squires. "Sir Gregory and all the knightly rank will only ever see me as a peasant. It won't matter how well I muck out his bloody horses."

The squires cheered as the two duelling squires began grappling in the centre of the clearing. The bigger of the two overpowered his opponent and tossed him to the ground. A Master-of-Arms Henri didn't recognise called out, "If you grapple with a stronger opponent, then you will die!" The squires applauded the victor as two more squires were called out to duel.

"The world will never let me forget my low birth." Henri said as he turned away from the squires and walked back under the canopy. "Come Rylan, we had better get back to our duties before I get you into trouble again." Henri added as though he was defeated and saddened.

Henri's words unnerved Rylan. Normally Henri was defiant to his low birth, and full of guile and determination to better himself. But something had suddenly changed, as though he knew something, something that made him no longer care about his place in Sir Gregory's retinue. He looked over to Henri and could see that he was thinking about something. "What are you planning?" Rylan asked.

Henri took out the brush from the bucket and began stroking the horse's flank. "Nothing." He answered evasively.

"I have known you since you were given a place in Sir Gregory's retinue." Rylan questioned Henri. "And never once have I heard you sound so defeated. So what are you planning?"

"It's better that you don't know." Henri replied as he ran the brush over the length of the horse's back.

"You're not planning on killing Sir Gregory are you?" Rylan asked with fear.

"No!" Henri said turning to face Rylan. "Don't say such things too loud, they would love nothing more than to string me up at the nearest tree!"

"Then what is it?" Rylan asked, pushing for an answer.

"I can't stay here anymore." Henri replied quietly.

"You're going to desert?" Rylan said, shocked and upset at Henri. "But why? You have a chance of one day becoming a knight."

"No I don't." Henri said placing a hand on Rylan's shoulder. "While I'm placed in this retinue, Sir Gregory will never give me my spurs."

"But why desert and not just ask to move to another knight's retinue?"

"You know that no other knight will allow a lowborn peasant to join their retinue." Henri turned back to the horse, more to avoid Rylan's awkward gaze then to continue brushing the horse. "It's better for everyone if I just go." He added.

"And where are you planning on going my young friend?" A familiar voice cut in.

Henri turned towards the familiar voice and saw a man dressed in a dark green tunic and trousers. His skin was dark like the easterners and his voice had a heavy accent. "Symond!" Henri said, both happy and concerned at his sudden appearance.

"We meet again my young friend." Symond said with a smile. "It has been too long."

The last time Henri had seen Symond was at Lhanwick where Symond had congratulated him and wished him well. But since then things had gone downhill fast. At first the lower ranks had cheered his crowning with the laurel of victory as it was said to give them hope. But now all that seemed to be forgotten and his elevation to squire seemed to be a constant embarrassment to both the king and all his knights. "What brings you here?" Henri asked, knowing that Symond was not simply just visiting to see how he was getting on.

Symond glanced at Rylan as if to say that he should leave them to talk more privately.

"Go Rylan." Henri said jerking his head. "I'll speak with you later."

"Very well." Rylan reluctantly said as he walked out of the canopy.

"The king is displeased with your resent conduct." Symond said once Rylan was out of earshot.

"Is that why you are here?" Henri said. "To tell me of the king's anger towards me?"

"The king has instructed me to issue you with a warning." Symond said in a serious tone. "If you persist in this unfit manner, then you shall be punished as befitting your rank."

"And what rank would that be!?" Henri said in a resentful tone. "A squire, or as the peasant that I'm seen as!?"

Symond smiled at Henri and said, "Where I come from, ones birth matters not. What matters is what knowledge he possesses."

Henri shook his head. "That may be Symond, but it is only the wealthy that can afford to be tutored. We poor must meaninglessly work so that the men of rank can keep their place."

"You have fared well enough." Symond said raising an eyebrow. "Born a peasant and yet you stand before me a squire."

Henri just shrugged. "I'm not a real squire, and I will never be knighted."

"No." Symond replied, looking sternly at Henri with his hazel eyes. "Not if you keep on with this conduct of yours."

Henri shook his head knowing that there was little hope of him ever becoming a knight, and a part of him wondered why he was even bothered. Did he really want to become part of a class he hated? It was said that the knightly class was honourable, virtuous and the keepers of the law of chivalry. But that law only applied to those of equal rank, and not to lowborn peasants. "So where have you been?" Henri asked Symond, wanting to change the subject.

"I have been given command of a small company of Arcani." Symond replied. "They are awaiting me by a small village to the north."

"Why so far?" Henri asked, knowing that the nearest village was miles away.

"A band of Langton's men that survived the battle have gathered there and have refused the king's offer of a pardon. My spies tell me that they plan on attacking the king's rear when he marches back north and the king has tasked me with eliminating the threat." Symond explained.

"Sounds like an adventure." Henri said sulkily.

"You should come with me." Symond said, seeing that Henri looked envious of the mission.

"I can't just leave my duties here." Henri said jerking his thumb at the horse he had been brushing. "Sir Gregory will never allow it."

"The Henri I know would not worry about such things." Symond turned and walked out of the canopy. "Now are you coming!?" He called back over his shoulder.

Henri, needing no further encouragement, followed Symond out where another member of the Arcani waited with Symond's horse. The squires were still holding their tourney and the crowd that had gathered to watch paid little attention to Henri or the Arcani. Henri mounted behind Symond and they rode out of the camp, heading north. After a couple of hours of riding across open grasslands, the terrain became rugged and began to climb up towards some hills that lorded it over the grassland below. The village was situated atop of a wooded hill that was overlooked by a larger hill to the east. It was on that hill that the band of Arcani had made their camp.

They had been there for a couple of days, carefully watching the village below. Not a single fire had been lit and their presence had been undetected by the remnants of Langton's men. Henri thought that the Arcani were grim men, all clad in grubby dark-green tunics and trousers. Though they looked ageing and scruffy, they were battle hardened and ready to swoop down the hill and kill at a moment's notice.

A man whose face was covered with scars from smallpox took the reins of Symond's horse as he and Henri dismounted. "Any movement to report captain?" Symond asked the man.

"The outskirts of the village have been scouted as you ordered." The captain answered as he pulled out a crudely drawn map from a pouch on his belt. "They are unaware of our presence and we may attack at nightfall."

"Have all buildings been plotted?" Symond asked as he took the crumpled up map from the captain.

"Yes commander. And it would seem that they are holding the villagers in the hall in the centre of the village."

"Do we know how many they number?" Symond asked, fearing that he would not have enough men to overwhelm them.

The captain shrugged his shoulders. "Twelve more joined their number an hour ago. By my reckoning we are outnumbered two, maybe three to one, but we have surprise on our side and the darkness of night."

Symond looked at the map, deep in thought. A night attack could go horribly wrong. Men could easily get lost in the dark, trip over tree roots and give away their position, or accidently end up killing each other in the confusion. But there was little choice. The king wanted the last of Langton's men dealt with quickly so that he could march north unhindered. "Gather the men." Symond ordered the captain.

The captain quietly summoned all of the Arcani, and together they sat in a circle around a makeshift map made of stones and branches. There was thirty Arcani, all grim and carrying the scars of many dark deeds. Quietly they sat awaiting their commander to make known his plans.

Symond stood over his crude map with a stick in hand, tapping the stones one by one to ensure that they were in the same place as drawn on the map the captain had given him. "There is only one road that leads in and out of the village." He said as he traced a scratched line in the ground. "I want three men covering it at all times to stop any fleeing." He then tapped a log in the centre of his makeshift map. "The villagers are being kept in the hall and are not to be harmed."

"Are we to free them?" The captain asked, interrupting Symond.

"Only once the battle is over." Symond answered as he looked around his company to ensure that they understood. "The last thing we want is for civilians to be running around in a blind panic in the dark."

"And what of any that might be still in their homes?" The captain asked, knowing that the soldiers would most likely keep the prettiest girls aside from the others.

"Tell them to remain where you find them until the battle is over." Symond turned from the captain and tapped at three points on the outskirts of the village. "We split into three groups and under the cover of darkness we shall move to these locations. Then two hours before sunrise I will give the signal to begin the attack. We move quickly and silently, killing as many of them as we can before the alarm is raised." Symond once again tapped each stone that represented a house. "Check each one, I don't want any enemy to spring any surprises of their own." Symond once again looked around his men. "It is simple, we go quietly and kill until the enemy is vanquished. Is that under stood?"

Henri looked around at Arcani nodding their agreement. They were dirty and scruffy, nothing like what one would

114

expect an elite military order to look like. Yet they were rough looking and Henri found himself glad that he would not have to fight such men, shadows of the night that brought fear and death.

"Go now." Symond ordered his men. "Eat and rest, for tonight we attack." Symond went and sat with Henri who was sat silently taking in his surroundings.

"A simple plan." Henri said as Symond came and sat beside him.

"Killing is such a simple thing. That is why it is so dangerous my young friend."

"So what of me?" Henri asked, wondering why Symond had asked him along. "What do you want me to do?"

"Nothing." Symond replied. "You must not get involved in the fighting."

"So why bring me?" Henri asked, disappointed at not being allowed to fight.

"I did not bring you, I invited you and you freely came." Symond pointed out with a smile.

"Don't play words with me Symond." Henri frustratingly said. "Why am I really here?"

"Sir Gregory has gone to the king and asked that you be removed from his retinue." Symond looked at Henri with sympathetic eyes. "Your elevation to squire has caused much discontent amongst the knightly class."

"And what will the king do?"

Symond shook his head. "I know not my young friend. That is why you are here…"

"To keep me out of the way!" Henri cut in with resentment.

Symond nodded. "You are to remain with me until the king has reached a decision."

Henri found that the news saddened him, yet he didn't know why. Since he had been placed in Sir Gregory's retinue he had found life as a squire hard. The other squires had resented him for his low birth and the Master-At-Arms had often picked on him. He should have welcomed being back with Symond, but a voice in his head whispered of failure and that the other knights and squires were right to doubt his elevation. And now all he wanted was to prove them all wrong, to prove that a man was not defined by his birth. But it seemed that the world would not give him a chance.

"I'm sorry my young friend." Symond said as he stood. "I will speak to have you given a suitable place somewhere. Now I must go and ready my men for battle."

The sun sank below the brow of the hills and a calm night descended. The sky was clear and the light of the full moon guided the Arcani into their positions. Silent as shadows they moved through the woods until to the outskirts of the village they came. There they waited until the early hours when the hooting of an owl, made by Symond, signalled them to attack. The soldiers in the village were asleep and caught completely by surprise. Many were killed in their beds by the silent blades of the Arcani as they systematically went from house to house.

The alarm was soon raised and the village erupted with the shouts and screams of battle.

Henri listened to ringing sound of clashing blades from the road that led in and out of the village. He thought it odd that Symond had called it a road as it was no more than a dirt track with a grass verge running down the middle. He had hoped that there would be a mass exodus of fleeing men come running down the road so that he had something to do, but so far there was nothing.

"Do not go too far!" The Arcani he was with said in a stern tone.

Henri ignored him, gripping the hilt of his small sword and willing for some of the enemy to come rushing down the road towards him. And he wasn't made to wait long. The first he saw was a red glow in the hands of a small boy being chased by a group of seven soldiers, shouting at him to stop.

"Stay back!" The Arcani snapped at Henri, his voice muffled by the steel cavalry mask he was wearing. "We shall deal with this!"

Henri drew his short sword ready, knowing that he would have to defend himself. The boy ran aside as the soldiers crashed against the three Arcani that kept watch over the road. Henri watched as the Arcani made short work of the soldiers, but one saw him and charged around the others straight at him. Henri quickly parried a lunge that would have pierced his heart and back swung his sword, catching the soldier's cheek with the edge of his blade. The soldier, angered by Henri's skill, launched a wild attack that Henri fended off with ease. The soldier staggered back as Henri smashed the pommel of his sword in his face then, exhausted and defeated, fell to his knees.

"Mercy, mercy." The soldier pled as he dropped his sword and held up his hands, blood pouring from his broken nose and cut cheek.

But before Henri could answer, an Arcani came up from behind the soldier and cut his throat. "Are you unharmed?" He asked Henri.

"Yes." Henri nodded. He looked over at the young boy who was sat with his back up against a tree, clutching a scroll that was glowing red. "I will see to him." He told the Arcani. As he walked over to the boy he heard him muttering, telling the scroll that he would be on his way soon. "Are you alright?" Henri asked the boy. The boy looked up and Henri was sure he saw a flash of red in his eyes.

"Yes, yes." The boy nodded. "Now I must be on my way."

As the boy rose to his feet, Henri caught the scent of the sea and fish on the boy's clothes. "Where have you come from?" Henri asked, knowing that the smell of sea salt could not have blown this far inland.

"Oldby." The boy said with a shudder. "I must deliver this to the king." He held up the scroll to show Henri. "Bad things have happened."

"What things?" Henri asked sensing the boy's fear and sorrow. But before an answer was given a horn blast signalled for the Arcani to gather in the village. "You had better come with me." Henri grabbed the boy's arm and led him up the road, back into the village.

Chapter 5

"You will make a hole if you scrub there any longer." A servant said to Catharine. She was a young, skinny girl with a freckled face and brown frizzy hair. Her cheeks were flushed and her forehead damp with sweat.

Catharine snapped out of her daydream and realised that she had been scrubbing the same patch of floor for some time, mindlessly rocking back and forth on her knees deep in a daydream. "Sorry Madge." She said as she dipped her hand brush in the bucket by her side. "The water has gone cold."

"Well I'm not surprised." Madge said with a playful smile. "You've been gone with the woodland fairies for some time."

"Have I?" Catharine asked, unsure if she had or was just being teased.

"My dear, in the time you have spent daydreaming, I have scrubbed most of the floor." Madge pointed towards the drying floor behind her. "Not that you could tell now." She added with a sigh.

The night before, the lord had held a feast to show all that he was well again and to douse the rumours that he was dying. The feast had gone on late into the night and the hall had been left in a sorrowful state. Platters and goblets had been scattered across the tables, food dropped onto the floor and candles burnt low in their harbourers. Many servant had laboured in the early hours to clear away the mess and all that now remained was to scrub clean the floor.

"Forgive me Madge, I don't know what's come over me." Catharine shuffled a little further along the floor and began scrubbing away at a sticky patch where someone had spilt wine.

"I know." Madge said with a teasing smile. "The lord has taken you as his mistress."

Catharine abruptly stopped and pointed at Madge with her hand brush. "You know that is not true!"

Madge giggled, knowing that Catharine disliked that the other servants were saying it. "It's alright, I won't tell anybody."

"There's nothing to tell." Catharine said placing the brush back on the floor and began scrubbing. "You shouldn't say such things, it could get me into trouble."

"So who is he?" Madge asked as she shuffled closer to Catharine.

"Who's who?" Catharine replied innocently.

"You know." Madge said, unable to hide the intrigue from her face. "The man that occupies your thoughts."

"There is no man." Catharine replied, annoyed with the constant gossiping amongst the servants. The lord's court was not a private place. Eyes and ears seemed to be lurking everywhere and malicious gossip was rife. "I was simply thinking on better days." Catharine explained.

"Fine, keep your secrets." Madge said as though she was annoyed with Catharine not confiding in her. "But I will find out, nothing stays secret for long around here."

"I have no secrets Madge." Catharine pulled out a handkerchief from the pocket on her apron and wiped the sweat off of her forehead. "It's so hot in here."

"You know Isabella once told me the same thing." Madge smiled at the memory. "So sure I was that she was up to no good, that one night I followed her."

"You did what?" Catharine said with disbelief that Madge would invade someone's privacy so readily.

"I followed her." Madge repeated as she giggled. "I suspected her to have a secret lover, and when I questioned her on my suspicions, she denied it."

"So you followed her to prove you were right." Catharine said, now eager to hear more.

Madge giggled and nodded her head. "It was during a winter's feast that the lord had held to attract more merchants to our market. One such merchant had spent weeks here, and he had took a liking to our Isabella." Madge leaned in closer to Catharine and lowered her voice so that she was not overheard. "I was collecting empty platters when I noticed the merchant in the corner with her. He was leaning on the wall and whispering in Isabella's ear. He then left and after a short time, so did Isabella. I followed her to a storeroom at the back of the kitchens. The door was slightly ajar and I had quietly snuck in." Madge once again giggled at the memory. "I saw them together as though they were husband and wife."

Catharine shook her head. "What became of it?"

"They would meet often, Isabella would deny it whenever I'd question her about it of cause, but the merchant eventually left. I later learned that he had promised to marry Isabella, yet he never came back for her."

"So what happened to Isabella?" Catharine asked as she did not know of any servant called Isabella.

"She was removed." Madge said nudging Catharine with her elbow. "They say she fell pregnant with the merchant's child and was sent away to avoid any scandal."

"Have you ever thought that he could have sent for her, and that they are now married?" Catharine said, annoyed that Madge only seemed to believe the worst.

"A rich merchant marrying a scullery maid." Madge said as though it was an impossible thing. "Such things do not happen, you know that."

Catharine knew this to be true. Marrying for anything other than position and power was considered foolish. "It's so hot in here." She said as she patted her forehead dry with her handkerchief.

"It is." Madge admitted. "Are you well? You look a little flushed."

"I'm fine." Catharine replied as she stood. "I'm going out to get some air."

"Well don't be too long." Madge said with a hint of anger. "I would like some help."

"I won't be long." Catharine promised. She walked out of the hall and down a corridor that had many small tapestries hanging from the walls that led out onto the cobbled courtyard. It was cooler outside as there was a light breeze that blew in from the west and Catharine sat on a wooden box that was beside the door. She leaned back and felt the warm stone on her back as she closed her eyes in an attempt to relieve her tiredness. All seemed calm and quiet. Normally the courtyard would be busy with people coming and going, but today all was quiet as if everybody was sleeping in. The sun's rays prickled her skin and she found herself once again daydreaming of better days. But her daydream was soon disturbed by the clip-clapping of a horse's hooves on the cobblestone. She immediately opened her eyes to see a messenger ride into the courtyard. Catharine watched as a stable boy rushed to take his reins as the messenger dismounted and ran up the stairs two at a time. He saw Catharine and took off his hat, bidding her a good morrow. "Good morrow." Catharine politely replied as the messenger rushed off into the keep. She wondered what news he carried and hoped that he might be carrying a letter from Elizabeth. No, she thought, Elizabeth would have wrote before now.

Minutes later the messenger came back out, carrying a leather bag filled with letters. As he remounted and sped off out of the gate, Catharine found herself longing for the freedom the messenger had. He was able to ride from place to place, seeing the countryside and meeting many different types of people. Adventure, that is what she wanted, an adventure so that she could get away from here. She quickly told herself off and reminded herself that Elizabeth had once thought like that, and look where it had got her. No, she would need to be more cunning then that if she was to ever become anything more than a servant and regain her family's lost wealth. She sat thinking of Elizabeth, wondering where she was and what she was doing. Then a memory of their childhood sprang to mind.

They had been young and Catharine had been playing in the garden of their family home, happily running away from a nursemaid that playfully chased her. Elizabeth had been sat under a tree quietly reading a book when Catharine had jumped out from behind the tree to scare Elizabeth.

"Catharine!" Elizabeth had shouted. "You're such a little terror!"

Catharine had giggled, taking great delight in scaring her sister. "Come and play with me." She said in the hope that Elizabeth would chase her.

"I'm busy." Elizabeth had abruptly replied.

"You're always too busy to play with me." Catharine had complained as she tugged on the sleeve of Elizabeth's dress.

"Catharine, I'm trying to read." Elizabeth had said sternly.

"You're always reading." Catharine complained further. "Why not put the book down and play like a normal child?"

"Because," Elizabeth said looking up from the pages, "I want to learn."

"Learn?" Catharine said pulling a face. "My tutor says that all women need to learn is needlework and good manners that shall reflect well upon their future husband."

"Well your tutor is a fool." Elizabeth had stood and looked into Catharine's eyes. "There may come a time when us women shake off the shackles of men and find ourselves their equals."

Catharine giggled. "Is that what you read about, silly thing that will never happen?"

Elizabeth had smiled at Catharine. "No, this book is about a dragon that once lived in a cave under the hill of the castle." She showed Catharine a vivid picture of a scaly dragon breathing fire at a solitary knight clad in golden armour. "This is Sir Arnoldus." Elizabeth had said, tapping on the knight with her finger. "Sir Arnoldus the dragon slayer."

"Did he defeat the dragon?" Catharine eagerly asked, the picture capturing her imagination.

Elizabeth had closed the book and took Catherine's arm, leading her further into the garden. "The book says that the dragon was the biggest and most ferocious of its kind. Sir Arnoldus was unable to defeat it in open battle and so he tricked it."

"How?" Catharine had asked.

"Dragons are said to have a fondness of flesh and can smell our fear from miles away." Elizabeth explained. "So Sir Arnoldus had all of the prisoners from the dungeon chained in a cave cut out into the side of the hill. The dragon, smelling the flesh of the fearful prisoners, spread its mighty wings and swooped down upon the cave where it devoured the prisoners' bones and all." Elizabeth had looked at Catharine and made chomping noises with her teeth. "While the dragon was busy chewing the flesh, Sir Arnoldus blocked up the entrance of the cave, trapping the dragon inside." Elizabeth had stopped and opened her book to a picture showing a blocked mouth of a cave. "They say that the dragon could still be heard for many years after, scratching at the walls with it spear-like claws."

"If its claws were so sharp how did it not manage to escape?" Catharine had asked sceptically.

"Maybe it did and is now descending down upon us." As Elizabeth said it there was a sudden breeze that stirred the leaves of the trees. "I'm going to find the entrance to the cave and discover if the tale is true." Elizabeth had said with excitement.

Catharine smiled at the memory as she remembered that she had spent that afternoon trying to persuade Elizabeth not to go looking for the dragon's cave. But she had failed. Elizabeth had asked Catharine to go with her before she had taken herself off. But Catharine had never been the adventurous one.

"The lord has summoned you." A groom to the lord said as he came and stood before Catharine. He was a thin, sly looking man with a haircut that looked as though someone had placed a bowl on his head and cut around it. "Come now." He said as Catharine was slow to move.

Catharine obediently followed the groom to the lord's bedchamber where he left her. She knocked on the thick, wooden door and entered. The lord was sat upright in bed reading reports that the messenger had brought him. The same tall, thin man with a long crooked nose tipped with small, round spectacles was stood beside his bed, holding a pile of parchments. They both stared at Catharine with suspicious eyes as she formally bowed. "You summoned me my lord."

126

The lord scribbled a quick note on the bottom of a letter he had read and handed it to his steward. "I'm to take a tour of the town to vanquish these vile rumours that I am dying." He said looking up from a report of supplies that he was to forward to the Duke of Baleford's army. "In my absence I want you to scrub clean this chamber." He scratched his signature on the report and passed it to his steward.

"Yes my lord." Catharine woodenly answered. She wondered why the lord had summoned her just to tell her this, and not have one of his servant do it.

"I want fresh linen and the walls scrubbed with soap." The lord ordered. "Is that understood?"

Catharine nodded. "My lord." She bowed and went to leave.

"I have not finished!" The lord angrily snapped. He began coughing in a fit and dropped the parchment in his hand.

Catharine could see that he was trying to not look weak in front of her, but despite his best efforts, he still looked frail. He had announced to his court that his illness had passed and had held a feast in his honour. But Catharine knew the truth, that he was still unwell. She watched as the lord held a handkerchief to his mouth and wiped away the blood he had coughed up.

The lord's coughing fit soon passed and he quickly hid the blooded handkerchief under the bedsheets. "I need not remind you of your need for discretion!" The lord stared at Catharine, his beady hawk-like eyes bloodshot and shallow, yet still hard and full of malice.

"No my lord, you need not." Catharine answered knowing what would happen to both her and her mother if she made public that the lord was still unwell.

The lord shifted in his bed to make himself more comfortable, never once taking his eyes from Catharine. "You and your mother are to attend my court." He said with a mocking expression on his face. "You both shall present yourself tonight, so make yourself look more presentable." He added as he looked Catharine up and down in a disproving manner.

Catharine was stunned, lost for words as to why the lord would suddenly allow her back to court as his guest.

"You must thank his lordship for his undeserved kindness." The steward said as he pushed his round spectacles up from the tip of his nose.

"I thank you my lord." Catharine said, unable to believe her sudden change in fortune.

"I shall leave within the hour." The lord said as though he was somehow displeased with Catharine. "You will clean my chamber and then take this letter of instruction to your mother." He waved his liver spotted hand to dismiss Catharine and returned to the pile of letters that required his attention.

Catharine dutifully curtsied and left the chamber. She went back to the hall and told Madge that she had been given other duties and that she would find someone else to help her. Madge had said that there was no point as she had already finished. So as the lord took his tour of the town, Catharine dusted, mopped and changed the linen on the bed. By the time she had finished in was mid-afternoon and the morning's quiet had given way to the usual hustle and bustle. Catharine went to the chamber she shared with her mother in hope of finding her there. But it was empty. "The graveyard." Catharine said softly to herself, knowing that it would be the only place her mother would leave the castle for.

The graveyard was on the outskirts of the town beside a small, circular shrine where it was said the spirits of the dead ascended to the stars. The shrine was white with a domed roof that was being held up by eight pillars with carvings of stars on them. Inside was a simple stone alter that had once been encased in gold where the people of the town had once left offering for the stars. But the gold had been long stolen and the offerings had long ago ceased, for the days of piety had long passed.

Catharine walked the familiar path, a simple dirt track that weaved around poorly attended graves, and over to the edge of the graveyard. There her father's grave was. Her mother was kneeling in front of the simple wooden stake with a small board nailed onto it that bore her father's name. Catharine stood watching her mother for a moment. She was dressed in a simple red dress that was brought in by a velvet cord that was tied around her waist. Her straw coloured hair caught the sun and looked gold. Catharine thought that she had looked different these last few days, like at long last she was moving on with her life. She was happy for her mother, and yet at the same time she was afraid of her sudden change.

Catharine's mother stood as Catharine walked over to her. "Daughter." She sombrely said. "What are you doing here?"

"I came to find you." Catharine replied. "The lord wants us to present ourselves at court tonight."

"I have been informed." Catharine's mother said as she took Catharine's arm and led her back down the path.

"I'm frightened mother." Catharine confessed.

"Afraid?" Catharine's mother stopped and turned to face Catharine. "Is this not what you wanted?"

"Yes, but why the change?" Catharine's face was genially puzzled as to why the lord would suddenly welcome them back to his court.

Catharine's mother lowered her blue eyes and pulled out a letter from a small pocket hidden in the folds of her dress. "Because of this." She handed the letter to Catharine and turned back towards the graves to avoid Catharine's puzzled gaze.

Catharine unfolded the letter and read its contents. "Mother is this true?"

"I had to do something." Catharine's mother said as she slowly turned to face her daughter.

"But he was father's rival!" Catharine protested.

"He is the only man that can help us!" Catharine's mother said sharply. "We have nothing."

"But what about father?" Catharine pled. "Do you not care for his memory!?"

"Your father is dead and can no longer help us!" Catharine's mother abruptly snatched back the letter. "Hubert Marcel can give us the life we want. He has promised to pay the lord a substantial sum if he allows our marriage."

"But mother, surely there is another way?"

Catharine's mother shook her head. "I wrote to him after I heard that his wife had died in childbirth in the hope that he still had feelings for me." She could see that Catharine was still unsure so continued on. "My marriage to Hubert will give us wealth and position."

"But why would the lord allow it?" Catharine asked, wondering why he would have brought their family down only to allow them to rise again.

"The lord," Catharine's mother explained, "has eyes on a greater prise then a lordship. And to achieve his ambitions he needs money and plenty of it."

Tears welled in the corners of Catherine's eyes, though in truth she wondered why the news saddened her as it would restore all the lord had taken from them.

"I will marry Hubert Marcel to restore our family's once good name." Catharine's mother embraced Catharine and looked her straight in the eye. "I will never forget the lord's mistreatment of us, and in time we shall move against him."

Catharine could see the resolve on her mother's face, and was comforted by it. "It is all settled then."

Catharine's mother nodded. "I shall marry Hubert and use the influence of being his wife to bring down the lord."

*   *   *

The sun rose from behind the hills, casting its warm rays on the sorrowful village below. It was a scene of carnage, a bloody massacre of lifeless bodies that lay where they were slain. Women and children cried at the sight as they were released from the hall, the men bemoaning that it would take a long time for the village to recover. Symond spoke with the village elder and gave him a bag of coins that had been collected from the pockets of the dead soldiers. The elder had thanked Symond and had invited him to stay and take a meal before leaving. But Symond had refused, saying that there was little enough food remaining to feed the villagers. So Symond ordered that what little provisions his men carried were to be left with the villagers.

Henri was sat on a rock, staring down across the lower land to the south. It was a clear day and Henri thought that he could make out Langton Castle in the distance. "That's where the king is." He said to the young boy that was sat next to him.

"Where?" The boy asked. He was still holding the scroll and had refused to hand it over to anyone other than the king.

"There." Henri said pointing at what he thought was Langton Castle. "That castle in the distance."

"I must go now." The boy said as he jumped off the rock. "I need to deliver this message quickly."

"We'll be leaving soon." Henri said as he too jumped off the rock. "You can't go alone, it's too dangerous."

"I've managed this far on my own." The boy pointed out.

"We will take you to the king." Henri said as a horn blast sounded in the village. "Come, it is time to leave."

Henri, with the young boy, went and joined the Arcani that were now leaving the village. The villagers waved and shouted their thanks to the masked demons that had come in the night, children running after them for a short time as they left. The journey back to Langton was uneventful and tedious. By the time they had set up a small camp a few miles away from Langton, the sun had sunk low on the horizon. Symond, with Henri and the young boy, rode on to the castle where they were to report to the king. When they had arrived they were told that the king was in council and that they were to wait.

Henri's stomach growled with hunger as he paced up and down the corridor they were made to wait in. "How much longer?" He said, holding a hand to his stomach. "I haven't eaten since yesterday."

Symond just shrugged. "None of us have my young friend."

The young boy was just sat quietly on a bench along the opposite wall, staring down at the dimly glowing scroll in his hands.

"We will report to the king and then take a meal my young friend." Symond looked at the young boy and could see that he was miming words that he was unable to lip-read.

A door at the end of the corridor opened and the king's councillors filed out. Henri stepped aside and noticed the look of utter disgust one of the councillors gave him. "What was his problem?" Henri asked, annoyed.

Symond stood from the bench he was sitting on and looked at Henri. "I know not. But you should not let such things trouble you."

The Duke of Hollington strode out of the door and gestured with his hand that they should enter. "The king will see you now."

The king was sat at the head of a long table littered with maps and lists of stores that would be needed for the long march back north. He was studying a map and never acknowledged Symond as he entered with Henri and the young boy.

"My king." Hollington said to gain the king's attention. "Commander Symond is here to make his report."

The king placed down the map and looked to Symond. "Commander, I trust that you bring news of victory." He looked from Symond and glanced at Henri, his eyes hard and unyielding as to what he might do with him.

"The band of Langton's men shall trouble you no longer." Symond announced. "Their bodies are now feeding the birds."

"Good." The king said, slapping the palm of his hand on the table. "And who is this?" He pointed at the young boy and raised an eyebrow.

"He was with the villagers." Symond explained. "And he carries a message that he will hand only to you my king."

The king waved the boy to step forward. "What is your name?" He asked as a strong scent of fish wafted over from the boy.

The young boy nervously stepped forward and held out the scroll, his hand shaking. "My name is Drugo and I have a message that I was told to deliver only to you."

"Drugo." The king repeated. "Tell me from where have you come?"

"Ol...Oldby." Drugo stuttered.

"The king glanced at the scroll in his hand and saw that it was dimly glowing red. "Who sent you?"

"Melanthius." Tears rolled down Drugo's thin, freckled face. "He...he came with monsters."

"Calm yourself." Hollington said as he walked from beside the king. "You are safe here." He stretched out his hand to take the scroll and a sudden flash of red briefly filled the room. All were awe-struck at the power the scroll processed.

"Only you may read it." Drugo said as he placed it on the table, in front of the king.

The king looked down at the scroll, mesmerised by the red mist that evaporated up from the scroll. "I have never seen or heard of such enchantments." The king said as he rolled the scroll so that the wax seal was facing up at him. The wax was black with a bull's head pressed into it. "Tell me." The king said looking up from the seal. "What happened?"

Drugo shuddered as the memory of that horrific night flooded his mind. "First, first came the fog." He momentarily closed his eyes and saw the piecing yellow eyes peering at him. "A thick mist that my father said was sent by the great Strabo."

"A mist." Hollington said as he stroked his bushy, grey beard.

"You have heard of such a thing." The king asked, seeing that Hollington was deep in thought.

"Only wet-nurses tales." Hollington said. "Once told to me as a child."

"Then the demon came!" Drugo went on with his tale. "They said it could leap over houses and run as swiftly as the wind blows."

"A demon?" The king said with doubt. He was a rational man and normally had little time for such superstitious nonsense. But the scroll had unnerved him, and he was filled with a sudden sense of dread. "Are you sure it was a demon and not some kind of trick?"

"I saw it." Drugo shifted from foot to foot and nodded his head. "So did many others. It stalked the village and attacked any who wondered alone in the mist. Then one night, they came."

"Who came?" The king asked, leaning forward in his chair.

"The monsters." Drugo lowered his voice to almost a whisper. "Horned monsters with the body of a man and the head of a bull. Their skin was black like a starless night and they were as tall as two men." Drugo exaggerated. "Their arms were as thick as tree trunks and their eyes an evil yellow that pierced the heart with fear."

"What happened to your village?" The king asked, already fearing the worst.

"Death and fire." Drugo replied as he lowered his head.

"Did they kill everybody other than you?" Hollington asked.

Drugo shook his head. "My father along with all the other men of the village. The women and children they rounded up on the beach."

"And they burned the village?" The king asked as he picked up the scroll and broke the seal.

Drugo sombrely nodded. "Nothing but ashes now remain."

The king unrolled the scroll and read its contents. "This Melanthius threatens to raid all the coastal villages if I do not pay a king's ransom in gold!" His anger flared up and he slammed the scroll back onto the table. "I will not give in to such demands!"

Hollington stepped over to the table and picked up the scroll, quickly scanning over the lines. "You cannot ignore this my king. You shall look weak if you were not able to protect you people."

"Commander Symond!" The king snapped. "Take the Arcani and kill all these so-called monsters! Show them no mercy!"

"Forgive me my king, but we should not be so hasty." Hollington said as he reread the letter.

"I should have the Arcani kill them all!" The king angrily shouted at Hollington. "This is yet another problem that I could do without!"

"My king." Hollington placed the scroll back in front of the king and tapped it with his finger. "This Melanthius asks for money, which means that he can be bargained with."

"So you reason that I should pay the money!?" The king said with raised eyebrows. "You know that as soon as I pay the money he will only want more!" He glanced over to Henri and gave a disgruntled grunt. "Leave us!" The king snapped at Symond. "I will send for you once plans have been made.

Symond bowed. "I shall await for your summons at the inn."

Drugo was made to stay so that he could be questioned further, but Symond and Henri were dismissed. Symond led Henri out of the castle and down into the town below built on the old bailey. The people of the town were loitering about the narrow streets, eagerly gossiping of recent events and of whom the king might appoint as their new lord. Symond led Henri to a red brick building with lead framed windows shaped like diamonds. It was close to the marketplace and many men stood outside in the last of the day's light drinking pots of ale. Above the door hung a faded wooden sign with a picture of an archer flexing his muscled arms.

"The Archer's Arms." Symond said as he opened the door and gestured for Henri to enter first.

Henri walked in and was instantly hit by the smell of stale beer and sweat. The room was small, dull and was being dimly lit by candles that were placed on the tables. The inn was full as many had gathered to hear all the latest rumours and all of the table were full.

A large woman with wild, frizzy hair and a round, flushed face saw them enter and strode over to welcome them. "A good evening." Her voice was high-pitched and whiney. "What can I get for ya?" She wore a green skirt and a low-cut grubby white shirt that revealed a glimpse her ample chest.

"Ale, food and a table." Symond said as he fished out a thick silver coin from a purse hanging from his belt and handed it to the woman.

"A table, a table." The woman muttered to herself as she glanced around the room. "Ah, follow me." She led them over to a corner where a drunk man was face down on the table sleeping. "Go home Walter." She grabbed him by the scruff and pulled him off the barrel he was using as a chair.

Symond and Henri sat at the table as the woman quickly pulled out a cloth that she had stuffed between her breasts and began wiping up the spilt beer. Henri uncontrollably glanced down her shirt as she was bent down wiping the table, then quickly away again as she noticed his glare.

"Bread and cheese with your ale?" The woman asked as she smiled at Henri, showing the gap between her two front teeth.

"Yes." Symond replied. "That will do."

Henri watched the woman walk off and noticed that they kept getting looked at by the locals. "I think there could be trouble." He said pointing over to a group of men clustered around a table, whispering and constantly looking over towards them.

Symond glanced over and saw that they were nothing more than disgruntled peasants fearing for their future. "We shall be fine my young friend." He smiled at Henri and his white teeth seemed to glow in the dull light. "They

139

will not risk the wrath of the king while his army is camped outside of the walls."

Henri caught the eye of one of them as he looked over and tapped the hilt of his short sword to show the man he was armed and ready should any trouble arise. But the man quickly looked away, not wanting any trouble.

The large women came back carrying two horn beakers in one hand and a platter of bread and cheese in the other. "There we go." She said as she place the beakers and platter on the table. "If you want anything else just call for me, Rosa." She winked at Henri before walking away to serve more waiting custom.

"It would appear that you have an admirer my young friend." Symond said with a grin spreading across his face.

Henri's face reddened as he grabbed the handle of one of the beakers and blew off the thick froth on top. "What do you know of these monsters Drugo spoke of?" He asked to change the subject.

Symond leaned forward and grabbed the remaining beaker. "Little." He admitted. "And what little I know comes from stories told in taverns like this one."

Henri took a swig of the warm ale and grimaced at its bitter taste. He found himself thinking of his father. He had often told tales to whomever would listen to him back at Heath Hollow, tales that were outright lies; and yet there had always been an element of truth hidden amongst the lies. "There is often some truth to every tale." Henri said before taking another swig.

"If what the boy and the stories say are true, then attacking them is not an option." Symond took a swig of his ale and he himself pulled a face at its taste. "They are mighty warriors that pride themselves on raiding and plundering. They have not been seen in this part of the island for many years, and their sudden appearance is somewhat disturbing."

"Will the king pay them off?" Henri asked as he took a hunk of bread from the platter and greedily bit into it.

"There is little choice." Symond replied in a hushed tone. "The king cannot waste the manpower trying to defeat them in battle."

The sun took a sudden plunge lower on the horizon and red light filed in through the lead framed windows, turning the inn even gloomier. Some spoke of it being an ill omen and that the king intended to go back on his gift of a pardon. One man claimed to have been told by one of the guards that the king intended to hang every tenth man in the town. Many dismissed this claim, saying that the king would have done it by now.

For an hour more did Henri and Symond listen to the grumbling of the townsfolk before an aide to the king summoned them back to the castle. They were led to a small chamber in the keep where the king was sat behind a desk, impatiently waiting for them. Henri entered first and instantly noticed the arrogant face of Sir Gregory Fitzwalter standing beside the fireplace.

The room was wooden panelled in dark oak and smelt musty as though it had not been used in years and lit by a handful of candles that filled the room with a dim yellow light.

"My king." Symond bowed.

"Commander." The king acknowledged Symond's formal bow. "You are to handpick four men from your company and join with Sir Gregory. He will lead a company to Oldby to negotiate with this Melanthius. Your mission is to prolong the negotiations long enough so that I can deal with the Duke of Baleford, then I shall turn my attention on these monsters. I want you ready to leave by morning, is that understood?"

Symond bowed once more. "My king." He asked. "What of Henri, is he to join me?"

Henri noticed Sir Gregory staring at him, a sinister smile upon his face.

"Henri step forward." The king ordered.

"My king." Henri said as he stepped before the king and clumsily bowed.

"It has been brought to my attention of your lack of decorum in your duties as a squire. Because of your low birth it was unwise of me to grant you such lofty titles." The king spoke in a pragmatic manner that showed he cared little for Henri. "I am hereby removing you from Sir Gregory's retinue and from the rank of squire."

Henri's anger rose, and he clenched his fists to control himself. He knew this would happen, that the world would not allow him to rise from his lowly birth. "So am I to join the ranks of the spear militia!?" He insubordinately asked as he aimlessly stared over the king's head.

"No." The king replied. "You are to report to the newly appointed lord of Langton's groom in the morning, he shall instruct you on your duties from there on."

Henri glanced over at Sir Gregory, who looked disgruntled at not being made the new lord, and was about to say what he thought of him when Symond interjected.

"We will go now to our duties my king." He said bowing and pulling Henri out of the door.

"Bloody bastard!" Henri spat with anger. "Bloody arrogant bastard!"

"Calm yourself my young friend." Symond said in the hope of calming Henri's anger. "You shall still hold a rank above a peasant. It is not as bad as you think."

"So instead of working the fields!" Henri roared. "I am to bloody….O' bugger this!" He angrily walked out of the castle's gate, back down towards the town.

"Where are you going?!" Symond called after him.

"To get bloody drunk!"

Chapter 6

The people of Market Barton watched sullenly as the Duke of Baleford's army erected their tents on the northern plain between the roads to Oldby and Baleford. The army had steadily marched down the Baleford road from Heath Hollow at a relaxed pace and in good order. The first to arrive was a company of skirmishers that questioned the locals and announced that The Grand Duke, as they referred to him, would be arriving at the town by mid-afternoon. The news of the Duke of Baleford's forthcoming arrival spread throughout the town like a wildfire. The locals rushed to the Baleford road where they watched column after column of Men-at-Arms arrive. It was a spectacular sight, men marching in unison to the beat to the drums, and yet it was worrying too. It was not that they were worried of the army sacking their town, but more of the trouble that masses of men brought. Crime would rise as soldiers stole, got drunk and fought with the locals. The Duke of Baleford, like the king before, would try to keep his soldiers disciplined. But there was always a handful of soldiers that pushed the rules of that discipline and would end up causing trouble.

When the king's army had camped outside of the town, he had forbid his men from entering the town without written permission from their captain. But despite the strict rules enforced by the king's constables, a group of soldiers had snuck into the town and got blind drunk. In their drunken state they had made lude comments to a woman passing the tavern and had tossed coins at her as though she were a whore. The woman had been surrounded by the men and taunted as they pulled and tore at her dress. She had been saved by the intervention of a mob of townsfolk that had heard the commotion and gathered to save the woman from being dishonoured. They had apprehended the men after a brief scuffle and had dragged them before the king's constables, who had them placed in chains. The next day a herald had summoned the townsfolk to the marketplace to watch as the men were flogged to the point of death. It had been a grim sight for any that were present, and the sound of the lash and its victim's screams was heard throughout the town.

The king's army had marched south soon after and the town had returned to its normal routine of trading. It was a wealthy town as it was situated on the crossroads that led to Baleford and the kingdom's capital, Elnaria, as well as Hollington and Lhanwick. Many merchants traveling between the cities would stop at Market Barton and buy and sell as well as share news and gossip of happenings on their travels. But it had not just been the marketplace that had benefitted from the constant stream of travellers, but the inns too as the traveling merchants needed a place to sleep, eat and drink. As a result of the town's wealth, the streets were wide and well cleaned by gangs of men that worked all day to sweep away the rubbish and nightly waste from chamber pots that were emptied from the windows above. At the centre of the town, where the four roads met, was the marketplace. That, like the streets, was wide and open, a flagstone square surrounded by stalls selling all manner of goods from all over the kingdom. The taxes collected by the town mayor had been used to build elegant buildings used by the town's council for meeting and administrate purposes. Many times the mayor had petitioned the king to make the town a lordship, but the king had refused as the town lacked a castle.

The townsfolk stood on the outskirts of their town, muttering of their thoughts of if the Duke of Baleford would be a better king then the one they already had. Maybe, some argued, the Duke would grant the lordship they wanted for their town. The truth was that they cared little for which noble sat on the throne and called himself king, but more for their unhindered trade. A handful of merchants disliked having yet another army on the town's doorstep as they feared that merchants would not risk traveling in such uncertain times. Yet many welcomed the sight of yet another army as it meant an opportunity to sell their wares to the soldiers. As the sun sank low on the horizon, the locals began to return to their homes, leaving the sounds of shouting men and clanking of wooded mallet on tent pegs behind them.

The Duke was sat on his warhorse, watching as his heralds assembled in front of him to hear his orders. "You are to ride into the town." He said as the last of his heralds rode up before him. "And decree that the town and its populace are safe and that I desire no quarrel with those that are rightfully my subjects. But should they resist and defy my right, then they shall be treated with the same manner in which they seek to give." The Duke looked at each of his heralds in turn to make sure all understood his orders. "Announce that on the morrow all men of worth are to gather in the marketplace and swear their loyalty to me." The heralds nodded their heads and rode forth into the town to make the Duke's announcement. The Duke turned his horse to see a smug looking man riding a pure-white horse towards him.

"My king." The smug looking man said as he came to a stop. "Permission to find quarters in the town."

"I am not yet king!" The Duke of Baleford replied, annoyed at the sudden appearance of John. "And you may not yet call yourself a prince!"

"As you insist your Grace." John replied with a sly smile, knowing that Baleford disliked him. "Now have I your permission to find quarters in the town?" He asked in a tone that suggested that he would regardless of what the Duke said.

"No!" Baleford said abruptly. "You are to remain with the army."

John shifted in his saddle and pulled out a folded piece of paper from his saddlebag. "This was delivered to me yesterday." He said, holding out the paper for the Duke to take. "It may be of some value to us."

Baleford leaned forward in his saddle and snatched the folded paper from out of John's hand. "What is it?" He asked as he unfolded the letter and read its contents.

"It asks that I meet with a man who claims that his master is displeased with the king, and has vital information of great importance to both me and the war effort."

"It is a trap!" Baleford said as though John was a fool for putting such trust in the unsigned letter.

"How can you be sure?" John asked, annoyed that it was so easily dismissed by the Duke. "Surely it would be better to investigate the matter."

"If the letter were true." Baleford stated. "And there was a disgruntled noble in the king's army, then why did the

148

letter go to you and not me. Surely I would need such important information."

"I think that we should look into this." John said, pointing at the letter.

"Do not be so foolish!" Baleford roared. "For all you know, the king could have assassins in the town. And this their method of drawing you away from safety."

John shook his head. "Then I will send one of my men in my place and have him brought before me so that I can weigh his words for truth."

Baleford stared long and hard at John as if he were a child that lacked understanding of the world. "You are to remain in camp and attend your duties. On the morrow we shall enter the town and you may have one of your men look into this then." He angrily tossed the letter at John and waved his hand to dismiss him.

"As you please." John said as he turned his horse and rode off.

The Duke of Baleford watched him go, full of hate for the man. He found that John's presence annoyed him and enflamed his anger. Too often had he discovered that things had gone wrong because of John neglecting his duties and leaving important matters to his aides. John was simply a man whom he disliked, an idle drunk that owed everything to his father's cunning ambitions. The thought of him marrying his daughter and calling himself prince, sickened him to his core. But a deal had been struck with the Lord of Heath Hollow, and Baleford was not a man to go back on his word.

The night passed uneventful and the sun rose in a near cloudless sky, promising another hot day. Baleford's heralds once more rode into the town, shouting and calling for the men of rank to gather in the marketplace. The heralds went on all morning, and by midday the marketplace was filled with the townsfolk, wealthy or not. All came to catch a glimpse of the man they called The Grand Duke. They were not kept waiting long as he came clattering down the Baleford road at the head of a procession of knights that were clad as if riding for battle. The people cheered and stood aside as he rode into the marketplace and dismounted to sit in the throne-like chair that had been placed on a wooden platform that had been hastily erected in the night.

Baleford sat, uncomfortable because of his armour, and addressed the crowd. "The town and people of Market Barton are safe!" He shouted so that all in the marketplace could hear him. "I come not as a conquering tyrant, but as a rightful liberator. The law wills that you pledge your allegiance to me and aid me by whatever means you are able! Do you will to pledge your allegiance unto me, the rightful king of Elnaria?!"

The town mayor was stood at the base of the platform and was the first to climb the few steps and pledge his allegiance to the Duke. "I can speak for both myself and the people in giving our allegiance to you, the rightful king." He was dressed in an expensive suit of red velvet and matching hat with a long white feather sticking out of the back.

For an hour more did the pomp continue as every man of rank went up onto the platform and knelt before the Duke of Baleford, swearing their loyalty. The truth was that the same men had done the same to the king when his army had passed through, and they would have sworn loyalty to any if it meant their businesses were left unhindered.

John had rode into town soon after the procession of knights. He wore an expensive blue trousers and tunic with a red feather upon his breast and knee-high boots that were so well polished that one could see their reflexion in them. During the night he had sent his most trusted knight to meet with the unknown messenger. The knight had gone from one inn to another, repeating the name Hendricks to the innkeepers. After searching many inns, and having no joy, an innkeeper to a tavern in the eastern part of the town had heard the name. He had explained to the knight that a man under that name was lodging there and had left instructions to give the person asking for him a letter, which he had left with the innkeeper. The letter contained instructions of a meeting to take place on the morrow, the second hour after the sun was at its height, at the same inn. The knight had rushed back to report his findings to John.

John now rode his pure-white horse down the narrower backstreets towards the inn where he was to meet with this Hendricks. The knight he had sent the previous night led the way, calling for people to move out of the way as they went cantering past. They came to the inn where John dismounted and handed the reins to his knight. "You remain here." He ordered. "I'll shout you if any trouble arises."

The inn was a large round building on the eastern outskirts of the town. It was a two storey building built in stone with a wooden roof that pointed up as though someone had placed a wizard's hat on top. There were no windows and even from the outside the inn looked gloomy.

151

John pulled open the thick metal studded door and entered the gloomy interior. Inside was lit by a huge chandelier that hung from the roof. The place was empty apart from the few people stood at the bar, which was itself a circle in the centre of the inn. John walked over toward the innkeeper, who stood watching his every move as he wiped clean horn beakers. "I'm here to see Hendricks." John said in a commanding tone.

The innkeeper was a suspicious looking man with a round face and bushy eyebrows and sideburns that ran to his chin. "Come now sir." He said in a burly, but cheerful voice. "Follow me." He led John up a set of stairs that curved up onto the floor above where there was rooms to rent. "It's just down here." The innkeeper said turning and smiling at John, showing that he had a tooth missing at the front of his mouth.

They came to a door at the end of a passageway and John gripped the hilt of his sword as the innkeeper knocked on the door.

"Will that be all sir?" The innkeeper asked.

John nodded. "For now."

"I'll leave you to it then." The innkeeper said as he turned and walked away, whistling a jaunty tune as he went.

John waited and was beginning to think that no one would answer when the door suddenly burst open. "Quickly come in." A voice said from behind the door.

John cautiously stepped in to the dark chamber lit by a single candle placed on a small table beside an unmade bed. "Well what have you to say?" He snapped.

"Were you followed?" A hooded man asked as he stepped closer to the light from the candle.

"I have armed men outside." John warned, knowing that he had only the one. "They'll kill you if anything should happen to me."

"Were you followed?" The hooded man asked more forcibly.

"No." John said, shaking his head. "Now what have you to tell me?"

"I have nothing to tell." The man removed his hood to reveal a slender face with thin lips and a long nose. His hair was dark and thinning on top, and his eyes tired and circled by black rings.

"Then why send me a letter saying that you have important information!?" John said, his voice rising in anger. "I'll have you whipped for the dog that you are!" He went to leave but the man grabbed his arm.

"Wait." The man let go of his arm and pulled out a folded letter from a hidden pocket stitched into his tunic. "I know nothing of its contents, save that it was written by my master whom ordered me to deliver it to you."

John took the letter and examined the wax seal. He didn't recognise it and began to doubt whether it was all worth his effort. "How do I know if I can trust this?"

"Read it." The man pointed at the letter. "You will soon see." He said as though he did know something of the letter's contents.

John cracked open the wax seal and unfolded the parchment. As he read the handwritten lines his heart lifted with the news it carried. "Is this true?" He asked, daring not to believe his good fortune.

"As I said." The man replied. "It was written by my master but a few days ago."

"You came from the king's camp?" John asked, suspicious at how fast the man had travelled.

"I was obliged with fresh horses by the messenger service the king has in place." The man rubbed at his tired face. "I rode day and night and as you can see, I have slept little."

"At Oldby." John repeated the last words he had read. "This contains information the Duke of Baleford should know." He folded the letter and stuffed it into his belt. "You are to come with me, as my guest."

Together they rode to the council building next to the marketplace, which the Duke of Baleford had made his headquarters. It was an elegant building, two storeys high, made of both stone and red bricks. The duke's purple banner with a golden stag's head hung above the entrance where two guards were posted. They dismounted and left their horses with the knight that had accompanied John to the inn. Inside was filled with waiting people, come to petition the Duke for numerous things. John, holding a high rank, was allowed to enter a room adjacent to the council's meeting chamber where the Duke was attending to his daily business.

"I wish to see the Duke." John said to a steward that stood dutifully by the door to the chamber. "I have urgent news of the king's movements."

The steward nodded and entered the meeting chamber to inform the Duke of John's arrival. "The Duke of Baleford permits you to enter." He said as he came back out.

John entered the meeting chamber with the man that claimed to have come from the king's camp. There was a large rectangular table littered with maps and reports in the centre flanked by high-backed chairs where the town's councillors would sit and argue over official matters.

"John." Baleford was sat at the table's head, placing wooden pieces on a map. "You have news for me?"

"I have." John answered as he stepped forward. "I have met with this informer whose master has sent me this." He pulled out the letter tucked into his belt and walked around the table, dropping it in front of Baleford. "This is of great worth to you and me."

Baleford gave John a suspicious look as he snatched up the letter and unfolded it. "This had better be good." He said, disbelieving that the letter could not tell him anything more than he already knew. As he read its contents he realised why john was so jubilant. "The king has defeated Lord Langton and captured his castle." He placed a small wooden piece over Langton Castle on the map. "It says that the king will soon march north to face me and that his army has dwindled in strength and moral." He took his eyes off the letter and looked up at John. "It also says that the king has sent a company to Oldby in an attempt to negotiate with the Minoton that have sacked the village."

John nodded and slyly smiled. "My wife is among their number and I ask your permission to take my men and disrupt these negotiations."

Baleford leaned back in his chair and thought about it. He disliked John and had often thought of sending him back to Heath Hollow, but that would have offended John's father and risked him allying back with the king. This letter now presented him with the opportunity to rid himself of John, who may even be killed. "Very well." Baleford said as he passed the letter back to John. "Do all you can to disrupt the king's plans."

"I will gather the men and leave at once." John inclined his head to the Duke and enthusiastically walked out of the chamber. For John, at long last, was going to rid himself of his wife so that he could marry the Duke of Baleford's daughter and become a prince.

*　　*　　*

Sir Gregory had left Langton Castle a couple of days ago with what he called a small company. But it was anything but small. He had taken all of his retinue of squires along with fifty mounted Men-at-Arms and a hundred infantry made up of mostly crossbowmen. His pages he left with the king, believing that they were too young to be of any used to him on his mission. It was not just fighting men that Sir Gregory had brought along, but three cooks, a musician and a physician with one of his aides. As well as all the men, there was the baggage. Six wagons, pulled by grumpy looking oxen, carried the supplies that would be needed on their mission.

Elizabeth was sat on the back of a wagon that carried the bandages and surgical equipment that would be needed should the company engage in battle. She was sat with her legs dangling over the edge of the wagon, watching the grumpy looking oxen pull the wagon behind them. The day was hot and she found herself feeling sorry for the oxen and the men that were forced to walk in their thick gambesons in the unrelenting heat. Sweat trickled down the nape of her neck and Elizabeth pulled at her white coif with a strip of cloth stitched around the bottom to cover her reddening neck. As the wagon slowly rumbled across the picturesque countryside, trampling down the knee-high grass that was mixed in with the spring yellow of many buttercups, Elizabeth found herself wondering why she was with the company.

She had been tending to the sick in the infirmary when the physician she was traveling with had told her that she was to accompany him as part of a company that was bound for Oldby. At first Elizabeth had been unwilling, unsure as to why the Duke of Hollington would allow her to leave his safety. She thought him a kind-hearted man who genuinely cared for her, and had often spoke with her to assure that she was being treated well. Confused as to why he would suddenly allow her to be part of a company that was to travel so far away from the army, she had asked to see him. But the physician had shown her an order signed by the king and told her that there was no need. So Elizabeth had begun to pack up the things the physician had instructed her to. The night before the company had departed, a drunken Henri had stumbled into the infirmary.

"Elizabeth!" Henri had drunkenly called. "Elizabeth!"

Seeing Henri, Elizabeth had rushed over to quieten him. "Shh." She hissed at him. "What are you doing here?"

157

Henri staggered a few steps and fell to the floor. "I came to see you." He said as he turned and sat up, his voice revealed that he was saddened by something.

"What has happened?" Elizabeth had asked as she sat on the cold floor next to him.

Henri had shook his head as tears rolled down his reddened cheeks. "Them bastards!" He spat out in anger. "They have taken it from me!"

Elizabeth had put her arm around Henri to try and soothe his anger. Since she had helped in the infirmary, Elizabeth had learned how best to soothe a man and she had used all of that skill to quell Henri's anger. "What have they taken from you?" She had asked in a soothing voice.

"I'm no longer a squire!" Henri had looked Elizabeth hard in the eye. "I'm to remain here as a servant to the newly appointed lord as Sir Gregory is to take a company to Oldby!" He had cuffed away his tears with the sleeve of his tunic and shook his head. "I should be going with them!"

"I know of this company." Elizabeth had admitted as she stroked the back of Henri's head. "I am to join it along with the physician and one of his aides."

"They will take you and not me!" Henri had unsteadily got to his feet, angered and in disbelief.

Elizabeth had stood and wrapped her arms around Henri. "Come, you look tired." She had led Henri by the arm and lay him down on an empty bed. "You should sleep now." She had pulled a blanket over him and soothingly stroked his hair. "We shall speak more in the morning."

"They are right about me." Henri had said as he tiredly closed his eyes. "I am nothing more than a peasant."

"Shh, sleep now." Elizabeth had waited for a while, watching Henri sleep, before she had returned to her duties. She had returned to Henri's bed in the morning before the company had left, only to find that he had gone.

Thoughts of Henri now troubled her as she wanted nothing more than to be with him and soothe his pain. She had known Henri for a long time now and had often felt his sorrow, even in times when she had been angered with him. She thought him a good man, though he had often found himself on the wrong side of the law, a man that was not weighed down by the heavy chains of society. He was born a peasant to a family of no value, and though he knew that, he never let it defeat his dreams of one day bettering himself. But Henri's sudden change that night before she had left Langton had deeply troubled her. Never had she seen Henri so defeated, destroyed by the world and its ignorance. Then she remembered her own. Back when Henri had been placed in the stocks by the marketplace in Heath Hollow, she had told him that she could never have married him; that he would never be able to provide the life she expected to have. But now she felt ashamed for saying such a thing, after all what was wealth and power next to love.

"Elizabeth!" The physician called from the bench at the front of the wagon. "Bring me my water!" He was a middle-aged man with a thick bushy beard and a round belly that he tried to conceal in a loose fitting tunic of undyed wool.

Elizabeth carefully swung her legs back up from over the edge and unsteadily rose to her feet. The wagon's motion made her stumble and she was forced to grasp hold of a rope that kept a large wooden box secure.

"Elizabeth! My water!" The physician impatiently snapped.

"I'm getting it." Elizabeth carefully stepped over a wooden box and knelt down beside another. She opened the lid and pulled out a round canteen made of tin. "Here you are." She said as she carefully leaned over and handed the canteen to the physician.

"Thank you." The physician said in a more cheerful tone. The tin canteen felt cool in his hands as he unstopped it and took a long dreg of the water inside. "Much better." He said as he handed the canteen back to Elizabeth.

Elizabeth took back the canteen and placed it back in the box she had taken it from. She leaned on a large box and looked ahead at the wagons in front. There was three of them to the front, each being pulled by two oxen, and two more following her wagon. Walking either side of the wagons was a line of crossbowmen that kept a watch for any sudden attack that might occur. At the front of the column rode the mounted Men-at-Arms with Sir Gregory leading them. Elizabeth could see that he was clad in his expensive armour as it shone in the sunlight, standing out against the mounted Men-at-Arms who wore simple, dull padded jerkins. The countryside seemed at peace and Elizabeth began to wonder if there really was a war being fought. The wagon bumped as it rumbled over a rabbit hole and Elizabeth tumbled, knocking a large wooden box. It seemed to balance close to the edge, teasing Elizabeth that it would not fall, before it crashed over the edge.

"Halt!" The physician cried. His face was red with anger as he abruptly turned to face Elizabeth. "You foolish girl!"

"I'm sorry." Elizabeth said in a daze. "I didn't mean to do it."

"Sorry!" The physician repeated in anger. "Sorry is not good enough!"

The column had come to an abrupt stop, and the crossbowmen on the side where the box had fallen began picking up the mess of bandages that had spilled out across the grass. Tangled in the mess was a young man dressed in the squire's uniform of Sir Gregory.

"Henri?" Elizabeth said as she saw a crossbowman pull him to his feet. "What are you doing here?"

Henri's eyes were closed and the front of his tunic was stained by sick. His legs were wobbly and his stomach churned as though rolling waves were crashing around inside of him. "Hello Elizabeth." He said as a smile spread across his face.

"Why the delay?" Sir Gregory asked as he reined his horse to a stop. He had cantered down the column to see what had cause the halt, expecting to see that a wagon had broken a wheel again. But instead he saw Henri, and was angered. "What is he doing here!?" He asked, casting Henri a look of utter disgust. "Someone had better explain!" His Master-At-Arms was at his side and he gave Henri a look even more disgusted than Sir Gregory's.

"He stowed himself away." The physician explained, fearing that he would be implemented in the crime. "I had no knowledge of it until now."

Sir Gregory gave the physician a look of disbelief. "I meant to believe you knew nothing of this!?"

"I swear it Sir Gregory." The physician said, holding out his hands as if pleading for mercy. "Upon my honour, I knew nothing of it until now."

Sir Gregory dismounted and walked over to face Henri. "You were ordered to report to the new lord of Langton. And have now deserted your post." He said with great delight. "For which death is the penalty."

Henri squinted at Sir Gregory. "So kill me and have done with me." He said in defiance.

"Remove that sword and tunic!" Sir Gregory snapped at the crossbowmen that were holding Henri up. "He is not worthy of such things." They dutifully did as they were ordered and left Henri's thin, pale body for all to see. "Bind his hands and tie him to the back of a wagon. I want us moving as quickly as possible."

"He is ill." Elizabeth interjected. "He needs to rest, not tied to a wagon and made to walk for miles."

Sir Gregory Ignored Elizabeth at first and remounted his horse. "He is to die anyway, so why bother with the act of kindness?"

"Because he has not yet been tried and found guilty of any crime." Elizabeth explained. "And until then he is eligible to every kindness that the king's law allows."

Sir Gregory shifted in his saddle as he weighed up his options. He could have Henri killed here where he stood, but that would not reflect well upon him. Had Henri still been a peasant, then he could have him killed without the need of a trial. But the king had granted him his independence along with the title of squire, and the law permitted every freeman the right to a trial. If he was to kill him now, he could find himself being tried for being unjust and un-chivalric. "Very well." Sir Gregory conceded, knowing that Henri's guilt was well established. "I will write to the king, detailing his crime and ask for the right to court-martial him. Until then he will be kept under guard."

Henri's wrists were tied and he was bundled onto the back of Elizabeth's wagon. The box that he had stowed away in was lifted back into place and the column began to move once more.

"You're a fool!" Elizabeth hissed at Henri. "How did you manage to hide in the box without anybody noticing?"

"It was that night I came to see you in the infirmary." Henri said as he wriggled up so that his back was against a wooden box.

Elizabeth angrily shook her head at him. "Look at the state of you! I can't believe that even you would do something so stupid!"

"Henri smiled. "It seemed a good idea at the time."

"You were drunk!" Elizabeth snapped back at Henri. "No good decisions are ever made when drunk!" She carefully rose to her feet and went to get a water canteen from the box they were kept in. "Here." She said as she handed Henri the canteen.

"Henri pulled the cork out with his teeth and dropped it onto his lap, before taking a long dreg of the cool liquid that soothed his dry throat. "Thank you." He bunged the cork back in and handed the canteen back to Elizabeth. "Where is Symond?" He asked, his voice still a little croaky.

"Out there somewhere." Elizabeth shrugged. "He is acting as a scout."

"I must speak with him." Henri closed his eyes as the bright sun was hurting them. "Only he can help me now."

"You could try helping yourself." Elizabeth said in a stern tone. "Your foolishness always gets you into trouble."

"I always get out of it though." Henri responded with a grin.

"Well how are you going to get out of being accused of deserting?!" Elizabeth knelt beside a small chest and opened the lid. "You're so foolish." She began to rummage through the folded up clothes and pulled out a plain black tunic that had been one of the physician's aide's. "Here put this on." She tossed the tunic down at Henri and quickly had to place a hand on a box to stop herself stumbling as the wagon suddenly jerked.

"I can't." Henri said, holding up his tied wrists. "My hands are tied."

Elizabeth tutted, more at her own folly for not thinking of that, and opened another chest to take out the physician's surgical tools that were wrapped in white linen to keep them clean. "Don't try anything foolish." She pulled out a small knife, used by the physician to cut through skin and muscle, and cut free Henri's bonds.

Henri pulled the tunic over his head and pushed his arms through the sleeves. "You had better tie me back up." He said holding out his wrists. "I don't want you getting into trouble because of me."

There was sudden shouts of men and Elizabeth stood to look at what all the commotion was about. To the column's right was a band of mounted men, lined up and

164

ready to charge. "Oh no." Elizabeth shook her head, deeply worried by the mounted men's sudden appearance.

"What is it?" Henri asked, knowing that it was danger by the ashen look on Elizabeth's face.

"Soldiers!" Elizabeth replied. "We're under attack."

Henri got to his feet, his legs still weakened from being cramped up in the box for days, and watched as the mounted men began to canter towards the column.

The sun reflected off their swords as they menacingly rode forwards to attack the column. But Henri knew it was all for show. If they attacked, most of them would be killed by the crossbowmen that now had weapon at the ready to loose their deadly bolts at the attackers. Sir Gregory's mounted Men-at-Arms knew this also as they charged the men and sent them fleeing back in the direction that they had appeared.

"They'll be back." Henri warned. "And in greater numbers."

"What will happen to us?" Elizabeth asked, suddenly realising the real dangers they faced.

Henri, though he was not the most experienced in battle, knew what defeated men would face. The chances were that they would not be spared, and put to death. But Elizabeth would face much worse. "We'll be fine." He answered, unwilling to tell her the truth. "We have enough men to defend ourselves."

Elizabeth, feeling suddenly very scared, watched as Sir Gregory rode down the column, shouting at the wagons to keep moving. "I hope you're right Henri."

The day went on in much the same manner with the mounted scouts of Baleford's army riding into sight and being chased off by Sir Gregory's mounted Men-at-Arms. Slowly the column rumbled across the countryside, heading further and further to the northwest towards Oldby, and away from the safety of the king's army.

Chapter 7

Catharine's mother quietly sighed as she looked out of a lead framed window that looked down upon the courtyard below. It was getting dark and the setting sun had turned the sky red, giving what remained of the day a red shade that discoloured all. For hours she and Catharine had been ready, as the lord had instructed them, yet they were made to wait in a dull corridor outside of the lord's audience chamber along with many others seeking an audience. When they had first arrived, the corridor was full and the air had been humid and sticky with the sound of many announcements and petitions, applauded by the courtiers filtering through the thick wooden doors that bared the entrance to the chamber. But as time slowly passed the people waiting were called in one by one until only they and another woman remained.

"How much longer?" Catharine asked her mother as she paced up and down a rug that only a few days ago she had been beating the dust off.

Catharine's mother turned from the window and looked at her daughter, thinking that she looked beautiful. She was dressed in an expensive pale-green dress with white lace that had been tailored to emphasize her figure. Her hair had been curled into ringlets and tied with silk ribbons that matched her dress, making her look even more youthful than she was. "I know not. But it shouldn't be too much longer." She added as she looked back out of the window.

Catharine blew out a long breath and slumped down on a bench pushed up against the wall. "Does that window open?" She asked her mother. "It's too hot in here."

"No." Catharine's mother replied as if she were annoyed with Catharine.

Catharine once again rose to her feet and began pacing up and down the rug. "How much longer?"

"You just asked that!" Catharine's mother said sharply as she turned to face Catharine. "Now sit down and be still!"

Catharine, like a sulky child, sat back down on the bench. Sitting on an opposite bench was another woman who gave her a disapproving look. She wore an elegant yellow dress that shone in the gloom of the corridor, and was sat with a straight back and hands together on her lap as Catharine herself had been tutored to do. But sitting upright in a dress laced up so tight that she thought she would pop out of was not comfortable. So Catharine constantly fidgeted and shuffled trying to find some comfort.

The door to the audience chamber opened and one of the lord's aides stepped into the corridor. "Avelyn Roseaman." He spoke in an educated voice as he glanced up and down the corridor. "The lord will grant you an audience now."

Catharine watched as the woman sitting opposite her rose and approached the lord's aide. She looked back towards her and gave her a look as if to say, I'm more important than you. Though in truth Catharine did not know if the woman had been thinking that. But one thing she had quickly learned from the lord's court, was that thinking the worst of others was often true. Catharine then looked to her mother, who herself looked beautiful. She was dressed in an expensive red dress with white lace that had been tailored in the latest fashion, and her hair had been tied up in a bun so that a matching triangular headpiece could be fitted. To Catharine she looked much like her former self, like in happier times when her father had been alive. It was odd to her how her mother was so calm and unaffected by the long wait. For all they had been through and were yet to go through, she appeared calm and controlled as if all was going as she expected it. A part of Catharine was disgusted by her mother's calmness, seeing it as though she was betraying her father's memory, and actually wanted to marry Hubert Marcel. But she'd had to battle those thoughts with the fact that they had little choice, and that it was a good marriage to restore some of the wealth and power that was taken from them.

"You should remember how a lady is to behave in public." Catharine's mother said as she walked away from the window and sat on the bench opposite Catharine. "You have been well tutored and know well enough what is expected."

Catharine straightened her back and placed her hands on her lap. "Yes mother." She said in a polite, but sarcastic manner.

The door at the far end of the corridor opened and a servant came in carrying a small box of candles. He was a small, frail man with bowed legs and a face full of brown freckles. Catharine recognised him from her time with the servants and had wanted to help him with replacing the molten candles. At one point she had begun to stand, when her mother gave her a stern glance that immediately changed her mind. As the man neared, he kept glancing over at Catharine as if he had wanted to speak with her. But unsure of if he should, he simply nodded and smiled.

"You must no longer associate with those of a lower class than yourself." Catharine's mother said as she had seen the man smiling at Catharine. "It would look ill upon us."

"Mother, we were ourselves counted among their number but a few days ago." Catharine reminded her mother.

"We were never truly one of them!" Catharine's mother said with distaste for Catharine's attitude. "We are set above them, remember that!"

Catharine nodded her agreement and remained upright in a graceful posture as a proper lady should. She still wondered why the lord would allow her mother to marry Hubert Marcel as it would mean that they would once again have money and position. Why take all they had only to grant her mother a good marriage that would restore all he had taken from them? She had asked her mother that very question, only to be told that the lord would receive a substantial sum from Hubert for the marriage, and that the lord needed money to fulfil his own ambitions. To Catharine, none of it made sense, and so she turned her thoughts towards her own selfish desires, a good marriage of her own that brought plenty of wealth.

"Catharine."

Catharine snapped out of her daydream of marrying a handsome, wealthy man and looked over towards her mother's stern face. "Yes mother."

"Stop fidgeting and be still."

"Sorry." Catharine said, unaware that she had been. "I'm just a little nervous." She then admitted.

"You know how to behave." Catharine's mother said, still looking sternly at her daughter.

"Mother how can you be so calm?" Catharine asked in disbelief that her mother was not at least a little bit nervous.

"I was well tutored on how to behave when being betrothed to a suitor."

"Yes," Catharine replied, "but this is no ordinary suitor. This is Hubert Marcel, father's rival. A man he had considered his enemy."

"I know who he is!" Catharine's mother stood and walked over to the bench Catharine was sat on. "But what choice do we have?" She said as she sat down.

"Something is off mother." Catharine said, looking into her mother's calming blue eyes. "I can feel it."

"Hush now." Catharine's mother looked over at the servant replacing the molten candles, and suspected that he was eavesdropping. "You speak too loudly."

"I just don't understand why the lord would allow you to marry Hubert." Catharine said in a hushed tone. "I mean, why would he take all we had to make an enemy of us, only to let us rise once more?"

"Catharine we have spoken of this." Catharine's mother looked over at the servant to make sure he could not hear what she was saying. "You are young, and still have much to learn."

"You should have learnt loyalty." Catharine said, angered by her mother's apparent ease with the betrothal.

"I will tell you what I told Elizabeth before she had married John." Catharine's mother's eyes narrowed, and her voice took a serious tone. "It may be men that rule the kingdom, but it is their wives that control them."

"What do you mean?" Catharine asked, unsure that she had understood.

"Men are foolish." Catharine's mother replied quietly. "They argue and fight like children, and would wonder around like a headless chicken without their wives." She could see that Catharine did not understand so she put it simply. "As the wife of Hubert Marcel, we would once again have position and wealth."

"I know that." Catharine interrupted. "But why would the lord allow it?"

"Because he is a fool with high ambitions." Catharine's mother took hold of her daughter's hand. "As I have told you before, he needs the money."

"But why you?" Catharine asked with raised eyebrows. "Surely he could get the money elsewhere."

"Since Elizabeth married John, we have been his family." Catharine's mother explained. "Though the lord will not admit it, there has been some unrest at our mistreatment." She stood back up and looked over at the servant, waiting for him to finish replacing the last of the candles. "As you know I wrote to Hubert and we came to an understanding." She said as the servant left the corridor through the same door that he had entered.

"What understanding?" Catharine asked, feeling as though she was nothing more than baggage tossed onto the back of a carriage and being taken for a ride.

"He has ambitions of becoming the next lord, and I wish to see the current lord and his son fall." Catharine's mother went back over to the window and stared out at the reddened sky. "So naturally that would make us allies."

"And what about me?" Catharine asked as she went and stood beside her mother. "Will Hubert then arrange a good marriage for me?

"Yes." Catharine's mother truthfully replied, not taking her eyes away from the window. "In time he will arrange a marriage for you, a marriage that will help us in our cause."

"So I am to be used." As Catharine had said it, she knew she sounded like Elizabeth. There was a time when she would have accepted it as that was the way of the world, after all she had told Elizabeth just that. But now it was expected from her, she felt affronted.

"In time you will have to learn how to manoeuvre a man to your will."

Catharine was unsure how she was to do that and was about to ask when the door to the lord's audience chamber opened.

"The ladies of house De'lacy." The aide said as he entered. He was a thin man, well-groomed and smelling as sweet as summer flowers. "The lord will grant you an audience now."

Catharine's mother brushed at Catharine's dress as though the few final adjustments would make all the difference. "Are you ready?" She asked with a smile.

Catharine nervously nodded. "Yes mother."

The aide led them into the audience chamber where he announced them to the many courtiers. "The ladies of House De'lacy!"

The chamber fell silent as Catharine and her mother walked before the lord's seat at the far end. The men looked on uninterested as they had nothing to gain from the impending announcement. But the women gathered together and muttered amongst themselves of all kinds of slanderous gossip. The malicious glances made Catharine feel uncomfortable and she found herself wondering why they would show such hostility towards them. She glanced at her mother and found comfort in her steadfastness as they neared the lord's seat.

"My lord." Both Catharine and her mother said as they formally curtsied before the lord.

The lord was dressed in his usual grim attire, an ankle length black robe that pointed up at the shoulders and a black tricorn hat with a long red feather sticking out of the back. His face was emaciated and ashen with age, yet his eyes still held all the venom of his youth. "I welcome you to my court." He said with a hint of malice in his voice.

"We thank your lordship for your undeserved kindness." Catharine's mother politely replied.

The lord's beady eyes scanned over the courtiers until they fell upon the man he was looking for. "Hubert Marcel!" He called, his voice still full of malice.

From the crowd of courtiers, stepped forward a grotesquely fat man wearing a bright orange robe that was so big, it could have been used as a bedsheet. "My lord." He struggled to bow as his round stomach got in his way. His face was red and blotchy, his curly hair wet with sweat, and his saggy cheeks wobbled as he spoke.

Catharine looked at her mother and pitied her for having to marry such an unpleasant looking man. But her mother looked unconcerned. She put that down to the fact that her mother had seen him before and she had not, though she had heard his name. The mere sight of Hubert was enough to turn her stomach, so she lowered her eyes to the floor to avoid making eye contact with him.

"May I introduce myself?" Hubert asked the lord as he glanced at Catharine and licked his lips.

"The lord raised an eyebrow as if he were intending on refusing Hubert's request. "You may." He said holding up his hand for Hubert to continue.

"Thank you my lord." Hubert struggled another bow to the lord before he slowly wobbled over to Catharine's mother. "We meet yet again." He said with a smile that showed the gap between his two front teeth.

Catharine's mother polity smiled back. "Only now we find that circumstances are more favourable towards us."

Sweat trickled down the side of Hubert's round face and he pulled out a smelly handkerchief from a pocket on his robe. "Indeed." He replied as he wiped his face.

"This is my daughter, Catharine." Catharine's mother introduced.

Hubert stepped before Catharine and looked her up and down as though she were a joint of meat waiting to be sampled. "You have your mother's beauty, the kind of beauty that would take many poets to do justice." He said as he placed his sweaty hand under her chin and forced her to look up at him.

Catharine could smell his warm, rancid breath and noticed that his eyes were constantly flickering from her face to her chest. He made her feel awkward, and it took all of her self-control not to turn away. "Thank you." She forced herself to say.

Hubert once again licked his lips and wiped his face. "It has been too long since I was last blessed with your presence." He said looking back at Catharine's mother. "And I must say that the years have been kinder to you."

Catharine's mother smiled at the compliment. "And I can see that in them years you have been very successful."

Hubert smiled and held up his wrists to show the many gold bracelets that adorned them. "Each one represents a business that I have seized." He said with much delight. "All of whom believed that they were greater than I."

The lord stood from his throne-like chair and held up his liver spotted hands. "Enough of the pleasantries." He waved forward an aide who was dutifully stood behind the lord's seat. "You, Hubert Marcel, have asked for my blessing to a proposed marriage." He took the rolled up parchment from the aide and held it up for the couriers to see. "I, as the Lord of Heath Hollow, willingly give my blessing for the proposed marriage, so long that all of these conditions are met." The lord passed the rolled up parchment back to the aide who dutifully went and handed it to Hubert.

Hubert already knew what terms were set out in the parchment as he had already agreed upon them in a meeting behind closed doors. But he nevertheless scanned over the document to ensure all was in order and to his liking. "The term set out are most agreeable." He said as he handed the parchment back to the aide.

The lord then looked to Catharine's mother. "Are you, Lady De'lacy, agreeable to the arranged marriage?"

Catharine's mother nodded. "Yes." She answered loud enough for all to hear.

It was then that Catharine noticed Hubert staring at her with lustful eyes as though he had an appetite for her flesh. "Disgusting." She said quietly as she lowered her eyes.

"Then I happily announce the betrothal of Hubert Marcel to Catharine De'lacy." The lord announced as he sat back on his throne-like chair, a sinister smile upon his face.

"That was not the agreement!" Catharine's mother snapped, unable to control her surprise. "I was supposed to marry! Not my daughter!"

The courtiers began to mutter and the lord had one of his aide silence them by banging the end of a heavy wooden staff they were holding on the floor. "It is done!" The lord said, glancing at both Catharine and her mother with a look of utter satisfaction.

"Mother." Catharine pleaded. "This cannot be right."

Hubert saw the distress on Catharine's face and wobbled over to her. "I shall treat you as though you were a princess." He said as he took her hand and kissed it.

"You agreed to marry me!" Catharine's mother said, unable to contain her anger.

Hubert looked to Catharine's mother and smiled. "You had your chance years ago. But you were not interested." He glanced back at Catharine and once again licked his lips. "Besides, you are past child bearing age. And the whole point of marriage is to produce children."

"You have children!" Catharine's mother angrily pointed out.

"More shall I need should the plague return." Hubert replied as though having children was just another part of his business.

The lord once more rose to his feet, his hand clutching at the pain in his stomach. "You shall remain here until a date for the ceremony can be set. And once the dowry is paid, you both shall take up residence with Hubert Marcel."

"My lord!" Catharine's mother pleaded. "Do not do this!"

But the lord was not in a mind to listen, and simply waved a dismissive hand. The aide that had led them in, now led them out. Catharine was at a loss for words and felt utter disgust at the thought of having to marry such a man.

"Catharine' I am so sorry." Catharine's mother said as they walked back into the corridor they had been waiting in. "This was not supposed to happen."

"No mother!" Catharine snapped back. "It's all your fault." She turned away from her mother, tears flooding from her eyes, and ran down the corridor.

"Catharine I'm sorry!"

But Catharine had gone.

*   *   *

The night was clear and crisp with dew dampening the ground the soldiers slept on. Small fires had been lit and many had now burned low to nothing more than glowing embers. All the previous day, the company had been constantly threatened by the Duke of Baleford's skirmishers. Though the infantry did not engage with the skirmishers, they were dog tired and fearful. Their fears were only enhanced as the mounted Men-at-Arms had not returned after last chasing away the skirmishers. And as the company made camp for the night, Sir Gregory had sent out his Master-At-Arms along with two squires to find any trace of them. But the Master-At-Arms had returned with no news. Talk of the mounted men being slain soon spread throughout the camp, and the soldiers were left feeling uneasy and fearing the worst.

Symond poked at the fire he was sat in front of with a stick, sending red embers up into the night. He had tried to sleep but found that his troubled mind would not allow him. Like the other soldiers, he was disturbed by the mounted men's disappearance, and played through multiple scenarios in his mind as to what may have happened to them. Wanting answers, he had earlier asked

Sir Gregory for his permission to scout for the missing men. But Sir Gregory had refused on the pretence that he was needed at camp. Symond knew that was odd, after all that is what Sir Gregory had used him for up until now. So why the change? He had then questioned the Master-At-Arms himself, only to be told that there was not one trace of the missing men and that it was most likely that they were attacked and killed by Baleford's skirmishers. But Symond knew that if that were true, there would be signs, blooded bodies and broken weapons, signs that at least would give some answers. But the Master-At-Arms had told Symond that he had not seen such signs as he was unwilling to travel too far from the camp. Symond had then gone back to Sir Gregory, saying that a greater search was needed. But Sir Gregory had angrily told him that it was not needed as it would most likely end in the killing of more of his company.

Symond laydown and closed his eyes in an effort to try and sleep, but his mind was active with ill thoughts and feelings. Unable to sleep, he sat up and blew out a frustrated breath that misted in front of him. The night was quiet, eerily quiet as though evil malice was not far away. Giving up on thoughts of sleep, he stood and walked over the wagon where Henri was tied to the wheel.

"So you can't sleep either." Henri said as Symond walked over and squatted in front of him.

"No my young friend." Symond solemnly replied. "Ill thoughts prevent such things."

"All seems quiet." Henri said as though it should have been easy to sleep in such circumstances.

"It is too quiet my young friend."

"Surely that is a good thing." Henri said, pulling at the rope that bound his hands in the hope of freeing himself.

Symond shook his head. "It is night, there should be the sound of animals hunting and foraging for food."

Henri listened and heard nothing more than the gentle snores of the soldiers that were supposed to be guarding him. "I feel the same." He admitted. "Something is odd."

Symond nodded. "The whole camp is the same. And the disappearance of the mounted men has only enhanced the fog of anxiety that surrounds us."

Did you find out anything from the Master-At-Arms?" Henri asked knowing that Symond had questioned him.

"No." Symond replied shaking his head. "He seemed reluctant to tell me anything, and what little he did was of no value."

"He's a bastard!" Henri said with scorn. "I'd bet a king's ransom that he knows something."

"That I am certain of my young friend." Symond replied as he stood. "But what it is he knows I would pay a king's ransom to know." He pulled out a small pocketknife from a pouch on his belt and tossed it down onto Henri's lap. "If we should be attacked and you find yourself in trouble, cut yourself free."

Henri picked up the knife and tucked it into his left boot to conceal it. "You expect us to be attacked?"

Symond nodded. "If the mounted men were killed then it will only be a matter of time." He glanced around at the soldiers lying beside smouldering fires, seeing how tired

181

and frightened they looked. "Any time now would be the best time to attack."

Henri felt Symond's apprehension as the night had taken a sinister turn, an eerie, still feeling as if the world had paused to take breath. "Elizabeth." He said as her face entered his mind. "She must be kept safe."

"I will do what I can my young friend." Symond replied. "But if the worst should happen and the camp is overrun, go straight for her and get far from here."

Henri doubted that he could get far as the Baleford's men would attack on horseback and mercilessly cut down any trying to flee. No, he thought, better to fend off any attack and then desert one night once it was safe. He wondered if Elizabeth would go with him, just give up all and start anew somewhere. A part of him wanted her to, and yet another believed it better to go on his own, that she would never agree to go with him. "There will be little choice but to stand and fight." Henri said. "Better to die with sword in hand rather than at the end of a rope as awaits me."

"Maybe the king will show leniency towards you my young friend." Symond said. "After all you are the saviour of the star oracle."

"It doesn't seem to matter." Henri shrugged. "All they will see is a peasant that has deserted."

Symond knew this to be true and felt a pang of pity for Henri. "I will do what I can for you my young friend, but it may be better for you to die in battle."

Henri looked down at the wet grass beneath his feet, deep in thought at his predicament. It had seemed simple when he had hidden in the box of bandages, simply just hide and then run away. But he had been drunk, and he very much doubted that he would have done it had he been sober. Now he reproved his stupidity and swore that he would never get drunk again. "I don't know what to do." He said dejectedly.

"You need not do anything yet." Symond said. "Now try and get some rest. I will speak with you more in the morning."

"Rest." Henri repeated the word. "I doubt that I will."

Symond smiled at Henri, his white teeth almost glowing in the moonlight. "You should try anyway my young friend." He thought that Henri looked well, remarkably well for saying how drunk he had been. Many years before, Symond had known of a man that had often drunk himself into such a state that he could no longer function. But each time he had, Symond knew it had taken him days to recover. Henri, however, looked as though he had never been drunk and Symond suspected that there was more to Henri then there seemed. "Now I must go and speak with the men on sentry."

The camp had been made on the reverse of a hill that over looked flat grassland to the east and a dense woodland to the west. Sir Gregory had argued that the high ground gave them the advantage should Baleford's scouts attack, and that they could retreat into the woods where men on horseback were ineffective. But as Symond strode up to the brow, where the sentries were posted, he had his doubts. Sir Gregory's plan would only work if they were attacked from the east, where they would see any approaching enemy. But what if they attacked west, from out of the woods? The thought troubled Symond as he knew the men would be forced uphill, slowing their escape as the swords of the mounted enemy would wreak havoc in the panic.

"Who goes there?!" A sentry called out, raising his crossbow.

"It is I, Commander Symond!" Symond called back, stepping closer so that he could be clearly seen.

"Oh." The sentry said as he lowered his crossbow. "What are you doing up here?" He was in his early fifties with an aged, tanned face and a broad, flat nose that had been broken.

"The night is uneasy and I can find no rest." Symond confessed. "Have you anything to report?"

"I have seen nothing to fear." The sentry shook his head. "The night is still and quiet."

Symond stepped over the brow of the hill and scanned over the grassland below. Moonlight illuminated the land below and as far as his eyes could see, there was no sign of enemy movement. Maybe they would not attack after all? "Something is ill this night." He said as he turned back towards the sentry.

"I knows how you feel." The sentry pulled up his sleeve on his right arm and showed Symond a deep scar on his wrist. "It's itching."

"What?" Symond replied, fearing that the sentry wanted him to scratch it.

"It's itching." The sentry rolled his blue eyes as if Symond should have known why it was itching. "Years ago," he explained, "I was escorting a merchants train to Silver Lake via Norlag's Pass."

184

"What evil made you use such a pass?" Symond interrupted.

"The merchants claimed that there were rare stones at the foot of the mountains." The sentry replied. "And they wanted to collect them to sell on for good profit."

"It must have been some profit to drive them through such a cursed place." Symond said with disbelief that one would risk entering such a treacherous place for profit.

Norlag's Pass was a simple dirt track that ran between the foot of the mountains of Azaroth and The Black Forest that concealed the ruins of Dimon Dor. No one knows why the Craft Master of the Gigantes cut the pass all those years ago. But if the stories of old were to be believed, it is where a secret door, hidden my magic, conceals a passage that leads deep down beneath the mountains. There it is said that the wisdom of the Gigantes lies, awaiting to be discovered. But all those that have searched the pass, return with tales of woe. Now many refuse to use the pass, preferring to use the safer passage that Langton Castle offered.

"I was young and foolish." The sentry went on. "And all seemed to be going well up until dog-like men attacked us."

"Dog-like men." Symond repeated. "Do you mean the Cynocephali?" He had heard of such creatures before, but had never seen one. The tales say that the Cynocephali are a war-like race that would rage war obstinately on any that attacked them and drink the blood of their foes when enraged. They had the body of a human and the head of a dog, and often roamed in small war bands close to the mountains were they dwelt.

"I that'll be them." The sentry scratched at his scar. "One of them tried to run me through and did this. Ever since it has itched when a battle is looming."

"And it itches now." Symond said watching he sentry scratch his scar.

"All night." The sentry pulled down his sleeve. "And it's getting worse."

There was a sudden flurry of birds that flew up from the woods to the west, and Symond instantly knew what it was. "Hold this ridge!" He barked at the sentry as he ran back down towards the camp. "Call out the alarm!"

A long horn blast sounded from the woods and a skirmish line of Baleford's scouts rode towards the camp, their swords reflecting the moonlight. Those soldiers that were asleep had been roused by the horn blast, and now franticly grabbed their weapons. They had barely made a hasty line of defence when Baleford's scouts crashed into them. Men were sent crashing to the ground, bones broken and blood flowing as the swords of Baleford's scouts fell upon them.

Henri watched as the soldiers guarding him rushed to the camps defence. Elizabeth, he thought, he must get to Elizabeth. He reached into his boot and pulled out the pocketknife that Symond had given him. The blade was small and thin, yet as sharp as a razor. But the rope binding Henri's hands was strong, and despite his best attempts, he could not free himself. He pulled angrily at the rope and desperately bit at the frayed edges.

"What are you doing?!" A voice shouted at Henri.

Henri looked up to see a crossbow being pointed at him. The soldier behind the crossbow was ugly, his face thin and rat like, his hair long and thinning. "Just make it quick." Henri said defiantly and unwilling to show fear of death.

"If I free you, will you fight?" The soldier kept his crossbow on Henri as he spoke. "Or just run like the traitor they say you are?"

"I'm no traitor!" Henri angrily snapped back. "I would rather die with sword in hand like a man than on my knees tied to a wagon." For a moment Henri thought that the soldier would squeeze the trigger and end his sorry existence. But the soldier lowered his crossbow and pulled his dagger from its scabbard.

"Go, we need every man." He said as he knelt down and cut Henri free.

Before Henri could thank him, he had ran towards the growing battle. Henri climbed onto the wagon and glanced around the camp, hoping to see the pavilion where Elizabeth tended to the physician's duties. Near to Sir Gregory's grand pavilion, in the centre, was a pavilion marked with a red and white painted pole that had been hammered into the ground outside of the entrance. Knowing that Elizabeth would be there, Henri jumped down off the wagon and ran straight towards the pavilion.

The hastily formed line of defence had now crumbled and Baleford's scouts had pushed further into the camp, mercilessly killing. Bodies were scattered between the campfires where men had fell back in hope of climbing up the hill to where the line of sentries offered some protection from the horsemen. Those horsemen that tried to charge uphill were killed by crossbow bolts carefully aimed by the sentries along the ridge.

Henri leapt over the body of a dead horse and dodged around another that had thrown its rider. He briefly stopped beside a body of a man that had a horrific gash on his head and snatched up his sword. Men were fighting outside of the pavilion he was heading for and Henri could see the body of the physician's aide lying face down in a pool of his own blood. A mounted man saw Henri approach and spurred his horse to meet him. At the last moment, Henri flung himself to the right and back swung his sword, catching the horse's rear leg. It stumbled to the ground and the rider was forced to jump out of the saddle before he got trapped. Henri ignored him and went straight into the pavilion.

Inside was a scene that showed there had been a struggle. A small wooden table was on its side and smashed pots were scattered across the ground. The body of the physician lay where he had been slain, his lifeless eyes open and looking up at Henri.

"Elizabeth!" Henri called as he looked around the pavilion. He walked into a curtained off part and saw a large wooden box beside a narrow camp bed. "Elizabeth!" He called again.

The box lid suddenly burst open and a startled Elizabeth climbed out. "Henri." She said as she shakily rushed over and wrapped her arms around him.

"Are you alright?" Henri asked, a sense of relief sweeping through his body.

"Yes." Elizabeth nodded. "They killed the physician and his aide, but I was able to hide." She pulled away from Henri and looked up into his weary face. "They were calling for me."

"That was me." Henri said grabbing Elizabeth's hand. "We must go now."

"No Henri, it was before I heard your voice."

Before Henri had chance to answer, a soldier rushed in through the entrance. It was the same soldier that he had unhorsed. He grinned at Henri, his face splatted with blood, and lunged with his blooded sword. Henri pushed Elizabeth back and parried the blow that was aimed for the soft flesh of his stomach. The soldier back swung his sword and caught Henri's upper arm with the tip of his blade.

"After I'm done with you, I'll take my pleasure with her." The soldier grinned and smiled at Elizabeth.

Henri, angered by the soldier, launched a ferocious attack. He quickly lunged to the right to fool the soldier to defend his left, then quickly spun his body around. His sword followed his body, and in one swift movement, he arched his sword around and struck down on the back of the soldier's head.

"Henri you're hurt." Elizabeth said as the soldier fell to the floor, his skull split.

"It's nothing." Henri replied as he grabbed Elizabeth's hand. "Now we need to get out of here." He led Elizabeth out into the sound of the persistent battle. The fight had moved on from the pavilion, leaving a trail of blooded bodies towards the ridge of the hill where the attack had been stalled. "We won't make it up there."

Along the top of the ridge was a hastily formed line, men armed with spears to the front and crossbowmen to the rear. Symond was on the ridge and it was he that had took charge, bellowing at the men to stay in line and for the crossbowmen to make every bolt count. And it had worked. At first the surprise attack had initial success as the camp scrambled to arms. The first line had been hastily made on the edge of the camp, but too few men had been ready and in position when the charge hit. Most of the men that had been in that line were now dead, and the rest of the camp would have shared their fate had it not been for Symond. He had gathered men together and sent them up the hill to where he had made the sentries stay. Though not all had made it to the safety of the hill. A few were caught between the tents and slain, though this only slowed the charge further as the horses stumbled over bodies.

"There!" Henri shouted above the shouts and screams of battle. He pointed over to Sir Gregory's pavilion that was only a stone's throw away.

A circle of men defended Sir Gregory who was stood in the centre shouting at his men. Though they looked like easy prey for the horsemen, they were well formed and offered great resistance. Horsemen cantered around the formation, their horses refusing to charge at the circle of spears.

"Come on!" Henri pulled Elizabeth, leading her towards the safety of the circle. At first he thought the men would not allow them in. But one of the soldiers recognised Elizabeth and moved aside to let them in.

"What are you doing opening up to allow such filth in!" Sir Gregory snapped at the man that had allowed them in. He looked at Henri, seemingly annoyed that he was still alive. "Bind his hands."

The Master-At-Arms, who was ever at Sir Gregory's side, stepped forward and hit Henri hard in the stomach, sending him doubled over to the ground.

"He saved me!" Elizabeth pleaded. "He deserves better treatment than this!"

Sir Gregory simply smiled at Elizabeth and said, "And now I shall save you from this wretched creature."

Another horn blast sounded and the horsemen, knowing that they could do no more damage, withdrew. Sir Gregory kept all his remaining men at the ready expecting another attack. But as the sun slowly rose, no attack came and the company was forced on, dog tired and in need of a rest.

Chapter 8

"I cannot marry now." Catharine whined as she slumped down on her bed. "The time isn't right and I'm not ready."

"The time is right." Catharine's mother replied in a tired voice. She had been over and over this with Catharine, several times already this day. "You are no longer a child and know what is expected from you."

"But mother." Catharine pleaded. "Can you not speak with Hubert and persuade him honour your original agreement, where you married him and not me?"

"I have told you before." Catharine's mother sat beside Catharine on the four-poster bed. "It is not just Hubert that I would need to convince, but the lord." The truth was that the lord knew that she was a cunning woman and would influence Hubert to move against him. So he had told Hubert that there would be no deal unless he married Catharine, a young woman he considered no threat to his power.

"But surely it's worth a try." Catharine looked into her mother's blue eyes, hoping to see a sympathetic look that showed she would speak with Hubert. But instead, her eyes were cold, calculated and refusing.

"Our plan is still working." Catharine's mother rose from the bed and walked over to a lead framed window and opened it, the warm air stirring the musty smell inside. The chamber they were now kept in was roomy, with space enough for two large four-poster beds, two large chests where they kept what little belongings they had, and a table with two chairs. The walls were a bare white plaster with two narrow arrow slits and one window to let in light, and the floor wooden with a red, threadbare rug placed between the two beds. The chamber was in the southwest tower and had been used for the storage of old recordings of the lord's council. It had been cleared and swept to accommodate them, but the musty smell of old parchments remained. It had not been out of the lord's kindness that they were kept there. But out of the lord's need to keep a tight control over them. Two guards were posted outside of their chamber, and they were only permitted to leave the castle so long as they were escorted by the two guards. Catharine's mother knew it was for appearance only that they were allowed to take walks into the town. The facade would show the lord to be merciful and quash any remaining unrest towards their mistreatment.

"Our plan?" Catharine said mockingly. "I don't remember being involved."

"Hush!" Catharine's mother scolded. "You speak too loudly." She briefly closed her eyes and felt the warm air prickle her pale skin. "Nothing has changed, save that it is you that is marrying Hubert and not me."

Catharine shook her head. "Do we really need wealth and power?" Not so long ago, that is exactly what she thought marriage and life was about. It had only been Elizabeth that had daydreamed of marrying for love, and Catharine had laughed at her for it. But the thought of having to marry Hubert, a man she considered fat and ugly, disgusted her. Whenever she had thought of marriage, it had been to some handsome son of a rich merchant. Not to an old, fat, pig-like man that was Hubert.

"What we had, what your father wanted us to have, was wrongly taken from us." Catharine's mother turned and looked down at her daughter, who looked more like a sulking child then a woman that was betrothed to a rich merchant. "I am not asking you to love him, but to marry him and use him to regain what is rightfully ours."

"Is that why you married father?" Catharine asked. "To aggrandise yourself?"

Catharine's mother turned away to avoid her daughter's awkward gaze. The truth was that when she had been betrothed to Catharine's father, she never loved him. That had come later, like a flower growing from a seed. "Yes." She confessed. "Your father offered a chance of wealth and I took it."

"So you didn't love him?"

"Not at first." Catharine's mother admitted. "It is impossible to love someone you do not know." She walked over to the table where a jug of water was placed. "Marrying for love is what the poor do." She poured herself a goblet and took a swig. The water was warm and unpleasant. "We of wealth must marry for greater wealth and position." She added as she placed the goblet back on the table.

"Then maybe the poor have more than us?" Catharine sombrely said. For the first time in her life, she found herself wishing that she were a peasant. Then she would not find herself being forced to marry a hideous man for money. Once she had heard a woman in the market saying that money was the root of all evil, and at the time she had dismissed it as nonsense. But now she felt trapped because of that need for money. It had been their family's wealth that had made them a target for the lord, and now it was the need for money that was forcing her to marry.

Catharine's mother's eyes narrowed as she gazed at her daughter. "But the poor are nothing more than dogs that must obey the word of their master. They have no purpose in life other than to work and die, all to the gain of their lord. Is that how you would want us?"

Catharine thought about it. Only days ago they had been like that, scrubbing floors and beating rugs. She herself had been made to tend on the lord through his sickness. All had been degrading for a family that not a year ago had their own house filled with their own servants to tend on them. And yet she had found the work, though hard, simple. There had been no pressure to act in a certain way nor any social pressure to conform to the latest fashion. It was simply do as you were told and nothing more. But that had also been the downside. For she had not been allowed to do as she pleased like before, and she very much doubted that she would be allowed once married to Hubert. "Maybe we would be better-off starting anew somewhere else" She said, still feeling trapped.

"I have told you before." Catharine's mother replied, annoyed at Catharine for bringing up such folly again. "The kingdom is at war and it would be unsafe for us to travel. Besides that, we have no money and the lord would surely send men after us."

Catharine knew this to be true. Where could they run to? There was little choice other than to marry Hubert, at the very least that would offer them protection from the lord. In one way a part of her told herself that her mother was right, that the marriage would restore all that the lord had taken from them. Their house, market stall, servants, everything. And yet even knowing this was not enough to convince her.

"Come." Catharine's mother said, seeing that her daughter looked deeply troubled. "Let us take a walk to briefly forget such things." She walked over to the closed door and knocked. The sound of a key scraping into the keyhole followed by a *clack* made Catharine's mother stand back as the door was opened.

"What do ya want?" The guard was tall and wide with a round, bold head and shallow eyes with thick black bags under them.

"We wish to take a walk." Catharine's mother said, looking suddenly very small and fragile. "As the lord has permitted us." She added, believing that the guard was about to refuse her.

"You wish to take a walk?" His voice was deep, burly, and his face flat and hardened by his rough upbringing.

"Yes." Catharine's mother replied, annoyed at the guards sluggishness. Whenever she had spoken with him he had been odd, as though he lacked understanding of what she said. She thought him simple and unintelligent enough to possess any attractiveness of his own, and she found that he was well suited for the simple task of guarding them, mindlessly following orders to the exact words given to him.

"A walk." The guard repeated, the expression on his face blank as though he did not understand.

"Yes, a walk" Catharine's mother repeated as though the guard was hard of hearing. "I wish to go to the marketplace."

"What, both of you?" The guard said as he waved his big, dirty finger at Catharine and then back to Catharine's mother repeatedly.

"Yes, we both wish to take a walk to the marketplace."

The guard rubbed at his jaw as he thought about it. "Well makes it quick." He ducked his head and walked out of the door.

Catharine and her mother followed the guard, who kept glancing back to make sure they were there, down the stairs and out into the courtyard. Normally both guards would escort them, but for an unknown reason only the big guard did today. Outside, the sun was shining and the day was hot. They both wore thin summer dresses that Hubert had sent them and their hair had been tied up to reveal their attractive necks.

The courtyard, as always was busy with people coming and going, and Catharine looked at a servant girl beating the dust off a rug hung over a wooden frame. She found herself relieved that it was not her, remembering how hard the work had been. As the servant pulled the rug off the frame, she turned and saw Catharine. It was a face Catharine recognised, a face that only days ago she had worked and gossiped with. "Madge!" She called out. But Madge simply turned away.

"You cannot speak with servants." Catharine's mother reminder her. "Only if you are giving them an order."

"But we were friend's mother." Catharine replied, upset that Madge had blanked her. "She was the only one that would befriend me."

"Those days are gone." Catharine's mother said as she linked her arm with Catharine's. "We must now look towards our future."

"Marrying a monster." Catharine sighed.

"Come now daughter, he is not that bad."

"Mother, he looks like a slimy toad."

Catharine's mother smiled as she agreed with her daughter's description of Hubert, though she would not openly say it herself. "He is wealthy and will keep you in the manner which will befit your status."

Status, Catharine thought, how odd and fickle the world was. Not long ago, her status was as low as it could be. Branded as a traitor and locked in a prison, then released to scrub floors and clean up after the wealthy. Her mother had given up and had consigned herself to death, but as circumstances changed, so too had her mother. Now she was much more like her former self and spoke of status and revenge. "How things change." She said aloud.

The guard called to the captain of the gate to open up. The gate was opened for them and the guard escorted them out. "Now no trying anything stupid." He warned, looking back at them.

"We are but simple women wishing to visit the market." Catharine's mother replied. "We could not fool one as strong as you."

The guard looked back with a raised eyebrow, unsure if Catharine's mother was mocking him or not. "Well don't." He grunted. "Or you'll not be allowed to leave again."

The streets were full of people going about their daily business and the rich were signalled out from the poor by their umbrellas that they used to shade themselves. Their skin was pale as it was seen as the mark of a poor person to be tanned, and many powdered their face just to look even paler than they were. The poor, however, were forced to work long days in the lord's fields in the hot sun. They could not afford thinner, lighter material for clothing like the rich wore, and wore their usual thick woollen garment that made them sweat. The rich complained that the poor smelt and should not be allowed in the streets at the same time as them. But it was a complaint that the lord cared little for as his concerns were with more pressing matters.

As Catharine and her mother neared the marketplace, the smell of bread and spices wafted past them. It was a smell that reminded Catharine of the days when she and Elizabeth had worked their father's stall. Back then she had complained and argued that it was beneath her, but her father had said that it would help her respect money and learn the way of the world. But the truth was that she had learned little, save how to speak with all manner of people, not that she had liked the poor. As then, the marketplace was a hive of activity with people shouting and bartering. The market square was awash with bright colours and potent smells, and Catharine drifted from one stall to another to look at their wares.

"Beautiful girl." A merchant said to Catharine. "I have the finest silk for you." He smiled, showing that one of his front teeth was missing. "You come look."

As Catharine stepped closer to his stall, she noticed that the man was an easterner. He was small, thin man with dark skin and a face that looked like an old cracked piece of leather. His nose was long and wide, and he wore a thin red robe that had not yet faded in the sun and a matching turban atop of his head. "Real silk." She asked suspiciously.

"Yes my lady. I sell only cloth of the highest quality." He smiled again and pulled out a folded cloth from a shelf under his stall. "This would make nice dress for you." He added as he looked at Catharine with his deep, brown eyes.

"Is it real silk?" Catharine asked again as she inspected the cloth.

"Yes, yes." The merchant nodded his head. "Very real."

Catharine's mother came over from the next stall selling silverware and inspected the cloth for herself.

"Ah, this your sister." The merchant smiled at Catharine's mother. "Very beautiful also." He clapped his hands together, making his silver arm rings jingle. "For you I sell for good price."

"It would make a fine dress mother." Catharine turned the cloth over in her hands and imagined herself dancing in a dress made from such beautiful silk.

"It would." Catharine's mother agreed. "Depending on the price." She looked at the merchant, who was stood smiling at them, and asked, "How good of a price?"

The merchant rubbed his jaw as he thought about it. "Come." He gestured for Catharine's mother to come closer. "I only whisper for if I was to say aloud, I fear there would be a stampede."

Catharine's mother leaned over the stall as the merchant whispered a price in her ear. His breath felt hot and tickled her ear, but the price was not as good as she thought it ought to be. "Too high a price." She handed the cloth back. "I could buy half the cloth in Elnaria for that price."

"You will not find this quality anywhere else in the kingdom." The merchant said, his smile fading as he realised that he would not make a sale.

"Come Catharine, let us get a little further."

"Can we not buy it mother?" Catharine asked as she linked her mother's arm.

"What with?" Catharine's mother replied. "We have no coin. Nor will we have any until you marry Hubert."

They went around the stalls, looking at their wares and Catharine was constantly reminded that they had no money and was forced to walk away from each one emptyhanded. They came to a stall selling flowers and the old woman behind it smiled as she saw them approach.

"My lady." The old woman said as she held out a bunch of purple and white flowers. She was a little lady with white curly hair and a face wrinkled up like an overripe orange.

Catharine's mother took the offered flowers and held them to her nose, breathing in the sweet scent. Whenever she had been in the marketplace, the old woman had given her a bunch of flowers to repay an old act of kindness that she had once showed her.

The old woman had once served in the bakery that Catharine's father had owned, serving there for many years. Then, when the plague had come, she and her husband and children had all fallen ill. She had been the only one to survive, though it had left her body weakened, and was left alone in the world to fend for herself. It had been Catharine's mother that had taken pity on her and paid to have her family properly buried and ensured that a basket of food and a few coins was delivered to her home each week. The old woman never forgot that kindness, and gave Catharine's mother flowers each time she saw her.

"Thank you." Catharine's mother said as tears welled in her eyes.

"Who is that?" Catharine asked. "And why does she always give you flowers?"

"Do you remember the bakery lady I told you about when you were a child?" Catharine's mother asked as she led Catharine out of the marketplace.

Catharine had to think hard as it had been a long time since she had heard the tale. "Vaguely."

"That is her." Catharine's mother turned to the guard who was now walking behind them. "We will go to the graveyard now."

"You said to the marketplace, nothing about visiting the graveyard." The guard grumpily replied.

"Well I'm telling you now, and I wish to pay my respects to my husband's grave." Without waiting for any response from the guard, she led Catharine on.

By the time they reached the graveyard, they were hot and bothered. A cobblestone path led between the richer graves and Catharine's mother commented that her husband should have been placed there. But John had refused to pay the price for a plot, and so Edgar De'lacy was buried with the poor. They walked past the rich section, the

203

cobblestone path giving way to a simple dirt track that led to the poor graves. Edgar's grave was marked with a simple wooden board that was nailed to a stake, which bore his name, the same as all the other poor graves. There were withered flowers on his grave and Catharine's mother picked them up and placed the fresh flowers down in their place.

"He deserves a better resting place than this." Catharine said looking around at the shabby graves. She disliked the graveyard as it was too quiet, a place when one could reflect upon life and ponder on their failures.

"Yes he does." Catharine's mother said, tears rolling down her cheeks.

"Mother." Catharine said in a questing voice. "Why did Hubert say that you once had your chance, but you refused him?"

There was a few minutes silence as Catharine's mother thought about what she should tell her daughter. "When I was younger." She said standing and looking at Catharine. "I was originally betrothed to him. But he was not the wealthy man that he is today, and so I rejected him and married your father."

"So that is why he held a grudge against my father."

"They once fought a duel over me." Catharine's mother shook her head. "I am sorry you have to marry Hubert. But it is a chance to restore all that was taken from us."

"Must we speak of this again mother?" Catharine said as though no good would come from it. "There is nothing we can do to change things."

"So you accept it?" Catharine's mother asked, surprised by Catharine's sudden change.

"No." Catharine replied. "But I will use it to our advantage."

Catharine's mother smiled. "We have been greatly wronged, and it is time we corrected those wrongs."

"You are right mother." Catharine was still unsure and hated the thought of having to marrying Hubert. But her mother was right, the lord had robbed them of their house, money and the chance of happiness. And Catharine was determined to avenge their losses. "Teach me how I can manoeuvre Hubert, and I will restore all that was taken from us."

Catharine's mother smiled at the determination in Catharine's voice. "Come then, we had better get started."

So it was that Catharine, full of the venom of determination and revenge, decided to use what fate had dealt her. She would learn all she could, and then take all she could. All it would take was to marry a monster, to bring down another.

*   *   *

"Hold your ground!" Symond yelled as he saw a few men take a step back. "They won't charge if you hold your ground!" Two of Baleford's scouts were riding parallel with the column, out of crossbow range, and Symond knew that the rest would be close by.

Throughout the day horsemen had been spotted on the horizon and the men in Sir Gregory's company had feared another attack. But no attack had yet come and they grew tired of the constant stop-starting whenever horsemen were spotted. They had rested little and had not eaten since the night before and their moral had sunk as low as it could be. The column was formed up with the wagons in the middle flanked by a line of crossbowmen, with spearmen in front of them. They had marched painfully slow in order to keep a tight formation as the enemy were never far away. Though despite their moaning, they knew the disciplined formation had kept them safe.

Over the horizon now rode a line of horsemen, swords drawn and ready to charge. They cantered forwards towards the column and it was then that Symond noticed that some carried small crossbows. "Take cover!" Symond yelled as the horsemen came into range. They loosed a volley and Symond watched as two men were snatched back by crossbow bolts. "Hold your ground!" He yelled, fearing that some men would try and seek shelter under a wagon, and cause gaps in the line, gaps that the horsemen would exploit. The horsemen, once loosed their bolts, turned and retreated back out of range to reload. "Stay in line!" He ordered as he saw that a few men had stepped forward to chase off the attackers.

Sir Gregory rode down the line, surrounded by his aides, and reined in beside Symond. "Can we not keep the men moving?" He asked as though he were irritated that the column had stopped.

"It would lead to confusion." Symond replied. "There would be stragglers as the men are tired."

"We're all tired!" Sir Gregory snapped. "And if we stay here, we will be picked off one by one!" As he said it, Baleford's scouts charged again and loosed another volley of bolts that killed a handful of men that could not duck behind their shields quick enough. A crossbow bolt whizzed past Sir Gregory's right ear and buried itself in an aide's neck that was behind him. "Prepare to march!" He shouted.

"We risk the company losing its cohesion." Symond warned. "We will be run down."

"And we risk being picked off if we do nothing." Sir Gregory gave Symond a look of utter disgust. He was not used to people questioning his orders, and his dislike for Symond only enflamed his anger. "Order the men!" He snapped as though Symond was a mere nothing but a tool to order about.

"But the dangers." Symond tried one last time to make Sir Gregory see sense.

"You will do as ordered, or be executed for disobedience!" Sir Gregory waved forwards his Master-At-Arms to show his seriousness.

"As you wish." Symond stubbornly replied.

The column went on and men that fell behind were mercilessly killed by the horsemen. Symond tried his best to keep cohesion, but the men were tired, and tired men were clumsy. Some tripped over the smallest of stones or simply did not react quickly enough to the volleys of bolts that the horsemen sent crashing into them. Men were needlessly dying as the column faltered and once more came to a halt. The horsemen, sensing victory, charged the ragged men. All cohesion was lost as men broke rank and tried to flee for their lives. Sir Gregory called them back, but it was of no use. Any that tried to run were slain and the oxen that were pulling the wagons were targets for the crossbow bolts.

Henri was on the medical wagon along with four other men that had collapsed on the march, and when the attack came he had laydown to avoid the crossbow bolts that flew overhead. Elizabeth was with him also, lying beside him with her hands covering her ears to block out the screaming of the dying.

"What's happening?" Elizabeth asked, fear making her voice quiver. "Is it all over yet?"

Henri, with his wrists and ankles tied, wriggled to the edge of the wagon and peered over. Men were everywhere fighting for their life and blooded bodies filled the gaps between the groups of fighting men. But it was not as bad as he thought. Though the company had been dog-tired, those that had fought back had killed many of the horsemen also. Clustered together, close to the rear of the column, was a small circle where he could see Symond and a handful of spearmen making their stand. There were bodies of men and horses at their feet, and he knew that they could hold their ground for many hours more so long as Symond led them. "No it's not over." He replied to Elizabeth. Crossbow bolts thudded against the side of the wagon and Henri was forced to quickly duck back down.

Elizabeth cried out as a crossbow bold thudded into the space between her and a soldier whose feet had badly swollen and was unable to stand. "What are we going to do?"

"There's nothing we can do." Henri said as he wriggled back down to Elizabeth. "Just keep your head down and hope for the best."

"Hold me." Elizabeth said as she placed her head on Henri's chest and closed her eyes, the sound of the battle ringing all around the wagon.

There, all the company would have met its end had it not been for a small company of the king's outriders who charged up from the southeast. For days had they traced Baleford's men in hope of engaging them, and now that they had caught up with them, they wasted no time. In a shape of an arrowhead they charged, unseen by Baleford's men who were taken by complete surprise by the outriders. Men and horse clashed, and the ringing of steel sang of the battle's ferocity. But Baleford's men, who had earlier sensed victory, were now trapped and almost cut down to a man. Only a couple escaped and three of the king's outriders gave chase to see them off.

"Many thanks." Symond tiredly said to an outrider reined in close to the defensive circle he had formed. He was covered in blood and his sword arm ached and felt as though it was on fire. "I feared all was lost until your timely arrival."

"I am Captain Adlard of the king's outriders." The captain said as he dismounted his horse. "Who are you?" He was dressed in a dark-green tunic and trousers, and wore knee-high, brown boots that were scuffed and scratched.

"I am Symond, a captain in this company."

"And who is in charge?" The captain asked.

"That would be Sir Gregory Fitzwalter." Symond replied as he bent down and wiped the blood off his sword on a dead soldier's tunic. "He is around here somewhere, dead or alive." He added, ramming his sword into its scabbard.

"Sir Gregory Fitzwalter." The captain repeated the name as though he had heard of him. "So you're the company the king sent to Oldby."

"Yes." Symond nodded, surprised that the captain knew of their mission.

"We were told to watch out for you and engage any threat." The captain glanced around and raised his eyebrows. "Where are your mounted men?"

"I know not." Symond replied. "They chased off some of Baleford's skirmishers and never returned."

"This is ill news." The captain said as he remounted his horse. "We cannot stay with you as we must report back to the king. But there are ruins of an ancient temple a few miles from here. I will speak with Sir Gregory and offer our assistance to the ruins."

The captain rode off to speak with Sir Gregory as the company regrouped. Sir Gregory agreed with the captain's advice and ordered the company on towards the ruins. After a few hours of tiredly marching, the company arrived at the foot of two broken statues, covered over with moss, which flanked a broken cobbled road with tuffs of grass poking up between the stones. That road led them to a ruin where only three high walls were left standing, walls that were crumbling and being pulled apart by the dense ivy that scaled it way up the stonework. There was a strange feel to the temple as if some sort of ancient curse lingered in the stones, and what remained of the company felt uneasy within its walls.

The company settled down on the cracked and broken tiled floor, taking the chance to rest, while the outriders fetched wood from a nearby woodland. Some made fires and began roasting meat while others searched the ruins. A hidden door that led down into dark vaults was found in a room along the north wall and two of the outriders went down to investigate.

Henri's stomach growled as his nose caught the smell of the roasting meat. He had been shoved in a corner where he was watched by men sat around a small fire close by.

"It looks fine!" Elizabeth said with shock. She had removed Henri's bandage expecting to see a red, sore looking gash. But instead it looked clean and had almost healed.

"It was just a scratch." Henri shrugged.

"I have seen men die from similar wounds." Elizabeth replied, looking suspiciously at Henri as if he were hiding something from her. "They became infected and they died a few days later. But yours has healed quicker than it should have."

"It wasn't that bad." Henri replied. Since he had drank from the chalice of knowledge, his wounds had quickly healed and he had been quick to learn new skills. A part of him wanted to tell Elizabeth that, but he had not told anybody through fear of what might happen to him, and Elizabeth was no exception. "I have just got lucky that's all." He said, looking away from her inquisitive gaze.

Elizabeth wrapped another bandage around his arm and continued looking at him suspiciously, her blue eyes seemingly trying to read his thoughts.

"Are you well my young friend?" Symond said as he came over, carrying two wooden platters of meat. "I was told that you were injured."

"At the camp. It was just a scratch." Henri replied, more to Elizabeth than Symond. "But never mind that. What is this place?"

"An old temple." Symond answered as he passed Elizabeth a platter and then Henri. "I know not its name nor what it was built for. I only know that we are to shelter here for the night before continuing on tomorrow."

Henri greedily bit off a chunk of meet, grease dribbling down his chin, and glanced around at the men slumped by the fire. "Have we enough men to go on?"

Symond shrugged. "I and the captain of the outriders have urged Sir Gregory to return to the king's camp, but he is determined to go on." He then looked to Elizabeth, his eyes tired and troubled. "I even asked if the outriders could escort you back to the king where it is safer."

"So I am to return?" Elizabeth asked, feeling unsure if that is what she wanted.

"No." Symond replied shaking his head. "Sir Gregory is insistent that you remain with the company."

"But why, I am of little use now that the physician and his aide have been killed." Elizabeth had felt something was off about being asked to go on this mission, as she felt certain that the Duke of Hollington would never have allowed such a thing.

"I have no answer to such a question." Symond replied. "But little of Sir Gregory's actions have made any sense. And I fear that doom shall meet us on this quest."

The two outriders emerged from the room where they had found the hidden door to the underground vaults. Being held by them was an old man wearing a dirty, navy-blue robe and a wide brimmed hat that flopped over at the top. They dragged him before Sir Gregory, who was sat at a makeshift table of a fallen stone, writing a report.

"Take your stinking hands off me!" The old man roared. "This is my home, you have no right to come and drag me away from my work!" He angrily snatched his arms out of the outriders grip and began flapping them. "Leave me alone!"

"Who are you, and what are you doing here?" Sir Gregory asked, placing down his quill and looking into the old man's colourless eyes.

"My name is Pagenellus!" The old man snapped as he tucked his long white beard back into his belt. "Pagenellus the wizard, the wise as I am called."

"The wise." Sir Gregory repeated as he stood and looked down at the short old man in front of him. He thought that the old man looked more mad then wise, and very much doubted that he was a wizard like he claimed. "And what are you doing here?"

"I just told you so." Pagenellus answered as he hopped from one foot to another, flapping his hands in frustration. "This is my home!"

"You said that I had no right to drag you away from your work."

"Yes, yes that's right." Pagenellus flapped. "Now let me get back to it." He went to turn around, but the outriders stopped him.

"What is it you're working on?" Sir Gregory asked, full of intrigue.

Pagenellus shook his head. "No, no, no say."

"Tell me!" Sir Gregory snapped.

"No, no, it's secret." Pagenellus violently shook his head. "I cannot say."

"You will tell me!" Sir Gregory yelled, his anger enflamed by Pagenellus's smiling and twitching face. "Tie him up." He ordered. "I have no time for this madman."

The outriders roughly grabbed Pagenellus's arms and tied his thin wrists. They then dragged him over to the corner where Henri was being kept.

"A madman!" Pagenellus said with utter disbelief as the outriders shoved him to the floor. "He called me a madman!"

"Pagenellus." Henri said as he placed down his empty platter and wiped his greasy mouth on his sleeve. "What are you doing here?"

"Why must everybody ask me the same foolish question?" Pagenellus's eyes narrowed as he tried to focus on Henri. "No, it cannot be. Henri it's you!" His white, bushy eyebrows wriggled with excitement. "They worked didn't they, didn't they?" He added as he nodded his head excitedly.

"What worked?" Henri asked, puzzled by what Pagenellus meant.

"At Lhanwick, my invention." Pagenellus wagged his head from side to side. "They worked really well."

The last time Henri had seen Pagenellus was at the temple at Lhanwick, where he had helped him with a secret weapon. The clay pots had been filled with a black powder that had exploded when lit, and Henri could remember the deadly effect that they'd had on the tight formations of the king's attacking men, and the noise that made his ears ring. But the worst, he remembered, was the thick smoke that stunk of rotten eggs. "They worked." Henri conceded. "But it was not enough to win the battle."

"So whatever happened to Robert Hawkwood?" Pagenellus asked, his right cheek twitching. "He lost the battle, not my pots of death."

"His body was found outside the entrance to the temple." Symond explained. "There were no other bodies around him and some say that he was wounded on the walls and retreated back to the temple to hide, where he met his end."

"That's not true." Elizabeth interjected. "He was killed by Dick as he was on his way to me." The memory saddened her. Although Robert had been her captor, he had treated her well and they had taken a liking for each other. "He was a good man at heart." She added, fearing that he would forevermore be branded as a traitor.

"Now that you are here," Pagenellus said after a moment's silence, "Maybe you could help me again."

"With what?" Henri said shaking his head. "What is it you are doing here?"

Pagenellus straightened his back and looked around to make sure nobody was eavesdropping. "Secret things." He replied quietly and raising a bushy eyebrow. "Things that would disturb the ignorance of men."

"What is it that you are doing here?" Symond asked wanting an answer.

"Men are weak." Pagenellus's voice was no more than a whisper. "Their flesh ages and their bones soften with time. Our bodies are delicate and the smallest of wounds can cause death." He pulled out a folded parchment from a hidden pocket inside his robe, his tied wrists making the task harder than it should have been. "Take a look." He said as he passed Henri the parchment and wriggled his eyebrows.

Henri, with the help of Symond, opened the parchment that had a diagram of a body along with instructions written in the eastern script. "What is it?" Henri shook his head and looked up into Pagenellus's grinning face.

"It is a stronger man." Pagenellus replied, unable to hide the excitement in his voice. "A man that won't need food nor water. A man that will not tire nor feel any pain."

"Necromancy." Symond said with distaste. "One should not delve into the black arts."

"I was unable to find a fresh body." Pagenellus said with raised eyebrows. "So I came here where there are many bones within the crypt below."

"You managed to give life to a skeleton?" Symond asked, fearing what evils Pagenellus could have released.

Pagenellus grinned as his right cheek twitched. "There are spirits trapped in these stones, and I have yet to find a way of freeing them. Only then could I make a skeleton walk."

"I think it was for the best that you were found." Symond said as he stood. "Before you unleashed an uncontrollable evil." He then looked at Elizabeth and said, "We had better tend to our other duties."

Elizabeth stood and nodded at Henri. "I'll come back and check on you later." She smiled down at him, then turned and walked off with Symond.

Henri passed the parchment back to Pagenellus, who was nodding his head and grinning as though he were over happy with his plans. Sir Gregory was right, Henri thought, Pagenellus was a madman. "I'm tired." Henri said as he turned away from Pagenellus and laydown, soon falling into an unsettled sleep.

Chapter 9

On Catharine and her mother's return to their chamber, news of the betrothal feast had waited for them, and that the formality of a feast would happen that very night. They were told to wear the two dresses that were lain flat on Catharine's bed, a gift that Hubert had sent for them, and to ready their manners. The news took Catharine by surprise and once again she felt unready for the marriage. But as they readied themselves for the feast, Catharine's mother had constantly reassured her that all would go well.

"This dress is too low." Catharine complained as wriggled to adjust herself. "Can I not wear something else?" She was dressed in a low-cut, red dress made of silk that emphasized her chest and slender neck. Her hair had been tightly curled and hung loose around her neck.

"It is a gift from your betrothed." Catharine's mother replied as though that were reason enough to wear the dress.

"But it shows too much."

"It shows what Hubert wants to see." Catharine's mother was as equally dressed as her daughter. She wore a pale-green dress embroidered with golden ivy that climbed up in elegant patterns. Her hair had been pulled back and plaited into a tail at the back of her head, making her face look rounder than it was. "He wishes all to see what a beautiful young woman you are, and all to know that it is he that possesses you."

"Possesses me." Catharine said with a chuckle. "I think that it will be me that possesses him." She added, trying to sound confident.

Catharine's mother smiled as she pulled out a red silk shawl from the chest beside her bed. "Wear this." She said as she walked over to Catharine and placed it around her shoulders. "Use it well."

"What do you mean by use it?" Catharine asked as she covered herself. "And where did you get this from?"

"Hubert brought you that dress because he desires to see you in it." Catharine's mother said as she made a few adjustments to the shawl and ignoring Catharine's question of how she had acquired it. "With this you can control what he can see."

"And at the same time, I am wearing what he wants." Catharine said, starting to realise what her mother meant by controlling Hubert. "Clever." She said with a smile.

"Now you can use it to your advantage." There was a knock on the door and Catharine's mother turned and walked towards the door.

"Ladies!" A voice called through the thick, metal studded door. "Are you ready?"

Catharine's mother pulled open the door to find the captain of the tower stood with the large guard that had escorted them to the marketplace earlier. "Yes." She answered with an authoritative voice.

The captain was a handsome man with a slender, youthful face and hazel coloured eyes that held your attention. "The guests have gathered and the lord has requested that you and your daughter join them in the great hall."

"Thank you captain, we need just a moment more." Catharine's mother partially shut the door and walked over to Catharine. "Are you ready?"

"I'm not ready." Catharine answered. "But I have to do this."

"One day we shall look back on this day and smile, seeing it as the moment we began to reclaim what was ours."

Catharine hoped that her mother was right, and that all went to plan. Though what that plan was she was unsure. "Let us get this over with." She said, forcing an unconvincing smile.

"Good girl." Catharine's mother said, returning the smile. "Our better future begins from this very moment."

They linked arms and walked out of their chamber. The captain of the tower then led them down the spiral stairs, which was a challenge for Catharine and her mother in their dresses. Once down the stairs, they were led through a thick wooden door that led out onto the courtyard. There was many elegant carriages parked up and awaiting their masters from the feast, and Catharine found herself picking one out and imagining herself riding out in the countryside.

"That one is Hubert's." Catharine's mother said as she pointed to a white carriage decorated with well-polished brass work that shone brightly in the moonlight. "Rumours say that he purchased it from the Satrap of Tallis."

"He travels far." Catharine said, impressed by the rumour. "Maybe as his wife he will take me to such exotic places?"

"Maybe." Catharine's mother replied, wondering if he would take Catharine. "If he does, imagine the wonders you shall see, the people you will meet."

"I have heard that the eastern kingdoms are too hot." Catharine said as she remembered a merchant that had once told her that her skin was far too pale to withstand the heat there.

"So they say." Catharine's mother replied. "It is why those that live there have darker skin."

They walked up the few stairs that led to the castles keep and the entrance was opened up for them by two of the lord's servants. The noise of the guests could be heard as soon as they entered the keep and the double doors that led to the great hall were pushed open to reveal the many gathered guests.

"The ladies of De'lacy!" A servant announced their arrival.

The muttering amongst the guests sat around the large rectangular table suddenly stopped as they turned and looked at Catharine and her mother. Their stares made Catharine feel uncomfortable and she looked down at the green tiled floor that only days ago she had been scrubbing clean. All of the guests were finely dressed and dripping with golden jewels that could have ended poverty in the town. But the lord was a forbidding contrast to the guests. He was sat at the head of the table, dressed in his usual grim attire of a black ankle length robe and his tricorn hat with a long red feather sticking out of the back. He sat rigid, stone-faced as his beady hawk-like eyes watched Catharine and her mother take their seats to his left hand.

"You're late!" The lord snapped as he cast his angered eyes on a nervous Catharine. "I wanted you here to greet the guest as they arrived!"

"Forgive us my lord." Catharine's mother replied, her voice confident and strong. "But we had to wait for the guards to unlock our door before we could attend the festivities."

"Sorry." Catharine said softly as she took her seat. She looked across the table and saw an empty chair and hoped that it was a sign that Hubert had changed his mind on the marriage. But she was to be disappointed. From a door that led to the privy came Hubert, his face already red and sweaty from too much drink. Catharine watched as her soon-to-be husband wobbled his way over to his seat, and felt a wave of disgust sweep through her. He wore a red robe that made him look even bigger than he was and his curled hair was matted to his round, sweaty head.

"That feels much better." Hubert said as he slumped down, his chair straining against the weight. "More wine!" He called to a servant refilling goblets at the far end of the table.

"Maybe now we can get on with this formality." The lord said grumpily as he gave Hubert a look that showed his annoyance with him. He rose from his high-backed chair and the hall fell silent as the guests awaited his words. "Honoured guest." His voice was full of astuteness and hid the pain that throbbed in his stomach. "We have gathered here tonight to celebrate the betrothal of my honoured friend, Hubert Marcel, and Catherine De'lacy. This marriage I freely give my blessings and shall personally attend the ceremony in the temple in two days' time." A few of the women began whispering amongst themselves, saying that it was a sham marriage and that Hubert only had eyes on the mother. But one stern look from the lord soon silenced them. "If anyone here should have reasons for me to denounce this marriage, then speak now." Though many of the guests knew the marriage would only further the lord's wealth and power, none spoke out and remained subjectively silent. "Good then let us raise a goblet and feast."

Catharine had watched the lord as he made his speech, noticing that he had kept a hand on his stomach. Though his voice was hard and full of all the malice of his youth, his body was frail and old. His face was emaciated and pale as if the reaper had marked him for death, his beady eyes were sunken into his head and his thin lips seemed to be constantly dry and cracked. She felt eyes watching her and she looked across the table to see Hubert staring at her with lustful eyes. "Why must he stare mother?" Catharine whispered quietly so she was not overheard.

"Smile daughter." Catharine's mother replied. "Smile as though you welcome his gaze."

Catharine looked back across the table at Hubert and forced a smile.

Hubert greedily gulped down his goblet of wine and belched. "May I now say a few words?" He drunkenly asked the lord.

The lord's hawk-like eyes narrowed as he was angered by Hubert's behaviour. "If you are able." He sat back in his chair and gestured to Hubert to continue.

"I thank you my lord." Hubert rose to his feet, his face red and sweaty, and his legs weak from the wine. "I welcome..." He paused and belched again. "I welcome your blessings and would ask you all to join me and my lady." He looked at Catharine and licked his lips. "Join us on our ceremonial day." The guests began to mutter of Hubert apparent drunkenness and he was forced to bang the base of his goblet on the table to regain their attention. "I thank you all for your attendance and bestow a vat of wine from Elon Dor to each and every one of you." The guests applauded happily at Hubert's generosity, for a vat of wine from Elon Dor was a princely gift.

The lord, however, was not pleased. He sat rigid, his beady grey eyes narrowed and staring at Hubert as though he willed death upon him. "Bring in the feast!" The lord waved a liver spotted hand at his servants and then gestured for Hubert to sit back down. "A very generous gift." He said as Hubert slumped back down on his chair. "A gift that you should have told me you would give!" The lord was deeply angered as the gift now reflected ill upon him, a lord less generous than a merchant was not a good thing.

"Forgive me my lord, the wine makes me forget myself." Hubert said as he pulled out a damp handkerchief from his pocket and wiped his face. "More wine!" He called over to a servant.

"I think that you have had enough already!" The lord picked up his own goblet, filled with water rather than wine, and took a swig.

"Nonsense." Hubert took the jug off of the servant and refilled his own goblet. "Tonight is a celebration."

The double doors opened and servants brought in platters of freshly baked bread, round cheeses surrounded by red berries, pies filled with a variety of meats, and exotic fruit from the eastern kingdoms. The last platter to be carried in was a large boar that had been roasted and stuffed with herbs and onions. The two servants carrying it placed it in the centre of the table and began carving it into portions.

Hubert's eyes widened as a servant placed a silver platter, overloaded with thick slices of the boar, in front of him. "Bring me some bread." He ordered as he greedily rammed a chunk of meat into his mouth. "And some of that pie."

Catharine watched him eat, disgusting her further, and thought him a pig. Often he would look up at her and smile, grease running down his double chin. She politely smiled back and looked away. "He eats like a starved pig." Catharine said quietly to her mother.

Catharine's mother looked over at Hubert who was ramming chunk after chunk of meat into his mouth. "Don't be so rude." She reproved, looking sternly at Catharine. "Though you are right."

Hubert grunted as he bit into a hunk of bread and looked over at Catharine. "You need to eat something my betrothed." He said with a mouthful, crumbs spaying out from his mouth as he spoke. "I don't want you getting too skinny." Hubert snatched up his goblet and drained his wine, a portion spilling down his double chin and onto to his robe. "Give her some more bread and meat." He ordered a servant as he wiped his mouth on the back of his flabby hand.

"I thank you for your concern." Catharine politely replied. "But I have eaten enough already." The truth was that she had only picked at a piece of bread and eaten a few slices of an apple, but the glances from the guests made her feel uncomfortable and she knew that the women would be gossiping about her.

"Nonsense." Hubert said, waving a servant over to fill Catharine's platter. "I like my wife like my chickens, plump and ripe for plucking." He picked up the jug of wine and once again refilled his goblet. "Come now my lord, let us share a drink in celebration."

The lord placed his shaky hand over his goblet. "No, I find that it dulls the better judgement."

"Well, all the more for me then." Hubert raised his goblet and smiled. "To an aggrandizing future." He drained his goblet and slammed down on the table, making the old merchant sat next to him jump. "Now my lord if I may be so bold as to ask about the gift as is customary from the lord?"

The lord's face was grim and locked in a battle to hide his anger and pain. "You forget your place Hubert!" He said, leaning menacingly forward in his chair. "You have drank too much and lost your good senses!"

Hubert felt suddenly very sober under the lord's hard gaze. If the lord's body looked weak, his eyes were not and still had all the malice of his youth. "Forgive me my lord." Hubert said soberly. "Prospects of this marriage overstimulates me."

The lord remained sinisterly quiet and many of the guests thought that he might order Hubert's execution at any moment. After an uneasy moment he rose to his feet, his grey eyes watching Hubert as a hawk watches its prey. "Honoured guests." The lord's voice was shaky because of the dull ache in his stomach and despite his attempt to hide it, all could see that something was amiss. "As the head of the De'lacy family, it is customary for me to bestow a gift upon the suitor." The lord's throat was dry and he felt a hot flush sweep up his frail body. He reached down and picked up his goblet, his shaky hand forcing him to spill some of his water before taking a sip. "The gift I bestow shall be a gift that benefits this town and its people." He said as he placed his goblet back on the table. "As all here know, Hubert has built a successful business and has good relations with the eastern merchants. Such a wealth of knowledge should be obtained for the betterment of the town. So as the Lord of Heath Hollow I do hereby appoint Hubert Marcel a place on the town's council."

The guests applauded the announcement, though they were not happy with it. The town's council had the power to grant licenses to build in the town and sell in the marketplace. Hubert's appointment caused unrest and many of the guests began to whisper of unjustness and greed, for surely Hubert would use the appointment to his own advantage and drive out his rivals from the marketplace.

The lord held up a hand, and the hall fell silent once more. Another hot flush swept up his body followed by a sudden stab of pain that forced him to cry out and fall back into his chair.

"My lord!" Hubert said with shock. "Fetch the physician!" He called out to no one in particular.

The guests were stunned and watched silently as the servants fretted over the lord. One removed his hat and fanned him while another held his goblet up to his lips. But the lord was unable to drink as he began a coughing fit that lasted a few minutes. A servant quickly wiped his mouth in an attempt to hide the blood, but all had seen and the gossip of a dying lord spread like an enraged fire.

"I'm fine!" The lord snapped as his strength returned. "I'm fine!" He snapped with more venom then before. He rose to his feet and cast his beady eyes over the on looking guests, daring any to comment on his health. "I am tired and have eaten something disagreeable to me. I give this marriage my blessings and will take to my chamber." Without another word, the lord walked around the table and out of the double doors, a hand clutching his stomach.

The guests burst in to excited gossip with some claiming that it was the ghost of the previous lord, come to avenge his murder. But most were more level-headed and spoke of more troubled times to come should the lord die and be succeeded by his son, the Lord Aide. Their fears were only enhanced by Hubert who smugly sat down on the lord chair and poured himself more wine, as though all were to his liking.

"Should we not delay our celebrations?" Catharine asked her mother, in hope that it would somehow delay the marriage.

"No need for that." Hubert answered, overhearing Catharine. "The lord has given us his blessing."

"You are quite right Hubert." Catharine's mother said with a hint of flattery in her voice. "There is no reason to keep love apart."

Hubert gulped down his wine and smiled. "You look delightful tonight."

"Do I not always?" Catharine's mother said flirtatiously.

"Quite so." Hubert answered as his eyes fell upon her ample cleavage.

"And what of my daughter, your future wife?" Catharine's mother placed her arm around Catharine's shoulder and pulled off the shawl. "Does she not look every bit as delightful as me?"

Catharine shook her head in disbelief, then noticed Hubert's lustful stare at her chest.

"She does." Hubert said, licking his lips as if she were a piece of meat awaiting to be sampled. "You know that both of you are to live in my manor?"

Catharine's mother nodded. "Yes, we know and cannot wait for the pleasure."

Hubert grinned, believing that he could bed both mother and daughter. "Tomorrow." He said as he leaned over and grabbed Catharine's hand. "Tomorrow you should both come and look at your new home." He rubbed his greasy thumb over Catharine's knuckles and once again licked his lips. "That is if the lord allows it, though I doubt that he has the strength to stop you."

Catharine removed her hand, revolted by Hubert's vulgar behaviour. It was all seemingly very real to her now. "Thank you." She forced herself to say. "I accept your kind invitation."

The feast went on for a little while longer, but most of the guest were eager to spread what they had seen and soon took their leave. For the news they spread was of a dying lord and a greedy merchant that will drive out all other merchants from the marketplace.

*   *   *

Henri jerked and shot up on to his feet. His wrists were no longer tied and his first thoughts were to run, get away and start anew somewhere else. He looked around the darkened ruins and saw that all were asleep. One of two soldiers that were guarding him was leaning upright against the wall, softly snoring while the other sat poking at the fire. Henri carefully took a step towards the soldier, hoping to creep up behind him and somehow knock him unconscious so that he could escape undetected. He took a breath to steady his drumming heart and took another step closer. The soldier turned and saw Henri, but instead of calling out to raise the alarm, he instead fell into a deep sleep. Henri, shocked and surprised by his good fortune, carefully stepped over Pagenellus's sleeping body and checked that the soldiers guarding him were asleep and not somehow tricking him. He nudged the soldier that had looked at him and watched as his slumbered body fell onto the floor. What was happening? Confused, Henri once more glanced around the ruins, hoping to see someone awake, but all were deep in a sinister slumber and silent.

"Pagenellus!" Henri shouted as he walked over to him. "Pagenellus wake up!" He knelt down and shook him, but Pagenellus would not wake.

The small campfires in the ruins suddenly died, giving way to darkness that was full of cruelty to the senses. A sudden chill in the air made Henri's teeth chatter and he pulled a blanket off one of the sleeping soldiers and wrapped it around his shoulders in an effort to stay warm. The sound of a woman's laughter was carried on the breeze that seemingly filtered from out of the door that led down to the vaults. Henri shuddered at the sound of the laughter, and despite his better judgement, he found himself walking towards the door as though unseen magic was alluring him.

"Who's there?!" Henri called down through the open door. There was no response, just darkness that concealed the way down. He placed his hand on the wall and began to descend the stairs, carefully placing one foot on the step below before moving forward. The stairs led him down to a corridor that had been lit up by mirrors that reflected in the moon's light from outside. "Who's there?!" Henri called as the sound of the woman's laughter echoed down the corridor.

"Clean, clean, clean to make it gleam." Came a croaked voice.

Henri walked down the corridor and came to a small room. It was dark and Henri feared what evil was lurking in the shadows. "Who's there?!" He called once more. From the blackness came a wisp of white smoke that shone so bright that it lit up the room. Henri held his hands to his face to shield his eyes from the intense light.

"Clean, clean, clean until it gleams." The crackled voice echoed all around him.

The light suddenly faded and Henri realised that he had been moved into the centre of the room. "What are you?!" He screamed out, a sudden sense of terror sweeping through him. "What do you want with me?!"

"Clean, clean, clean until it gleams." The croaky voice echoed.

Henri heard footsteps behind him and he instinctively ran back into the corridor. He stopped and looked back, seeing a white shadow of a woman wearing a long, flowing gown. "What are you?!" Henri yelled in hope that his angered voice was enough to scare the ghost off. But scare it off, he did not. It began to float menacingly towards him, its arms stretched out in an attempt to grab him. Fear now uncontrollably swept through Henri and he turned to flee back up the corridor.

"Clean, clean, clean until it gleams." The ghost sang as it chased Henri down the corridor.

Henri sprinted as fast as he could and leapt up the stairs two at a time. He glanced back over his shoulder as he felt an ice-cold hand wrap around his ankle and pull him back. He stumbled and painfully fell on the stairs.

"Clean, clean, clean until it gleams." The ghost sang as it retreated back down the stairs.

Henri rushed to his feet and climbed the remaining stairs and found that the door had closed. "Open up!" He yelled as he beat his fist against the decaying wood. The door felt warm and covered the bottom of his fist with soot. "Open up!" Henri yelled once again. The door suddenly fell from its hinges and crashed down onto the floor, sending up a thick cloud of soot that concealed Henri's view. After a brief moment, the soot settled and Henri was met by a scene straight from the underworld.

The ruins were gone, giving way to a scorched land covered over with ash. The sky above was blood-red with fire, and the air hot and toxic. In the distance was a creature that one only heard of in the old stories told to frighten children. Its mighty wings beat a wild wind that stirred up the ash, causing an ash-cloud that choked Henri. Its teeth were sharp like swords, its claws as long as spears, and its black scales were as strong as armour. A dragon, huge and furious, bent its long neck and looked back down at Henri with its white narrowed eyes. It gave a terrifying screech as it turned and flew above Henri.

Henri, filled with terror, fell to his knees and watched helplessly as the dragon landed before him. Its white eyes flickered with a flame of bloodlust and its claws turned up the ash as a plough cuts through a field. There it stood for a moment, menacing and mighty as it stared down at him. For a moment Henri thought that he would not be devoured. But no sooner had he thought it, the dragon reared up on its back legs and splayed its mighty wings. Its eyes turned red as it opened its mouth and spewed fire down upon Henri.

Henri jolted upright, sweating and full of fear. He quickly glanced around and saw Pagenellus's smiling face looking straight at him. "Are you real?" Henri asked, unsure whether he was still dreaming.

"Real?" Pagenellus said as he wiggled his bushy eyebrows. "Are you alright?"

Henri shook his head. "I don't know. I think so."

"You were dreaming." Pagenellus grinned. "And I don't think that it was a pleasant one."

"No." Henri confessed. "There was a ghost of an old woman that kept saying; *clean, clean, clean until it gleams*."

Pagenellus's face twitched. "Did she chase you?"

Henri nodded. "You know of her?"

"There was once a woman that served the temple here." Pagenellus said in a quiet tone. "An efficient woman that spent many years cleaning after the other temple maids."

"How do you know of this?" Henri interrupted.

"I read about this place many a year ago." Pagenellus explained. "And what I read said that the woman went mad in her later years. She claimed to see faces in the floor and that the more she washed them away, more would appear. After her death, many claimed to see her ghost scrubbing the floors and singing; *clean, clean, clean until it gleams*."

"That was not the worst of it." Henri said as thoughts of the dragon swirled around in his head.

"You saw something else?" Pagenellus asked with excitement.

Henri nodded. "I saw a dragon."

"A dragon!" Pagenellus's face twitched as he excitedly shook his legs against the floor. "What did it look like?"

Henri told him about the rest of his dream and Pagenellus listened keenly, nodding his head and grinning as though he knew something.

Pagenellus's face went into an uncontrollable spasm and he excitedly clapped his hands. "Baptized by the fire of a dragon!" He said loud enough to wake a soldier close by.

"Quieten down!" The soldier yelled at Pagenellus as he rolled over, quietly grumbling to himself.

Henri shook his head in disbelief that Pagenellus could think that being scorched to death was a good thing.

"There is more to you Henri, more than eyes can see." Pagenellus said, wagging a suspicious finger at Henri.

A cold blast of air swept through the ruins, waking many of the soldiers. The night had taken a sudden sinister turn and many grabbed their weapons ready.

"What was that?" Henri asked, feeling a sudden sense of dread.

"A stirring." Pagenellus replied, his face ashen and his eyes wide with fear. "Something had disturbed the spirits, something powerful."

From the dark depths of the vaults came a long, terrifying screech that drove the company mad. Soldiers fell to their knees and covered their ears in an attempt to block out the deafening noise. Then, up from the ground came the bones of the dead. The company fled in all directions, losing their courage and abandoning any sense of discipline. The skeletons tackled down soldiers as they tried to flee and systematically started to tear away their limbs. Soldiers dropped their weapon so that they could run unhindered, weapon that the skeletons now picked up and used against them.

"It worked!" Pagenellus said with excitement. "It really worked!"

"Never mind that!" Henri snapped. "We need to get out of here!" A soldier stumbled and fell close by, killed from a deep gash across his stomach. Henri quickly wiggled over to the body and grabbed the sword that the soldier had dropped. "Quickly, cut me free!"

Pagenellus scrunched his face up as he wrapped his hand around the blooded handle and cut Henri free. "Now we must go!" He said as he dropped the sword and wiped his hand on the skirts of his robe.

"Now I need to find Elizabeth!" Henri grabbed the sword and rushed to his feet, dashing off into the chaos. All around him was death, lifeless bodies that had been mutilated so bad that you could not tell one body from another. "Elizabeth!" Henri called as he frantically cast his eyes around the ruins. A soldier with a blood splatted face bumped into him, almost knocking him over. "Where is Elizabeth?" Henri asked. But the soldier never replied and kept on running. "Elizabeth!" He called again. More soldiers passed him, but none stopped to offer any assistance.

A skeleton saw Henri and rushed towards him wielding a sword above its skull. Its bones were stained yellow with age and covered in moss that gave it a greenish tint. It lunged at Henri, quick and furiously, almost disembowelling him. But Henri had seen the threat and was able to parry the blow with ease and counter with a swift attack that forced the skeleton back.

"Elizabeth!" Henri yelled as he hacked down on the skeleton's skull, splitting it in two. "Elizabeth where are you?!"

"Henri help me!" Elizabeth's voice called over the chaos.

"Where are you?!" Henri called as he frantically tried to distinguish where her voice came from. Another skeleton rushed at him, wildly swinging a broken sword. But despite their terror and speed, they were clumsy and their bones brittle. Henri parried and stepped to his right, leaving his left foot sticking out. The skeleton tripped and crashed to the ground, breaking ribs. Henri quickly stepped over it and struck a blow that shattered its skull. "Elizabeth where are you?!"

"Help me!" Elizabeth's voice cried.

Elizabeth's voice was coming from the doorway that led to the underground vaults. Henri ran over and poked his head through the open door. "Elizabeth are you down there?!"

"Henri, they've got me!" Elizabeth's voice echoed up the stairs.

"I'm coming!" Henri rushed down the stairs as quick as he could. It was dark and Henri had to tread carefully so not to trip. Unlike his dream, the stairs never took him to a passageway, but straight to a dark vault with many columns and arches to stop it from collapsing in on itself. There was a dim glow in the corner and Henri could make out the outline of Elizabeth facing the wall. "Are you unharmed?" Henri asked as he cautiously walked over to her. As he got closer his instincts told him something was wrong, that he was foolish for entering the vaults. "Elizabeth?" He said as he went to touch her shoulder.

238

Suddenly Elizabeth vanished and there was a crackle of a laugh that echoed all around him.

"Your blood shall be my power." An orb of white light danced around the columns and disappeared into a wall.

Henri rushed back towards the stairs to find that they were now nothing more than ruins, like the rest of the temple. His heart was racing and he began to panic. "Hey!" He yelled up. "Anybody!"

"Clean, clean, clean to make it gleam."

A fresh wave of fear swept through Henri as he recognised the voice from his dream. Do something, he told himself, anything would be better than dying in this dismal place. With the fear of death driving him on, he dropped his sword and began climbing the broken stairs, but an unseen hand pulled him back down. He crashed on to the stone floor and lay winded as the walls around him began to dimly glow.

"Clean, clean, clean to make it gleam." The voice echoed all around him as faces of an old hag appeared in the walls and floor. "Clean, clean, clean to make it gleam." They said in unison, over and over again.

Henri, clutching his bruised ribs, staggered to his feet. "Be swift!" He yelled. "I'll not ascend to the stars with fear swelling inside me!"

The vault suddenly fell dark and silent. From the archway that led to the adjacent vault came a white orb of light that manifested into the ghost of the old temple maid that Pagenellus had spoken of. Her hair was long and straggly, her white robe torn to reveal her emaciated, grey body. She looked at Henri with her black eyes and stretched out her arms as she slowly walked towards him, her feet flapping on the stone floor.

Henri closed his eyes, refusing to look and cause himself fear, when a familiar voice called down to him.

"Henri!"

"I'm here!" Henri called back. He looked up towards the door to see Symond holding a torch. "Get me out!"

"Clean, clean, clean to make it gleam." The ghost of the old woman said as it slowly stepped closer.

"Hurry!" Henri yelled as he climbed up the stairs as far as he could.

Symond had found a long log that two soldiers now carried in. They placed it down and slid it down to Henri.

"Clean, clean, clean to make it gleam." The ghost was now at the foot of the stairs, reaching out with its arms.

Henri wasted no time in crawling across the log to safety. "Where is Elizabeth?" He asked as he rose to his feet.

"She is safe my young friend." Symond replied. "She is with the Sir Gregory and the remainder of our company."

There was a sudden flash of light followed by a long drawn-out screech. Loose stones fell and the floor vibrated as the ghost let out its frustration.

"Let's go." Symond said as he grabbed Henri by his arm and led him out.

The ruins were now littered with bloody bodies and bones from the battle with the skeletons. The stone floor was slippery from the blood and Henri would have lost his footing had it not been for Symond pulling at his arm to keep him up. They ran clear out of the ruins and back up the dirt road where the remainder of the company had gathered.

Who goes there?" A soldier keeping watch called out as he saw men running toward him.

"It's me." Symond called back. "I have more survivors."

The soldier allowed them past and soon they came to what remained of the company. Many were tending their wounds and paid no attention to Symond, Henri and the two others with them as they came to a stop.

"Henri." Elizabeth rushed over and wrapped her arms around him. "I thought that you were lost."

"No." Henri replied. "Thanks to Symond."

"It worked, it worked." Pagenellus saw Henri and danced over. "All it needed was some power, magic power that you must possess."

"Henri what is he talking about?" Elizabeth asked.

Henri shook his head. "I don't know."

"I know that there is more to you." Pagenellus flapped his hands and hopped from foot to foot. "I know it, I know it."

"Tie him up!" Sir Gregory snapped as he pointed at Henri with his sword. "I want us ready to move as soon as we can."

"Surely we should report back to the king?" Symond said. "We no longer have the men to continue on with our mission."

Sir Gregory had started out with a large force, large enough for the mission given to them. But with the disappearance of the mounted men, and the number now killed, the company resembled more of a small band of men rather than a whole company.

"I have sent word to the king." Sir Gregory explained. "With the outriders that left us earlier, asking to send us reinforcements." He rammed his sword into its scabbard, scowling at Symond as though he were crossing some line by urging him to go back. "We will make for an abandoned farmstead a few miles from Oldby, and there we shall await for further orders."

The Master-At-Arms pulled Henri away from Elizabeth's arms and tied his wrist.

"Now let's move on!" Sir Gregory called.

Under the cover of darkness, the remainder of the company limped off. Though all were frightened and wanting to return home, none spoke out and dutifully marched on toward Oldby, where further dangers awaited them.

Chapter 10

If one could fly, as a bird, and look down upon the road north to Market Barton, they would see the king's army marching, like a giant snake slowly slivering its way north. Though the road was well maintained and made the march much easier than going across countryside, the men were tired from the long hot days and their moral had sunk.

When the army had first marched out of Langton Castle, moral was high as the men were as fresh as the supplies that they carried in their packs. But now their feet were blistered and their supplies depleting and stale. But it was not just the blisters and their food that caused their misery. Rumours of the Duke of Baleford's larger army had spread amongst the common men, saying that the Duke's forces were already at Market Barton and were fresh and well-fed. But if that news was not enough to sink one's moral, then news of men deserting in the night sank even the most experienced men's. A whisper amongst the common men spoke that the Duke was offering any man that deserted the king and join his forces one golden crown, a coin that many of the lower ranks would never see in a lifetime. Many now spoke ill of the king, with some even going as far as to call him a tyrant.

The day had been long and hot with little time to rest, and by the time that the army had arrived at their camp, the lower ranks discontent had worsened. The king's outriders had rode well ahead of the army and erected the pavilions that belonged to the men of rank so that they were ready for the army's arrival. But the common men could not afford such luxury and were forced to bed down on the hard ground. The sun sank and thick clouds trapped in the day's heat as soldiers made Small fires, more for their light than heat. Men slumped down on the ground and grumbled about their ill treatment and spoke quietly of better treatment in the Duke's army.

"It's not right." An older man said as he opened his pack to see a chunk of bread and a small lump of cheese that had almost turned completely blue. "A full day's march with these meagre rations."

"Yeah." Another soldier agreed as he turned his pack upside-down and shook out crumbs. "We need some meat, a nice plump chicken will do." He was young and stick thin with long, greasy hair and blue eyes that sat atop of a long, slender nose. "Maybe we would be better-off with the Duke."

"Careful now." The older soldier warned, raising a finger. "Talk like that will get you hung."

"It's only what most others are saying." The younger soldier replied as though his words were justified. "By all accounts he feeds his men well."

"And how do you know that?" The older solider asked, suspiciously shaking his head with doubt.

"Everybody is saying it." The younger soldier dropped his pack and sat beside the fire. "You must have heard what others are saying."

"Heard it yes." The older soldier broke his chunk of bread in half and tossed the younger soldier a piece. "But I do not believe it."

"Bloody bastards!" Another soldier spat in anger as he came and sat beside the older soldier.

"What's wrong Baret?" The older soldier asked.

"Bloody supply wagons are miles behind." Baret, like the two others sat around the fire, was poor and had been conscripted into the spear militia because he owed his lord service. "It's going to take at least two hours for them to reach camp."

"Bah!" The old soldier waved a dismissive hand. "The usual mess."

A waft of roasting meat passed with the breeze. "It smells as though the bloody better half of the army have their supplies!" Baret said with scorn. "To think that they have been riding their noble horses all day while we have to walk to the point of exhaustion, and it is they that have the meat, and us told we must wait for the bloody wagons!"

"It could be worse Baret." The old soldier said, knowing that it could get much worse than this.

"Worse." The young soldier said with shock, his stomach grumbling. "I don't see how."

"You're young and know little." Baret replied. "My grandfather once served with a garrison that was forced to eat the dead."

"He ate the dead?" The young soldier shuddered at the thought. "Really?"

Baret nodded. "He was part of the garrison of Fort Varus during the harsh winter of 1047. The snow blocked all roads and supply wagons ceased their vital deliveries. Rations soon dwindled and the men began to starve. At first they slaughtered the dogs and commander's horse, but soon their meat was exhausted. Then out of desperation or madness, they began eating the flesh of those that had died." Baret chuckled. "My grandfather told me that their commander was so fat that they feasted on his flesh for many days. He told me that at the onset of winter, the fort had a garrison a hundred strong, but come spring only five of them remained."

"We're more likely to be killed in battle then starve on this campaign." The old soldier said as he bit into his stale bread. "Though those wagons had better hurry up." He added as he broke a tooth chewing on the hard crust.

The wagons arrived later that night to a disgruntled camp. They carried boxes of apples and vegetables to make a stew, but no meat. Cooking pots were filled with water and chopped up vegetables to make a thin stew that would briefly keep the hunger away. As the moon hit its height, its light piecing through the clouds, men laydown and tried to sleep.

Beside a fire that was burning low was a small group of men, whispering of deserting and claiming the reward of a gold crown offered by the Duke of Baleford.

"I know of two that went last night." A soldier said, sticking up two fingers. He wore a long, grubby gambeson and a steel cap of a crossbowman. "Two that managed to escape." His face was weatherworn and his teeth broken, the traits that marked him out as poor, and yet his voice betrayed that he was educated.

There was a few murmurs around the fire and one soldier stood, looking around to make sure none of the king's constables was close by. "If we're caught they will hang us

and leave our bodies for the crows to peck out our eyes."
He jabbed his finger out in a warning gesture. "Just like
the others they caught."

Two nights ago, a small group had snuck out of camp,
deserting on the promise that the Duke would welcome
them and offer better food and pay. But the king's
constables had rode out the next morning and apprehended
them. A makeshift scaffold was erected and the common
men were massed around it as all of the deserters were
hung as an example. The king had hoped that it would end
any talk of desertion, but it only made the men believe that
he was a tyrant and that maybe they would be better-off
with the Duke.

"I." The crossbowman agreed. "Those that were caught,
was hanged. But not all were caught."

"But how are we to make it past the picket line?" A soldier
called out a little too loudly. All around the fire hushed,
some even got up and walked away.

"You speak too loudly." The crossbowman warned. "Do
you want us all hung?"

One of the king's constables, who was patrolling the camp,
saw the group and walked over, his navy-blue tunic and
white trousers a stark contrast to the grubby men he
passed. "What's going on here then?" He asked in a stern
voice that showed that he was suspicious.

"Just us men idling and talking of women." The
crossbowman innocently answered.

The constable held up his lantern and suspiciously cast his
eyes over the group of men. He was an experienced man
with solid eyes and thick sideburns that ran all the way

down to his pointed chin. "I'll be watching you." He warmed as he began to walk away. "All of you."

The crossbowman waited until the constable was out of earshot before he continued. "I have a friend who is on duty tonight. A friend that is sympathetic to those wishing to desert." He spoke in a hushed tone and glanced around at the worried faces staring back at him. "Head for the western picket and say that Kendrick sent you."

"And what of the swine." A soldier nervously asked, meaning the constables. "Surely they will come after us."

Many in the group nodded their agreement and thought that it would be pointless to even try. "Some may be caught." Kendrick said as he held up is hands in admittance. "But not all, not if you split up." Kendrick could see that some were convinced, but many others were still reluctant. "Why stay and fight for a king that cares little for you or your families. The Duke of Baleford would personally welcome each and every one of you, and bestow a gift of a golden crown. Just imagine what you could do with such wealth." Kendrick paused to let them think, seeing the glint in their eyes at the mention of money. "Money enough for ale, women, land of your own to farm, whatever you want." Kendrick saw a few nodding and knew that fewer still would attempt to run. But his mission was to cause discontent amongst the king's army, and that he had done by spreading lies and causing men to desert. "I wish you all the best of luck." He said as he walked away.

The camp had an apprehensive feel as if trouble was stirring, yet all seemed normal. Kendrick nodded his head to soldiers as he passed them by, soldiers that were grumbling about the king and his ill treatment of them. He knew that all soldiers suffered the same no matter who commanded them. But the king's army was tired from the long marches and lack of food. The truth was that Baleford's army fed on much the same as the king's, but it was not forced on long marches and was freshly awaiting the king at Market Barton, thus their moral was high and the king's low. Though the king's army was not deserting in droves as the Duke of Baleford wanted. Kendrick knew that they would not fight hard for the king and make the looming battle easier for the Duke.

"Kendrick." A hushed voice said. "Kendrick."

Kendrick turned to see one of his fellow spies rushing towards him. "Roger, what's wrong?"

"A meeting has been called." Roger said as he came to a stop before Kendrick. He was a short man with a bold head and a thick chest that looked as though he had spent years forking hay bales onto carts.

"A meeting?" Kendrick asked with raised eyebrows.

Roger fished into his pocket on his brown tunic and pulled out a note. "This was left in my pack." He explained as he passed Kendrick the note.

"I have had no such note." Kendrick said suspiciously, not even bothering to look at it. "Is it genuine?"

Roger shrugged. "All of the others have already gathered by that large rock we passed earlier."

Kendrick tapped the piece of paper against his knuckles as he thought about it. Why meet now? Had Baleford sent fresh orders for them? Was it a trap? The more Kendrick thought about it, the more his head ached. He reasoned with himself that it couldn't be a trap as there was no way the king could have known that there were spies in his army, they had made sure to be extra careful whenever they spoke to others about deserting. "Come on Roger, we had better see what this is all about."

They walked over to the western part of the camp, where they hoped to find their friend on sentry duty. But he was not there, and Kendrick reasoned that he must have already gone to the meeting. A group of the king's constables was sat around a fire, ready for anybody trying to desert.

One of the constables saw them and pointed. "What are you doing?!" He called.

"We have orders to take up sentry duty!" Kendrick called back. His heart was racing as he expected the constable to see through the lie.

"I need to take your names!" The constable walked over with a scrap piece of paper and pencil to hand. "And your names are?" He asked, licking the nib of his pencil.

"Simon and Will." Kendrick smoothly lied.

"Simon and Will." The constable repeated as he made a note of the names. "I take it Will is short for William?"

Roger nodded. "That's right."

The constable pulled out a folded parchment that contained a list of names that were to go on sentry duty. "Ah." The constable exclaimed as he ran a finger down the columns names. "There you are."

Kendrick had been confident as he had been able to gain a copy of the list and prepare for such an event, but at the same time he feared the worst.

"Carry on." The constable said as he turned and went back to the others sat around the fire, convinced by the lie.

Kendrick and Roger walked up and down the line of sentries trying to find the best place where they could pass undetected. Men were posted at regular intervals and made to walk back and forth to quell any surprise attack. They found that every so often two of the sentries would stop their patrols and talk, leaving a gap in the line. So, keeping low, they took their chance and slipped past the sentries. After a while they came to a large rock that had eroded and looked like the shape of a hand, there the other spies had gathered.

"You two are late!" One of the spies hissed. His face was heavily wrinkled and his two front teeth were missing. "We have been waiting hours!"

"They are many constables to avoid." Kendrick explained. "We had to give false names in order to pass."

"It has been the same for all of us!" The spy angrily snapped. "But now that we are all here, maybe we can get to business."

"Wait." Another spy said, looking at both Kendrick and Roger. "Were you followed?"

"No." Kendrick answered. "But what I want to know is who called this meeting? It is too dangerous for us all to gather like this."

The spies looked around at each other's faces, all looking confused. "I found a note in my pack, saying that you wanted us all to meet here. So I gathered us all here."

Kendrick shook his head. "I never sent the notes."

Horror swept through the spies as they realised the error of their mistake. They stood frozen, looking to each other on what they should do. "Let's get away from here." One of them said.

But it was too late.

Emerging from the darkness were men dressed in black tunics and trousers and sinister looking cavalry masks made of steel. They were armed with readied crossbows which they aimed at the spies. "Your weapons!" An Arcani said as he stepped forward from the others. "Drop them!"

One of the spies, fearing days of torture followed by being hung, tried to make a run for it. But he only made it a few paces before he was shot in the back by a well-aimed crossbow bolt. He crashed to the ground and was killed by an Arcani that stood over him and shot a crossbow bolt into his head.

"Drop your weapons." The Arcani ordered again.

Kendrick glanced around, seeing that their position was hopeless. He unbuckled his belt that had a long dagger tied to it and dropped it to the ground. The others followed his lead and dropped their weapons.

"On your knees and place your hands on your head."

The spies did as they were instructed. Two Arcani collected up their weapons as two more began shackling their hands and feet. Once all were secure, the king and Hollington rode up and cast their eyes over the spies.

"Is this all of them?" The king asked Hollington, his voice trying to contain his anger.

Hollington quickly counted the spies. "That we know about anyway." He replied.

"Prisoners shackled and secure my king." An Arcani said as he stood dutifully before the king.

"Take them to your camp and have them interrogated." The king ordered. "Report all your findings to me on the morrow."

"It will be as you order my king." The Arcani bowed and signalled to the others to get ready to move out.

"Mercy my king, mercy!" Roger desperately called out.

But the king was in no mood for mercy. Ignoring the plea, he turned his horse and rode away. "Have the heralds announce that spies have been caught and that the rumours they spread were false."

"Yes my king." Hollington replied. "And maybe now would be the right time to double the men's rations?"

The king thought about it and nodded his agreement. He had been holding back rations in the hope of causing discontent amongst his army, discontent that had drawn the spies out as they tried to make men desert. Now he knew that he needed to heal the rifts caused by the spies, and by doubling rations was a good start. Once the men's bellies were full and they learned of the spies lies, all would be right. Fickle, the king thought, how the common men were fickle. "Have a company of the outriders catch some game and have it distributed among the men when we make camp tomorrow."

"And the spies my king?" Hollington asked, already knowing the answer.

"Hang them all." The king coldly replied. "And have the men watch so that they know the punishment for such traitorous actions."

"Yes my king." Hollington replied. "And if I may ask what you have decided regarding Henri?"

On hearing that Henri had failed to report to the new lord of Langton, the king had issued a warrant for his arrest. His constables had searched the town and the nearby surroundings, but had not found a trace of him. Hollington had urged the king to show mercy, but the king had a deep detest for those that deserted.

"He will hang for his crime." The king spoke as though it was pointless for Hollington to plea for Henri's life. "One more day's march and we will be at Market Barton." The king said to change the subject. "Then the battle that shall decide upon the fate of the kingdom." He twisted in his saddle and looked at Hollington sternly. "I want the men ready to fight, not run. Is that understood?"

Hollington nodded. "A gentle march tomorrow followed by meat will lift their spirits."

"Good." The king hoped that Hollington was right and his men would quickly regain their moral. For in two days' time there would be a battle, a battle that he needed to win.

* * *

The morning was dull, overcast with dark-grey clouds that threatened rain. The night had been hot and humid with many of the townsfolk waking in a groggy mood. But despite the mood of the town, the people gathered along the road from the castle to the temple to catch a glimpse of the bridal carriage.

Catharine was sat on a wooden stool staring into a mirror that a servant held up in front of her. As she looked at herself, she thought that she looked pale, thin and deeply troubled. She was still being kept in the tower with her mother, and was still not liking having to marry Hubert. Over the past couple of days her mother had tutored her how she was to manipulate Hubert. Little things, subtle things her mother had constantly told her. Catharine was unsure if her mother's methods would work, but there was little other choice. She thought back to the betrothal feast, and how Hubert had constantly looked at her with lustful eyes. Use it to your advantage her mother had urged, but that thought sickened her. It had been a blushing talk as her mother explained to her how a woman could use her body to sway the minds of men.

"Permission to brush your hair my lady?" Another servant said as stepped up behind Catharine. She was a middle-aged woman, heavily set and grumpy looking. Her cheeks were flushed and her red, frizzy hair poked out from her white servant's cap.

Catharine silently nodded and continued to aimlessly stare at herself in the mirror. The chamber was silent as the servant brushed her hair, and she once again found herself thinking of Hubert. He was so fat, sweaty and uncouth. The thought of having to marry such a grotesque man was not a pleasant thought, so instead she condoled her thoughts to the wealth and better life she would soon have.

The chamber door opened and Catharine's mother entered, her head held high and her back as straight as a spear. "Are you well daughter?" She asked as she took the hairbrush off the servant and softly ran it down the length of Catharine's hair. "You look a little off colour."

"I'm fine mother." Catharine replied solemnly. "I'm just a little nervous."

"There is nothing to be nervous of my daughter. I will be at your side." Catharine's mother handed the hairbrush back to the servant so that she could style Catharine's hair.

"You look beautiful mother." Catharine said, staring at her mother's reflection in the mirror.

"Thank you daughter." Catharine's mother replied as she smiled and twirled to show-off her pale-blue dress. It was low-cut and pulled in at the waist by a white sash made of silk that gave her an hourglass figure. Her hair had been plaited and rolled into buns that were pinned one either side of her head. "Many have gathered in the streets, so I wanted to look my best."

"They have?" Catharine said with surprise, her face looking suddenly very anxious.

"More so than when Elizabeth married." Catharine's mother smiled. "But this will be a far grander day."

"How so mother?" Catharine asked as the servant began to pin her hair up so that her headpiece could be fitted.

"I have been told that Hubert has decorated his house with flowers and has organised a feast filled with exotic fruits from the east to honour the occasion."

Catharine sighed as a wave of doubt swept through her. "Are you sure that there is no other way than this?"

"You know that there is not." Catharine's mother replied. "I thought that you understood this."

"I do mother, it's just…"

"Nerves." Catharine's mother interrupted. "Nerves and nothing more."

There was a knock on the chamber door and the servant pinning Catharine's hair went and opened it. Two more servants entered, one carrying a cushion with a silver head-dress encrusted with pearls and a white vail on it, the other carried a white dress with silver lace embroidered into elegant spirals that ran the length of the dress.

"Oh mother." Catharine said as the dress was placed on her bed. "It's wonderful."

"I have not seen such an elegant dress for a long time." Catharine's mother said as she inspected the droplets of pearls stitched on to it.

Any doubts that Catharine had, soon disappeared with the arrival of the dress. Now her thoughts were of riches and revenge, and she would do anything to achieve gaining both of them, even if it meant marrying a man she thought looked like a slimy toad.

"Come." Catharine's mother clapped her hands to usher the servants on. "My daughter needs to be readied."

The servants removed Catharine's nightgown and fitted her corset, pulling the laces so tight that Catherine had flinched with pain every time the servant pulled on the laces. "Stay still my lady." The middle-aged servant said as she finished lacing up the corset. Next they pulled up two chairs which they used to stand on as they pulled the dress over Catharine's head. They took extra care as not to ruin her hair as they pulled and laced the dress into place. "The headpiece." The middle-aged servant snapped the order to one of the younger ones. The headpiece was pinned into place and final adjustments to her hair were made to hold it in place.

"Beautiful." Catharine's mother said as she walked over beside her. "You look beautiful."

Catharine looked at herself in the mirror, thinking that she did look beautiful. The dress fitted well and made her look shapelier and her hair had been styled to show her attractive neck, but something was missing. Before she could figure out what, the middle-aged servant stood in front of her holding a box.

"Must have a bit of rouge on your wedding day." The servant said as she placed down the box and carefully placed a large cloth around Catharine's shoulders to stop the powder from ruining her dress. She then opened the box and brushed a small amount of the red powder on Catharine's cheeks. "There." The servant said as she placed the brush back into the box. "A little colour to make your husband smile. That's what my mother told me."

Catharine looked at herself in the mirror and thought that she looked stupid. Her face was pale with rosy red cheeks that made her look as though she had been slapped. "I think it's a little too much."

The middle-aged servant put her grumpy face directly in front of Catharine's. "It just needs a little more brushing." She said as she examined her work.

"Give me the brush." Catharine's mother ordered. The servant took the brush back out of the box and handed it to her. She gently brushed along Catharine's cheek bone until the rouge blended into her skin and looked more subtle. "There, much better." Catharine's mother handed the brush back and gestured for the younger servant to remove the cloth from Catharine's shoulders.

There was a loud knock on the door and the middle-age servant rushed over and opened it. "Who is it?" She said as she poked her head around the door.

"It is the lord's steward." An educated voice replied. "I have come to escort the ladies of De'lacy to the temple." He was dressed in scarlet tunic with white buttons shaped liked flowers that were tightly buttoned up to a stiff collar where more white flowers were embroidered.

The middle-aged servant turned to Catharine's mother. "Are you ready my ladies?"

Catharine took a breath to calm her nerves and nodded her head. "I am ready." She forced herself to say.

The steward entered the chamber and formally bowed to Catharine and her mother. "Your carriage await you in the courtyard."

Catharine recognized the steward from when she had served on the lord during his illness. She thought him a pompous man who had little time for pleasures or niceties. A man that spent long days fulfilling the lord's orders so that he might rise with him. They dutifully followed him down the stairs and out into the courtyard where a red carriage with well-polished brass fittings waited for them.

The morning had turned sunny with the earlier grey clouds thinning into small patches that blotched a near perfect sky. It was promising to be another hot and sweaty day, and in the blue sky above a flock of birds circled. Catharine looked up at the birds and tried to make out what they were. Sparrows, she thought, no they were too big to be sparrows. She found herself thinking of her grandfather, he had like birds and had spent hours watching them in his garden. And if he were here now, he would have told her what they were.

"Daughter?" Catharine's mother said, seeing her looking up at the birds.

"I am alright mother." Catharine replied, seeing the concern on her mother's face. "I was just thinking of grandfather."

Catharine's mother looked up at the birds and smiled. "He did love them."

"Ladies if we could keep moving." The steward said as he turned his head back towards them, a flash of light reflecting off his spectacles.

They quietly walked the short distance to the carriage, where the driver stood beside the open door. He was wearing black trousers and tunic, and Catharine thought how hot he would get having to wear such garments. They climbed into the comfortable interior and took their seats as the driver raised the steps and closed the door.

The carriage ride to the temple was smooth and steady. The town's guard lined the streets and pushed back the crowds that had gathered. For Catharine it was strange to hear people shouting blessings and waving bits of cloth in the air in celebration of the occasion.

"Thank you my lady!" A woman's voice called out from the crowd. "Thank you!"

"Why are they thanking me mother?" Catharine asked. "I have done nothing."

"I do not know." Catharine's mother answered. "I know only what is expected of you during today's events."

"Your soon-to-be husband, has had his household servants' distribute bread and ale amongst the common mass as a gift to mark the occasion." The lord's steward said with a hint of distaste for Hubert's actions. "An action his lordship advised him against."

The carriage continued on towards the temple with the townsfolk cheering and merrymaking the whole way. Many times along the way Catharine thought about opening the door and trying to make a run for it. But her common-sense had told her that it was foolish, that it was something Elizabeth would try, and look where her foolishness had got her.

The carriage came to a stop and the driver jumped down and opened the door. The lord's steward was the first to climb out, swiftly followed by Catharine's mother who respectively bowed to the temple maid that awaited for them.

"I bid thee blessings." The temple maid said. She was dressed in a white hooded robe that clung to her athletic body and her face was powdered white with a red stripe that ran from the middle of her forehead, down her nose and lips, to her chin. In her hands she carried a small silver bowl filled with white rose petals that she would sprinkle out in front of her as she led Catharine into the temple.

Catharine stepped out of the carriage and looked up at the temple, a sudden sense of dread sweeping through her. The temple was highly built in a circular shape with a domed roof that was held up by thick marble pillars. The town's guards kept the cheering crowds back, jostling back and forth to keep the path to the temple clear.

"You are to follow me into the temple." The temple maid said as she turned and ceremonially walked towards the temple, tossing handfuls of the petals before her.

Catharine, with her mother at her side and the lord's steward behind, dutifully followed the temple maid. Inside was made to look like the sky at night; the walls and ceiling were black with varied sized white stones dotted around in irregular patterns. Sparkles of light reflected off the stones as hundreds of candles lit up the interior. The guests were seated in wooden pews that circled around a raised centre where the High Priest with Hubert Marcel now waited. The temple maids that were stood around the wall, holding flickering candles, began to sing a soft melody that sent cold shivers down the guests' backs. But Catharine hardly noticed the beauty of the temple or the song, as the sight of Hubert distracted her.

Hubert was stood smiling as Catharine walked towards the raised centre. He wore a white robe that was already yellowed under the armpits from sweat and a large, floppy beret with two ostrich feathers sticking out of the back. "You look beautiful." He said as Catharine climbed the two steps onto the raised centre.

"Who brings this woman for holy matrimony?" The High Priest asked in a hoarse voice. He was old, very old and his wispy, pure white hair and his wrinkled face was proof of it. The red robe he wore hung off his frail body and he leaned heavily on a staff to stop himself falling.

"I do." The lord's steward said stepping forward. "In the name of the Lord of Heath Hollow, I bring Catharine De'lacy to marry Hubert Marcel."

It was then that Catharine noticed that the lord was not present. His place on the front bench was empty, and Catharine knew that would spark rumours and reflect badly upon the marriage.

"And do you Lady Catharine De'lacy, consent to marrying Hubert Marcel?" The High Priest raised his bushy white eyebrows as he spoke.

Catharine looked to her mother, who gave her a stern look back, before she answered. "I do." She said quietly.

"You will have to speak up." The High Priest wheezed. "I have become hard of hearing with age."

"I DO!" Catharine said again, loud enough for all to hear.

The old priest turned to Hubert's smiling face. "Is this the woman you wish to wed?"

"Yes it is." Hubert replied as he licked his lips. "I wish to marry Catharine De'lacy."

The old priest took Catharine's hand and led her to face Hubert. He placed Hubert's hand over hers and said. "You came to this temple as two willing to become one. Today before these witnesses and the stars, you shall swear the sacred oath of matrimony." The High Priest spoke loud enough for all to hear. "Do you, Hubert Marcel swear before the stars that from this day on, till death shall part you; that you shall love and honour Catharine De'lacy and no other, as befitting the title of wife."

Hubert looked into Catharine's eyes and once again licked his lips, "With all my free heart, I so swear to treat her well, as befits the title of wife."

The High Priest then looked to Catharine. "And do you Catharine De'lacy also swear before the stars that from this day on, till death shall part you; that you shall love and honour Hubert Marcel and no other, as befitting the title of husband."

Catharine looked away from Hubert's sweaty face, feeling disgusted by what she must do. "Yes, I swear it." She nervously replied, looking to her mother in hope that she would stop the marriage at the last moment. But Catharine's mother just stood politely smiling, knowing what must be done.

The High Priest raised his wrinkled hands into the air. "From this day forward, let the light of the havens bless the oath you have both sworn this day. Go now in union as one body, as one voice and of one mind. I hereby declare you Husband and wife."

The guests stood and applauded as Hubert leaned in and kissed Catharine. "Come now!" Hubert said with gusto. "Let us feast and drink together to honour the occasion."

Catharine resisted wiping her mouth and forced a smile, trying to appear that she was happy as Hubert led her out to his awaiting carriage. A servant dutifully opened the door and lowered the steps as they approached, bowing to the new lady of the household.

"Wife." Hubert gestured for Catharine to enter the carriage first, his bulging eyes full of lust.

Catharine, feeling deflated of any will to resist, climbed into the carriage. Her mother climbed in after her and sat on the seat opposite, giving her a sympathetic look.

"Now let's go home." Hubert said as he climbed in, the carriage tilting because of his weight. He thudded down next to Catharine with the smell of his sweat fouling the air.

Fortunately for Catharine, the carriage journey was not far. Hubert's house was in the rich quarter of the town, high up and close to the castle. It was a three storey building built in stone that had been painted white to make it stand out from the other dull homes along the street. The carriage passed Catharine's old home and both Catharine and her mother were filled with emotion as memories of the past whirled around their heads.

"Are you well mother-in-law?" Hubert asked, seeing tears in her eyes.

"Can a mother not shed a tear on her daughter's wedding day?" Catharine's mother replied, staring out of the carriage window at her former home passing by.

Hubert smiled as he wiped sweat off of his forehead with his smelly handkerchief. He knew why she was crying, and it gave him great satisfaction to know that he had triumphed over the De'lacy's, even though it had taken him years to do so.

The carriage rumbled up before the wrought iron gates that bared the entrance to Hubert's home. Two servants dressed in yellow tunics pulled open the heavy gates and the carriage continued on up toward the mansion.

Catharine's first thoughts were that it was impressive, a grand home as befitting for a lord. Her former home had been large, but Hubert's was twice as big. There was a circular courtyard before a grand entrance of elegantly carved doors flanked by a marble façade. In the centre of the courtyard was a fountain, a brass fish curled up at the head and tail, ejecting water out of its mouth. Servants opened the door of the carriage as it came to a stop before the entrance.

The guests were awaiting Hubert and Catharine in the grand hall, gossiping of the lord's none attendance. Many spoke of the lord being gravely ill, with some even claiming that he had died and it was being kept a secret to avoid panic. But the truth was unknown and so they drank and made merry for the occasion.

Catharine spent the afternoon greeting guests and making polite conversation with the other merchants' wives. They all wished her well and smiled to her face, but Catharine knew that they would whisper all sorts of slander behind her back. As the hours passed, Hubert drunk and ate more and more, quickly becoming the topic of detrimental gossip. Catharine began to feel uneasy about the night ahead. Her mother had told her what to expect, and that was a lot of pain. But the pain was not what was bothering her, it was the thought of having to share a bed with such a grotesque man.

Hubert wobbled over to Catharine, his face was red from drink and his eyes greedy for his conjugal rights. "Shall we take to bed wife?" Hubert spoke loud enough for those close by to hear.

"Wife." Catharine quietly said to herself. It suddenly dawned on her that she was no longer a De'lacy, but a Marcel. And so she dutifully followed her husband to his chamber.

Chapter 11

The remainder of Sir Gregory's company had taken refuge in an abandoned farmstead a few miles southeast from Oldby. The owners had saw the pillars of black smoke rising from the village and had fled, leaving all of their possessions behind. The house was large and rectangular with a thatched roof that was supported with thick wooden beams inside. The thick walls were built with cobblestone and mortar with white plaster skimmed over the stonework on the inside with six small square windows to let in air and light. Outside was a large vegetable patch that the owners had worked, and a small, stone kraal where a few sheep had been kept, but the wooden gate that had closed them in was now broken and the sheep were gone. The farmstead itself had been built beside a narrow dirt road that led off the main road to Market Barton, where the Duke of Baleford's army was now camped. There was no other homes within sight and the nearest neighbours were those that dwelt in Oldby.

On the company's arrival, Sir Gregory had told his men that they were to wait at the farmstead for reinforcements before continuing on. And so the company nervously waited in the gloomy interior. The night was cool with a clear sky in which the stars and moon illuminated the world below with their soft white light. A sentry walked up and down the road, softly whistling to himself as he kept a watch for the promised reinforcements. The remainder of the men were inside, where a fire crackled and spat in the fireplace, resting and eating what little provisions they had left.

"No food for us!" Pagenellus said with anger. "I don't even know why they have tied me up!"

"A lot doesn't make sense." Henri replied. His wrists were cut from the rope and his mood was dark. He, with Pagenellus, had been shoved in a damp corner where the plaster was crumbling away and were given no food or water. What he didn't understand, was why he was still with the company and not being taken back to the king with the outriders. Surely Sir Gregory would willingly send him back to be hung? Why have the trouble of keeping watch on him? Was it just so that Sir Gregory could have the pleasure of watching him being hung? These questions troubled Henri's mind, and the more he tried to reason with himself, the more troubled be became.

"I have much work to be done." Pagenellus complained. "I have no time to be tied up and dragged around. Especially as I have done nothing wrong."

Henri leaned back and felt loose plaster come away from the wall, sighing in frustration. The waiting and unknowing was playing on his mind, and he felt certain that danger was looming.

"Henri." Elizabeth said to gain his attention. "Henri."

Henri snapped out of his dark thoughts and looked up into Elizabeth's calming face. "Elizabeth." He said tiredly.

"I brought you some water." Elizabeth knelt beside Henri and passed him a tin canteen, half filled with water.

"Thank you." Henri said as he pulled out the cork and took a drink, the water warm and unpleasant. "Where is Symond?"

"He is outside talking with Sir Gregory." Elizabeth replied. "He's trying to convince him to allow him to go looking for the reinforcements."

Henri shook his head. "He has more chance of persuading a temple maid to become a whore."

Pagenellus chuckled at the comment and wriggled his eyebrows. "More chance of persuading a temple maid to become a whore." He repeated, chuckling and wagging his head from side-to-side.

The door opened and a glum looking Symond entered. He walked straight over to Henri and sat, anger seeping out of him. "Pompous fool!"

"I take it he didn't listen." Henri said as he passed the canteen to Symond.

"Because he is a knight, he thinks he knows it all!" Symond pulled out the cork and took a sip. "This water is on the turn." He said as his face scrunched up with distaste.

"So we are to just wait?" Henri asked, his feelings of danger growing ever stronger.

Symond shrugged. "I know not my young friend, but he seems steadfast on waiting here."

Henri looked around at the faces of the other soldiers that were lying around on the wooden floor. They lay silent, their faces ashen and full of fear. After the attack at the ruined temple, they now numbered less than thirty men, and Henri knew that would not be enough should the Minoton choose to attack them. "Have the Minoton learnt of out arrival here?" Henri asked, looking back at Symond.

Again Symond shrugged. "I know not. But it will not be long before they do."

"The Minoton." Pagenellus said with excitement. "They have returned?"

Symond nodded. "They attacked the village of Oldby and have threatened to attack others if the king does not pay the gold that they have asked for."

"So that is why your company is heading for Oldby." Pagenellus said as he wriggled his eyebrows. He would have known this had his mind not been fixed on his experiment back in the ruined temple. "The power of the mask." He added as he excitedly wagged his head from side-to-side.

"You know of this Melanthius?" Symond asked.

Pagenellus nodded his head, broadly smiling as though he were proud of himself for knowing. "An elf that lived long ago."

"An elf." Symond said with wonder. "Tell me more."

"More." Pagenellus said with wide eyes and raised eyebrows.

"Yes, it may help when I have to negotiate with him." Symond explained.

"Negotiate." Pagenellus chuckled. "There will be no negotiating with Melanthius, he is powerful in the lore of magic, magic that he used to trap his own spirit within his mask." Pagenellus leaned forward and spoke in a hushed tone. "If what I have read is a true account of his life, it reads as quite the tragedy."

272

"Tell me." Symond said, intrigued by the tale.

"The account says that Melanthius's father was the chieftain of a faction of elves called the Tryon, and that his mother was a nameless woman that took shelter one night with the elves. I read that Melanthius was tall like men and slender of build with pointed ears like the elves. The tale reads that he was never accepted as a true elf and that he was banished from his home with the elves." Pagenellus wagged his head from side-to-side. "A long story short, he went in search of his mother, only to find that the very elves he had once called friends, had cursed the village where his mother had dwelt, killing all. Melanthius then took refuge with a giant, who crafted him his mask." Pagenellus's eyes once again widened. "A mask of great power that the Minoton fell under its magic, a mask that upon his death trapped his spirit." Pagenellus turned his head and looked at Henri. "It is written that whoever wears the mask will become possessed by Melanthius's spirit, and that only one of true power could resist its power."

"Is it really possible that one could kill this Melanthius and use the power of controlling the Minoton without being possessed?" Symond asked, hoping that he could simply kill Melanthius and order the Minoton back to their home.

Before Pagenellus could answer, the door opened and Sir Gregory walked in. He was followed by his Master-At-Arms who instantly started waking the men that were sleeping by nudging them with his dirty boot.

"You are all to remain here." Sir Gregory ordered, his hand resting upon the hilt of his sword. "I and the Master-At-Arms shall go ahead and scout the village. I maybe even able to begin the negotiations with the Minoton if at all possible."

"I think that I should go with you." Symond said as he shot up onto his feet, feeling annoyed. "It is what the king has assigned me to this company for."

Sir Gregory gave him a scathing look. "You will wait here for the reinforcements, and if I have not returned by the time that they have arrived, you are to move on Oldby."

"I think that I should go ahead and begin the negotiations as the king ordered." Symond said with confidence that the king's orders would prevail.

"You will do as I command!" Sir Gregory roared back at Symond. "I merely wish to scout ahead and weigh up our options!" All fell deathly silent apart from the fire that crackled and spat in the fireplace. "You will remain here and wait for the reinforcements." Sir Gregory said, restoring his calm. "I will return soon enough." He pointed a finger towards Symond and added, "If any leave this farmstead, I will treat it like a desertion, and I myself will hang the transgressors." Sir Gregory looked around at his remaining men to ensure them that he was serious. "I will be back soon." He signalled for his two remaining squires to follow him, and he strode calmly back out of the door.

"You know your orders." The Master-At-Arms said with a warning voice, and glancing sternly at the men before he followed his master out.

"Pompous fool!" Symond spat in anger as he slumped back down.

"Something is wrong." Henri said, unable to figure out what. "I can feel it."

"Feel it can you." Pagenellus said with raised eyebrows. "It must be some sort of magic." He added suspiciously.

"I don't have magic powers Pagenellus." Henri replied with a hint of frustration in his voice. Since they had escaped the ruined temple, Pagenellus had questioned him on his previous adventures and had once even asked him if he could conduct an experiment to measure the magic within him. But Henri had told him little and had declined to have himself experimented on, much to Pagenellus's annoyance. "It's more of that feeling you get before a storm."

"The calm before the storm." Symond said. "I feel it also." None of it made any sense to him. How could Sir Gregory be so sure that reinforcements would be coming? It would take days for the outriders to return to the king and get back to them, days that had not yet passed. "I am not convinced that any reinforcements are coming." Symond said quietly.

"But Sir Gregory said that they were." Elizabeth said innocently, believing it to be unthinkable that a knight, who spoke only truth, would lie.

"Let us think about it." Symond spoke with a hushed tone so that he was not overheard. "If Sir Gregory sent word to the king with the outriders, it would take them days to even reach his camp. And at least another day while the king organised some men to reinforce us. Still then it would take days more for them to reach us here."

"But if they used the main road from Market Barton and had fast horses." Elizabeth offered an explanation of how it could be done.

Symond shook his head. "The Duke of Baleford's army will already be there, and any reinforcements would have

275

to go miles around, then they would have to avoid any of his scouts."

"Maybe the king has defeated Baleford and is resting his army at Market Barton?" Henri interjected with hope.

"Maybe." Symond conceded. "But what of Sir Gregory taking himself off to scout Oldby?"

"What is so bad with that?" Elizabeth asked, not understanding what Symond was getting at.

Henri shook his head. "Never." He said, realising that Sir Gregory had never once volunteered himself for such a task. "Never has Sir Gregory done anything for himself. He always sends his squires or others under his command."

"Exactly." Symond said as a flash of horror swept across his face. "So why the change?" Inside the farmstead took a sinister turn as the fear of uncertainty was felt by all. He pulled out his dagger from its scabbard on his belt and cut Henri free. "We need to be ready."

"What about me, what about me?" Pagenellus said as he wriggled his body excitedly.

Symond then leaned over and cut Pagenellus's wrists free. "Now do not do anything stupid."

"Stupid." Pagenellus said shaking his head and holding a finger up to make a point. "Stupidity often leads to great discoveries."

"Hey!" A soldiers with a flat nose and bold head called over. "You're not supposed to do that!" He was wearing a studded leather jerkin that had a split on his left shoulder and a brass badge of a sword that marked him as a captain of the Men-at-Arms.

"So report me when Sir Gregory returns." Symond said sarcastically.

"Henri, your wrists." Elizabeth said, taking his hands and inspecting the sores where the rope had rubbed.

"I'm fine." Henri pulled his hands out from Elizabeth's grip and stood. "It will soon heal."

Pagenellus's face twitched and he excitedly clapped his hands. "Magic, magic, magic."

Henri shook his head and walked over to the door, none of the soldiers bothering to stop him. He pulled it open and a gush of cold air blew in, much to annoyance of the other soldiers.

"You heard Sir Gregory's orders." The flat nose captain said, not bothering to get up to try and stop him. "Anybody that leaves this farmstead will be hung as a deserter."

Henri just shrugged. "I'm only going to get hung anyway." He walked out into the night and the first thing he noticed was how sinisterly quiet it was. The moonlight was still bright and he could see further up and down the dirt road than if it had been cloudy. There was no sign of any reinforcements and all seemed still. Then it dawned on him. Where was the soldier on sentry duty? He quickly glanced back up and down the road to make sure that he was not there. Then, from the corner of his eyes, he saw yellow eyes watching him from overgrown bushes on the opposite side of the road. He quickly turned his head back towards the place in the bushes where he had seen the eyes, only to find that they were gone. "Symond!"

277

"What is it?" Symond asked as he rushed out of the door.

"Over in those bushes." Henri pointed. "I saw yellow eyes watching me."

Symond glanced over at the bushes, but saw nothing. "Are you sure it was not your mind playing tricks on you?"

Henri shrugged. "It looked real enough, though I never got a good look."

Symond stared over at the bush, sensing that they were being watched. "Come on my young friend, if anything had been there it would have left some trace."

They walked over to the bushes and Symond repeatedly poked his sword into leaves, hoping to scare out anything that might be lurking. Nothing. He rammed his sword back into its scabbard and began pulling aside branches to inspect the ground. The ground was hard and at first he could see no trace of anything. Then, just as he was about to give up, he saw some markings.

"Hoof prints." Symond said as he let go of the branches.

"A goat?" Henri offered an explanation.

"No." Symond replied, looking confused. "They are too big to be a goat's"

The distant sound of a horse neighing pierced the silence and Henri and Symond instinctively ran back inside, closing the door behind them.

"What is it?" The flat nosed captain asked, rising to his feet and gripping the hilt of his sword.

"Horses." Symond replied as he shut the door.

"The reinforcements?" The captain walked over to the door and went to open it, but Symond stopped him.

"Why would the reinforcements be traveling at night?" Symond stated the obvious. "It is far too dangerous."

The sound of horses' hooves loudened as they cantered up the dirt road and came to a stop outside of the farmstead. Symond pulled the door ajar and peered out. The horsemen were wearing blue tunics that he never recognised, and one carried a blue banner with a red feather in the centre. At the head of the horsemen rode their commander. A fist on his hip and head held high as though he were a conquering hero.

"Come out and surrender!" The commander called.

Henri felt a sudden sense of dread as he recognised the voice. He rushed to a window that looked out onto the road and pushed open the wooden shutters. "John!"

Elizabeth rushed to Henri side as she heard him say the name of her husband. "No." She said with horror. "It cannot be."

"Surrender now and you will be all spared!" John called, a smug smile creeping across his face. "Even you Henri!"

Uncertainty clouded the minds of the men in the farmstead. Some were of a mind to stand their ground and fight to the death, but others were wanting to lay down their weapons and surrender. Men began to argue as to what they should do and the noise they made gave John every confidence that they would not make a stand.

"If we go out there, we're dead." Henri said to try and convince others that they should fight. "That bastard isn't going to let us live."

"Silence!" Symond roared as he watched another man step forward from behind the horsemen. He was short and stocky with recognisable curly hair. "Sir Gregory."

"He has been captured." The captain said with alarm.

"I think that you should come out!" Sir Gregory called to his men. "No harm shall befall you!"

"Well that settles it." The captain said. "We surrender as ordered."

"But we haven't been ordered." Henri said with suspicion, noticing that Sir Gregory had said *think* and had not actually commanded them. "And I don't see any rope binding his hands."

"Well you can stay here if you want, but I'm taking the men out." The captain unbuckled his belt and dropped his weapons onto the floor. "Lady Elizabeth I shall escort you out." But she simply shook her head and clung on to Henri's arm. "As you wish." He said as he waved his men to follow him.

"I think that you are making a mistake captain." Symond tried one last time.

"We're coming out!" The captain yelled, ignoring Symond's warning. "We surrender to your mercy!" He pushed Symond aside and led his men out.

Henri and Symond helplessly watched as they were forced onto their knees. For a moment it looked like John would keep his word and spare the men's life, but instead he

280

ordered them killed. The horsemen quickly surrounded the kneeling men and began shooting crossbow bolts until all were dead, their blooded bodies heaped together in death.

"Elizabeth!" John called. "Come out now and I will send you back home."

"You're a liar!" Elizabeth shouted back. "You will kill me like you had Dick try and kill me at Lhanwick!"

John smiled and laughed, long and hard. "Do not take it so personal my love. You are no longer of any value to me. But if you come out and agree to a divorce, I will take you back to your mother."

Elizabeth looked at Henri as though she was considering the offer, after all, what else could she do?

"No" Henri said shaking his head. "He will kill you." He rushed over to a window along the back wall and pushed open the shutter to see if they could climb out and escape that way. But a crossbow bolt thudded into the wooden frame, missing Henri's head by inches. "We're surrounded." He said rushing back to Elizabeth and grabbing her hand.

"What shall we do?" Elizabeth asked, fear now causing her to panic.

Symond looked to Henri, his face full of doom. "It looks as though our end is here my young friend."

"This is your last chance!" John said growing tired of trying to persuade them. "Come out!"

"Maybe we should just have the men storm through the door." Sir Gregory suggested.

John turned his horse away from the farmstead and shook his head. "If we do that, I will lose a couple of men, men that we shall need if we're to face the Minoton."

"Then what are we to do?" Sir Gregory pushed for an answer. "We cannot stay here for long."

"Set fire to the house." John ordered. "And when they try to run out, put a bolt through them." His men quickly lit torches and tossed them up onto the thatched roof. "But leave Henri, I wish to kill him myself." John added, feeling self-satisfied.

Flames quickly engulfed the dry thatch, weakening the wooden beams that held it up. Burning debris fell, and smoke quickly filled the inside.

"We need to make a run for it!" Symond called, coughing and spluttering because of the smoke.

Henri, with Elizabeth beside him, slumped down on the floor. "I'd rather die here than give that bastard the pleasure of killing me."

Elizabeth's face was blackened from smoke and her hair singed in places because of the falling embers. "I'm staying with Henri." She said as she closed her eyes and placed her head on Henri's chest, waiting for death to come and claim them.

The flames flickered high into the air as the beams groaned and collapsed in on themselves, sending a blast of flames and smouldering embers out towards John and his soldiers.

"Let's move out." John ordered, knowing that nothing could have survived that inferno. His men formed a column and rode on toward Oldby, a pillar of black smoke raising high into the night behind them.

*   *   *

The village of Oldby was now nothing more than burned down ruins. The many fishing huts and hall that had made up the village were now just thick blackened beams lying in small mounds of smouldering ash. Nothing had been spared and no stone left unturned as the Minoton had searched for anything of value. Large burgundy pavilions had been erected close to the shore where the Minoton's longship was beached. In the centre of their camp was a makeshift cage made from blackened beams pulled from the ash. The remainder of the villagers were imprisoned there, and their faces were as black as their mood. None of the men had been spared by the Minoton and the women and children faced an unknown future as slaves.

The single road that led into Oldby was constantly being guarded by two of the Minoton. John stared at them though his telescope, and his first thoughts were of their impressive size. "They are bigger than I thought that they would be." Never in all of his days did he think to see such creatures. As a child he had heard of many mythical beast, but he had never believed in their existence and now he wondered what other creatures were true.

"How many?" Sir Gregory asked, nudging his horse up beside John.

"Two guarding the road in." John answered. "But they'll be more in the village."

Sir Gregory took out his own telescope from his saddlebag and glanced at the road ahead. It was a narrow road with tufts of grass growing up between the cobblestones, with rolling grassland on either side. "There will be nowhere to hide past this point." He warned as his gaze fell upon the Minoton, who stood like statues, holding wicked looking axes at the ready.

"I don't plan on hiding." John announced as though he was not in the least bit scared. "I plan on riding straight towards them."

"You plan on charging straight into their camp?" Sir Gregory said, shocked by the foolishness of the plan and thinking that the sea air had addled his head.

"No." John snapped shut his telescope and tucked it in his belt. "We shall ride forward on the pretence of wanting to negotiate. Your Master-At-Arms shall remain here with the men, then an hour before sunrise he will attack."

"Surely we cannot win against such monsters?" Sir Gregory replied, still staring at the Minoton through his telescope.

John shuddered at the thought of having to fight such beasts. But he knew the rewards of gaining the mask would by far outweigh the risks. "If what you say is true, I would gain a great power. A power that I could use to advance my family further."

"I thought that you were to negotiate on the Duke of Baleford's behalf?" Sir Gregory said as he took his eye from the eyepiece of his telescope and looked at John. "You gave me your assurance that you would have the Duke give me a lordship."

"And I will." John said with a sly smile. "But if you help me gain that mask, then we may both look to even loftier titles."

Sir Gregory snapped shut his telescope, greed now blinding his better judgement. He had been well educated and knew what John meant; and he fully intended to aggrandise his position. "You plan on taking the throne for yourself?"

"I was born to be more than a mere lord." John turned his horse and could see the look of concern on Sir Gregory's face. "And those that help me rise, shall rise with me."

"I myself would like to think of becoming more than a lord." Sir Gregory hinted that John should make his offer.

John smiled. "I will make you a Duke."

"And if it doesn't go to plan?" Sir Gregory asked with a raised eyebrow.

"Now that I have finally rid myself of my wife, and I am now free to marry Baleford's daughter. The worst that could happen is that we don't gain the mask and are forced to negotiate with the Minoton on Baleford's behalf. I will still marry his daughter and you will still be given a lordship." John gave Sir Gregory a self-assured smile. "We shall gain either way."

"What if they just kill us on sight?" Sir Gregory turned his horse and began to ride alongside John.

"They won't." John confidently replied. "I have read that they are a greedy race and have a great yearning for the riches in the world. They will want to hear what we have to say."

Sir Gregory shuddered at the thought of trying to reason with such beasts and wanted nothing more than to simply ride away and join with the Duke of Baleford's army. "So your plan is to attack them and take the mask?"

"We will ride ahead." John began to explain his plan in more detail. "And begin the negotiations with this Melanthius. Your Master-At-Arms shall begin the attack an hour before sunrise. With a bit of luck we shall be with this Melanthius at the time of the attack and I will use the distraction to kill him and take his mask."

"But surely they will take our weapons." Sir Gregory said as though John were foolish for not thinking of such a simple floor in the plan.

John pulled a dagger from its scabbard. It was an old dagger, twelve inches long with a black handle bound with silver wire, and was rumoured to be worth a king's ransom. Despite the dagger's age, it looked new and had razor-sharp edges that flanked Gigantic runes that formed words along the centre of the blade. "I will conceal this and use it when the time is right."

Sir Gregory was still unsure, but had little other choice. He had betrayed the king for want of a lordship, and should the king be victorious, he would be executed for his crime. No, he thought, it would be better for John to gain the mask and defeat the king. "Then let's get this plan of yours into motion."

With the Master-At-Arms informed, and the men ready, John and Sir Gregory steadily rode down the road towards Oldby. The distant figures of the Minoton gradually grew along with their fear as they approached. At first they wandered if the Minoton guarding the road were real as they never moved and stood frightfully motionless with their wicked looking axes ready in hand. Then, quicker than a bolt of lightning, the Minoton sprung to life.

"Who dares approach the domain of the Minoton?" One of the Minoton said as it swung its doublehanded axe at the horses. It was large with black, thick, cow-like skin and yellow eyes. Its armour was made of bronze and shaped to give him a more menacing look.

John's horse, like Sir Gregory's, reared up and tossed him onto the road before running off in a blind panic. "Wait!" John cried, holding up his hands to show that he meant no harm. "I have come to parley with your leader, Melanthius." His heart was racing and he felt certain that the Minoton stood over him would smash his skull with the axe that menacingly hovered inches above his face. "We wish to parley with your leader, Melanthius." John said again, unsure if they had understood what he was saying.

"Weapons." The Minoton stood over John said, his yellow eyes narrowed, his voice menacing and his muscles twitched with want of delivering a deathly blow.

John looked over at Sir Gregory and slowly unbuckled his belt. "They want us to surrender our weapons."

"I understood that." Sir Gregory replied, his voice and ashen face full of fear.

The Minoton ripped their weapons from their hands and tossed them well out of reach. They then roughly pulled John and Sir Gregory to their feet before shoving them towards the ruins that were once the village of Oldby. They walked through the ash and burned remains of the buildings until they came to a makeshift cage where the remaining villagers were being kept. Another Minoton kept guard over the cage and unlocked the door as he saw the new prisoners approach. The Minoton tossed John and Sir Gregory into the cage as though they were nothing more than sacks of hay.

John knelt, clutching his ribs, and glanced around at the blackened faces that stared at him. They looked terrified and most were crying, their eyes puffy and red.

"Have you come to save us?" A young boy asked. He was only five with a mop of brown hair and missing teeth.

John ignored the boy and rose to his feet, looking through the timber bars at the longship on the shoreline. He began to think that perhaps his plan was not a very good one, and that he would have been better-off staying with Baleford's army at Market Barton. But then he reminded himself of what was to gain. If he were to gain the mask, then he could control the Minoton and use them as his own personal army. A smile spread across his face as he imagined the Duke of Baleford being made to kneel before him.

"What are we to do now?" Sir Gregory asked, fearing why they had been imprisoned.

"Now we wait." John said, his voice low and waning in confidence. "There is little else we can do."

They sat together in a corner and waited for hours before a Minoton returned. The door was opened and they were dragged out of the cage and tossed at the hooves of a mighty looking Minoton. He was big, heavily muscled and wore a bronze breastplate and greaves with a golden torque around his thick neck. Strapped across his back were two cruel looking longswords, and the horns on his head were pierced with thick golden rings.

"I Etor." The Minoton said, slamming his fist into his chest. "Chieftain of the Minoton and descendant of the last king of my people." His yellow eyes narrowed on John and Sir Gregory. "Who are you, spies?"

"We are no spies." John gave answer, his shaky voice showing his nerves. "I am John Kinge, the Lord Aide of Heath Hollow and this is Sir Gregory Fitzwalter." John slowly rose to his feet and tried to make himself look more dignified. "We have been sent by the Duke of Baleford to negotiate with Melanthius."

"Why do talkers need weapons?" Etor asked as he had been told that the prisoners had been carrying weapons.

"The kingdom is at war and it is dangerous to travel unarmed." John explained, his voice beginning to quiver even more with fear as he looked up into the bull face of Etor.

"Two puny men traveling alone." Etor laughed long and menacingly deep. "Too dangerous, even with weapons." He stretched out his massive hand and grabbed John around his throat, lifting him off of his feet. "Tell me where the others are." John wiggled and choked like a chicken as Etor slowly began to strangle the life out of him.

"There are no others!" Sir Gregory shouted desperately. "There is only us!"

Etor dropped John and rounded on Sir Gregory. "Speak truth or I will rip off your arms."

"I do speak the truth." Sir Gregory flinched, his hands quickly shot up to protect his face. "I am a knight, and a knight speaks only truth."

"It is unwise to anger the Minoton." Etor shoved Sir Gregory to the ground and drew one of his longswords. "Speak now or you shall find your end."

Sir Gregory, fearing death, was about to confess that their company was awaiting to attack, when another Minoton came and spoke with Etor. Neither John nor Sir Gregory knew what was being said as they spoke in a language that had not been heard in the kingdom for many a year. Etor sheaved his longsword and grabbed both John and Sir Gregory by the scruff, tearing John's blue tunic. With no explanation of what was happening, they were dragged towards the longship.

The longship was a hundred feet long and made from blackened beams that were shaped to cut through choppy waters. A figurehead of a bull looked out from the bow of the ship, its eyes yellow glow-stones and its horns sharp steel. Erected over the deck was a burgundy pavilion that was tied to the mast and riggings for the sail. Over the edges were placed tall, squared shields painted red with a black bull's head in their centre.

Etor walked up the gangplank, pulling and shoving John and Sir Gregory. Once at the top, he shoved them through the pavilion's entrance, and they crashed onto the wooden deck. Inside, there was an oppressive atmosphere that clouded the mind and made it difficult to think properly.

"You come to offer me great riches?" A muffled, sinister voice spoke.

John looked up and saw a masked figure sitting on a high-backed chair in front of a blue flame that magically hovered above the deck. "I have come to speak with Melanthius." John managed to answer, his mind a haze and distant.

"Then speak, for I am Melanthius."

"They claim to have come alone, to negotiate with you." Etor said as he knelt before Melanthius. "I think they lie."

"Go Etor, find their company." Melanthius stood, his red robes looking more like purple because of the blue light as he walked over to John.

"I will leave none alive." Etor rose and walked out to gather some of the Minoton, the sound of his hooves clacking heavily on the wood.

"What have you to say?" Melanthius asked.

"His Grace, the Duke of Baleford, would like to offer a truce." John had to fight the strong urge to tell Melanthius all. It was not out of want, but more as if unseen magic were willing him to speak the truth of his plans. "In return of a truce, he will grant you an annual tribute of gold and jewels."

"I need not you terms." Melanthius said as he stepped before Sir Gregory, who was kneeling on the floor with his head down. "I have already sent terms to the king, and I am assured that he will grant me the gift of gold."

Sir Gregory shook his head, unable to resist the urge to speak the truth any longer. "The king sent me." He spat out. "The king sent me, but not to negotiate."

"He sent you with a company to eliminate me?" Melanthius said as though he had known all along. "I have heard whispers of the war between the king and the Duke, but never thought to find those on opposing sides to be traveling together." Melanthius knelt down so that his mask was level with Sir Gregory's face. "Tell me how you became companions."

"I betrayed the king." Sir Gregory answered. "I betrayed the king for land, wealth and for the title of lord."

"What of you company?" Melanthius asked, his voice becoming more menacing. "Where are they?"

Sir Gregory's face scrunched up as he tried to stop himself from talking, but the unseen magic was too great. "Dead, we killed them all."

"We have come to offer anything you ask." John interjected in a last-ditch attempt to conceal the truth.

Melanthius, being no fool, shot back up and pointed a finger at John, removing his ability to speak. "Your mouth speaks flattery, and yet it hides the truth." He raised a hand above Sir Gregory's forehead and the light from the blue flame began to get brighter. "Now tell me the truth of your plans."

Sir Gregory's eyes widened and turned white, seeing only an intense light and hearing only Melanthius's voice. "Our company will attack an hour before sunrise." A penetrating pain burned in his head. "We will kill you and take the mask for our own ends."

John, swallowing his fear, seized his opportunity. He pulled out his dagger that was concealed down his trousers and plunged it into Melanthius's thigh. It should not have been a deadly wound, but Melanthius screeched as beams of light shot out from the eyeholes on his mask. There was a sudden flash as his lifeless body fell to the floor. John's head suddenly cleared, and he quickly crawled over to Melanthius's body. Only it was no longer Melanthius. In his place lay the body of an easterner with dark hair and a weatherworn face. The mask lay beside the body and John quickly snatched it up, shocked and disbelieving that his plan had worked. From outside came the sound of battle, men screaming as they clashed steel, and John told himself to make good his escape in the confusion of battle.

"Sir Gregory." John said, his voice now returned as the magic had faded.

But Sir Gregory was dead.

John stood and looked down at the mask in his hands, a broad smile spreading across his face. He had done it, rid himself of his wife, and now holding a power that would make all bow before him. But first he needed to escape and hide until the battle was over, then he would take control of the Minoton.

Chapter 12

Fire engulfed all around Henri and Elizabeth as they huddled together in a corner. Symond was close by, lying on the floor and uttering an eastern prayer as smoke consumed him, while Pagenellus was sat, cross-legged and muttering softly to himself as though the danger of being burnt alive did not affect him. The stones at Henri's back were becoming hot and he was forced to move, disturbing Elizabeth.

"What's happening?" Elizabeth deliriously asked, her eyes shut and her face black.

"Shh." Henri hushed. "Just rest" He said as he stroked her singed hair with a blackened hand. So this was it he thought, death by being burnt or choking on the thick smoke that gathered above his head. Memories of his mother flooded his mind and he found himself hoping that the religious men were right, that all souls would ascend to the stars where loved ones would meet again. The thought of seeing his mother again comforted him as he closed his eyes and awaited for death to come and claim him.

The beams above their heads began to creek as the fire weakened them. After a moment of cracking and groaning, one came crashing down. A part of the floor had been broken and Henri saw that there was a gap. He quickly wriggled out of Elizabeth's grasp and rushed over to inspect if they could somehow crawl under the farmstead and escape. But what he saw was not a gap between the raised floor and the ground, but a small tunnel.

"Symond!" Henri turned and quickly grabbed Elizabeth. "Pagenellus!"

Symond, only half conscious, mustered his remaining strength and sprang to action. He saw the hole that Henri was now halfway down and crawled over. "Quickly." He urge Henri on as the groaning of the other beams grew louder.

Pagenellus flapped his hands as he rushed over to the hole. "We must get safe, we must get safe!"

Henri pulled Elizabeth down the hole and instantly he could feel a draft. "It has to lead out somewhere." He wrapped his arms around Elizabeth and dragged her down the tunnel. "I can't see." Henri said as the tunnel was low and dark.

"Follow the draft." Symond said as he dropped through the hole along with Pagenellus, just as the entire roof collapsed. "Keep it on your face."

The tunnel was straight and began to slope up, making the task of carrying Elizabeth even harder.

"She has inhaled too much smoke." Pagenellus said as he excitedly hopped up and hit his head on stone, flattening his pointed hat.

The tunnel suddenly steepened and Henri saw a distant grey light. "We're nearly there." His legs burned with the effort of carrying Elizabeth and by the time he reached the top, he felt ready to collapse from exhaustion.

The exit was overgrown with tufts of grass and bushes that concealed the tunnel, but Symond made short work of clearing the way with his sword. The tunnel had brought them out to a hilltop that overlooked the farmstead and the road, and they fell to the ground and looked back at the wild flames and pillar of smoke that rose high into the air, each realising how close to death that they had come.

"Elizabeth." Henri said as he tried to wake her. "Elizabeth."

"She needs some water." Symond said as he took a small canteen strapped to his belt and tossed it to Henri.

Henri uncorked the canteen and dribbled water into Elizabeth's mouth. "Elizabeth."

Elizabeth coughed and spluttered up the water Henri had given her. "What's happening?" She asked as she opened her eyes and wiped her mouth on the back of her hand.

"Are you alright?" Henri asked as he sat Elizabeth upright.

"Was I dreaming?" Elizabeth asked, feeling unsure. She looked at Henri and saw that his face was black and that he smelt of smoke. "John." She said with fear. "Don't let John take me."

"You're safe now." Henri said as he hugged her. "You're safe now." Though he had said it, he didn't believe it. There was now just the four of them, with no food and the only water they had was what was in Symond's small canteen. They all looked tired, their face stained by smoke and their eyes bloodshot.

"We must gather what we can and report back to the king." Symond said as he stood. "He must know of our failure and Sir Gregory's treachery."

"You can go back if you want to." Henri said as he handed the canteen to Elizabeth. "But I'm going to kill that bastard."

"My young friend, you are not thinking straight." Symond replied as though he were speaking with a child. "We cannot possibly go on." He pointed at Elizabeth and Pagenellus. "We are a band made up of an old man, a woman, you and I. Hardly a band of warriors." Symond shook his head. "I am sorry my young friend, but we must go back."

"If I return, I'll be hanged." Henri rose to his feet and looked down at the burning farmstead, not realising the distance the tunnel had taken them until now. "But if I can somehow redeem myself by making this mission successful, then maybe the king will spare me."

Symond doubted it. The king was not a man to easily forgive those that deserted, and he knew that Henri would at the very least face imprisonment. "We are weak." Symond pointed out. "And the only weapons we have is my sword and dagger."

Henri pointed back at the burning farmstead. "Those men that were killed, their weapons will still be with the bodies."

Symond walked up beside Henri and placed a hand on his shoulder, looking him straight in the eye. "Even with weapons, we cannot take on a company of men."

But Henri was full of anger and wanted his revenge on John, a man that had imprisoned him and taken the woman he loved. "I'm going on." He stubbornly said as he shrugged off Symond's hand. "On my own if I have to."

Symond shook his head. "It is not an advisable action my young friend, but we have travelled this far together and I shall not abandon you now."

Henri nodded his thanks and looked back to Pagenellus and Elizabeth. "You don't have to come, you can wait here until we return."

Pagenellus shot up onto his feet and began flapping his hands. "I want to see the Minoton, I want to see the Minoton!" He said in a child-like manner.

"Well," Elizabeth forced a smile, "I cannot stay here on my own."

With all agreeing to go on together, they walked back to the farmstead where they salvaged whatever they could. From the heaped bodies they collected five water canteens that were half full and a few dried up strips of meat that they ate. Henri unbuckled a sword belt from a body and strapped it around his own waist, drawing the sword a few inches from its scabbard to check that the edges were sharp. After a small rest they began to walk towards the village of Oldby, keeping off the road to avoid being detected. Their plan was simple, to get ahead of John's company without being seen and negotiate with Melanthius. Then when John and his men turned up, they would have the Minoton apprehend them. So using the rolling grassland that raised up and down in gentle slopes as cover, they crept towards the strong smell of the sea.

"There!" Pagenellus pointed to the left of them. "Over there!"

"Hush now." Symond said sternly. "We wish to remain undetected."

"I've seen it again." Pagenellus's face twitched as he hopped from foot to foot, pointing over at a small hill. "It looked over the ridge at us."

Symond glanced towards the hill, but saw nothing. "We do not have time for this."

"Did it have yellow eyes?" Henri asked, wondering if it was what he had seen back at the farmstead.

Pagenellus flapped his hands and nodded. "You saw it too?"

"I don't know what I saw." Henri shrugged. "But I thought I saw yellow eyes watching me back at the farmstead."

"I think that we should rest here for the night." Symond said as a plan to capture the creature formed in his mind.

Symond whispered his plan and they all laydown and pretended to sleep. Henri, with Elizabeth at his side, kept one eye open, but could see little over the grass. They waited for what seemed hours before they heard the soft sound of hooves on the hard ground. Slowly it got closer and closer until they could hear the creature's breath wheezing in the still air. Symond waited. The creature stopped between Symond and Henri, sniffing at the air, and it was then that Symond made his move. He quickly reached out and wrapped his arms around the creature's bowed legs, trying to force it onto the ground. But the creature was stronger than it looked, and it defensively began scratching down at Symond with its claws.

Henri shot up onto his feet and tackled the creature. For a brief moment it looked as though it would free itself and slip off into the night. But Symond gritted his teeth and held on as it crashed onto the ground. It was a creature straight from the old stories told to frighten children, a creature with scaly grey skin like a snake, wide, terrifying yellow eyes, and bowed legs with hooves instead of feet. It had a flat face with a broad nose with two sharp tusks that grew up from its lower jaw, and it wore a knee length dark-green tunic and a brown hooded cloak.

It took all of Symond's and Henri's strength to hold the creature down, and after minutes of struggling, it gave up trying to free itself.

"What a creature!" Pagenellus excitedly said as he knelt down and looked the creature up and down in amazement. "What a magnificent creature!"

"Who are you?" Symond asked, his face scratched by the creature as it had tried to free itself.

The creature didn't answer and began to violently shake its head, distressed by his capture.

"You're hurting it." Elizabeth said as she walked over and knelt down beside the creature. "It's frightened, can you not see that."

"It's scared?" Henri said with surprise. "I think we're more afraid of it then it is of us."

Elizabeth ignored Henri and looked down at the creature, seeing the fear in its face. "Can you understand me?" She asked in a soothing voice.

The creature seemed to calm as it looked at Elizabeth, nodding its head. "I understand your words." It replied in a high-pitched and croaky voice.

Elizabeth smiled down at the creature and nervously placed her hand on its scaly forehead. "We don't want to hurt you." She assured the creature. "We just need some answers."

"Yesss." The creature nodded. "I answer."

"Good." Elizabeth said as she stroked the creature's forehead. Not so long ago, she would not have dared speak with such a creature, but her time helping in the infirmary had given her the confidence that she had sometimes lacked before. "Now do you have a name?"

The creature shook its head. "No name."

"What are you?" Pagenellus interjected, excited to know the answer.

The creature looked to Elizabeth for approval before it answered. "I am a Gromling."

"A Gromling?" Pagenellus said as he stroked his beard, deep in thought. "No, I've never heard of a Gromling before."

"I was spawned from the ashes of the fire mountain." The creature hissed. "Spawned to scout for the Minoton. My task is to instil fear and report back information to Melanthius before he arrives."

"How are you able to communicate before Melanthius arrives?" Symond asked, knowing that it would be a difficult task.

"He seesss what I see." The creature explained. "I knowsss not how."

"Magic." Pagenellus said clapping his hands. "How I wish that I had parchment and quill to record all you say."

302

"You said you are a Gromling and that you have no name." Elizabeth said, wondering why it hadn't been given a name.

The creature nodded. "No name given, Gromlings never given names." The truth was that Gromlings were few in number, and were spawned by the Minoton for the sole purpose of serving them. Their small build and great agility made them perfect for scouting, and too few ever lived long enough to ever be given a name.

"Then if you are agreeable, I would like to name you." Elizabeth smiled. "As a token of our friendship."

"You name me?" The creature seemed disbelieved to be named, as being named was considered a great honour amongst the Gromlings.

"You say that you are a Gromling." Elizabeth smiled. "So I shall name you... Grom."

"Grom." The creature repeated its name. "Grom."

"Now Grom." Elizabeth said as she stood. "We are going to let you up. But you must first promise not to harm anybody."

"No, Grom no harm anybody." Grom replied. "Must never lie to my name giver."

Henri and Symond cautiously let go of Grom's arms and allowed him to rise upright on his hooves.

"What a magnificent creature!" Pagenellus said with a smile on his face, hopping from foot to foot. "I have so many questions."

"And we have little time." Symond interjected. "Are the Minoton still at Oldby?" He asked, looking at Grom.

Grom nodded. "They await for word from the king of men."

"We were sent by the king." Symond said with a hint of urgency. "We must get to Oldby and speak with your master, Melanthius."

"Grom." Elizabeth said stepping closer. "We need your help. A company of men that tried to kill us are heading toward Oldby, and we need to get there first."

Grom agreed to take them the quickest way he knew and sprang off. "This way, this way!" It called back to them.

It was a struggle to keep up with Grom as he could run as swiftly as the wind blows, but even though he was running a lot slower than he could, it was a still a struggle. Many times they stopped to take breath and have a sip of water. Then a little before sunrise, they came to the outskirts of Oldby. The sea air rang with the sound of battle, as the distant shadowy figures fought amongst the ruins.

"We are too late." Symond said. "We must turn back and report to the king."

"No." Henri replied. "John and Sir Gregory will be down there, we must stop them."

Symond shook his head. "It is too dangerous my young friend."

"Grom, where is Melanthius's pavilion?" Henri asked ignoring Symond and glancing at the few pavilions that he could see.

"He staysss on the boat." Grom replied. "Over there on the shore."

"Take me." Henri drew his sword and looked back at Elizabeth's flushed face. "Stay here with Pagenellus until I return." Without another word, he rushed off into the chaos with Grom.

"He will be the death of me." Symond uttered to himself as he dashed off behind them.

The route Grom had taken them was close to the shoreline where there had been little fighting. From the looks of where the dead bodies lay, it looked as though John's company had charged straight down the road into the heart of the village. Some of the bodies were so badly mutilated that one could not tell whether it had been a person or a joint of meat carved up by a butcher. But no bodies of Minoton lay with the dead. The Minoton's longship could be seen on the shore and Henri carefully made his way over towards it, using the burnt down ruins as cover.

"It looks clear." Henri said as he poked his head up over charred remains of a wall, the sound of the waves slapping against the shore mixing with the ringing sound of battle.

Symond took a look for himself. The longship was not far, maybe about two-hundred feet away. But it was open and they could be seen easily by anyone looking towards the longship. "Let us hope that the battle is enough to keep them occupied."

"It has so far." Henri shrugged. He felt uneasy and a part of him wanted to turn back like Symond had suggested. But his bitter hatred of John had forced him on. Then there was Sir Gregory, a man that had resented him and often

305

rebuked the king for making a lowly peasant a squire. He was unsure why, but he felt that if he somehow got his revenge, then maybe he could earn his redemption for deserting his post. "Let's go." He said as he dashed over the ruined wall towards the longship. As he ran up the gangplank, he looked back over his shoulder to check that they had not been spotted. No one moved in their direction and he could see large figures of the Minoton swinging their wicked axes at men desperately try to flee. Henri ran into the gloomy interior of the pavilion that had been erected on the deck of the longship. There was two bodies lying close together, one was Sir Gregory and the other was a body of an easterner that he didn't recognise.

"The blood is still warm." Symond said kneeling beside the body of the easterner and pulling out the dagger buried in the body's thigh.

"NOOOO!" Grom screeched. "No, it cannot be!"

"Grom what is it?" Henri asked, alarmed by the creatures distress.

"The mask, it has gone!"

Symond stood and walked over to Henri, his boots sounding heavy on the wood. "You remember this my young friend?" He said holding up the dagger.

Henri took the dagger and recognised it immediately. It was the same dagger that he had found in the woods next to the village of Raven Wood. "John." He said as it dawned on him that he had taken the mask.

"He has the mask!" Grom cried. "The Minoton will do whatever he desires if he has the mask!"

"Then we must get it back." Henri said as he rushed back out of the pavilion. "Hurry he can't have got far."

Elizabeth waited with the sound of battle unsettling her. Long menacing war-cries from the enraged Minoton made her shudder and she found herself feeling sympathy for the men that fought such beasts. She had not yet seen a Minoton, but their noise was enough to frighten her.

"Dangerous." Pagenellus said jumping up and down. "It's getting too dangerous."

"We must move from here." Elizabeth said with fear for their safety.

"No, no." Pagenellus shook his head. "We were told to wait here."

"But it's not safe." Elizabeth said as the sound of men screaming grew louder and she began to step backwards.

"Wait." Pagenellus said, waving at Elizabeth to standstill. "Someone is coming."

"Is it Henri?" Elizabeth asked, fear causing a haze in her head.

Pagenellus's eyes narrowed as he tried to focus on the figure that ran toward them. It was then that he noticed the figure was not alone, and that there was four more with him. "Quickly, hide!" They quickly ran behind a dune with long tufts of grass poking up through the sand and ducked low. Soldiers ran past, struggling to keep going as their feet sank into the soft sand. Pagenellus poked his head over the bank and caught a glimpse of a Minoton giving chase. "What a strong creature." He muttered quietly as it passed.

"We must find somewhere safe." Elizabeth said as she crawled up next to Pagenellus and gazed over at a burnt hut close by. "We can wait for Henri and Symond there." She pointed.

"You go." Pagenellus said, hoping to see more of the Minoton. "I'll join you in a moment."

Elizabeth was unsure at first if she should go alone, but fear of being found by a Minoton forced her on. She pulled up the skirts of her dress and made a dash for the hut, granules of sand finding its way into her shoes. The hut was a small, round building that had been used to smoke fish. Only the outer stone wall remained, and instead of running around to the entrance, Elizabeth climbed over the blackened stones where a section of the wall had collapsed. She jumped down and crashed onto the floor inside, sending ash high into the air.

"Elizabeth?" A familiar voice cut through the ash.

"Who's there?" Elizabeth said with horror, unable to see anybody because of the ash. A figure stepped closer and Elizabeth could make out that he was wearing a torn blue tunic with a red feather on his chest. "John." She said with horror.

John came to a stop, his face in disbelief of what he saw. "Well it would appear as though you have as many lives as a cat, my dear wife."

"No." Elizabeth shook her head as tears welled in her eyes. "Please don't harm me."

A sinister grin spread across John's face as he slowly drew his sword from its scabbard. "So I can assume that scum, Henri is still alive?"

"If you harm me, he will kill you!" Elizabeth spat, finding some courage. She reached out behind her, feeling for anything that she could use as a weapon, and pulled a long nail from out of the ash.

John laughed. "I doubt it, he is a lowborn peasant. Scum that will end up on the gallows."

"He is a better man then you!" Elizabeth rose to her feet and took a defiant step towards John, her fist clenched around the nail behind her back. "And once I'm free of you, I will marry him and reveal to the whole town what a monster you really are!" Elizabeth grabbed hold of a strap around John's shoulder and hit him in the face with the nail, causing a deep cut that ran from his forehead, over his right eye and down to his chin.

Blood gushed from the wound and John, fuelled by anger, lunged forward with his sword, piecing Elizabeth's stomach. "This is the only way you will be rid of me!"

Elizabeth fell to the floor, her blood spilling onto the ash. She tried to cry out, but the pain was too great and all she could do was lay still holding her wound. In the tussle, the strap she had grabbed had broken and the small bag had fallen to the floor, unnoticed by John.

"Goodbye my dear." John said with scorn, holding a hand to the cut on his face and running out of the hut, his blooded sword still in hand.

Elizabeth knew her time was up, and could feel her life slowly slipping into darkness. Then, unknowing how much time had passed, a young face with short, dark hair and a scar under his right eye looked down on her. "Henri." She managed to say.

"Elizabeth." Tears rolled down Henri's cheeks. "Elizabeth."

"Henri….I'm sorry." Elizabeth winced with pain. "I'm so sorry."

"Stay still." Henri said looking at the wound. "Pagenellus is going to heal you."

But Pagenellus knew the horrible truth, and took off his pointed hat. "I'm sorry Henri, there is nothing I can do." He lowered his head, feeling Henri's pain.

"No." Henri sobbed. "No there must be something."

"Henri." Elizabeth wheezed. "Forgive me, forgive me for all the bad things I said to you." She reached up with her hand and stroked his face. "You are a good man…and I should have married you." She felt another shudder of pain as she closed her eyes, her hand dropping.

"Elizabeth." Henri said as he took her hand. There was so much more that he had wanted to say, but he could not find the strength to speak. He felt numb, cold and unable to contemplate his life without Elizabeth. His head was filled with memories and emotions, like a cooking pot filled with water that was bubbling over the side, yet nothing came out.

The hut fell silent.

"My young friend." Symond said in a soothing voice as he held out the bag that had fallen from John. "The mask."

Henri snatched the bag and pulled out the mask. "John!" He hissed as sorrow gave way to raw anger.

"What are you doing?" Symond asked as Henri stood up and walked out of the hut.

But Henri was no longer himself. Filled with a burning fire of rage he placed the mask over his face and summoned the Minoton to him. For now he had the power to gain his vengeance.

*   *   *

The morning was dull, overcast with grey clouds and a warm breeze that stirred the leaves on the tree outside of Catharine's chamber. She had been given a room in the west wing of Hubert's mansion that overlooked the garden where many colourful flowers grew beside a stony path that led to a central plaza with an elegantly built summerhouse which housed a small fountain. Catharine's room was large and comfortable with a four-poster bed made of dark oak with white sheets and a red blanket. The walls were painted green and decorated with tapestries that depicted the countryside, the floor polished wood with a red and white striped rug at the end of the bed. When Catharine had been shown to her chamber, on the night of her wedding, the chamber had been filled with flowers and gifts of expensive dresses and matching jewels, gifts that marked Catharine as a married woman.

Catharine sat at her small table, staring at herself in the oval mirror that was framed with dark wood and carved into the shape of flowers. Her troubled thoughts were of

Hubert and his nightly visits. First he would go to his own chamber where his servants would undress him and wash his stinking, flabby body. They would then dress him in his nightgown and escort him to her chamber, where her servant had prepared her. His face was always red from drink and he always smelt sweaty, even after his servants had washed him. The thought of him climbing on top of her made Catharine shudder as she remembered the pain that followed. Her mother had warned her of what to expect, and all she could do was lie still with her eyes closed as Hubert took his pleasure. Luckily it had been brief and Hubert had left to take to his own bed, puffing and sweating as though his skin was melting. But the worst was not the pain, it was Hubert's rancid breath and sweat that dripped on her from his forehead, and the thought that he would visit her chamber again the night after. Each night after the wedding, he had come to her and took his marital rights, and each night was the same disgust that she had to suffer.

Catharine was thankful that his visits were brief, and wondered why anybody spoke of it as being a pleasurable thing. During her time within the servants' quarters, many of the girls had stopped up late, whispering and giggling as they compared secret lovers and spoke of who was the most vigorous. But Catharine had found no pleasure from Hubert's visits, only pain and disgust, nothing like what the servants had giggled about.

Catharine sighed softly to herself as she rose from her chair and walked out of her chamber, her stomach grumbling with hunger as she descended the stairs. She was dressed ready for a warm day in a yellow summer dress with white lace, and her hair had been pinned up and curled, the way that Hubert liked. The dining hall's doors were open and the air was scented with the smell of freshly baked bread.

"Good morning my lady." A servant said as he saw Catharine entre the hall. "I trust that you had a good night's sleep." He was a tall, thin man with white powdered hair that was pulled back and tied with a red ribbon at the back of his head. His narrow eyes that sat atop of a slender nose and thin lips watched Catharine as she took the seat that he had respectfully pulled out for her.

"No." Catharine replied. "The wind whistling through the tree outside of my chamber window kept me awake."

"I'm sorry to hear that my lady." The servant dutifully replied as he tucked the chair in under Catharine. He was dressed in a long, crimson tunic, tight white trousers with stockings and shiny black shoes with a squared brass buckle.

"And the window rattles." Catharine added as she glanced around the empty table. "Has my mother eaten yet?"

"No my lady." The servant poured Catharine a goblet of water. "I expect your lady mother shall join you presently."

The hall was a rectangular shape with a long, well-polished table surrounded by many high-backed chairs that ran down the centre. The walls had been painted light-blue with a border of white flowers that ringed around the top. On the walls hung old and cracked paintings of Hubert's family members that had long passed from this world.

Catharine disliked the paintings and was sure that their eyes seemed to move as if they were alive. "You must have someone see to my window so I am not disturbed the next time the wind blows at night."

"Yes my lady." The servant answer uninterestingly. "Will you be having your usual breakfast my lady?"

"Yes." Catharine nodded.

"If you will excuse me my." The servant bowed. "I shall procure your breakfast."

Catharine watched the servant walk out, feeling uneasy and distrustful of him. She felt sure that he reported back to Hubert on things she has said and her actions. She believed that she was now no better than when she scrubbing floors as a servant herself, even though Hubert had told her that she was now free. But that freedom was just an illusion. Yes she now had fine dresses and wealth, but she was being watched and was once again trapped by the unwritten rules of society. A prison comes in many shapes and forms, she thought, she may once again have wealth, but like the servant, she had very little control, and that was not true freedom.

The doors to the hall opened and Catharine's mother entered, smiling as though she were overjoyed. "Good morning daughter." She said as she sat on the chair next to Catharine. Like her daughter, she wore a thin summer dress, only hers was pale blue with darker blue lace.

"You seemingly appear to be in a good mood mother?" Catharine said in a questioning tone. "Is all well?"

"Yes." Catharine's mother smiled. "All is very well."

"What is it mother?" Catharine asked, seeing that her mother wanted to tell her something. "We are alone, the servant has gone for my breakfast."

Catharine's mother glanced around and shook her head. "One can never be too careful." She looked at Catharine, her blue eye glinting with excitement.

"Can you not whisper it to me?" Catharine said, eager to hear what her mother knew.

The doors to the hall once again opened and the servant returned carrying a silver tray with fresh bread and two long, curved yellow fruits. "Lady Mother." He said as he placed the tray in front of Catharine. "I trust you slept well."

"Very well until I was awoken by someone hammering on the door." Catharine's mother said with suspicion. Her room was at the front of the house above the main entrance, and in the early hours she had been awoken by someone banging on the door and yelling to see the master of the house. Intrigued by the commotion, Catharine's mother had climbed out of bed and crept over to the window, opening it a little so that she could hear what was said. "Will the master not be joining us this morning?" She asked in a cunning voice.

"The master of the house has breakfasted early this morning and left to attend on business." The servant replied as he poured another goblet of water and placed it in front of Catharine's mother.

Catharine's mother knew that the servant was lying as she had watched Hubert leave with the lord's servant that had hammered on the door. And what she had heard had given her hope. "Bring me some toasted bread and butter." She ordered. "And some honey."

"Yes my lady mother." The servant inclined his head and walked back out of the hall.

Catharine bit into her bread and looked up suspiciously at her mother. "What is it you know?"

"Do not speak with a mouthful." Catharine's mother reproved. "What I know is that you must have a son for Hubert."

Catharine swallowed and placed her bread back onto the tray. "He already has a son mother."

"Yes I know that." Catharine's mother replied, waving a dismissive hand. "I know of his boy that is being schooled in Elnaria and is Hubert's heir apparent." She lowered her voice and leaned closer to Catharine. "But I have been told that he is a sickly child, weak minded and easy to manipulate."

"Is that why you are so happy this morning?" Catharine said as she picked up one of the long, yellow fruits and began peeling off the skin. "Because you have learnt how weak Hubert's son is?"

"No, that is not why I smile." Catharine's mother leaned back in her chair and snatched up her goblet of water. "Though Hubert does need another son as a spare."

The thought of having to bare Hubert a son was not a pleasant one and Catharine sighed, placing the half eaten fruit back on the tray. "I have lost my appetite."

"I'm sorry daughter." Catharine's mother said sympathetically. "Does it still hurt?"

Catharine's face reddened. "A little." She admitted. "But the worst is having to suffer the smell of his sweaty body.

"Our time is coming." Catharine's mother replied. "The winds of change are afoot."

The servant brought in Catharine's mother's breakfast and they ate silently together. After they had finished they took a stroll through the garden, the gravel path crunching beneath their feet as they passed raised borders with herbs planted in them. Though the sun was hidden behind the clouds, the day was still warm and both Catharine and her mother were grateful for wearing thin dresses.

"So tell me mother." Catharine said impatiently. "What is it you know?"

Catharine's mother glanced behind them to make sure that no servants were close enough to overhear. "Last night a man came, a man dressed in the livery of the lord."

"So?" Catharine said knowing that the lord's servants often came to the house.

"I heard what was said." Catharine's mother stopped and turned so that she was facing her daughter. "They said the lord was dying and that an emergency meeting of the town's council had been called."

"I knew that he had been unwell." Catharine said. "But I don't think that it was that serious." Her thought trailed back to when she had served on him, remembering the blood he had coughed up and his anger towards her for seeing it.

"From what I heard, he could already be dead." Catharine's mother turned away and watched as a bee landed on a lavender plant.

Catharine shook her head. "So what does that mean for us?"

"What it means, is that John is likely to be named the new lord." Catharine's mother turned and linked her arm with Catharine's and they continued along the gravel path. "From what I have seen and heard, John is disliked by the council and seen as being unfit to be lord."

"So the council will not allow John to claim the title of lord?" Catharine said, wondering why her mother was so interested in the town's plights.

Catharine's mother stopped and turned her daughter to face her. "Don't you see?" She spoke softly. "Your husband is now on that council, he could use his wealth and influence to move against John and claim the lordship for himself." Catharine's mother smiled and grabbed Catharine's hands. "You must manoeuvre his mind to thinking that way."

Catharine doubted that she had that sort of influence over Hubert, surely he would only take advice from his advisors. "I don't see how I can, and to openly speak out against the rightful lord is treason."

"Publicly yes." Catharine's mother cunningly replied as she let go of Catharine's hands and walked on.

"Mother?" Catharine said as she walked after her.

"When you are alone with him tonight, mention that you have heard grumblings amongst the people in the marketplace, and that they would favour a lord that is not so easily distracted from his duties like John."

"But what if he gets mad?" Catharine asked, fearing that he might have her arrested and thrown back into prison.

"You simply apologize and say that it is simply what you heard in the marketplace."

"But we don't know for sure if the lord is dead, there has been no announcement." Catharine looked down at her feet and kicked a stone that went bouncing into the flower-filled borders.

"We will do nothing until we know for sure." Catharine's mother said, seeing that her daughter looked frightened. "Now let us go back inside, it's getting a little chilly out here."

The breeze had cooled and the temperature had plunged as a result. As Catharine and her mother walked back into the house, the town's bells rang. The servant with the white powdered hair was waiting for them and handed Catharine a sealed letter.

"What is it?" Catharine said as she broke the wax seal of her husband and read the hastily written letter.

"Daughter." Catharine's mother said with pretence that she never knew what the letter said.

"The lord has died." Catharine replied. "And the king's army has reached Market Barton."

Catharine's mother's face tried to hide her delight at the opportunity that fate had bestowed on them. "The winds of change." As she said it, a distant clash of thunder sounded. "The winds of change are afoot."

Chapter 13

The king's standard was unfurled and raised, its bright purple silk and silver crown of stars a contrast to the overcast sky above. Men clamoured and clashed their weapons on shields in a bravado that they hoped would frighten the army apposing them. Many of the younger men made jokes and boasted of what gallant feats they would dare in the looming battle. But the older, more experienced men, knew that their boasts were a facade to cover their fear. Though the king's army looked to be in good spirits, it was tired from the long march from Langton Castle and its moral was low. The men from Langton that the king had spared, had been split up into different battles so that they would not simply swap sides during the battle. But this had only spread discontent amongst the men as they deemed it dishonourable to have men that had rebelled within their ranks. But It was not just that factor why moral was low. The night before the men had been sullen at the sight of Baleford's camp. Many fires were dotted across the plain to the west of Market Barton and the men in the king's army had counted the fires and knew that they were heavily outnumbered. The older men knew this two be an old trick to dishearten them and that the enemy had lit more fires than was needed to fool them into believing their army was far greater than it really was. Though they spoke of the trick, all knew that even if half of those fires were needed, they were still outnumbered.

As the morning had dawned the king had marched his army forward, taking position between the roads to Elnaria and Lhanwick, on a northeast to southwest alignment, to mirror the position of Baleford's army to the northwest. To the north was the town of Market Barton where Baleford had placed a battle of men with two small wedges of crossbowmen in support and cavalry formed up on the east side to stop the king from using the narrow streets to flank his army. Both the king and Baleford knew that those streets would become killing grounds for trapped men. There would be no room for manoeuvring and it would simply become a stalemate of pushing as neither side would gain the advantage. So Baleford had his army formed up to the west of the town where he hoped to gain a decisive victory.

"He wishes to keep the fighting away from the town." The king said as he scanned over Baleford's army with his telescope. They were a mix of colour with banners blazon above the neatly formed up men. Drummers beat and men raised weapons into the air as they shouted in a stirred up frenzy.

"Better not to get trapped in those narrow streets." Hollington replied. He wore a simple padded gambeson with a black boar on his chest and was mounted on an unarmoured warhorse, preferring speed over protection.

"We are outnumbered at least two to one." The king wore shining plate armour which was gilded with golden stars and rode a heavily armoured horse that had been trained to stamp and bite. He took his eye from his telescope and looked back towards the road to Lhanwick. "There will be nowhere to hide if we should lose." The land to the south of the king's army was open, a vast rolling plain where Baleford's pursuing cavalry would cut down the king's army as it tried to flee. The king let out a soft sigh, knowing that it was a battle that he had to win, or he would lose his crown.

"Battles have been won against greater odds." Hollington nudged his horse forward a few paces and pulled open his own telescope. He cast his experienced eye to the left of Baleford's line, where mounted men were positioned, and saw that they were screening another formation of mounted men. "We will have to watch our left flank." Hollington warned, lowering his telescope and pointing.

The king raised his telescope's eyepiece to his eye and looked to the left of Baleford's line. "Mounted Men-at-Arms." He said with relief. "Our knights will have to hold them."

Hollington nodded, knowing that the mounted Men-at-Arms were no match for heavily armoured knights. But he also knew that there was enough of them to keep the king's knights engaged and stop them from being effective in the battle. He traced Baleford's battle line to find the knights, passing men formed up in battles and crossbowmen in wedges between the battles, until he came to the gap between the town and Baleford's left flank. It was there that the knights were positioned, their armour and silk jupons gleaming against the dull morning. "There." Hollington pointed as he took his eye from the eyepiece. "To the right."

The king trained his telescope to the right of Baleford's line and saw the threat that the knights posed. On his right flank was a wedge of crossbowmen that would become vulnerable to the knights when the line advanced. Further out to the king's right he had positioned two small battles supported by a wedge of crossbowmen to guard against Baleford's men that were positioned in front of the town.

Then further east was his own mounted Men-at-Arms which guarded from a flank attack by more of Baleford's mounted Men-at-Arms that were formed up ready on the eastern flank. "I will have to commit my reserve should they charge."

Hollington nodded, knowing that the king had little other men to manoeuvre against the threat. "Baleford means to pin us down while he uses his knights to charge our exposed right. His infantry will be his shield, and his cavalry will be his sword."

The king grunted his frustration. "I cannot advance my line without causing a gap for Baleford to exploit."

"We will have to fight a defensive battle." Hollington said as he snapped shut his telescope and placed it back in his saddlebag. "Let them wear themselves out on our lines."

The king sat silent as he cast his eye back over Baleford's line. "Have we heard anything from Symond?"

Hollington shook his head. "No my king. Nothing."

"Damn it!" The king slapped his armoured thigh in anger. "How I could use those extra men now."

"What of the Arcani?" Hollington asked. "Can you not call them up to fight?"

"They are holding the road to Elnaria." The king replied. "Should I find defeat then we are to retreat west, the Arcani will act as a rear-guard while we make good our escape." The king closed his telescope and tossed it at an aide that was mounted close by. "I have no choice other than to win this day." He turned his horse and spurred it into a trot, riding towards his right flank where he stopped again to survey the field of battle.

The battlefield was almost flat with a gentle slope that led up to the northwest where the Duke of Baleford's army was positioned. Midway between the two armies was the road to Elnaria, a road that the king would need to retreat down should the battle turn bad for him. The town itself was north of his position, a market town that had been built around a crossroads at its centre. The northeast road led to Baleford and was guarded by mounted men to stop the king from cutting off Baleford's retreat.

"Damn you sun, will you not make an appearance?" The king said looking up at the grey clouds that covered the sun. His hope had been that it would be a clear day and the sun would be at his army's back and in the faces of Baleford's men, blinding them and giving his own men a small advantage. But the sky above was filled with rolling grey clouds as far as the eye could see.

"Look." Hollington pointed as a great cheer came across from Baleford's army. "He wishes to parley."

The king looked over to where Hollington was pointing and saw the Duke of Baleford riding out from his line with an entourage of advisors and aides. He wore gleaming plate armour covered over with a tight, purple jupon with a golden stag on his chest. Behind him rode two aides carrying banners, one was the plain white banner of parley, the other matched Baleford's jupon. "This should be interesting." The king said as he rode out to meet Baleford.

Both parties met at the road, the aides holding back either side while Baleford and the king met face-to-face.

"Cousin." Baleford greeted, his tone mocking.

"I trust, cousin." The king replied, staring at Baleford's white, left eye. "That you wish to negotiate your surrender and beg for my mercy."

Baleford chuckled and scratched at his short, greying beard. "That's funny, I was just about to say the same to you."

The king's anger flared and it took all of his self-control not to let it show. "My terms are simple." He held a straight back and spoke as though winning the battle was a certainty. "You and your men are to surrender and stand trial for treason."

"Treason." Baleford repeated the word. "It's only treason if I lose, which I don't intend on doing."

"You have rebelled against your rightful king!" The king snapped, angered by Baleford's confidence. "If you surrender now I promise you a fair trial."

"A fair trial." Baleford scoffed as he waved a dismissive hand. "We both know that to end this war, one of us will need to die."

The king shifted in his saddle, uncomforted by the thought. "You have heard my terms."

"Heard them and reject them." Baleford leaned menacingly forward in his saddle and looked at the king with his one good eye. "Many men have died because of this war, good men that should have been at home minding their crops."

"You started all this." The king reminded Baleford. "By claiming that you have a greater right to the throne than me."

"Then hear my terms." Baleford said, sitting back upright and placing an armoured fist on his hip. "Let us not waste more unnecessary blood and settle this the old way."

"The old way." The king said with surprise. "You mean single combat?"

Baleford nodded with a sly smile across his face. "You and I, one-on-one, and let the gods above decide the victor."

The king looked back at Hollington, who waited with the other aides a few paces away from the road. Hollington shook his head and the king knew why. Baleford was said to be an excellent swordsman and as the king looked at the short, stocky man mounted on a great warhorse, he never doubted it. "I reject your terms."

"You really are the weak coward the nobles call you." Baleford said with disgust. "You would let your army find death and defeat, just so you can wear a crown and polish the throne with your arse."

"There is nothing more to be said." The king nudged his horse, turning his back on Baleford. "This day shall see the end of your rebellion."

With the negotiations at an end, both parties rode back to their own battle lines. Trumpets sounded and drummers beat a rhythmic tattoo to stir the men's courage. A cool breeze blew from the east, snatching at bright banners as the men below them anxiously awaited for the battle to begin. And they were not made to wait long.

Ba-boom, Ba-boom, Ba-boom-boom-boom.

From Baleford's line, advanced three wedges of crossbowmen that once clear of their battle line, formed into a loose skirmish line. The king sent forward his own crossbowmen, and the battlefield erupted into the sound of many crossbows being loaded and fired. Men fell, snatched back by deadly bolts that found their mark, as others desperately reloaded in hope of gaining the upper hand. At first the king's men had some success and were able to inflict casualties upon the opposing crossbowmen, but Baleford's greater numbers were now starting to tell. The king's crossbowmen began to edge back, stepping over their fallen comrades. Captains all along the line yelled and pushed men back into place to try and maintain discipline.

"Stay in line!" A captain yelled. He was a short man with thinning hair and a burly voice that could have awoken the dead. "Fight damn you!"

All along the king's skirmish line captains struggled to keep the men in place. They knew that they were being beaten and would soon have to retreat back, or else face death.

The short captain snatched up a crossbow from a body with a crossbow bolt through his eye and began to load it. "Don't just cower!" He yelled as he placed his foot through the stirrup and cocked the string over the spool. "Fight back!" The captain pulled a bolt from his quiver at his waist and placed it in the groove. "Don't cower!" He then aimed towards the enemy and squeezed the trigger, instantly reloading as soon as his bolt was in flight. The men around him took heart from his courage and began to vigorously load, loose and reload.

The skirmish went on with both sides sending crossbow bolts back and forth in hope of forcing their opponents back. Casualties mounded on both sides, but it was the king's men that bore the brunt, and continued to edge back.

"Recall the men." The king ordered an aide that was mounted on a grey horse behind him.

The aide put his trumpet to his lips and gave two long blasts. On hearing the recall, the crossbowmen fell back to the battle line where they regrouped.

"Have them reform into their wedges." The king ordered. "We will defend our line."

"My king!" Hollington shouted as he reined his horse to a stop. "They're advancing!"

Ba-boom, Ba-boom, Ba-boom-boom-boom.

The king looked across the field and saw that the whole of Baleford's battle line was advancing. They advanced as far as the road where they halted, their crossbowmen then advanced within rage. Men fell to the ground as Baleford's crossbowmen began to pepper his line in a constant barrage of raining death.

"Take cover and shoot back!" Hollington roared at the men.

The king's line was now under threat.

Baleford knew that the king had a bad temper that once invoked would blind him to reason. His hope had been that the king would see the threat to his right flank and decide upon fighting a defensive battle so not to spread his forces too thinly. With his own battle line out of range from the king's crossbows, his plan was to weaken the king's line and force him to attack. Then in the chaos of battle his knights on his left flank would charge the gap that would inevitably open. And this far his plan was working.

"My king, my king!" A squire said as he ran towards the king waving his arms in the air.

"What is it?" Hollington asked as he turned his horse, knowing that it could be nothing good.

"Our horses." The squire panted. He wore a blue and black stripped tunic covered over with a simple leather breastplate. "They're being killed by the crossbowmen." His face was youthful and flushed, his eyes and voice full of fear.

"Have them retreat back out of range!" The king snapped, his anger building.

But it was too late.

The knights seeing only crossbowmen and mounted Men-at-Arms in front of them, jabbed their spurs into their horses' flanks and charged. It was a sight that squires dreamed of taking part in, poets wrote of their gallantry, and fair ladies admired. But to the king it was folly. They thunderously rode, the horses' hooves cutting up the ground as they went, with levelled lances at the ready. Their charge smashed into Baleford's mounted Men-at-Arms with the leading knights piecing into the fifth rank of Baleford's formation. The king's knights hacked and killed many of the lighter armoured men they fought. But the mounted Men-at-Arms far outnumbered the knights and the momentum of the charge came to a stop. Behind the men that they had charged, was another formation of mounted men who swept around the knights and attacked their flanks. They became trapped in a mass of horsemen and those that were not killed were taken as prisoners to be ransomed back to their families.

"Call them back!" The king shouted at his aides. "Call them back!"

"My king." Hollington said, seeing that the king was losing his calm. "It is too late."

A handful of knights had managed to escape from the melee and the king angrily watched them flee down the road to Elnaria. "Damn them!" The king slapped his thigh in anger and pointed to an aide. "I want to know who gave them the order to charge!" A barrage of bolts suddenly rained down, killing two aides and wounding his horse. It reared up and the king fell. "I'm alright." He said as aides fussed over him checking for wounds.

"My king." Hollington winced with pain, a bolt deeply embedded in his right thigh.

"Get him to the infirmary!" The king snapped. "Quickly now before he bleeds to death!"

"My king." Hollington said as he stumbled off his horse. "Take my horse." He handed his reins to an aide and watched the king mount his steed. "We need to be cautious." He warned.

"You need to see the physician." The king could see blood oozing out of Hollington's wound and felt concern as he had known men die of such wounds.

Hollington nodded. "I will be back as soon as it is bandaged."

The king's line was taking many casualties from the constant barrage of bolts that rained down upon them. Men crawled back from the line and lay wounded, calling for help to get to the infirmary. It was now a simple choice for the king, keep his position and lose most of his men to the crossbow bolts, or he could advance and take the fight to Baleford's army in a do or die attack.

*   *   *

The Duke of Baleford cheerfully watched as his crossbowmen punished the king's army for their indecisiveness. His own battles of men, he had kept back out of range and were yet to take any casualties. The mounted men on his right flank had been hit hard by the king's knights with many of them killed. But it was a price worth paying as now the king's left flank was vulnerable to the remainder of his mounted Men-at-Arms. Soon, he thought, the king must attack soon or simply flounder as his army slowly diminished to the deadly bolts.

Ba-boom, Ba-boom, Ba-boom-boom-boom.

The king's drummer beat and Baleford smiled, knowing that his time had come. He watched the king's army advance, their crossbowmen racing ahead of the main battle line. "Forward!" He yelled, rising in his saddle and waving his hand towards the king's advancing army. His army marched forward with their own drums beating and captains shouting at the men to keep their cohesion.

Ba-boom, Ba-boom, Ba-boom-boom-boom.

The gap between the two armies narrowed as men tightened their grip around weapons, kissed lucky charms and pulled on armour straps to make sure nothing was loose. Crossbowmen loosed a few bolts at close range before falling back to their advancing lines where they reformed into their wedges. The two lines met on the road like two waves crashing upon the shore, and the struggle began. The day quickly filled with the sounds of battle, screams of the wounded, weapons clashing on steel and wooden shields, captains yelling at men to push forward. All this mixed with the constant beat of the drums.

Ba-boom, Ba-boom, Ba-boom-boom-boom.

Baleford watched the battle, his one good eye narrowed and his blood stirring from the sound of the battle. He never knew why, but he had always liked the thrill of battle; the adrenalin that the blazon banners and rhythmic drums gave him was unmatched by any other pleasure to be had. Now he wanted nothing more than to draw him sword and charge into the fray. But he had to wait. That pleasure would come once he had secured his victory, and seeing that his men were gaining the upper hand, he knew it would be soon.

"My Duke, my Duke!" A rider shouted as he approached.

Baleford turned his attention from the battle and watched the lonely rider as his bodyguards stopped him. "Who are you?"

"I bring word from John Kinge, the Lord Aide of Heath Hollow." The rider replied.

"Let him through." Baleford ordered. His bodyguards opened up and allowed the rider to approach.

"I thank you my Duke." The rider was travel worn, his face dirty with a distinctive scar on his left cheek that gave him a constant mocking expression.

"Spare me the pleasantries and get to your point." Baleford snapped, eager to get on with the battle. He looked at the blue tunic with a yellow lion standing on its back legs the rider was wearing and didn't recognise it.

"I was the Master-At-Arms for Sir Gregory Fitzwalter." The rider explained, seeing that the Duke was looking at the sigil on his tunic. "He was killed at Oldby and I now serve John Kinge."

"What of John and his company?" Baleford asked, growing impatient.

"I am to report that John has succeeded in disrupting the king's plan with negotiating with the Minoton, but has suffered heavy losses and retreated back to Heath Hollow. John himself was wounded."

Baleford, who had a deep dislike for John, knew what that could mean. "Has John negotiated with the Minoton?"

"He tried my Duke, but they forced a battle on him." The rider lied, unwilling to tell the Duke of the true events. "We were only just able to escape with our lives."

Baleford wished that they hadn't and felt annoyed at John's luck of having escaped. "Where are the Minoton now?" He asked, knowing that he would have to engage them once he had defeated the king.

"They are still at Oldby." The rider lied. The truth was that he was unsure as they had simply fled.

Baleford glanced back at his battle line and saw that his men had pushed past the road, leaving blooded bodies on the ground behind them. "Ride to Heath Hollow and tell your master to come to here. I wish to speak with him."

"As you wish my Duke." The rider went to turn his horse.

"Stay." Baleford said holding up his hand. "See the ending of the battle, so that you have something to report to you new master." His battle line was pushing the king's back by sheer weight of numbers. Many had been killed and many more would yet have to fall before the battle's ending and he could claim the throne.

Ba-boom, Ba-boom, Ba-boom-boom-boom.

The slaughter was horrific, a stark contrast to the epic poems resonated in great halls that sang of heroic deeds and courageousness that all should aspire too. The once dry ground was now wet with the blood of the fallen and littered with bodies and broken weapons, and the sky above was blackening as if the gods above were ashamed by the battle below.

"Now!" Baleford shouted to an aide holding a long, brass trumpet. "Sound the charge." The aide dutifully placed the trumpet to his lips and sounded the charge.

On Baleford's left flank were his knights, who on hearing the trumpet blast, lowered their visors and spurred their horses forward. They charged at the king's right flank, where a wedge of crossbowmen were desperately trying to hold ground. The crossbowmen saw the threat and many simply turned and ran. The charge crashed home and the king's entire line was routed. The knights rode unopposed, their swords and lances killing many as the king's men fled in a blind panic.

In a last ditch attempt to salvage his army, the king had formed his reserve battle into a hollow square to defend against the knights. To the right of his square were two small battles and a wedge of crossbowmen that were yet to engage in the fighting and further right, north of the road to Hollington, was his mounted Men-at-Arms. He sent an aide to order them into a defensive square and for the mounted men to counter charge the knights. But the mounted Men-at-Arms saw that the king was defeated, and simply fled the field.

Baleford smiled. "Victory." He announced to his aides, all of whom applauded. "Master-At-Arms."

"Yes my Duke." The Master-At-Arms nudged his horse forward.

"Ride to my mounted Men-at-Arms and tell them to encircle those squares and complete the victory." Baleford ordered, wanting his victory complete.

"At once my Duke." The Master-At-Arms said as he turned his horse and rode off.

The battle paused as both side reorganised their forces for the final assault that would end one king and crown another. A clash of thunder rumbled overhead and a heavy rain burst from the black clouds above, a sure sign that the king was doomed.

Then from the northwest came a long, terrifying horn blast followed by the war cry of the Minoton.

*   *   *

"What are your orders my master?" Etor said, kneeling before Melanthius.

Melanthius stood, looking at the distant battle, with a host of battle-ready Minoton at his back. The king's army was in peril and the field of battle was both bloody and grim. But Melanthius cared little for the king or his men, he had come for vengeance, because his anger yearned for blood. He had come for John. "We find John Kinge." He said as he gazed down at Etor. "He is to be brought to me, alive."

After the events at Oldby, the Minoton had given chase to John and his remaining men. But as swift as the Minoton were, they could not catch up with the horses John's men rode. The ground was hard from the baking sun and tracking the fleeing horsemen became impossible. But Melanthius knew that the king was moving his army to Market Barton and as they neared, the sound of the battle allured them.

"It will be as you command, my master." Etor rose and drew his wicked looking longswords from across his back, giving a mighty war cry that the other Minoton took up.

A crack of thunder sounded overhead followed by a flash of lightning that forked across the black clouds. Rain poured, blurring the distant bright banners and the men that formed up to meet the threat of the Minoton.

"Kill Baleford and his men." Melanthius ordered. "But spare the king and the fools that he commands." He rose his hand into the air and the Minoton scuffed at the wet ground with their hooves, eager to charge. "Forward now and turn the day red with the blood of our foe!"

The Minoton charged, their war cries and yellow eyes striking fear into the two battles that Baleford had hastily formed up to protect his rear. They each carried tall rectangular shields that were painted red with a black bull's head in the centre, and cruel looking swords or axes that were as sharp as a razor. Their armour was bronze and simple, covering their body and lower legs only. The ground shook beneath their hooves and they crashed into Baleford's men with the force of a rock, flung from a trebuchet, smashing into a wooden fence.

Men cried out with fear as the Minoton made short, bloody work of their resistance. The braver men foolishly tried to fight, but they were mercilessly cut down and trampled into the mud. Now there was chaos as men tried to flee in all directions from the savagery, dropping weapons and shields as they went.

The Duke of Baleford's reserve battles were routed.

The whole battlefield once again erupted as the king seized his chance and had his men charge Baleford's line in a desperate hope of clinching a victory form the jaws of defeat. Men slipped in the blood and mud, trampled over as the pushing and shoving began. Melanthius calmly walked amongst the dead and discarded weapons, looking for John or any of the faces he would recognise from Sir Gregory's retinue. But none were whom he sought.

"Etor!" Melanthius summoned.

Etor rushed over and knelt, his armour and weapons splattered with blood. "Yes my master."

"Send a message to the king, tell him that his men are safe and not to attack us." The breeze stirred his red robe and softly whistled as it blew through his mask's eyeholes. "Now let us finish off Baleford's army."

"As you command my master." Etor rose and dashed off to carry out Melanthius's orders, taking two other Minoton with him.

Close to the town of Market Barton was Baleford's knights that had earlier routed the king's men. They were now formed into a two rank deep line over the road to Elnaria, barring the way northeast to the crossroads of the town. It was there that the Duke of Baleford was now positioned, knowing that the Minoton had seized his victory. Other of his units were falling back in good order, heading for the safety of Heath Hollow.

Melanthius could have ended the war by ordering the Minoton to attack their retreat. But he was not interested in the Duke of Baleford, or the war. He was interested in what he saw amongst a mass of horsemen. Fighting on the Duke's right flank were mounted Men-at-Arms, and in the blur of the rain and battle, Melanthius saw a blue tunic with a distinctive yellow lion standing on its back legs on it that he recognised. It was the Master-At-Arms. Without another thought he dashed towards the man, the Minoton following him into the fray. The mounted men's horses reared up and tossed their riders, the smell of the Minoton causing the horses to panic. No mercy was shown and many were killed.

"Mercy, mercy!" A fallen rider pled as he tried to crawl away. "Please, mercy!"

Etor, who had quickly returned from the king, placed a hoof on the rider's back to stop him squirming and slammed his sword down on his head, splitting it in two. "Puny whelp." He said as he pulled free his sword, blood dripping from the tip.

Baleford's line broke in a panic, and men fled in all direction trying to escape the carnage that was the Minoton. The king halted his line and watched the massacre that the Minoton inflicted upon Baleford's army. And later scribe would record that he shed a tear at the bloody sight.

"Do you not recognise me?" Melanthius said as he approached the Master-At-Arms, his voice deep and angered.

The Master-At-Arms horse had tossed him off and fled, leaving him in a mucky puddle mixed with blood. "Spare me, and my master will pay a ransom."

"Your master." Melanthius said as he stood over the Master-At-Arms. "Where is he?"

"He was wounded at Oldby and has returned to Heath Hollow." The Master-At-Arms replied, holding up his hands to show he was surrendering.

Another clatter of thunder sounded and the sky was briefly lit up by a flash of lightning.

"Do you not know me?" Melanthius asked, his anger beginning to boil over his control.

The Master-At-Arms shook his head and began to slide away, fearing for his life.

"Maybe this will help." Melanthius pulled back the hood of his red robe and took off his mask. There was a sudden flash that blinded all close by.

"Henri!" The Master-At-Arms said with disbelief, his eyes bloodshot and blurred. "How can this be?"

"This will be the last face you ever see!" Henri said, his voice full of malice.

"No wait." The Master-At-Arms pled. "You are a squire and must obey by the laws of chivalry."

Henri pulled out a dagger with Gigantic runes written into the blade and smiled. "But you always told me that I was never really a true squire." He fell on top of the Master-At-Arms, filled with a blind rage of hate, and repeatedly stabbed down over and over until he was too tired to continue. Henri tiredly stood, his head a haze, and looked around at the dead and dying.

The field was a killing ground, slippery from the rain and blood. Baleford had escaped with a small number of men, but most were now killed and their bodies lay scattered across the blood soaked field of battle. The Minoton quickly finished off any that dared to stand, and as suddenly as the battle had erupted, it fell eerily silent with the soft patter of rain falling on the sorrow of battle below.

Rain poured, washing the blood into the mud, as thunder rumbled overhead. The king's army began helping the many wounded that lay amongst the dead and piled up discarded weapons. A sense of calm and relief swept over the battlefield, with many of the king's men standing awestruck by the Minoton. They knew that they had come close to death and defeat, and many now called out their thanks to the Minoton.

"The mask." Etor said as he strode over to Henri, his longsword dripping with blood and his yellow eyes fixed on the mask.

Henri looked down at the blooded mask in his hands, feeling unsure. He held power, power that he could use to gain vengeance for Elizabeth, but that same power would also consume him, enslave him. And that was not what he wanted. "Here." Henri said tossing the mask over to Etor. "Be free."

"You would willingly give the Minoton the mask." Etor stepped closer to Henri, his yellow eyes narrow and unpredictable.

Before Henri could answer, the king and his remaining entourage rode over. They were all weary and blooded, none mounted upon the same horses that they had begun the battle with.

"Many thanks." The king said as he reined his horse to a stop. He cast his eyes over the Minoton that gathered around, trying to distinguish which was their leader. But among their number was a face he recognised. "Henri!" He said with surprise.

"I have been a slave in all but name." Henri replied, looking at the king with anger. He turned his back and began walking away. "Never will I suffer that fate again, nor doom any to it." Soldiers parted to allow him passage through, whispering of an age old prophecy.

"I was told that men have a vast yearning for power." Etor called after Henri, his voice deep and menacing. "Why would you give up such power?"

Henri stopped, finding it odd that his thoughts could be so clear amongst the bloody aftermath of battle. He felt almost as if the gods above had given him a purpose. "Because I am unlike any other man."

The king's men that had gathered around the Minoton began to chant, "Henri! Henri! Henri!" as they punched the air with their weapons. To them he was their saviour, an age old prophecy that spoke of a man that would yield power and end serfdom.

"Where are you going?!" The king shouted, his voice drowned out by the chanting of his men.

But Henri was oblivious to the exaltation that he was being given by the king's men. He walked on, stepping over the dead, with a heavy heart that was grieved and full of sorrow.

Etor looked at the king, his eye hard and steadfast. "Your thanks and your survival, you owe to this Henri." He turned from the king and Followed Henri, the other Minoton doing the same.

So it was that on the blood soaked fields of Market Barton, amongst the debris of battle, that the common men found hope. The news of Henri giving up great power so that the Minoton were free, spread quicker than any plague, and the talk of an old prophecy gave hope where there was none before. For from the jaws of defeat, Henri had given the king his victory and the battlefield rang with the sound of his name. Henri, not a lord nor knight, but a commoner of low birth was said to be the man who would end serfdom. And so the men chanted, "Henri! Henri! Henri!"

Epilogue

In the days that passed since the battle, the rain had been heavy and unrelenting as if the gods above were crying out at the savagery of the battle. Where once there had been dried-up brooks, had now become floods plains that the people welcomed and children slashed and played in. The people of Market Barton spoke of ill omens that the gods were displeased with the battle and the number of men that had been killed. But that number had not been known as each day new rumours were spread, and the numbers grew.

Henri had stayed at a tavern in the town the night of the battle before travelling back to Oldby the next morning with the Minoton. Like many of the town's people, he had plundered the many bodies, finding himself a matching pair of black trousers and tunic. From a dead captain of Men-at-Arms he took a pair of boots that fitted as though they had been made for him. Then from under a dead horse he had found a broadsword that had once belonged to a knight that had been killed by a crossbow bolt fired at close range. It was three and a half feet long, made of the highest quality steel, with a brown leather handle bound with silver wire that was protected with a steel cross guard and circular pommel. Henri had stood studying the sword for some time before deciding that it was not a sword for him, preferring something smaller and lighter. This sword was for someone of wealth and status, not a lowborn peasant like him, and so he decided to take a shorter sword that the crossbowmen carried. Close by there had been a group of people scavenging the dead who violently told an old woman dressed in rags to wait her turn. Henri, knowing that there would be nothing left once the others were finished, walked over and gave the old woman the sword. She had thanked him and called him sir, but Henri had replied that he was no knight, but a simple peasant like her before walking off. He plundered a few more bodies before he left for Oldby, taking some coins and a simple brass telescope that he placed in his pack.

The journey back to Oldby had been sombre, the grim weather a reflection of Henri's broken heart. He had ate and spoke little as his sorrow overwhelmed him. His mind was filled with memories of Elizabeth, the sunny days as she had worked her father's stall in the marketplace, her smile, and the way she frowned when angry. All brought tears to his eyes. Then came the thoughts of John, and his tears would turn to bitter anger.

He returned to Oldby to find that Symond, with the help of Grom and Pagenellus, had buried Elizabeth's body on a hilltop that overlooked the village and sea. There was a solitary tree beside the grave which Henri now sat at the base of as memories flooded his mind. Rain poured, saturating Henri and the world below as if the gods were trying to wash away the great many sins of men. But Henri hardly noticed the rain and sat, dripping wet, deep in troubled thoughts.

"I'm sorry." He managed to say after hours of silently sitting. "It's my fault." His thoughts had been of the ruined temple at Dimon Dor, when he had drank from the chalice.

"If thee doth not flee the path thou has set upon, then thou heart shall know pain." That is what the spirit had warned. Yet Henri had foolishly continued on and drank from the chalice. Since then he had known nothing but pain. Tom, his best friend had been killed, his mother had died and he

had been imprisoned by John. Then Elizabeth had married John only for him to unjustly kill her. Woe and pain.

"I'm sorry." Henri cried. "It's my fault, I should never have drank from the chalice." But his tears quickly turned to anger as John's smug face came into his mind. No, he told himself, it was John's fault. He and his father had sent him with the Arcani to retrieve the chalice and then imprison him. It was John that had fooled Elizabeth into marrying him and then kill her. And it would be John who would pay the price for it. Henri took out the Gigantic dagger that he had found in the woods beside the village of Raven Wood and scratched a hole in the soil where he placed the blade. He had been told that it was worth a king's ransom, and that the money it would fetch would set him up for life. But when Henri thought of his future, it had always been with Elizabeth. Now that had been taken from him, great wealth seemed pointless. Now his future seemed blank, a dark unknown where he must venture alone into a howling wilderness of sorrow.

"Good bye my love." He said as he covered over the blade.

Henri stood, angered and swearing revenge, when he noticed a boat out on the grey water, a longship with black beams and a red sail of the Minoton. Etor had named him a friend and given Henri his torque as a symbol of their friendship as well as promising to let Grom keep his name. The villagers of Oldby had been released and the plunder taken from their homes had been returned to them so that they could rebuild their destroyed village. On the ships prow stood a large shadowy figure of a Minoton that held something up above its head. Henri took out the telescope he had plundered from the battlefield and cast his eye towards the ship. The Minoton were rowing and Grom sat at the stern of the ship beating the pace of the oars on a drum. The shadowy figure at the front was Etor, holding up an artefact of power. Power that consumed the soul of any that wore it. But Henri had resisted that power and given it back to the Minoton who swore to leave the kingdom and return to their homeland. Now his gaze lingered on that artefact until it faded from sight.

It was the Mask of Melanthius.

Appendix
Races and monastic orders of the island of Valhanor

Men: Human kind have inhabited the island of Valhanor for thousands of years. It remains lost in time as to when men first arrived on the island, and as to where it was they came from. An ancient tale told of a lonely giant that carved a smaller image of himself and of his recently deceased wife from a single block of stone. It was said that the Star Gods took pity on his loneliness and gave life to the carvings, thus mankind came to be. Later scholars dismissed the tale as myth, unreliable folklore from a long lost age. Over the centuries, men lived alongside other races of the island, learning to build and govern over themselves without the aid of giants or imps watching over them. They built vast stone cities with huge step pyramids that they dedicated to the Star Gods. Each city-state had its own king and laws, unique to their own culture and traditions. Trade flourished and the ancient cities prospered with peace and wealth.

Then came the darkness.

Nobody knows what the darkness is, or from where it came. Wise men said that it was sent by the Star Gods to test men's loyalty to righteousness. The darkness corrupted men's souls, and greed and power took the place of the needs of the people. Kings began to close their city gates to all but their own citizens and began to distrust their neighbours. Over the passing years, men became lesser and fell from righteousness, desiring greater wealth and power for themselves. The city-states of Dimon Dor and Balharoth grew to their heights of power, conquering nearby towns and villages to bring them greater wealth and power. The wise men of the island searched for a cure to the darkness that had corrupted men. They searched for many years before an answer was found.

After years of traveling from city to city, and reading countless old scrolls, a wise man named Adullam believed that he had found the answer. He united the ancient kingdoms and races together in a great council, in the hope of restoring the diminishing righteousness that had once thrived throughout the island. The great council agreed to the creation of a blessed chalice so that all races could gain a true knowledge to vanquish the darkness. The great kings of Balharoth and Dimon Dor, along with the other members of the great council went atop mount Gannim where the Craft Master of the Gigantes called down a star from the night sky, splitting in two as it fell. From the sea a young boy was found washed up on the shore. Adullam proclaimed the boy of heavenly decent, and that he had been sent by the gods to lead mankind back into the light. But another wise man named Baal disagreed, and demanded that they continued with their plan of crafting a magical chalice from the star rock. The chalice of knowledge was thus crafted and an ancient spell of knowledge placed upon it. All kings drank from the chalice, but it carried the curse of too much knowledge. Men became evermore greedy for power, and now understood how to gain it.

Adullam took the young boy found washed up on the shoreline and took him as his apprentice, naming him Elnar. Elnar grew up in the chalice temple built in the mountains to the southeast of the island, where the chalice of knowledge was supposed to have been safeguarded. But the chalice never made it there. The war for the chalice erupted and the kingdom of Balharoth fell to ruin. After the death of Adullam, Elnar was forced to flee west where many people believed in his divinity.

After gathering support, Elnar raised an army and marched on Dimon Dor, who now held the chalice. The two armies met on the Plains of Pendor and Elnar's forces were able to deal the forces of Dimon Dor a crushing defeat. The city of Dimon Dor was cursed and fell to ruin.

Elnar took the chalice of knowledge and founded the Order of the Star to safeguard it, ordering that no one should ever consume from it again. The city of Elnaria was founded in his name and soon the western part of the island came under Elnar's control. With the war won, the kingdom of Elnaria flourished as peace was restored to the island. The remaining city-states in the east continued on with their traditions and grew in power. Many spoke of uniting the eastern kingdoms to rival that of Elnaria, but no king was able to unite them. Soon the eastern kingdoms abandoned kings in favour of electing the strongest citizen to lead them, giving them the title of satrap. The eastern city-states went on independently from the kingdom of Elnaria and refused to believe in Elnar's divinity.

The kingdom of Elnaria declared a new age, the age of the chalice, and began counting the years from the coronation of Elnar and labelled it AC, for after the chalice was reclaimed. Elnar commissioned the construction of the great library in Elnaria and appointed an army of scribes to record the history of the kingdom. Much of what is now known of the island comes from those old scrolls.

Blessed with long life Elnar reined for many years, but in 84AC Elnar the great came to pass. His dying words were of a fading light within his bloodline and the hope of one whom the gods shall choose to come forward and bring light back to the kingdom.

The line of kings lessened as the centuries passed, and kings became less pious and more tainted by the darkness. The kingdom of Elnaria became structured so that those at the top reaped all the wealth for themselves, and those at the bottom were no better than slaves to their lords. Thus the kingdom remained until the coming of the one who would bring the kingdom back to the light, and to a new age.

Gigantes: Gigantes were giants, famous for their size and strength. They stood between 9 – 13 feet tall and had the strength of twenty men. As a race, the Gigantes were generally righteous characters and lived in peace alongside the other races on the island for many years. Though a cattle farmer from Attaroth once claimed that a giant had stolen two of his cows by running past and picking them up (one under each arm) without stopping. They resided mainly in rocky hills or the mountains where they honed their skill in the crafting of metal tools and carving of stonework, which was considered to be the finest on the island.

It is generally believed that the Gigantes were the first race on the island and were believed to have built The Great Mountains to the east of the island. Nothing is known of their origin as they never kept any written records of their own, and what little is known, was written by various different scribes that lived centuries after men first settled on the island. One scribe said that the Gigantes were gods cast out of the heavens for their yearning to build a paradise of their own. Another wrote that they were the gods' first creation. Another that they were mere slaves, created to shape the world. The truth may never be known as the Gigantes were secretive and kept much of their knowledge to themselves. They did have a written language, straight lined runes that they carved into stone. But only a handful of men were ever able to read them.

Unlike men, the Gigantes were not led by a king to rule over the race, instead they were mostly left to make decisions for themselves. The giant they considered to have the most knowledge in craftwork was given the title of Craft Master, who gave wisdom to any giant seeking it. Over the passing centuries, they built huge stone circles, for what purpose nobody knows for sure, though it was widely believed that they were used to map the stars. As the population of men began to rise the Gigantes began to teach them how to build, but kept their greater knowledge for themselves.

By the time the darkness came to the island, their numbers had begun to dwindle. Where once there had been elegant halls carved under a mountain that were filled with generations of families, were now left abandoned. Nobody really knows as to why their numbers declined, though one scribe later recorded that it was because they were so deeply engrossed with their craftwork, that they had simply forgot to reproduce. A later scribe dismissed that claim and wrote that the Gigantes simply left the island to find a new home across the Sea of Rune. Over time, as the kingdoms of men grew, sightings of the Gigantes lessened.

After the creation of the chalice of knowledge, Craft Master Norlag urged men to come to peaceful terms with each other, to stop the bloody war that had erupted amongst men, but they did not heed his wisdom. Nothing after the war is known as the Gigantes had little more dealings with men. There were a few remote sightings and one woman called Eleanor claimed that she had become friends with a giant who lived in the hills near to Heath Hollow. In the years that passed, the Gigantes passed into legends, myths and stories told to children by the fireside. But their stonework remained and their finely crafted swords and daggers became highly sought after. Much of their craftwork and knowledge remains hidden, and awaits discovery in their long abandoned caves.

Imps: Imps were a small, lesser folk then the Gigantes, and stood no bigger than a child. They had little love for the hot furnaces used for the smelting of metals like the Gigantes did. Instead they had a fondness for the growing of trees. A scribe recorded that when the races of Imps and Gigantes first met, it was agreed that they would share the island. The Imps grew many woodlands where they joyfully dwelt for centuries. Like the Gigantes, they kept no written records, but had an oral tradition that they passed down from generation to generation.

Over the centuries they built villages, little mud huts with thatched roofs, deep in the forests where they honed their skills in the lore of magic and of healing potions. At the coming of spring every year all Imps from across the island would travel to the northern most forest where they had planted their first tree. For three days they would drink potions that made them hallucinate, and chant a magical spell which brought the trees around them to life. The trees would then pick out an Imp they deemed worthy and named him as Grand Imp.

When the darkness descended upon the island, men began to take Imps and keep them against their will to try and harness with their lore of magic. This resulted in many Imps becoming mischievous and distrusting of men. Over time the Imps became mysterious and placed powerful spells upon the woods in which they dwelt to keep men away from their villages. At first they refused to help in the crafting of the chalice of knowledge, preferring to stay hidden deep in the woods. Norlag the Craft Master of the Gigantes was able to persuade the Grand Imp Georus otherwise, saying that their lore of magic was greatly needed to repel the darkness.

Georus the Grand Imp reluctantly agreed and took the chalice deep into the woods, where the Imps placed a powerful spell of knowledge upon it. In the war that broke out after, the Imps were blamed for it. The kings of men accused the Imps of placing a curse on the chalice that made men evermore ambitious and distrusting of each other.

In the years that followed, many Imps left the island. Nobody knows as to how many remain on the island, if any. But their powerful spells on the woodlands remains strong. One such spell can be seen at the ruins of Balharoth, which was cursed to be barren by the Imps. To this day it remains an eerie place where not even a weed will grow in its memory.

Elves: Elves were often mistaken for Imps because of their similar size and appearance. Like the Imps they too had a love for the woods, and dwelt alongside the Imps for centuries before men appeared on the island. Elves, however, were generally more mischievous then Imps. When men first built small dwellings, intrigued by them, they often snuck in while the inhabitants were out and stacked all of their belongings into a pile in the middle of the room. An early recording told of an Elf that had terrorised a family for years, each night he came, constantly knocking on the door and running away. Then he would sit on a tree stump outside of the house, menacingly laughing until dawn.

The Elves had no king or chieftain who ruled over them. A scribe that lived long ago recorded that they were a nomadic race that travelled from forest to forest, ever searching for a paradise they would never find. They had a lore of magic, though not as great as that of the Imps. Instead they became the masters of trickery and curses. They would shoot their cursed arrows at any who walked the woods where they dwelt and watched as their victim fell to madness.

Little more is known of them and many believe that they no longer dwell on the island. Though there were still a few reports, from people traveling though woods, of hearing sniggering as stones are thrown at them. But over the years these reports lessened to where, eventually, only a handful of villages claimed that Elves still inhabited the nearby woods.

Baobhan Sith:
The Baobhan Sith were cursed women that could shapeshift into ravens at their desire. Originally they were temple maids that served the temple in Dimon Dor, famed for their beauty and piety. After the war for the chalice had ended and the city of Dimon Dor fell to ruins, they were cursed by a spell cast by the Imps for their yearning to stay young and never grow old. They were cursed to wonder the forest for all eternity, never being able to feel or taste pleasures again, growing older and older, yet never dying.

According to a scribe who lived in Elmham Castle centuries of years later, the Baobhan Sith were able to capture an Imp wondering alone in the forest, and torture him until they had gained the knowledge to restore their beauty. They learned that if they drank the blood of the living, that it would revitalise their withered bodies. They stalked the forest or the nearby roads for any man they might find. Any they came across, they butchered and drained their blood.

As the years passed, tales of bloodthirsty witches spread throughout the kingdom. A man that had travelled near to the black forest (the forest around Dimon Dor as it became known) came back telling a tale of beautiful women seducing his foolish younger friends and drinking their blood. He described them as witches wearing revealing dresses that spoke to stir a man's resolve. He said that he had only managed to survive as he was wearing well-polished armour, saying that when the witches saw their reflection in his breastplate, they gave a deathly screech and shapeshifted into ravens and flew off back towards the forest. For it was said that the only thing they feared was their own reflection. Many similar tales sprang up over the

357

years, and the forest became a place where no man would enter. The Baobhan Sith were then forced to venture further out of the forest to finds their victims.

The scribe from Elmham Castle recorded that instead of biting, they used their long sharp fingernails that grew out from their fingertips that they stuck into the back of their victims' neck to suck out their blood. Although they had the ability to shapeshift their feet always remained like that of ravens. That was why they were always reported as wearing long dresses to cover their true identity. If one was to ever vanquish a Baobhan Sith, it was said that a cairn of stones should be placed over the spot where they were vanquished to stop their spirit returning to the world. Though most that have encountered these blood thirsty witches never lived to tell the tale.

To this day they still dwell in the black forest, hunting any that dare enter. Some say that the Baobhan Sith have long since departed the world, but many travellers report of large black ravens watching them from the edge of the forest, but none of sound mind get to near to that evil place, for fear of the blood thirsty witches that dwell there.

Woodland Wraiths:
Woodland Wraiths, or Shadow Wraiths as they are more commonly known, tended to dwell in a place filled with negative energy. They came to existence after the coming of the darkness and fed off the negative energy of its surroundings in order to grow stronger. The Elves had managed to keep them at bay by using what little lore of magic they had, and now that many Elves have departed from the world, the wraiths had grown stronger.

Old Records said that the wraiths were agents of the darkness, used to collect the souls of the living. Nobody knows for sure if this is true, and some claim that they are no more than stories to frighten children. Yet many reports of people seeing the shadowy figures lingering near cursed woods and graveyards had reached the ears of the king himself. In 425AC, King Edward III launched an investigation into the reports. His scribes recorded that only a handful of the hundred agents sent by the king returned. The few that did return told tales of black mists roaming the woods where elves had once dwelt. The wraiths were described as a floating black mist that filled whoever set eyes upon them with terror. A list of places where the wraiths were reported to have been seen was drawn up, and King Edward decreed that no man should enter such places until someone found a way of vanquishing the wraiths.

As the years passed, no such answer was found, and reports of the wraiths began to fall silent. Many learned men have studied the old scrolls on the wraiths, and searched for an answer for what they truly are. But to this day nobody truly knows much about them, other than that they are evil creatures that dwell in evil places.

Wild folk of Dimon Dor:
The Wild Folk of Dimon Dor were once citizens of the city from where they took their name, and had lived in peaceful worship of the Star Gods. They built a huge step pyramid in the centre of the city and dedicated it to the Star Gods, who they believed created them. Up until the coming of the darkness the people of Dimon Dor thrived and freely shared their knowledge with others. But, over time, the darkness

tainted them. Distrusting the neighbouring city-states, they closed their gates and planted a forest of trees to hide their city.

After the city was sacked by Elnar's victorious army, and the chalice taken, the imps placed a powerful spell upon the people. The spell made them one with the forest, and over time they lost their human appearance and looked more tree like than human. An eastern scribe, whose scrolls now lay gathering dust in the library of Elon Dor, recorded that their skin had become like tree bark and that branches with thick black leaves grew up out of their backs. It was also recorded that they would sink into the depths of the forest in deep slumber, and that if one was to enter their ruined city it would awaken them along with their anger. Other sources claimed that the Star Knights had secret dealings with a spirit that dwells in the temple there. But the Star Knights have remained silent whenever asked about it.

What little is known about the Wild Folk comes from ancient scrolls and folklore. Nobody can say with certainty whether they truly exist or not, as not even the bravest of men would enter the cursed ruins of Dimon Dor.

Star Knights: Star Knights were a monastic order founded by Elnar the Great in the year of his coronation, 1 AC. Their order was originally made up of Elnar's most loyal men that he knighted after the battle of Pendor plains. Elnar granted them a charter to build and recruit more men to the order, and soon, the handful of knights became a formidable army. Naming himself as the Grandmaster, Elnar had complete control over the order and could rely on them in times of war. Over time the order built up and became a noble cause that many would join. Rich merchants and nobles alike would donate money to their cause, and soon the Star Knights hoarded an abundance of wealth which they used to build a vast stronghold atop mount Gannim (where the great council had called forth a star from the sky) to safeguard the chalice.

Elnar, knowing that that he should not have complete control over the order, appointed a council of elders who could veto the grandmaster if they felt he was abusing his position. The elders first set out a code in which all knights of the order must follow. This code became known as the Rule of the Star. Over the passing centuries the order went from strength to strength, and the Star Knights became famed for their piety and courage on the battlefield. Their long black surcoats with a white eight-pointed star became a symbol of hope that one day the darkness shall be banished from the kingdom.

As the line of kings became tainted by the darkness, the council of elders began to speak of removing the right for kings to inherit the title of Grandmaster and that it should be appointed to one whom they deemed worthy. Things came to a head in 611AC when King Edward the Fifth died. The council deemed his son to have been corrupted by the darkness and unworthy of the title of Grandmaster. From then on kings were no longer given the title and a candidate was chosen from amongst the elders. The then new king Philippe the Third demanded that the order give up the chalice, but instead Grandmaster Everard of Beolog had the chalice hidden, fearing that the king would use it for himself.

In the years that followed, the people of the kingdom grew suspicious as to what the Star Knights' true motives were. People no longer willingly joined (unless desperate) the order that locked themselves up in their strongholds and never helped those in need as they had sworn to do. Instead, the Star Knights hoarded their wealth and served the order's own interests. The order became self-sufficient and exclusive to those who had heritage within the order. Those who could prove their lineage would become knights after many years of training. Those few who chose to join could only achieve the rank of a sergeant, but their children could one day become knights.

To this day the Order of The Star keeps the whereabouts of the Chalice of Knowledge a closely guarded secret. They remain in their strongholds, refusing to get involved in the kingdom's troubles and hoard their wealth and knowledge for themselves.

Arcani: The Arcani are a secret order that answer only to the king himself. Unlike the Star Knights they have no code of conduct to abide by, and swore only to obey the king's orders. Founded by Phillipe III in 615AC as a force to counter the Star Knights, they quickly became agents used as assassins and gatherers of intelligence for the king. They worked in the shadows of secrecy, carrying out the king's orders and safeguarding the royal family.

Little records of the Arcani's missions were ever kept as the king forbid them from doing so, through fear of their discovery. But others recorded of seeing men dressed in dark-green and wearing a steel cavalry mask wherever the king held his court. Soon whispers of a secret order used by the king to quiet any opposition to his rule, spread throughout the kingdom. Whenever asked about a secret order at his privy council, the king would deny their existence, save to those he deemed worthy of knowing.

As the centuries passed, the Arcani became feared by the king's enemies, and were often referred as demons of the night, or demons with silver faces. Though in truth one could never tell who was a member of the Arcani, as they were masters of deception and could blend in with all levels of society.

An eastern scribe, writing in the year 874AC, claimed that the Arcani snatched babies from their cribs in the night, and groomed them into killers for the western king. Nobody knows if these claims are true as it is uncertain how members of the Arcani are recruited into their ranks.

As the darkness grew, King Henri IV ordered a band of Arcani to reclaim the Chalice of Knowledge so that he could banish the darkness, but the mission failed and only one member of the band had returned. Rumours that the Star Gods had abandoned the king quickly spread throughout the kingdom, and many lords rose up in rebellion against him. But the Arcani remained steadfast in their loyalty. To this day they serve only the king and his ambitions to hold on to power.

Star Gods: The Star Gods are a deity that the ancient people of Valhanor worshiped. Before the age of the chalice (what is often called the Dark Age) the many city-states dotted all over the island built vast temples to honour the Star Gods. The temple at Lhanwick was considered to be the grandest, and it was believed to be the place where the Star Gods first came to the island and where their spirit speaks with the oracle.

An ancient scroll, written by an unknown scribe, recorded that the Star Gods rode on stars across the sky a millennia before men came to be, and that it was they who created mankind at the dawning of the world. For centuries many believed this, and the old scrolls from Dimon Dor claimed that the Star Gods would descend from the sky and give them light (knowledge). The ancient scrolls describe them as tall, thin with elongated heads and large, dark eyes that could read a man's thoughts. Then one year, as the people of Dimon Dor stood ready to receive them, they never returned and the darkness came.

Many learned men later discredited the ancient scrolls and claimed that there was no evidence to support their theory, saying that gods could not simply disappear. Though many still believed in them. The east and west divided over Elnar, as the east did not believe in his divinity and continued on with their worship of the Star Gods. The western kingdom's beliefs in the Star Gods faded over the passing centuries. Many of its people still believe in them and in became customary for the king to uphold certain traditions (like seeking light from the oracle at Lhanwick).

The centuries passed and the eastern city-states still hold firm that the Star Gods will one day return, but to this day all that remains of them is the ruined temples and the crumbling statues in the ruins of Dimon Dor and sunken images in the swamps of Balharoth.

Temple maids of Lhanwick: The temple maids have served the temple at Lhanwick for thousands of years. Every spring, when the temple was first built, there would be an annual gathering of women from all over the island. From amongst the gathering ten or more women were chosen to serve the temple. But now, the temple has become a place where lost women would seek sanctuary from the life they had fled from. Nobody knows exactly when the temple was built as little records were kept on its founding. But what little records there are, says that the Gigantes helped in its construction around 2074 BC (before the chalice was reclaimed by Elnar).

An eastern chronicler, writing centuries after the temple was founded, claimed that the first oracle's bones lay buried beneath the foundations of the temple, and that it is her spirit to whom the oracle really speaks with, not the Star Gods. The oracles that followed dismissed the claim as heretical, and many throughout the island agreed. As the years passed, the temple maids became famed for their piety and their appearance of having a blue painted face with a silver star on their foreheads. Many people from all over the island would travel to seek the oracle's wisdom, carrying gifts to help maintain the temple, though many left feeling less enlightened than when they went in.

After the war for the chalice, the temple became part of the kingdom of Elnaria. The temple maids were given a charter from Elnar to continue with their worship and traditions. The great king himself payed homage to the temple once every year, and it soon became customary for all kings that followed to follow the example set by Elnar.

The temple maid led a secluded life of prayer and discipline. It was forbidden for them to leave the temple unless instructed to by the oracle. Each day started in the early hour of the morning when the temple maids would gather in the temple's main chamber to offer prayers to the Star Gods. The remainder of the day was spent doing mundane chores and offering yet more prayers. It was often said that the temple maids spent most of their lives in prayer, hence the old proverb, I have the knees of a temple maid, said by those who suffer with their knees.

To this day the temple maids still dwell in the ancient temple at Lhanwick, partaking in their old customs and awaiting the return of righteousness. It was said that so long as the temple maids safeguarded the temple, then the kingdom would never fall.

Minoton: Much about the Minoton is unknown and in the few written accounts that have survived the passing of time, each gave a differing opinion as to their nature. One scribe recorded that they were warlike in manner and cared little for beauty, preferring a tough and simple life where the weak perished and the strong flourished. But an older scroll spoke of horned demons from the eastern island being merchants, excellent smiths, and that the weapons they forged were second only to that of the Gigantes. The same scroll recorded that they were peaceful traders (despite their demon like appearance) and once travelled far and wide to sell their wares, but over time their appearance and wares in the marketplace faded from memory and sight.

Where the few accounts would differ over their nature, there was one thing that was recorded in all of the remaining scrolls, that was their appearance. The writings all recorded that they stood eight feet tall with a thick, heavily muscled body of a man and a horned head of a bull with black cow-like skin. It was said that they possessed the strength to crush the skull of a man with their bare hands and that their yellow eyes could instil fear into the bravest of warrior's heart. But these accounts were dismissed by learned men from Elnaria who claimed them to be nothing more than ancient folklore, stories told to frighten children on a warm summer's night.

However, in the east, the stories were given some acclaim and men would tell their children of an age-old tale of the Minoton falling under the spell of a half-elf and how they had terrorised coastal towns, plundering much wealth and taking it back to their ash covered homeland. The tale was a favourite among the eastern city-states and many adventurers had went in search of the ancient tomb where an artefact of power was said to lie, but few had returned and over time it had become a fool's errand to even attempt such an adventure.

So it was that the Minoton faded from the passages of history, until the time came when they would venture from their layer and once more wreak havoc upon island of Valhanor.

Cynocephali: There is many records of these creatures, records that speak of men with the head of a dog and an unquenchable lust for blood once provoked into war. Their stature is similar to that of men, save only their dog-like head, and their nature was mainly peaceful. But as peaceful as they could be, they would rage unrelenting war on any that threatened them and quaff on the gore of those that they defeated.

The learned men offer two explanations as to the origins of the Cynocephali, the first being that they were an experiment that went wrong, and the second that they were an ancient race of shapeshifters come forth to reclaim their ancestral homeland. The truth was that no one knew for sure as the old scrolls recorded a differing history of the race. But one scribe offered yet another explanation, recording that Cynocephali were the product of a god that descended from the heavens and took the form of a wild dog. The writing says that the god would roam the wild and force himself upon any woman he came across and that the offspring were the dog-headed men that came to be known as the Cynocephali. The same scribe explains that the unnamed god committed this foul act in order to raise an army and forge his own kingdom among men, though want of being worshiped.

In the early years of men the Cynocephali were believed to be a myth, a mere misunderstanding of a race of people with strange customs. Then in the year 868Ac the Cynocephali sprang up from the mines under the city of Beolog, killing all that were trapped with its walls. To this day they dwell there, keeping to themselves, with none daring to venture near the city through fear of awakening their wrath.

Many reports have been heard in the halls of kings, reports that tell of dog-like men with the body of a human and the head of a dog, often roaming in small war bands close to the mountains were they dwell.

Gigantic Runes

A	⋀	J	⋋	S	⟋
B	▷	K	⟝	T	⊦
C	⟨	L	⊥	U	⊔
D	⊲	M	⋏	V	⋁
E	⋲	N	⋔	W	⋁⋁
F	⊤	O	⬦	X	×
G	⟅	P	⊦	Y	⋎
H	⋏	Q	⋔	Z	⋜
I	⋋	R	⋀		

TH	⋔	Silent E	⋈	CH	⋁
ND	⋎	IS	⋲	SH	⊓
NG	⬥	AND	⊠	GN	⋏
NN	⋔	IT	⋈	Silent G	⋈

0	⊠	5	N	10	⋇
1	I	6	NI	50	⬦
2	II	7	NII	100	⋈
3	III	8	NIII	1000	⋈
4	IIII	9	I⋇		

369

Map of Baden Hill

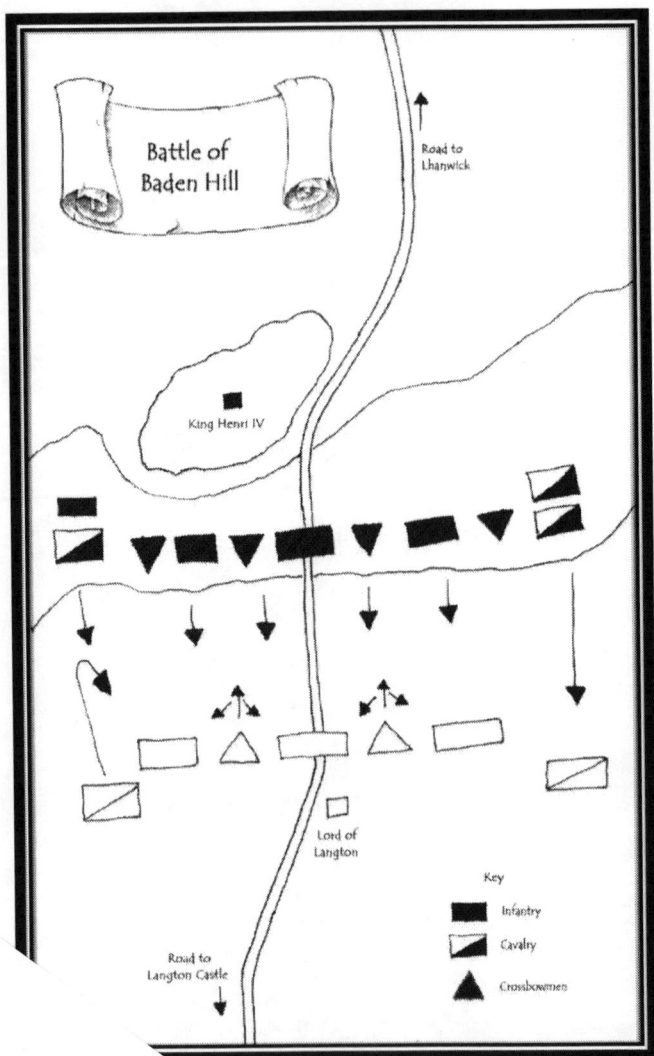

Battle of
Baden Hill

Road to
Lhanwick

King Henri IV

Lord of
Langton

Road to
Langton Castle

Key

Infantry

Cavalry

Crossbowmen

Map of Valhanor

Made in the USA
Columbia, SC
27 October 2017